PROLOGUE

Perfect Crimes

Casanova

Boca Raton, Florida, June 1975

For three weeks, the young killer actually lived *inside the walls* of an extraordinary fifteen-room beach house.

He could hear the whispery Atlantic surf outside, but he was never tempted to look out at the ocean or the private white-sand beach that stretched to three hundred feet or more along the shore. There was too much to explore, to study, to accomplish, from his hiding place inside the dazzling Mediterranean-revival-style house in Boca. His pulse hadn't stopped hammering for days.

Four people lived in the huge house: Michael and Hannah Pierce and their two daughters. The killer spied on the family in the most intimate ways, and at their most intimate moments. He loved all the little things about the Pierces, especially Hannah's delicate seashell collection and the full fleet of teak sailboats that hung from the ceiling in one of the guest rooms.

He watched the elder daughter, Coty, day *and* night. She attended St Andrews High School with him. She was stunning. No girl in school was as beautiful or as smart as Coty. He was also keeping his eye on Karrie Pierce. She was only thirteen, but already a budding fox.

Although he was more than six feet tall, he easily fit into the air-conditioning ducts of the house. He was wire thin and hadn't started to fill out yet. The killer was handsome in an Eastern preppy way.

Stashed in his hiding place were a handful of dirty novels, highly erotic books he had found during fevered shopping trips to Miami. He had become addicted to *The Story of O, School Girls in Paris*, and *Voluptuous Initiations*. He also kept a Smith and Wesson revolver in the walls with him.

He went in and out of the house through a casement window in the cellar that had a broken latch. Sometimes he even slept down there, behind an old, gently purring Westinghouse refrigerator, where the Pierces kept extra beer and soda pop for their gala parties, which often ended with a bonfire on the beach.

Truth be told, he was feeling a little extra weird that night in June, but nothing to worry about. No problema.

Earlier in the evening, he had handpainted his body in bright streaks and splashes of cherry red, orange, and cadmium yellow. He *was* a warrior, a hunter.

He huddled with his chrome-plated 22-caliber revolver, flashlight, and grope-books in the ceiling over Coty's bedroom. Right on top of her, so to speak.

Tonight was the night of nights. The beginning of everything that really mattered in his life.

He settled in and began to reread favorite passages from *School Girls in Paris*. His pocket flashlight cast a dim light on the pages. The book was definitely a major turn-on, but also a big yuk. It was about a 'respectable' French lawyer who paid a buxom headmistress to let him spend nights inside a hotsy-totsy boarding school for girls. The story was filled with the hokiest language: 'his silver-tipped ferrule,' 'his faithless truncheon,' 'he gamahuched the ever-willing schoolgirls.'

After a while he got tired of reading, and peeked at his wristwatch. It was time now, almost 3:00 A.M. His hands were shaking as he put the book aside and peered through the cross-hatching of the grill.

He could barely catch his breath as he watched Coty in bed. The very real adventure was now before him. Just as he had imagined it.

He savored a thought: *My real life is about to begin. Am I really going to do this? Yes, I am!* . . .

He was *definitely* living in the walls of the Pierce beach house. Soon that nightmarish, eerie fact would dominate the front page of every major newspaper throughout the United States. He could hardly wait to read the *Boca Raton News*.

THE BOY IN THE WALLS!

THE KILLER WHO ACTUALLY LIVED IN THE WALLS OF A FAMILY'S HOUSE!

A STARK-RAVING HOMICIDAL MANIAC COULD BE LIVING IN YOUR HOUSE!

Coty Pierce was sleeping like the most beautiful little girl. She had on an oversized University of Miami Hurricanes T-shirt, but it had moved up and he could see the pink silk bikini panties underneath.

She slept on her back, one sunbrowned leg crossed over the other. Her pouty mouth was just slightly open, forming the tiniest o, and she looked all innocence and light from his vantage point.

She was almost a full-grown woman now. He'd watched her preen in front of the wall mirror just a few hours before.

5

Watched her take off her pink lacy push-up bra. Watched her as she stared at her perfect breasts.

Coty was unbearably haughty and *untouchable*. Tonight he was going to change all that. He was going to take her.

Carefully, silently, he removed the metal grill in the ceiling. Then he crawled out of the wall and down into Coty's sky-blue-and-pink bedroom. His chest felt constricted, and his breathing was quick and labored. One minute he felt hot, the next he was shivering and cold.

Two small plastic trash bags covered his feet and were secured around his ankles, and he wore the light blue rubber gloves that the Pierces' maid used for housecleaning.

He felt like a sleek Ninja warrior and looked like Terror itself with his naked handpainted body. The perfect crime. He loved the feeling.

Could this be a dream? No, he *knew* it wasn't a dream. This was the real deal. He was actually going to do this! He took a deep breath and felt a burning inside his lungs.

For a brief moment, he studied the peaceful young girl he'd admired so many times at St Andrews. Then he quietly slipped into bed with the one-and-only Coty Pierce.

He took off a rubber glove and gently caressed her perfect, sun-bronzed skin. He pretended that he was smoothing coconut-scented suntan oil all over Coty. He was rock-hard already.

Her long blonde hair was sunbleached and felt as soft as rabbit's fur. It was thick and beautiful and smelled forest-clean, like balsam. *Yes, dreams do come true.*

Coty suddenly popped open her eyes. They were shiny emerald green gems, and they looked like priceless jewels from Harry Winston's in Boca.

She breathlessly said his name – the name she knew him

by at school. But he had given himself a new name; he'd *named* himself, re-created himself.

'What are you doing here,' she gasped. 'How did you get in?'

'Surprise, surprise. I'm *Casanova*,' he whispered against her ear. His pulse was racing off the charts. 'I chose you from all the beautiful girls in Boca Raton, in all of Florida. Aren't you pleased?'

Coty started to scream. 'Shush now,' he said, and smothered her small lovely mouth with his own. With a loving kiss.

He also kissed Hannah Pierce on that unforgettable evening of mayhem and murder in Boca Raton.

Shortly after, he kissed thirteen-year-old Karrie.

Before he was finished for the night, he knew that he really was Casanova – the world's greatest lover.

The Gentleman Caller

Chapel Hill, North Carolina, May 1981

He was the perfect *Gentleman*. Always a *Gentleman*. Always unobtrusive and polite.

He thought about that as he listened to the two lovers talking in sibilant whispers as they strolled near University Lake. It was all so dreamily romantic. It was so right for him.

'Is this a good idea, or is this too dumb for words?' he heard Tom Hutchinson ask Roe Tierney.

They were maneuvering into a teal blue rowboat that was gently rocking alongside a long dock on the lake. Tom and Roe were going to 'borrow' the boat for a few hours. Sneaky college mischief.

'My great-granddaddy says drifting downstream in a rowboat doesn't count against your life span,' Roe said. 'It's a great idea, Tommy. Let's go for it.'

Tom Hutchinson started to laugh. 'What if you do other things in said boat?' he asked.

'Well, if that includes aerobics of any sort, it might

actually extend your life span.' Roe's skirt rustled against her smooth thighs as she crossed her legs.

'Then stealing off in these nice people's boat for a moonlight ride is a good idea,' said Tom.

'*Great* idea.' Roe held her ground. 'The best. Let's do it.'

As their rowboat left the dock, the Gentleman slipped into the water. He made no sound. He listened to every word, every movement, and every nuance of the lovers' fascinating courting ritual.

There was almost a full moon, and it looked serene and beautiful to Tom and Roe as they slowly paddled out into the glistening lake. Earlier in the evening they had gone out for a romantic dinner in Chapel Hill, and they were both dressed to the hilt. Roe had on a pleated black skirt, a cream-colored silk blouse, silver shell earrings, and her roommate's dress pearls. Perfect boating attire.

The Gentleman's best guess was that Tom Hutchinson didn't even own the gray suit that he had on. Tom came from Pennsylvania. He was an auto mechanic's son who had made it to captain of the Duke football team, and had also managed to keep a grade index bordering on 4.0.

Roe and Tom were the 'golden couple.' It was just about the only thing that students from Duke and the nearby University of North Carolina could agree on. The 'scandal' of Duke's football captain dating Carolina's Azalea Queen made the romance even spicier.

They fumbled with uncooperative buttons and zippers as they slowly drifted on the lake. Roe wound up wearing only her earrings and the borrowed dress pearls. Tom had on his white shirt, but it was open all the way, making a kind of tent as he went inside Roe. Under the moon's watchful eye, they began to make love.

Their bodies moved smoothly as the boat rocked gently and playfully. Roe made tiny moaning sounds, which intermingled with a chorus of cicadas playing shrilly in the distance.

The Gentleman felt a column of rage welling up inside him. His dark side was bursting through: the brutal, repressed animal, the modern-day werewolf.

Suddenly, Tom Hutchinson flopped out of Roe Tierney with a tiny *thup*. Something powerful was pulling him out of the boat. Before he hit the water, Roe heard him yell. It was a strange noise that sounded like *yaaagghh*.

Tom swallowed lake water and gagged violently. There was a terrible pain and stinging in his throat, localized pain, but very intense and frightening.

Then, whatever powerful force had pulled him backwards into the lake suddenly released him. The choking pressure left him. Just like that. He was being set free.

His large strong hands, quarterback hands, went up to his throat and touched something warm. Blood was gushing out of his throat and spreading through the lake water. A terrible fear, a feeling close to panic, gripped him.

Horrified, he felt his throat again and found the knife embedded there. *Oh, Jesus God*, he thought, *I've been stabbed. I'm going to die at the bottom of this lake, and I don't even know why.*

In the rocking, drifting rowboat, meanwhile, Roe Tierney was too confused and shocked even to scream.

Her heart was pounding so rapidly and fiercely, she could hardly breathe. She stood up in the boat frantically searching for some sign of Tom.

This must be a sick joke, she thought. *I will never go out with Tom Hutchinson again. Never marry him. Never in a million years. This is not funny.* She was freezing, and she began to grope for her clothes in the bottom of the boat.

Swiftly, close to the boat, someone or something burst out of the black-looking water. It felt like an explosion under the lake.

Roe saw a head bobbing above the surface. Definitely a man's head . . . but it wasn't Tom Hutchinson.

'I didn't mean to scare you.' The Gentleman spoke softly, almost conversationally. 'Don't be alarmed,' he whispered as he reached for the gunwale of the rocking boat. 'We're old friends. To be perfectly honest, I've watched you for over two years.'

Suddenly Roe started to scream as if there were no tomorrow.

For Roe Tierney, there wasn't.

PART ONE

Scootchie Cross

1

Washington, D.C., April 1994
I was on the sun porch of our house on Fifth Street when it
all began. It was 'pouring down rain' as my little girl Janelle
likes to say, and the porch was a fine place to be. My grandmother had once taught me a prayer that I never forgot:
'*Thank you for everything just the way it is.*' It seemed right
that day – almost.

Stuck up on the porch wall was a Gary Larson *Far Side*
cartoon. It showed the 'Butlers of the World' annual banquet.
One of the butlers had been murdered. A knife was in his
chest right up to the hilt. A detective on the scene said, 'God,
Collings, I hate to start a Monday with a case like this.' The
cartoon was there to remind me there was more to life than
my job as a homicide detective in D.C. A two-year-old drawing
of Damon's tacked up next to the cartoon was inscribed: '*For
the best Daddy ever.*' That was another reminder.

I played Sarah Vaughan, Billie Holiday, and Bessie Smith
tunes on our aging piano. The blues was having its sneaky-
sad way with me lately. I'd been thinking about Jezzie

15

Flanagan. I could see her beautiful, haunting face sometimes, when I stared off into the distance. I tried not to stare off into the distance too much.

My two kids, Damon and Janelle, were sitting on the trusty, if slightly rickety, piano bench beside me. Janelle had her small arm wrapped across my back as far as it would stretch, which was about one-third of the way.

She had a bag of Gummi Bears in her free hand. As always, she shared with her friends. I was slow-sucking a red Gummi.

She and Damon were whistling along with my piano playing, though for Jannie, whistling is more like spitting to a certain preestablished rhythm. A battered copy of *Green Eggs and Ham* sat on top of the piano, vibrating to the beat.

Both Jannie and Damon knew I was having some trouble in my life lately, for the past few months, anyway. They were trying to cheer me up. We were playing and whistling the blues, soul, and a little fusion, but we were also laughing and carrying on, as children like us will.

I loved these times with my kids more than I loved all the rest of my life put together, and I had been spending more and more time with them. The Kodak pictures of children always remind me that my babies will be seven and five years old only one time. I didn't plan to miss any of it.

We were interrupted by the sound of heavy footsteps running up the wooden stairs of our back porch. Then the doorbell rang: one, two, three tinny rings. Whoever was out there was in a big hurry.

'Ding-dong the witch is dead.' Damon offered his inspirational thought for the moment. He was wearing wraparound shades, his impression of a cool dude. He was a cool little dude, actually.

'No, the witch isn't,' countered Jannie. I'd recently noticed that she had become a staunch defender of her gender.

'It might not be news about the witch,' I said, with just the right timing and delivery. The kids laughed. They get most of my jokes, which is a frightening thought.

Someone began to pound insistently against the door frame, and my name was shouted in a plaintive and alarming way. *Goddammit, leave us be. We don't need anything plaintive or alarming in our lives right now.*

'Dr Cross, please come! Please! Dr Cross,' the loud shouts continued. I didn't recognize the woman's voice, but privacy doesn't seem to count when your first name is Doctor.

I held the kids down, my hands fastened onto the tops of their small heads. 'I'm Dr Cross, not you two. Just keep on humming and hold my place. I'll be right back.'

'I'll be back!' said Damon in his best Terminator voice. I smiled at his joke. He is a second-grade wiseguy already.

I hurried to the back door, grabbing my service revolver on the way. This can be a bad neighborhood even for a cop, which I am. I peered out through the foggy and grimy windowpanes to see who was on our porch steps.

I recognized the young woman. She lived in the Langley projects. Rita Washington was a twenty-three-year-old pipehead who prowled our streets like a gray ghost. Rita was smart, nice enough, but impressionable and weak. She had taken a very bad turn in her life, lost her looks, and now was probably doomed.

I opened the door and felt a cold, wet gust of wind slap against my face. There was a lot of blood on Rita's hands and wrists and on the front of her green fake-leather carcoat.

'Rita, what in hell happened to you?' I asked. I guessed that she'd been gut-shot or stabbed over some drugs.

'Please, please come with me.' Rita Washington started to cough and sob at the same time. 'It little Marcus Daniels,' she said, and cried even louder. 'He been stabbed! It be real bad! He call your name. He ask for you, Dr Cross.'

'You stay there kids! I'll be right back!' I shouted over Rita Washington's hysterical cries. 'Nana, please watch the kids!' I yelled even louder. 'Nana, I have to go out!' I grabbed my coat and followed Rita Washington into the cold, teeming rain.

I tried not to step on the bright red blood dripping like wet paint all over our porch steps.

2

I ran as fast as I could down Fifth Street. I could feel my heart going *whump, whump, whump*, and I was sweating profusely in spite of the nasty, steady, cold spring rain. Blood was pounding furiously in my head. Every muscle and tendon in my body was straining, and my stomach clenched real hard.

I held eleven-year-old Marcus Daniels in my arms, clutched tightly against my chest. The little boy was bleeding badly. Rita Washington had found Marcus on the oily, darkened stairway leading to the basement in his building and had taken me to his crumpled body.

I ran like the wind, crying inside, holding it back as I've been taught to do on The Job and most everywhere else.

People who don't normally stare at much in Southeast were staring at me as I rumbled forward like a ten-axle semi on the loose in the inner city.

I outpaced gypsy cabs, shouting at everybody to get out of my way. I passed ghost store after ghost store boarded up with dark, rotting plywood that was scrawled with graffiti.

I ran over broken glass and rubble, Irish Rose bottles, and occasional dismal patches of weeds and loose dirt. This was our neighborhood; our share in The Dream; our capital.

I remembered a saying I'd heard about D.C.: '*Stoop down and you'll get stepped on, stand tall and you'll be shot at.*'

As I ran, poor Marcus was throwing off blood like a soaking-wet puppy dog shedding water. My neck and arms were on fire, and my muscles continued to strain.

'Hold on, baby,' I said to the little boy. 'Hold on, baby,' I prayed.

Halfway there, Marcus cried out in a tiny voice, 'Doctor Alex, man.'

That was all he said to me. I knew why. I knew a lot about little Marcus.

I raced up the steep, freshly paved asphalt drive of St Anthony's Hospital, 'St Tony's Spaghetti House' as it's sometimes called in the projects. An EMS ambulance rolled past me, heading toward L Street.

The driver wore a Chicago Bulls cap pulled sideways, its brim pointing strangely in my direction. Loud rap music blared from the van, and it must have been deafening inside. The driver and medic didn't stop, didn't seem to consider stopping. Life in Southeast goes like that sometimes. You can't stop for every murder or mugging that you come across on your daily rounds.

I knew my way to St Anthony's emergency room. I'd been there too many times. I shouldered open the familiar swinging glass door. It was stenciled EMERGENCY, but the letters were peeling away and there were nail scratches on the glass.

'We're here, Marcus. We're at the hospital,' I whispered to the little boy, but he didn't hear me. He was unconscious now.

'I need some help here! *People, I need help with this boy*!' I shouted.

The Pizza Hut delivery man would have gotten more attention. A bored-looking security guard glanced my way and gave me his practiced, flat-faced stare. A shabby stretcher clattered loudly down the halls of medicine.

I saw nurses I knew. Annie Bell Waters and Tanya Heywood, in particular.

'Bring him right here.' Annie Waters quickly cleared a way once she sized up the situation. She didn't ask me any questions as she pushed other hospital workers and the walking wounded out of our path.

We sailed past the reception desk, with SIGN IN HERE in English, Spanish, and Korean. I smelled hospital antiseptic on everything.

'Tried to cut his throat with a gravity knife. I think he nicked the carotid artery,' I said as we rushed down a crowded, puke-green corridor that was thick with faded signs: X-RAY, TRAUMA, CASHIER.

We finally located a room about the size of a clothes closet. The young-looking doctor who rushed in told me to leave.

'The boy's eleven years old,' I said. 'I'm staying right here. Both his wrists are cut. It's a suicide attempt. Hold on, baby,' I whispered to Marcus. 'Just hold on, baby.'

3

Click! Casanova popped the trunk latch of his car and peered into the wide, shiny-wet eyes staring out at him. *What a pity. What a waste*, he thought as he looked down at her.

'Peekaboo,' he said. 'I see you.' He had fallen out of love with the twenty-two-year-old college student tied up in the trunk. He was also angry at her. She had disobeyed the rules. She'd ruined the fantasy du jour.

'You look like absolute hell,' he said. 'Relatively speaking, of course.'

The young woman was gagged with wet cloths and couldn't answer back, but she glared at him. Her dark-brown eyes showed fear and pain, but he could still see the stubbornness and spunk there.

He took out his black carrying bag first, then he roughly lifted her one hundred twelve pounds out of the car. He made no effort to be gentle at this point.

'You're welcome,' he said as he put her down. 'Forgotten our manners, have we?' Her legs were shaky and she almost fell, but Casanova held her up easily with one hand.

She had on dark green Wake Forest University running shorts, a white tank top, and brand-new Nike cross-training shoes. She was a typical spoiled college brat, he knew, but achingly beautiful. Her slender ankles were bound with a leather thong that stretched about two and a half feet. Her hands were tied behind her back, also with a leather thong.

'You can just walk ahead of me. Go straight unless I tell you otherwise. Now *walk*,' he ordered. 'Move those long, lovely gams. Hut, hut, hut.'

They started through the dense woods that got even thicker as they moved slowly along. Thicker and darker. Creepier and creepier. He swung his black bag as if he were a child carrying a lunch box. He loved the dark woods. Always had.

Casanova was tall and athletic, well built, and good-looking. He knew that he could have many women, but not the way he wanted them. Not like this.

'I asked you to listen, didn't I? You wouldn't listen.' He spoke in a soft, detached voice. 'I told you the house rules. But you wanted to be a wiseass. So be a wiseass. Reap the rewards.'

As the young woman struggled ahead she became increasingly afraid, close to panic. The woods were even denser now, and the low-hanging branches clawed at her bare arms, leaving long scratches. She knew her captor's name: Casanova. He fancied himself a great lover, and in fact he could maintain an erection longer than any man she had ever known. He had always seemed rational and in control of himself, but she knew he *had to be* crazy. He certainly could act sane on occasion, though. Once you accepted a single premise of his, something he had said to her several times: '*Man was born to hunt . . . women.*'

He had given her the rules of his house. He had clearly

warned her to behave. She just hadn't listened. She'd been willful and stupid and had made a huge, tactical mistake.

She tried not to think of what he was going to do to her out here in these bewildering Twilight Zone-type woods. It would surely give her a heart attack. She wouldn't give him the satisfaction of seeing her break down and cry.

If only he would ungag her. Her mouth was dry, and she was thirsty beyond belief. Perhaps she could actually talk her way out of this – of whatever it was that he had planned.

She stopped walking and turned to face him. It was draw-a-line-in-the-sand time.

'You want to stop here? That's fine with me. I'm not going to let you talk, though. No last words, dear heart. No reprieve from the governor. You blew it big time. If we stop here, you *may not like it*. If you want to walk some more, that's fine, too. I just love these woods, don't you?'

She had to talk to him, get through to him somehow. Ask him *why*. Maybe appeal to his intelligence. She tried to say his name, but only muffled sounds made it through the damp gag.

He was self-assured and even calmer than usual. He walked with a cocky swagger. 'I don't understand a word you're saying. Anyway, it wouldn't change a thing even if I did.'

He had on one of the weird masks that he always wore. This one was actually called a death mask, he'd told her, and it was used to reconstruct faces, usually at hospitals and morgues.

The skin color of the death mask was almost perfect and the detail was frighteningly realistic. The face he'd chosen was young and handsome, an all-American type. She wondered what he really looked like. Who in hell was he? Why did he wear masks?

She would escape somehow, she told herself. Then she would get him locked up for a thousand years. No death penalty – let him suffer.

'If that's your choice, fine,' he said, and he suddenly kicked her feet out from under her. She fell down hard on her back. 'You die right here.'

He slid a needle out of the well-worn black medical bag he'd brought with him. He brandished it like a tiny sword. Let her see it.

'This needle is called a Tubex,' he said. 'It's preloaded with thiopental sodium, which is a barbiturate. Does barbiturate-sounding things.' He squeezed out a thin squirt of the brown liquid. It looked like iced tea, and it was not something she wanted injected into her veins.

'*What does it do? What are you doing to me?*' she screamed into the tight gag. '*Please take this gag out of my mouth.*'

She was covered with sweat, and her breathing was labored. Her whole body felt stiff, anesthetized and numb. Why was he giving her a barbiturate?

'If I do this wrong, you'll die right now,' he told her. 'So *don't move.*'

She shook her head affirmatively. She was trying so hard to let him know that she could be good; she could be so very good. *Please don't kill me*, she silently pleaded. *Don't do this.*

He pricked a vein in the crook of her elbow, and she could feel the painful pinch there.

'I don't want to leave any unsightly bruises,' he whispered. 'It won't take long. Ten, nine, eight, seven, six, *five, you, are, so, beautiful*, zero. All finished.'

She was crying now. She couldn't help it. The tears were streaming down her cheeks. He was crazy. She squeezed her eyes shut, couldn't look at him anymore. *Please, God, don't let me die like this*, she prayed. *Not all alone out here.*

The drug acted quickly, almost immediately. She felt warm all over, warm and sleepy. She went limp.

He took off her tank top and began to fondle her breasts, like a juggler with several balls. There was nothing she could do to stop him.

He arranged her legs as if she were his art, his human sculpture, stretching the leather thong as far as it would go. He felt down between her legs. The sudden thrust made her open her eyes, and she stared up at the horrible mask. His eyes stared back at her. They were blank and emotionless, yet strangely penetrating.

He entered her, and she felt a jolt like a very powerful electric shock running through her body. He was very hard, fully aroused already. He was probing inside her as she was dying from the barbiturate. He was watching her die. That's what this was all about.

Her body wriggled, bolted, shook. As weak as she was, she tried to scream. *No, please, please, please. Don't do this to me.*

Mercifully, blackness came over her.

She didn't know how long she'd been unconscious. Didn't care. She woke up and she was still alive.

She started to cry, and the muffled sounds coming through the gag were agonizing. Tears ran down her cheeks. She realized how much she wanted to live.

She noticed that she'd been moved. Her arms were behind her and tied around a tree. Her legs were crossed and bound, and she was still tightly gagged. He had taken off her clothes. She didn't see her clothes anywhere.

He was still there!

'I don't really care if you scream,' he said. 'There's absolutely nobody to hear you out here.' His eyes gleamed out of the lifelike mask. 'I just don't want you to scare away the hungry birds and animals.' He glanced briefly at her truly beautiful body. 'Too bad you disobeyed me, broke the rules,' he said.

He took off the mask and let her see his face for the first time. He fixed the image of her face in his mind. Then he bent down and kissed her on the lips.

Kiss the girls.

Finally, he walked away.

4

Most of my rage had been spent on the furious footrace to St Anthony's with Marcus Daniels cradled in my arms. The adrenaline rush was gone now, but I felt an unnatural weariness.

The emergency-room waiting area was noise and frustrated confusion. Babies crying, parents wailing out their grief, the PA incessantly paging doctors. A bleeding man kept muttering, 'Ho shit, ho shit.'

I could still *see* the beautiful, sad eyes of Marcus Daniels. I could still *hear* his soft voice.

At a little past six-thirty that night, my partner in crime arrived unexpectedly at the hospital. Something about that struck me as wrong, but I let it pass for now.

John Sampson and I have been best friends since we were both ten years old and running these same streets in D.C. Southeast. Somehow, we survived without having our throats slashed. I drifted into abnormal psychology, and eventually got a doctorate at Johns Hopkins. Sampson went into the army. In some strange and mysterious manner, we both ended up working together on the D.C. police force.

I was sitting on a sheetless gurney parked outside the Trauma Room. Next to me was the 'crash cart' they had used for Marcus. Rubber tourniquets hung like streamers from the black handles of the cart.

'How's the boy?' Sampson asked. He knew about Marcus already. Somehow, he always knew. The rain was running down his black poncho in little streams, but he didn't seem to care.

I sadly shook my head. I was still feeling wasted. 'Don't know yet. They won't tell me anything. Doctor wanted to know if I was next of kin. They took him to Trauma. He cut himself real bad. So what brings you to happy hour?'

Sampson shrugged his way out of his poncho, and flopped down beside me on the straining gurney. Under the poncho, he had on one of his typical street-detective outfits; silver-and-red Nike sweatsuit, matching high-topped sneakers, thin gold bracelets, signet rings. His street look was intact.

'Where's your gold tooth?' I managed a smile. 'You need a gold tooth to complete your fly ensemble. At least a gold star on one tooth. Maybe some corn braids?'

Sampson snorted out a laugh. 'I heard. I came,' he said offhandedly about his appearance at St Anthony's. 'You okay? You look like the last of the big, bad bull elephants.'

'Little boy tried to kill himself. Sweet little boy, like Damon. Eleven years old.'

'Want me to run over to their crack crib? Shoot the boy's parents?' Sampson asked. His eyes were obsidian-hard.

'We'll do it later,' I said.

I was probably in the mood. The positive news was that the parents of Marcus Daniels lived together; the bad part was that they kept the boy and his four sisters in the crack house they ran near the Langley Terrace projects. The ages of the children ranged from five to twelve, and all the kids worked in the business. They were 'runners.'

'What *are* you doing here?' I asked him for the second time. 'You didn't just happen to show up here at St A's. What's up?'

Sampson tapped out a cigarette from a pack of Camels. He used only one hand. Very cool. He lit up. Doctors and nurses were everywhere.

I snatched the cigarette away and crushed it under my black Converse sneaker sole, near the hole in the big toe.

'Feel better now?' Sampson eyed me. Then he gave me a broad grin showing his large white teeth. The skit was over. Sampson had worked his magic on me, and it *was* magic, including the cigarette trick. I was feeling better. Skits work. Actually, I felt as if I'd just been hugged by about a half-dozen close relatives and both my kids. Sampson is my best friend for a reason. He can push my buttons better than anybody.

'Here comes the angel of mercy,' he said, pointing down the long, chaotic corridor.

Annie Waters was walking toward us with her hands thrust deeply into the pockets of her hospital coat. She had a tight look on her face, but she always does.

'I'm real sorry, Alex. The boy didn't make it. I think he was nearly gone when you got him here. Probably living on all that hope you carry bottled up inside you.'

Powerful images and visceral sensations of carrying Marcus along Fifth and L streets flashed before me. I imagined the hospital death sheet covering Marcus. It's such a small sheet that they use for children.

'The boy was my patient. He adopted me this spring.' I told the two of them what had me so wild and crazed and suddenly depressed.

'Can I get you something, Alex?' said Annie Waters. She had a concerned look on her face.

I shook my head. I had to talk, had to get this out right now.

'Marcus found out I gave help at St A's, talked to people sometimes. He started coming by the trailer afternoons. Once I passed his tests, he talked about his life at the crack house. Everybody he knew in his life was a junkie. Junkie came by my house today . . . Rita Washington. Not Marcus's mother, not his father. The boy tried to slit his own throat, slit his wrists. Just eleven years old.'

My eyes were wet. A little boy dies, somebody should cry. The psychologist for an eleven-year-old suicide victim ought to mourn. I thought so, anyway.

Sampson finally stood up and put his long arm gently on my shoulder. He was six feet nine again. 'Let's head on home, Alex,' he said. 'C'mon, my man. Time to go.'

I went in and looked at Marcus for the last time.

I held his lifeless little hand and thought about the talks the two of us had, the ineffable sadness always in his brown eyes. I remembered a wise, beautiful African proverb: '*It takes a whole village to raise a good child.*'

Finally, Sampson came and took me away from the boy, took me home.

Where it got much worse.

5

I didn't like what I saw at home. A lot of cars were crowded helter-skelter around my house. It's a white shingle A-frame; it looks like anybody's house. Most of the cars appeared familiar; they were cars of friends and family members.

Sampson pulled in behind a dented ten-year-old Toyota that belonged to the wife of my late brother Aaron. Cilla Cross was a good friend. She was tough and smart. I had ended up liking her more than my brother. What was Cilla doing here?

'What *the hell* is going on at the house?' I asked Sampson again. I was starting to get a little concerned.

'Invite me in for a cold beer,' he said as he pulled the key from the ignition. 'Least you can do.'

Sampson was already up and out of the car. He moves like a slick winter wind when he wants to. 'Let's go inside, Alex.'

I had the car door open, but I was still sitting inside. 'I live here. I'll go in when I feel like it.' I didn't feel like it suddenly. A sheen of cold sweat was on the back of my neck. Detective paranoia? Maybe, maybe not.

'Don't be difficult,' Sampson called back over his shoulder, 'for once in your life.'

A long icy shiver ran through my body. I took a deep breath. The thought of the human monster I had recently helped put away still gave me nightmares. I deeply feared he would escape one day. The mass killer and kidnapper had already been to Fifth Street once.

What in hell was going on inside my house?

Sampson didn't knock on the front door, or ring the bell, which dangled on red-and-blue wires. He just waltzed inside as if he lived there. Same as it's always been. *Mi casa es su casa.* I followed him into my own house.

My boy, Damon, streaked into Sampson's outstretched arms, and John scooped up my son as if he were made of air. Jannie came skating toward me, calling me 'Big Daddy' as she ran. She was already in her slipper-sock pajamas, smelling of fresh talcum after her bath. My little lady.

Something was wrong in her big brown eyes. The look on her face froze me.

'What is it, my honeybunch?' I asked as I nuzzled against Jannie's smooth, warm cheek. The two of us nuzzle a lot. 'What's wrong? Tell your Daddy all your troubles and woes.'

In the living room I could see three of my aunts, my two sisters-in-law, my one living brother, Charles. My aunts had been crying; their faces were all puffy and red. So had my sister-in-law Cilla, and she isn't one to get weepy without a good reason.

The room had the unnatural, claustrophobic look of a wake. *Somebody has died*, I thought. *Somebody we all love has died.* But everybody I love seemed to be there, present and accounted for.

Nana Mama, my grandmother, was serving coffee, iced tea, and also cold chicken pieces, which no one seemed to be eating. Nana lives on Fifth Street with me and the kids. In her own mind, she's raising the three of us.

Nana had shrunk to around five feet by her eightieth year. She is still the most impressive person I know in our nation's capital, and I know most of them – the Reagans, the Bush people, and now the Clintons.

My grandmother was dry-eyed as she did her serving. I have rarely seen her cry, though she is a tremendously warm and caring person. She just doesn't cry anymore. She says she doesn't have that much of life left, and she won't waste it on tears.

I finally walked into the living room and asked the question that was beating against the inside of my head. 'It's nice to see everyone – Charles, Cilla, Aunt Tia – *but would someone please tell me what's going on here?*'

They all stared at me.

I still had Jannie cradled in my arms. Sampson had Damon tucked like a hairy football under his massive right arm.

Nana spoke for the assembled group. Her almost inaudible words sent the sharpest pain right through me.

'It's Naomi,' she said quietly. 'Scootchie is missing, Alex.' Then Nana Mama started to weep for the first time in years.

6

Casanova screamed, and the loud sound coming from deep inside his throat turned into a raspy howl.

He was crashing through the deep woods, thinking about the girl he had abandoned back there. The horror of what he had done. *Again.*

Part of him wanted to go back for the girl – *save her* – an act of mercy.

He was experiencing spasms of guilt now, and he began to run faster and faster. His thick neck and chest were covered with perspiration. He felt weak, and his legs were rubbery and undependable.

He was fully conscious of what he had done. He just couldn't stop himself.

Anyway, it was better this way. She had seen his face. It was stupid of him to think she would ever be able to understand him. He had seen the fear and loathing in her eyes.

If only she'd listened when he'd tried to talk to her. After all, he was different from other mass killers – *he could feel everything* he did. He could feel love . . . and suffer loss . . . and . . .

He angrily swept away the death mask. It was all her fault. He would have to change personas now. He needed to stop being Casanova.

He needed to be *himself*. His pitiful other self.

7

It's Naomi. Scootchie is missing. Alex.

We held the most intense Cross family emergency conference in our kitchen, where they've always been held. Nana made more coffee, and also herbal tea for herself. I put the kids to bed first. Then I cracked opened a bottle of Black Jack and poured stiff drinks of whisky all around.

I learned that my twenty-two-year-old niece had been missing in North Carolina for four days. The police down there had waited that long to contact our family in Washington. As a policeman, I found that hard to understand. Two days was pretty standard in missing-person cases. Four days made no sense.

Naomi Cross was a law student at Duke University. She'd made Law Review and was near the top of her class. She was the pride of everyone in our family, including myself. We had a nickname for her that went back to when she was three or four years old. *Scootchie.* She always used to 'scootch' up close to everybody when she was little. She loved to 'scootch,' and hug, and *be* hugged. After my brother Aaron died, I helped Cilla to raise her. It wasn't hard – she was always sweet and funny, cooperative, and so very smart.

Scootchie was missing. In North Carolina. Four days now.

'I talked to a detective named Ruskin,' Sampson told the group in the kitchen. He was trying not to act like a street cop, but he couldn't help it. He was on the case now. Flatfaced and serious. The Sampson stare.

'Detective Ruskin sounded knowledgeable about Naomi's disappearance. Seemed like a straight-ahead cop on the phone. Something strange, though. Told me that a law-school friend of Naomi's reported her missing. Her name's Mary Ellen Klouk.'

I had met Naomi's friend. She was a future lawyer, from Garden City, Long Island. Naomi had brought Mary Ellen home to Washington a couple of times. We'd gone to hear Handel's *Messiah* together one Christmas at the Kennedy Center.

Sampson took off his dark glasses, and kept them off, which is rare for him. Naomi was his favorite, and he was as shook up as the rest of us. She called Sampson 'His Grimness,' and 'Darth One,' and he loved it when she teased him.

'Why didn't this Detective Ruskin call us before now? Why didn't those university people call me?' my sister-in-law asked. Cilla is forty-one. She has allowed herself to grow to ample proportions. I doubted that she was five feet four, but she had to be close to two hundred pounds. She'd told me that she didn't want to be attractive to men anymore.

'Don't know the answer to that yet,' Sampson told Cilla and the rest of us. 'They told Mary Ellen Klouk *not* to call us.'

'What exactly did Detective Ruskin have to say about the delay?' I asked Sampson.

'Detective said there were extenuating circumstances. He wouldn't elaborate for me, persuasive as I can be.'

'You tell him we could have the conversation in person?'

Sampson nodded slowly. 'Uh-huh. He said the result would be the same. I told him I doubted that. He said okay. Man seemed to have no fears.'

'Black man?' Nana asked. She is a racist, and proud of it. She says she's too old to be socially or politically correct. She doesn't so much dislike white people as distrust them.

'No, but I don't think that's the problem, Nana. Something else is going on.' Sampson looked across the kitchen table at me. 'I don't think he *could* talk.'

'FBI?' I asked. It was the obvious guess when things get overly secretive. The FBI understands better than Bell Atlantic, the *Washington Post*, and the *New York Times* that information is power.

'That could be the problem. Ruskin wouldn't admit it on the phone.'

'I better talk to him,' I said. 'In person would probably be best, don't you think?'

'I think that would be good, Alex.' Cilla spoke up from her end of the table.

'Maybe I'll tag along,' Sampson said, grinning like the predatory wolf that he is.

There were sage nods and at least one hallelujah in the overcrowded kitchen. Cilla came around the table and hugged me tight. My sister-in-law was shaking like a big, spreading tree in a storm.

Sampson and I were going South. We were going to bring back Scootchie.

8

I had to tell Damon and Jannie about their 'Auntie Scootch,' which is what the kids have always called her. My kids sensed something bad had happened. They knew it, just as they somehow know my most secret and vulnerable places. They had refused to go to sleep until I came and talked to them.

'Where's Auntie Scootch at? What happened to her?' Damon demanded as soon as I entered the kids' bedroom. He had heard enough to understand that Naomi was in some kind of terrible trouble.

I have a need always to tell the kids the truth, if it's possible. I'm committed to truth-telling between us. But every once in a while, it is so hard to do.

'We haven't heard from Aunt Naomi in a few days,' I began. 'That's why everybody is worried tonight, and why they came over to our house,' I said.

I went on. 'Daddy's on the case now. I'm going to do my best to find Aunt Naomi in the next couple of days. You know that your daddy usually solves problems. Am I right?'

Damon nodded to the truth in that, and seemed reassured

by what I had told them, but mostly by my serious tone. He came into my arms and gave me a kiss, which he hasn't been doing as much lately. Jannie gave me the softest kiss, too. I held them both in my arms. My sweet babies.

'Daddy's on the case now,' Jannie whispered. That warmed my spirits some. As Billie Holiday put it, 'God bless the child who's got his own.'

By eleven the kids were sleeping peacefully, and the house was beginning to clear. My elderly aunts had already gone home to their quirky old-lady nests, and Sampson was getting ready to leave.

He usually lets himself in and out, but this time, Nana Mama walked Sampson to the door, which is a rarity. I went with them. Safety in numbers.

'Thank you for going down South with Alex tomorrow,' Nana said to Sampson in confidential tones. I wondered who she thought might be listening, trying to overhear her intimacies. 'You see now, John Sampson, you *can* be civilized and somewhat useful when you want to be. Didn't I always tell you that?' She pointed a curled, knobby finger at his massive chin. 'Didn't I?'

Sampson grinned down at her. He revels in his physical superiority even to a woman who is eighty. 'I let Alex go by himself, I'd only have to come later, Nana. Rescue him *and* Naomi,' he said.

Nana and Sampson cackled like a pair of cartoon crows on an old familiar fencepost. It was good to hear them laugh. Then she somehow managed to wrap her arms around Sampson and me. She stood there – like some little old lady holding on to her two favorite redwood trees. I could feel her fragile body tremble. Nana Mama hadn't hugged the two of us like that in twenty years. I knew that she loved Naomi as if she were her own child, and she was very afraid for her.

It can't be Naomi, Nothing bad could happen to her, not to Naomi. The words kept drifting through my head. But something had happened to her, and now I would have to start thinking and acting like a policeman. Like a homicide detective. *In the South.*

'*Have faith and pursue the unknown end.*' Oliver Wendell Holmes said that. I have faith. I pursue the unknown. That's my job description.

9

Seven o'clock in the evening was a busy time in late April on the stunningly beautiful campus of Duke University. The physical impressiveness of the students was visible everywhere at the self-proclaimed 'Harvard of the South.' The magnolia trees, especially along Chapel Drive, were plentiful and in full bloom. The well-kept and striking orderliness of the grounds made it one of the most visually satisfying campuses in the United States.

Casanova found the fragrant air intoxicating as he strolled between tall graystone gates and onto the university's West Campus. It was a few minutes past seven. He had come for one reason only – to hunt. The entire process was exhilarating and irresistible. Impossible to stop once he had begun. This was foreplay. Lovely in every way.

I'm like a killer shark, with a human brain, and even a heart, Casanova thought, as he walked. *I am a predator without peer, a thinking predator.*

He believed that men loved the hunt – lived for it, in fact – though most wouldn't admit it. A man's eyes never stopped searching for beautiful, sensual women, or for sexy men and boys, for that matter. All the more at a prime location like the Duke campus, or the campuses at the University of North Carolina at Chapel Hill, or North Carolina State University at Raleigh, or many others he'd visited throughout the Southeast.

Just look at them! The slightly uppity Duke coeds were among the very finest and most '*contemporary*' American women. Even in dirty cutoffs, or ridiculous holey 501s, or baggy hobo's pants, they were something to see, to watch, occasionally to photograph, to fantasize about endlessly

Nothing could be finer, Casanova thought, whistling a bar of the beamish old tune about a life of leisure in the Carolinas.

He casually sipped an icy Coca-Cola as he watched the students at play. He was playing a game of skill himself – several complicated games at once, actually. The games had become his life. The fact that he had a 'respectable' job, another life, no longer mattered.

He checked *each passing woman* who even looked like a faint possibility for his collection. He studied shapely young coeds, older women professors, and female visitors in the Duke Blue Devils T-shirts that seemed de rigueur for outsiders.

He licked his lips in anticipation. Here was something splendid up ahead . . .

A tall, slender, exquisite black woman leaned against a shapely old oak in the Edens Quad. She was reading the Duke *Chronicle*, which she'd folded into thirds. He loved the smooth shine of her brown skin, her artistically braided hair. But he moved on.

Yes, men are hunters by nature, he was thinking. He was off in his own world again. 'Faithful' husbands were oh-so-careful and furtive with their looks. Fresh-eyed boys of eleven and twelve appeared very innocent and playful. Grandfathers pretended to be above the fray, and were just 'cute' with their affection. But Casanova knew they were all watching, constantly selecting, obsessed with mastering the hunt from puberty to the grave.

It was a biological necessity, no? He was quite certain of that. Women nowadays were demanding that men accept the fact that their female biological clocks were ticking . . . well, with men, it was their biological *cocks* that were ticking.

Constantly ticking, those cocks.

That was a fact of nature, too. Everywhere he went, at virtually any time of day or night, he could feel the pulsing beat inside. *Tick-cock. Tick-cock.*

Tick-cock!

Tick-cock!

A beautiful honey-blonde coed sat crosslegged on the grass intersecting his path. She was reading a paperback, Karl Jaspers's *Philosophy of Existence*. The rock group Smashing Pumpkins was contributing mantralike riffs from a portable CD player. Casanova smiled to himself.

Tick-cock!

The hunt was relentless for him. He was Priapus for the nineties. The difference between him and so many gutless modern men was that he acted on his natural impulses.

He relentlessly searched out a great beauty – and then he took her! What an outrageously simple idea. *What a compellingly modern horror story.*

He watched two petite Japanese coeds chowing down on greasy North Carolina barbecue from the new Crooks Corner II restaurant in Durham. *They* looked so delicious eating their dinner, wolfing their barbecue like small animals. North Carolina BBQ consisted of pork cooked over a fire, seasoned with a vinegar-laced sauce, then finely chopped. You *couldn't* eat BBQ without slaw and hush puppies.

He smiled at the unlikely scene. *Yum.*

Still, he moved on. Sights and scenes caught his eye. Pierced eyebrows. Tattooed ankles. Lalapalooza T-shirts. Lovely flowing breasts, legs, thighs everywhere he looked.

He finally came to a small Gothic-style building near the Duke University Hospital, North Division. This was a special annex where terminally ill cancer patients from all over the South were cared for during their final days. His heart began to pound, and a series of small tremors shook his body.

There she was!

10

*There was the most beautiful woman in the South! Beautiful
in all ways. Not only was she physically desirable – she was
extremely smart. She might be able to understand him. Maybe
she was as special as he was.*

He almost said the words out loud, and believed them to
be absolutely true. He had done a great deal of homework
on his next victim. Blood began to pump and rush into his
forehead. He could feel a throbbing all through his body.

Her name was Kate McTiernan. Katelya Margaret
McTiernan, to be as precise as he liked to be.

She was just walking out of the terminal cancer wing,
where she had worked to help pay her way through medical
school. She was all by her lonesome, as usual. Her last
boyfriend had warned her that she was going to 'end up a
beautiful old maid.'

Fat chance of that. Obviously, it was Kate McTiernan's
decision to be alone as much as she was. She could have
been with nearly anyone she chose. She was stunningly beautiful, highly intelligent, and compassionate, from what he

could tell so far. Kate *was a grind, though*. She was incredibly dedicated to her medical studies and hospital duties.

Nothing was overdone about her, and he appreciated that. Her long, curly brown hair framed her narrow face nicely. Her eyes were dark blue, and sparkled when she smiled. Her laugh was catchy, irresistible. She had an all-American look, but not banal. She was a hardbody, but she appeared so soft and feminine.

He'd watched other men hit on her – studly students and even the occasional jaunty and ridiculous professor. She didn't hold it against them, and he saw how she deflected them, usually with some kindness, some small generosity.

But there was always that devilish, heartbreaking smile of hers. *I'm not available*, it said. *You can never have me. Please, don't even think about it. It's not that I'm too good for you, I'm just . . . different.*

Kate the Dependable, Kate the Nice Person, was right on time tonight. She always left the cancer annex between a quarter to eight and eight. She had her routines just as he did.

She was a first-year intern at North Carolina University Hospital in Chapel Hill, but she'd been working in a co-op program at Duke since January. The experimental cancer ward. He knew all about Katelya McTiernan.

She was going to be thirty-one in a few weeks. She'd had to work three years to pay for her college and medical-school expenses. She had also spent two years with a sick mother in Buck, West Virginia.

She walked at a determined pace along Flowers Drive, toward the multilevel Medical Center parking garage. He had to move quickly to keep up with her, all the while watching her long shapely legs, which were a little too pale for his liking. *No time for the sun, Kate? Afraid of a little melanoma?*

She carried thick medical volumes against one hip. Looks and brains. She planned to practice back in West Virginia, where she was born. Didn't seem to care about making a lot of money. What for? So she could own *ten* pairs of black high-topped sneakers?

Kate McTiernan was wearing her usual university garb: a crisp white med-school jacket, khaki shirt, weathered tan trousers, her faithful black sneakers. It worked for her. Kate the Character. Slightly off-center. Unexpected. Strangely, powerfully alluring.

On Kate McTiernan, almost anything would have worked, even the most homespun interpretation of cheap chic. He particularly loved Kate McTiernan's irreverence toward university and hospital life, and especially the holier-than-thou medical school. It showed in the way she dressed; the casual way she carried herself now; everything about her lifestyle. She seldom wore makeup. She seemed very natural, and there was nothing phony or stuck-up about her that he'd noticed yet.

There was even a little of the unexpected klutz in her. Earlier in the week, he had seen her flush the deepest red after she tripped on a guardrail outside Perkins Library and crashed into a bench with her hip. That warmed him tremendously. He *could* be touched, could feel human warmth. *He wanted Kate to love him . . . He wanted to love her back.*

That was why he was so special, so different. It was what separated him from all the other one-dimensional killers and butchers he had ever heard or read about, and he had read everything on the subject. He could feel everything. He could love. He knew that.

Kate said something amusing to a fortyish-looking professor as she walked past him. Casanova couldn't hear it from where he was watching. Kate turned for some quick repartee, but kept on walking, leaving the professor with her luminous smile to think about.

He saw a little jiggle action as Kate whirled around after her brief interchange with the prof. Her breasts weren't too large or too small. Her long brown hair was thick and wavy, shiny in the early evening light, revealing just a touch of red. Perfect in every detail.

He had been watching her for more than four weeks, and he knew she was the one. He could love Dr Kate McTiernan more than all the others. He *believed* it for a moment. He *ached* to believe it. He said her name softly – *Kate* . . .

Dr Kate.

Tick-cock.

11

Sampson and I took shifts at the wheel on the four-hour haul from Washington, down into North Carolina. While I drove, the Man Mountain slept. He wore a black T-shirt that bluntly said SECURITY. Economy of words.

When Sampson was at the controls of my ancient Porsche, I put on a set of old Koss headphones. I listened to Big Joe Williams, thought about Scootchie, continued to feel hollowed-out.

I couldn't sleep, hadn't slept more than an hour the night before. I felt like a grief-stricken father whose only daughter was missing. Something seemed wrong about this case.

We entered the South at noon. I had been born around a hundred miles away, in Winston-Salem. I hadn't been back there since I was ten years old, the year my mother died, and my brothers and I were moved to Washington.

I'd been to Durham before, for Naomi's graduation. She had finished Duke undergraduate summa cum laude, and she received one of the loudest, cheeriest ovations in the history of the ceremony. The Cross family had been there in full force. It was one of the happiest, proudest days for all of us.

Naomi was the only child of my brother Aaron, who died of cirrhosis at thirty-three. Naomi had grown up fast after his death. Her mother had to work a sixty-hour week for years to support them, so Naomi was in charge of the house from around the time she was ten. She was the littlest general.

She was a precocious little girl, and read about Alice's adventures in *Through the Looking-Glass* when she was only four. A family friend gave her violin lessons, and she played well. She loved music, and still played whenever she had time. She graduated number one in her class at John Carroll High School in D.C. As busy as she was with her studies, she found time to write graceful prose on what life was like growing up in the projects. She reminded me of a young Alice Walker.

Gifted.

Very special.

Missing for more than four days.

The welcome mat wasn't out for us at Durham's brand-new police headquarters building, not even after Sampson and I showed our badges and IDs from Washington. The desk sergeant wasn't impressed.

He looked something like the TV weatherman Willard Scott. He had a full crewcut, long thick sideburns, and skin the color of fresh ham. After he found out who we were, it got a little worse. No red carpet, no Southern hospitality, no Southern comfort.

Sampson and I got to sit and cool our heels in the duty room of the Durham Police Department. It was all shiny glass and polished wood. We received the kind of hostile looks and blank stares usually reserved for drug dealers caught around grade schools.

'Feel like we just landed on Mars,' Sampson said as we waited and watched Durham's finest, watched complainants come and go. 'Don't like the feeling I get from the Martians. Don't like their beady little Martian eyes. Don't think I like the new South.'

'You think about it, we'd fit in the same anywhere,' I told Sampson. 'We'd get the same reception, same cold stares, at Nairobi Police Headquarters.'

'Maybe.' Sampson nodded behind his dark glasses. 'But at least they'd be black Martians. At least they'd know who John Coltrane is.'

Durham detectives Nick Ruskin and Davey Sikes finally came down to see us an hour and a quarter after we arrived.

Ruskin reminded me a little of Michael Douglas in his dark-hero cop roles. He wore a coordinated outfit: green-and-tan tweed jacket, stonewashed jeans, yellow pocket T. He was about my height, which would make him six three or so, a little bigger than life. His longish brown hair was slicked back and razor-cut.

Davey Sikes was well built. His head was a solid block that made sharp right angles with his shoulders. He had sleepy, oatmeal-brown eyes; almost no affect that I could discern. Sikes was a sidekick type, definitely not the leader. At least not if first appearances meant anything.

The two detectives shook hands with us, and acted as if all were forgiven, as if they were forgiving us for intruding. I had the feeling that Ruskin especially was used to getting his way inside the Durham PD. He seemed like the local star. The main man around these parts. Matinee idol at the Durham Triplex.

'Sorry about the wait, Detective Cross, Sampson. It's been busy as a son of a bitch around here,' Nick Ruskin said. He had a light Southern accent. Lots of confidence in himself.

He hadn't mentioned Naomi by name yet. Detective Sikes was silent. Didn't say a word.

'You two like to take a ride with Davey and me? I'll explain the situation on the way. There's been a homicide. That's what had us all tied up. Police found a woman's body out in Efland. This is a real bad one.'

12

This is a real bad one. A woman's body in Efland. What woman?

Sampson and I followed Ruskin and Sikes out to their car, a forest-green Saab Turbo. Ruskin got in the driver's seat. I remembered Sergeant Esterhaus's words in *Hill Street Blues:* *'Let's be careful out there.'*

'You know anything at all about the murdered woman?' I asked Nick Ruskin as we headed onto West Chapel Hill Street. He had his siren screaming and he was already driving fast. He drove with a kind of brashness and cockiness.

'I don't know enough,' Ruskin said. 'That's our problem, Davey's and mine, with this investigation. We can't get straight-dick information about much of anything. That's probably why we're in such a good mood today. You notice?'

'Yeah, we noticed,' Sampson said. I didn't look over at him. I could feel the steam rising in the back seat, though. Heat coming off his skin.

Davey Sikes glanced back and frowned at Sampson. I got the feeling they weren't going to become best buddies.

Ruskin continued talking. He seemed to like the spotlight, being on the Big Case. 'This entire case is under the control of the FBI now. The DEA got in the act, too. I wouldn't be surprised if the CIA was part of the 'crisis team.' They did send some kinky crackerjack down from their fancy outpost in Sanford.'

'What do you mean this *entire case?*' I asked Ruskin. Warning alarms were sounding in my head. I thought of Naomi again.

This is a real bad one.

Ruskin turned around quickly and looked at me. He had penetrating blue eyes and they seemed to be sizing me up. 'Understand we're not supposed to tell you anything. We're not authorized to bring you out here either.'

'I hear what you're saying,' I said. 'I appreciate the help.'

Once again, Davey Sikes turned and looked at us. I felt as if Sampson and I were on the other team, looking over the line of scrimmage, waiting for the ball snap, the crunch of bodies.

'We're on our way to the *third* murder site,' Ruskin went on. 'I don't know who the victim is. Goes without saying that I hope the victim isn't your niece.'

'What's this case all about? Why all the mystery?' Sampson asked. He sat forward in his seat. 'We're all cops here. Talk straight to us.'

The Durham homicide detective hesitated before he answered. 'A few women, let's say *several*, have disappeared in a three-county area – Durham, Chatham, and Orange, which you're in now. The press has reported a couple of disappearances and two murders so far. *Unrelated* murders.'

'Don't tell me the media is actually cooperating with an investigation?' I said.

Ruskin half smiled. 'Not in your wildest wet dreams. They only know what the FBI's decided to tell them. Nobody's actually withholding information, but nothing's being volunteered, either.'

'You mentioned that several young women have disappeared,' I said. 'How many exactly? Tell me about them.'

Ruskin talked out of the side of his mouth. 'We believe eight to ten women are missing. All young. Late teens and early twenties. All students in college or high school. Only two bodies have been found, though. The one we're going to see could make three. All the bodies were discovered in the last five weeks. The Feebies think we're in the middle of what could be one of the worst kidnapping and murder sprees ever in the South.'

'How many FBI in town?' Sampson asked. 'Squad? Battalion?'

'They're here in full force. They have "evidence" that the disappearances extend beyond state lines – Virginia, South Carolina, Georgia, down into Florida. They think our friendly squirrel abducted a Florida State cheerleader at this year's Orange Bowl. They call him 'The Beast of the Southeast.' It's as if he's invisible. He's in control of the situation right now. Calls himself Casanova . . . believes he's a great lover.'

'Did Casanova leave mash notes at the murder scenes?' I asked Ruskin.

'Just at the last one. He seems to be coming out of his shell. He wants to communicate now. Bond with us. He told us he was Casanova.'

'Were any of the victims black women?' I asked Ruskin. One trait of repeat killers was that they tended to choose their victims along racial grounds. All white. All black. All Spanish. Not too much mixing, as a rule.

'One other missing girl is black. Student from North Carolina Center University. Two bodies we found were white. All the women who've disappeared are *extremely* attractive. We have a bulletin board up with pictures of the missing girls. Somebody gave the case a name: "Beauties and the Beast." It's on the board in big letters. Right over the pictures. That's another handle we have for the case.'

'Does Naomi Cross fit his pattern?' Sampson asked quietly. 'Whatever the crisis team has established so far?'

Nick Ruskin didn't answer right away. I couldn't tell if he was thinking about it, or just trying to be considerate.

'Is Naomi's picture up on the FBI bulletin board? The Beauties and the Beast board?' I asked Ruskin.

'Yes, it is.' Davey Sikes finally spoke. 'Her picture is on the big board.'

13

Don't let this be Scootchie. Her life is just beginning, I silently prayed as we sped to the homicide scene.

Terrible, unspeakable things happened all the time nowadays, to all kinds of innocent, unsuspecting people. They happened in virtually every big city, and even small towns, in villages of a hundred or less. But most often these violent, unthinkable crimes seemed to happen in America.

Ruskin downshifted hard as we curled around a steep curve and saw flashing red and blue lights. Cars and EMS vans loomed up ahead, solemnly gathered at the edge of thick pine woods.

A dozen vehicles were parked haphazardly along the side of the two-lane state road. Traffic was sparse out there in the heart of nowhere. There was no buildup of ambulance-chasers yet. Ruskin pulled in behind the last car in line, a dark blue Lincoln Town Car that might as well have had *Federal Bureau* written all over it.

A state-of-the-art homicide scene was already in progress. Yellow tape had been strung from pine trees, cordoning off the perimeter. Two EMS ambulances were parked with their blunt noses pointed into a stand of trees.

I was swept into a near out-of-body experience as I floated from the car. My vision tunneled.

It was almost as if I had never visited a crime scene before. I vividly remembered the worst of the Soneji case. *A small child found near a muddy river*. Horrifying memories mixed with the terrifying present moment.

Don't let this be Scootchie.

Sampson held my arm loosely as we followed detectives Ruskin and Sikes. We walked for nearly a mile into the dense woods. In the heart of a copse of towering pines, we finally saw the shapes and silhouettes of several men and a few women.

At least half of the group were dressed in dark business suits. It was as if we had come upon some impromptu camping trip for an accounting firm, or a coven of big-city lawyers or bankers.

Everything was eerie, quiet, except for the hollow popping of the technicians' cameras. Close-up photos of the entire area were being taken.

A couple of the crime-scene professionals were already wearing translucent rubber gloves, looking for evidence, taking notes on spiral pads.

I had a creepy, otherworldly premonition that we were going to find Scootchie now. I pushed it, shoved it away, like the unwanted touch of an angel or God. I turned my head sharply to one side – as if that would help me avoid whatever was coming up ahead.

'FBI for sure.' Sampson muttered softly. 'Out here on the Wilderness Trail.' It was as if we were walking toward a mammoth nest of buzzing hornets. They were standing around, whispering secrets to one another.

I was acutely aware of leaves crumpling under my feet, of the noise of twigs and small branches breaking. I wasn't really a policeman here. I was a civilian.

We finally saw the naked body, at least what was left of it. There was no clothing visible at the murder scene. The woman had been tied to a small sapling with what appeared to be a thick leather bond.

Sampson sighed, 'Oh, Jesus, Alex.'

14

'Who is the woman?' I asked softly as we came up to the unlikely police group, the 'multijurisdictional mess,' as Nick Ruskin had described it.

The dead woman was white. It was impossible to tell too much more than that about her at this time. Birds and animals had been feasting on her, and she almost didn't look human anymore. There were no fixed, staring eyes, just dark sockets like burn marks. She didn't have a face; the skin and tissue had been eaten away.

'Who the hell are these two?' one of the FBI agents, a heavyset blonde woman in her early thirties, asked Ruskin. She was as unattractive as she was unpleasant, with puffy red lips and a bulbous, hooked nose. At least she'd spared us the usual FBI happy-camper smile, or the FBI's famous 'smiling handshake.'

Nick Ruskin was brusque with her. His first endearing moment for me. 'This is Detective Alex Cross, and his partner, Detective John Sampson. They're down here from D.C. Detective Cross's niece is missing from Duke. She's

Naomi Cross. This is Special Agent in Charge Joyce Kinney.' He introduced the agent to us.

Agent Kinney frowned, or maybe it was a scowl. 'Well, this is certainly not your niece here,' she said.

'I'd appreciate it if the two of you would return to the cars. Please do that.' She felt the need to go on. 'You have no authority on this case, and no right to be here, either.'

'As Detective Ruskin just told you, my niece is missing.' I spoke softly, but firmly, to Special Agent Joyce Kinney. 'That's all the authority I need. We didn't come down here to admire the leather interior and instrument panel of Detective Ruskin's sports car.'

A thick-chested blonde man in his late twenties briskly stepped up beside his boss. 'I think y'all heard Special Agent Kinney. I'd appreciate it if you leave now,' he announced. Under different circumstances, his over-the-top response might have been funny. Not today. Not at this massacre scene.

'No way *you're* going to stop us,' Sampson said to the blonde agent in his darkest, grimmest voice. 'Not you. Not your Dapper Dan friends here.'

'That's fine, Mark.' Agent Kinney turned to the younger man. 'We'll deal with this later,' she said. Agent Mark backed off, but not without a major-league scowl, much like the one I'd gotten from his boss. Both Ruskin and Sikes laughed as the agent backed down.

We were allowed to stay with the FBI and the local police contingent at the crime scene. *Beauties and the Beast.* I remembered the phrase Ruskin had used in the car. Naomi was up on the Beast board. Had the dead woman been on the board as well?

It had been hot and humid and the body was decomposing

rapidly. The woman had been badly attacked by forest animals, and I hoped that she was already dead before they came. Somehow, I didn't think so.

I noted the unusual position of the body. She was lying on her back. Both her arms appeared to have been dislocated, perhaps as she twisted and struggled to free herself from the leather bonds and the tree behind her. It was as vicious a sight as I had ever seen on the streets of Washington or anywhere else. I felt almost no relief that this wasn't Naomi.

I eventually talked up one of the FBI's forensic people. He knew a friend of mine at the Bureau, Kyle Craig, who worked out of Quantico in Virginia. He told me that Kyle had a summer house in the area.

'This shitheel's real savvy, real smooth, if nothing else.' The FBI forensic guy liked to talk. 'He hasn't left pubic hairs, semen, or even traces of perspiration on either of the victims I've examined. I surely doubt if we'll find much here to give us a DNA profile. At least he didn't eat her himself.'

'Does he have sex with the victims?' I asked before the agent went on a tangent about his experiences with cannibalism.

'Yeah, he does. *Somebody* had repeated sex with them. *Lots* of vaginal bruises and tears. Bugger's well equipped, or he uses something large to simulate sex. But he must wear a cellophane body bag when he does it. Or he dusts them somehow. No pubes, no trace of body fluid yet. The forensic entomologist has already collected his samples. He'll be able to give us the exact time of death.'

'This could be Bette Anne Ryerson,' one of the gray-haired FBI agents within earshot said. 'There was a missing-person report on her. Blonde-haired gal, five six, about a hundred and ten pounds. Wearing a gold Seiko when she disappeared. Drop-dead gorgeous, at least she used to be.'

'Mother of two kids,' said one of the female agents. 'Graduate English student at North Carolina State. I interviewed her husband, who's a professor. Met her two children. Beautiful little kids. One and three years old. Goddamn this bastard.' The agent started to choke up.

I could see the wristwatch, and the ribbon that tied back her hair had come undone and rested on her shoulder. She was no longer beautiful. What was left of her was bloated and suffused. The odor of decomposition was pungent even out in the open air.

The empty sockets seemed to be staring up into a cresent-shaped opening at the tops of the pine trees, and I wondered what her eyes had looked at last.

I tried to imagine 'Casanova' cavorting around in these deep dark woods before we had arrived. I took a guess that he was in his twenties or thirties, and physically strong. I was afraid for Scootchie, much more than I had been, in fact.

Casanova. The world's greatest lover . . . God save us.

15

It was well past ten o'clock, and we were still at the grisly, highly disturbing murder scene. The dazzling amber headlights of official cars and emergency vehicles were used to illuminate a footworn path into the shadowy woods. It was getting colder outside. The chill night wind was a gritty slap in the face.

The corpse still hadn't been moved.

I watched the Bureau's technicians dutifully strip search the woods, collecting forensic clues and taking measurements. The immediate area had been cordoned off, but I made a sketch in the dim light, and took my own preliminary notes. I was trying to remember what I could about the original Casanova. Eighteenth-century adventurer, writer, libertine. I had read parts of his memoirs somewhere along the line.

Beyond the obvious, why had the killer chosen the name? Did he believe that he truly loved women? Was this his way of showing it?

We could hear a bird somewhere let out an unearthly scream, and also the sounds of small animals all around us.

Nobody thought of Bambi in these woods. Not under the circumstances of the gruesome murder.

Between ten-thirty and eleven, we heard a loud roar like thunder in the eerie woods. Nervous eyes looked up into the blue-black sky.

'There's a familiar old tune,' Sampson said as he saw the fluttering lights of an incoming helicopter approaching from the northeast.

'Probably mediflight finally coming for the body,' I said.

A dark blue helicopter with gold stripes finally swirled down onto the blacktop highway. Whoever was piloting the copter in was a real pro.

'Not mediflight,' Sampson said; 'more likely be Mick Jagger. Big stars travel in copters like that one.'

Joyce Kinney and the regional Bureau director were already headed back to the highway. Sampson and I followed along like uninvited pests.

We received another rude shock right away. Both of us recognized the tall, balding, distinguished-looking man who stepped from the helicopter.

'Now what the hell is *he* doing down here?' Sampson said. I had the same question, the same uneasy reaction. It was the deputy director of the FBI. The number two man, Ronald Burns. Burns was a real hummer inside the Bureau, a bigtime cage rattler.

We both knew Burns from our last 'multijurisdictional' case. He was supposed to be political, a bad guy inside the Bureau, but he had never been that way with me. After he had looked at the body, he asked to speak to me. It was getting stranger and stranger down in Carolina.

Burns wanted to hold our little talk away from the big ears and small minds of his own people.

'Alex, I'm real sorry to hear your niece might have been kidnapped. I hope that isn't the case,' he said. 'Since you're down here, maybe you can help us out.'

'Can I ask *why you're* down here?' I said to Burns. Might as well skip right to the sixty-four-thousand-dollar question.

Burns smiled, showing off his capped, very white front teeth. 'I *do* wish you had accepted our offer of that VICAP position.'

I had been offered a job as a liaison between the Bureau and the D.C. police after the Soneji kidnapping case. Burns was one of the men who interviewed me.

'I like directness more than anything in a senior officer,' Burns continued.

I was still waiting for an answer to my direct question.

'I can't tell you as much as you'd like to hear,' Burns finally said. 'I will tell you that we don't know if your niece was taken by this sick Johnny. He leaves very little physical evidence, Alex. He's careful and he's good at what he does.'

'So I've heard. Leads us into some obvious areas for suspects. Policemen, army vets, amateurs who study the police. That could be misdirection on his part, though. Maybe he wants us to think that way.'

Burns nodded. 'I'm here because this has become a high-priority mess. It's large, Alex. I can't tell you why at this time. It's *classified* large.' Spoken like a true FBI honcho. Mysteries wrapped in more mysteries.

Burns sighed. 'I will tell you one thing. We believe that he might be a *collector*. We think he could be keeping a few of the young women nearby . . . a private harem maybe. His very own harem.'

It was a scary, startling idea. It also gave me hope that Naomi might still be alive.

'I want to be in on this,' I told Burns, holding eye contact with him. 'Why don't you tell me everything?' I gave him my terms. 'I need to see the whole picture before I start giving out any theories. Why does he reject some of the women? If that's what he's doing.'

'Alex, I can't tell you any more right now. I'm sorry.' Burns shook his head and closed his eyes for a second. I realized that he was exhausted.

'But you wanted to see how I would react to your collector theory?'

'I did,' Burns admitted, and finally had to smile.

'A modern-day harem would be possible, I guess. It's a common enough male fantasy,' I told him. 'Strangely, it's a prevalent female fantasy, too. Don't rule that out yet.'

Burns catalogued what I'd said and left it at that. He asked me to help again, but was unwilling to tell me everything he knew. He finally walked back to be with his own people.

Sampson came up beside me. 'What did His Rigidness have to say? What brings him to this unholy forest with us mere mortals?'

'He said something interesting. Said that Casanova might be a collector, maybe creating his own private harem some-where near here,' I told Sampson. 'He said the case is *large*. His choice of words.'

'Large' meant it was a very bad case, probably worse than it already seemed. I wondered how that could be, and I almost didn't want to know the answer.

16

Kate McTiernan was lost in an odd, but nicely illuminating, thought. *When the strike of a hawk breaks the body of its prey*, she considered, *it's only because of timing.*

That was the insight from her latest kata in black-belt class. Exquisite timing was everything in karate, and also in so many other things. It also helped if you could bench-press almost two hundred pounds, which she could.

Kate dawdled along busy, funky, rambunctious Franklin Street in Chapel Hill. The street ran north and south, bordering the picturesque campus of the University of North Carolina. She passed bookstores, pizza shops, Rollerblade rentals, Ben & Jerry's ice cream. The rock group White Zombie was blaring from the ice-cream store. Kate wasn't a dawdler by nature, but the evening was warm and pleasant, so she stopped to window-shop for a change.

The college-town crowd was familiar, friendly, and very comfortable. She loved her life here, first as a medical student and now as an intern. She never wanted to leave Chapel Hill, never wanted to go back and be a doctor in West Virginia.

But she would go. It was her promise to her mother – just before Beadsie McTiernan died. Kate had given her word, and her word was good. She was old-fashioned about things like that. A small-town mensch.

Kate's hands were thrust into the deep pockets of a slightly wrinkled hospital medical jacket. She thought that her hands were her bad feature. They were gnarled, and she had no fingernails to speak of. There were two reasons for that: her job as slave labor at the cancer ward and her avocation as a second-degree black belt, a Nidan. It was the one tension releaser she allowed herself; karate class was her R & R.

The name pin on the upper left pocket of her jacket said *K. McTiernan, M.D.* She liked the tiny irreverence of wearing that symbol of status and prestige with her baggy pants and the sneakers. She didn't want to seem like a rebel, and she really wasn't, but she needed to keep some small individuality inside the large hospital community.

Kate had just picked up a paperback copy of Cormac McCarthy's *All the Pretty Horses* at the Intimate Book Shop. First-year interns weren't supposed to have time to read novels, but she made time. At least she promised to make time tonight.

The late April night was so fine, so perfect in every way, that Kate considered stopping off at Spanky's on the corner of Columbia and Franklin. She might sit at the bar and just read her book.

There was absolutely no way she would let herself meet somebody on a 'school night' – which meant most nights for her. She usually had Saturdays off, but by then she was too bushed to deal with pre- and post-mating rituals.

It had been that way ever since she and Peter McGrath

had severed their on-again, off-again relationship. Peter was thirty-eight, a doctor of history and close to brilliant. He was handsome as sin and way too self-absorbed for her taste. The breakup had been messier than she had expected. They weren't even friends now.

It had been four months without Peter now. Pun intended. Not good, but not in the top ten worst things she'd had to deal with. And besides, she knew the breakup was really her fault and not Peter's. Breaking up with lovers was a problem she had; it was part of her secret past. Secret present? Secret future?

Kate McTiernan raised her wristwatch to her face. It was a funky Mickey Mouse model that her sister Carole Anne had given her, and it was a swell little timekeeper. It was also a reminder to herself: Never get a big head because you're a DOCTOR now.

Damn! Her farsightedness was getting worse – at *almost* thirty-one years old! She was an old lady. She'd been the grandam of the University of North Carolina Medical School. It was already nine-thirty, past her bedtime.

Kate decided to pass on Spanky's and head back to the hacienda. She'd heat up some fourth-degree chili, and maybe have hot chocolate with about an inch topping of Marshmallow Fluff. Curling up in bed with some junk food, Cormac McCarthy, and maybe R.E.M. didn't sound half bad, actually.

Like many of the students at Chapel Hill – as opposed to the wealthier crowd up Tobacco Road at 'Dook' – Kate had a major cash-flow problem. She lived in a three-room apartment that was the top floor of a frame house, a North Carolina 'country' house. All the paint was peeling, and the house looked as if it were molting. It was at the ass-end of

Pittsboro Street in Chapel Hill. She had gotten a good deal on the rent.

The first thing she had noticed about the neighborhood were the exquisite trees. They were old and stately hardwoods, not pines. Their long branches reminded her of the arms and fingers of wizened old women. She called her street 'Old Ladies Lane.' Where else would the old lady of the medical school live?

Kate arrived home at about a quarter to ten. Nobody was living downstairs in the house that she rented from a widowed lady who lived in Durham.

'I'm home. It's me, Kate,' she called to the family of mice who lived somewhere behind the refrigerator. She couldn't bring herself to exterminate them. 'Did you miss me? You guys eat yet?'

She flipped on the overhead kitchen light and listened to the irritating electric buzz that she hated. Her eyes caught the blowup of a quote from one of her med-school teachers: 'Medical students have to practice humility.' Well she was definitely practicing humility.

Inside her small bedroom, Kate pulled on a wrinkled black polo shirt that she never ever bothered to iron. Ironing clothes was not a priority these days. It was one reason to have a man around, though – someone to clean, maintain, take out the trash, cook, iron. She was fond of a particular old feminist line: '*A woman without a man is like a fish without a bicycle.*'

Kate yawned just thinking about the sixteen-hour day that would start for her at five the next morning. Dammit, she *loved* her life! Loved it!

She fell onto the creaking double bed that was covered with plain white sheets. The only flourish was a couple of colored chiffon scarves which hung from the bedpost.

She canceled her order for chili and hot chocolate with Marshmallow Fluff, and she set *All the Pretty Horses* on top of unread copies of *Harper*'s and *The New Yorker*, Kate flipped off her lamp and was asleep in five seconds. End of wonderfully illuminating discussion with herself for the night.

Kate McTiernan had no idea, no suspicion, that she was being watched, that she had been followed ever since she'd walked down crowded, colorful Franklin Street, that she had been chosen.

Dr Kate was next.

Tick-cock.

17

No! Kate thought. *This is my home.* She almost said it out loud, but she didn't want to make a sound.

There was someone in her apartment!

She was still half asleep, but she was almost sure about the intruding noise that woke her up. Her pulse was already racing. Her heart floated up into her throat. *Jesus God, no.*

She stayed very still, huddled near the head of her bed. A few more nervous seconds passed slowly, like centuries. Not a move from her. Not a breath. Bone-white slants of moonlight played across the windowpanes, creating eerie shadows in her bedroom.

She listened to the house, listened with total concentration to every creak and crack the old building made.

She didn't hear anything unusual now. But she was sure she had. The recent murders and the news stories about the kidnappings in the Research Triangle area made her fearful. *Don't be gruesome,* she thought. *Don't get melodramatic.*

She sat up slowly in bed and listened. Maybe a window

had blown open. She had better get out of bed and check the windows and doors.

For the first time in four months, she actually missed Peter McGrath. Peter wouldn't have helped, but she would have felt safer. Even with dear old 'Peter-out.'

Not that she was totally frightened or vulnerable; she could hold her own with most men. She could fight like hell. Peter used to say that he 'pitied' the man who messed with her, and he meant it. He had been a little physically afraid of her. Well, prearranged fighting in karate dojos was one thing. This was the real thing.

Kate slipped silently out of bed. *Not a sound.* She felt the roughness and coolness of the floorboards under her bare feet. It sent a wake-up call to her brain, and she moved into a fighting stance.

Whap!

A gloved hand came down *hard* over her mouth and nose, and she thought she heard cartilage crack in her nose.

Then a large and very strong male body tackled her. All of his weight was pressing her into the cool, hard floorboards, pinning her down.

Athlete. Her brain was computing every bit of information. She tried to stay clear and focused.

Very powerful. Trained!

He was cutting off her air supply. He knew precisely what he was doing. Trained!

It wasn't a glove that he was wearing, she realized. *It was a cloth.* Thick with dampness. It was suffocating her.

Was he using chloroform? No, it was odorless. Maybe ether? Halothane? Where would he get anesthetic supplies?

Kate's thinking was getting fuzzy, and she was afraid she was going to black out. She had to get him off of her.

Bracing her legs, she twisted her body hard to the left and threw all of her weight away from her attacker, toward the pale, shadowy bedroom wall. Suddenly, she was out of his grasp, free.

'Bad idea, Kate,' he said in the darkness.

He knew her name!

18

The strike of a hawk . . . timing was everything. Now, timing was survival, Kate understood.

She tried desperately to stay alert, but the powerful drug from the dampened cloth had started to act. Kate managed a three-quarter-speed sidekick, aiming at his groin. She felt something hard. *Oh, shit*!

He was prepared for her. He had on an athlete's cup to protect his mushy genitals. He knew her strengths. *Oh, God, no*. How did he know so much about her?

'Not nice, Kate,' he whispered. 'Definitely not hospitable. I know about your karate. I'm fascinated by you.'

Her eyes were wild. Her heart was hammering so loudly she thought he might hear it. He was scaring the living shit out of her. He was strong and fast, and knew about her karate, knew what her next move would be.

'Help me! Somebody, please help!' she shrieked as loudly as she could. Kate was just trying to scare him off with her screams. There was nobody within half a mile of the house on Old Ladies Lane.

Powerful hands like claws grabbed at her and managed to catch her arm just above the wrist. Kate howled as she ripped herself away.

He was more powerful than any of the advanced black belts at her karate school in Chapel Hill. *Animal*, Kate thought. *Savage animal . . . very rational and crafty. Professional athlete?*

The most important lesson her sensei at the dojo had taught her broke through the numbing fear and chaos of the moment: *Avoid all fights. Whenever possible, run from a fight.* There it was – the best of hundreds of years of experience in martial arts. *Those who never fight, always live to fight another day.*

She ran from her bedroom and down the familiar, narrow, twisting hallway. *Avoid all fights. Run from a fight*, she told herself. *Run, run, run.*

The apartment seemed darker than usual that night. She realized that *he'd closed every curtain and blind.* He'd had the presence of mind. The calmness. The plan of action.

She had to be better than him, better than his plan. A saying of Sun-tzu's hammered through her head: '*A victorious army wins its victories before seeking battle.*' The intruder thought exactly like Sun-tzu and her sensei. Could it be someone from her karate dojo?

Kate managed to reach the living room. She couldn't see a thing. He had closed the curtains in there, too. Her vision and sense of balance were definitely way off. There were *two* of just about every shape and shifting shadow in the room. Goddamn him! Goddamn him! . . .

Floating in the soft, drug-induced haze, she thought of the other women who had disappeared in Orange and Durham counties. She'd heard on the news that another body had been found. A young mother of two children.

She had to get out of the house. Maybe the fresh air would help to revive her. She stumbled to the front door.

Something was blocking her way. He had pushed the sofa against the door! Kate was too weak to shoulder it away.

In desperation she screamed out again. 'Peter! Come help me! Help me, Peter!'

'Oh, shut up, Kate. You don't even see Peter McGrath anymore. You think he's a bloody fool. Besides, his house is seven miles away. Seven point three miles. I checked.' His voice was so calm and rational. Just another day at the office of psychopathology. And he definitely knew her, knew all about Peter McGrath, knew everything.

He was somewhere close behind her in the electrifying darkness. There was no urgency or panic in his voice. This was a day at the beach for him.

Kate moved quickly to her left, away from the voice, away from the human monster inside her house.

Excruciating pain suddenly shot through her body, and she let out a low groan.

She'd clipped her shin on the too-low, too-dumb-for-words glass table her sister Carole Anne had given her. It was Carole's well-meaning effort to class up the place. Ohhh, Christ, goddammit, how she hated that table. There was a shooting, throbbing pain in her left leg.

'Stub your toe, Kate? Why don't you stop trying to run around in the dark?' He laughed – and it was such a normal-sounding laugh – almost friendly. He was enjoying himself. This was a big game for him. A boy-girl game, in the dark.

'*Who are you?*' she screamed at him . . . Suddenly, she thought: *Could it be Peter? Has Peter gone mad?*

Kate was close to passing out. The drug he had given her left her little strength to run anymore. He knew about her karate black belt. He probably knew she spent time in the weight room, too.

She turned – and a bright flashlight shone right in her eyes. *Blinding light was beaming at her face.*

He moved the flashlight away, but she still saw residual circles of light. She started to blink, and could barely make out the silhouette of a tall man. He was more than six feet tall, and had long hair.

She couldn't see his face, just a glimpse of his profile. *Something was wrong with his face. Why was that? What was the matter with him?*

Then she saw the gun.

'No, *don't*,' Kate said. 'Please . . . don't.'

'Yes, do,' he whispered to her intimately, almost like a lover.

Then he calmly shot Kate McTiernan point-blank in the heart.

19

Early on Sunday morning it got even worse on the Casanova case. I had to drive Sampson to Raleigh-Durham International Airport. He needed to be back on The Job in Washington that afternoon. Someone had to protect the capital while I was working down here.

The investigation was getting hotter and nastier now that the third woman's body had been found. Not only local police and FBI, but also field-and-game officials had joined in the physical search at the homicide site. *Deputy Director Ronald Burns had been here last night. Why was that?*

Sampson gave me a bear hug at the American Airlines security gate. We must have looked like a couple of Washington Redskins linebackers after they won the Super Bowl, or maybe after they didn't even get into the play-offs in 1991.

'I know what Naomi means to you,' he whispered against the side of my skull. 'I know some of what you're feeling. You need me again, you call.'

We gave each other a quick kiss on the cheek, like Magic

Johnson and Isiah Thomas used to before their NBA basketball games. That drew a few stares from the peanut gallery milling around the metal detectors. Sampson and I love each other, and we're not ashamed to show it. Unusual for tough-as-nails men of action like the two of us.

'Watch out for the Fed Bureau. Watch your back with the local folk. Watch your front, too. I don't like Ruskin. I *really* don't like Sikes,' Sampson continued to give me instructions. 'You'll find Naomi. I have confidence in you. Always have. That's my story, and I'm sticking to it.'

The Big Man finally walked away, and never once looked back.

I was all alone down South.

Chasing monsters again.

20

I walked from the Washington Duke Inn to the Duke campus at around one o'clock on Sunday afternoon.

I had just eaten a real North Carolina breakfast: a pot and a half of hot, good coffee, very salty cured ham and runny eggs, biscuits and redeye gravy, grits. I'd heard a country song playing in the dining room, 'One Day When You Swing That Skillet, My Face Ain't Gonna Be There.'

I was feeling crazy and on edge, so the pretty, half-mile hike to the campus was good therapy. I prescribed it for myself and then listened to the doctor. The crime scene the night before had shaken me.

I vividly remembered a time when Naomi was a little girl, and I'd been her best friend. We used to sing 'Incey Wincey Spider' and 'Silkworm, Silkworm.' In a way, she'd taught me how to be friends with Jannie and Damon. She had prepared me to be a pretty good father.

At the time, my brother Aaron used to bring Scootchie with him to the Capri Bar on Third Street. My brother was busy drinking himself to death. The Capri was no place for his little girl but, somehow, Naomi handled it. Even as a child, she understood and accepted who and what her father was. When she and Aaron would stop at our house, my brother would usually be high, but not really drunk yet. Naomi would be in charge of her father. He would make the effort to stay sober when she was there. The trouble was, Scootchie couldn't always be around to save him.

At one o'clock on Sunday, I had a meeting scheduled with the dean of women at Duke. I went to the Allen Building, which was just off Chapel Drive. Several administration offices were housed there on the second and third floors.

The dean of women was a tall, well-built man named Browning Lowell. Naomi had told me a lot about him. She considered him a close adviser and also a friend. That afternoon I met with Dean Lowell in his cozy office that was filled with thick, old books. The office looked out across magnolia and elm-lined Chapel Drive to the Few Quad. Like everything else about the campus, the setting was visually spectacular. Gothic buildings everywhere. Oxford University in the South.

'I'm a fan of yours through Naomi,' Dean Lowell said as we shook hands. He had a powerful grip, which I expected from the physical look of him.

Browning Lowell was well muscled, probably in his mid-thirties, and good-looking. His sparkling blue eyes seemed relentlessly cheerful to me. Once upon a time he'd been a world-class gymnast, I remembered. He had attended Duke as an undergraduate, and was supposed to star for the American team in the 1980 Olympics in Moscow.

In the early part of that year an unfortunate news story had broken that Browning Lowell was gay, and having an affair with a basketball player of some renown. He had left the American team even before the eventual Olympic boycott. Whether the story was true had never been proved to my knowledge. Lowell had married, though, and he and his wife now lived in Durham.

I found Lowell to be sympathetic and warm. We got down to the sad business of Naomi's disappearance. He had all the right suspicions and appropriate fears about the ongoing police investigation.

'It seems to me that the local papers aren't making simple, logical connections between the murders and the disappearances. I don't understand that. We've alerted all the women here on campus,' he told me. Duke coeds were being asked to sign in and out of dorms, he elaborated. The 'buddy system' was encouraged whenever students went out at night.

Before I left his office, he made a phone call to Naomi's dorm house. He said it would make access a little easier, and he wanted to do everything he possibly could to help.

'I've known Naomi for almost five years,' he told me. He ran his hand back through his longish blonde hair. 'I can feel a small fraction of what you're going through, and I'm so sorry, Alex. This has devastated a lot of us here.'

I thanked Dean Lowell and left his office feeling touched by the man, and somewhat better. I went off to the student dorms. *Guess who's coming to high tea?*

21

I felt like Alex in Wonderland.

The main dormitory area at Duke was another idyllic spot. Smaller houses, a few cottages, rather than the usual Gothic buildings. Myers Quad was shaded by tall ancient oaks and spreading magnolias, surrounded by well-kept flower gardens. Glory be to God for dappled things.

A silver BMW convertible was parked in front of the place. The sticker on the Bimmer bumper read: MY DAUGHTER AND MY MONEY GO TO DUKE.

Inside, the living room of the dorm had polished hardwood floors and respectably faded oriental rugs that could pass for the real thing. I took in the sights while I waited for Mary Ellen Klouk. The room was filled with overstuffed 'period' chairs, couches, mahogany highboys. Bench seats were under both front windows.

Mary Ellen Klouk came downstairs a few minutes after my arrival. I had met her half a dozen times before that Sunday afternoon. She was nearly six feet tall, ash blonde, and attractive – not unlike the women who had mysteriously disappeared. The body that was found half-eaten by birds and animals in the woods around Efland had once been a beautiful blonde woman, too.

I wondered if the killer had checked out Mary Ellen Klouk. Why had he chosen Naomi? How did he make his final choices? How many women had been chosen so far?

'Hello, Alex. God, I'm glad you're here.' Mary Ellen took my hand and held it tightly. Seeing her brought on warm, but also painful, memories.

We decided to leave the dorm and stroll out onto the rolling grounds of the West Campus. I had always liked Mary Ellen. She'd been a history and psych major as an undergraduate. I remembered that we'd talked about psychoanalysis one night in D.C. She knew almost as much about psychic trauma as I did.

'Sorry I was away when you arrived in Durham,' she said as we walked east among elegant Gothic-style buildings that were built in the 1920s. 'My brother graduated from high school on Friday. *Little* Ryan Klouk. He's over six feet five, actually. Two hundred and twenty pounds if he's an ounce. Lead singer for Scratching Blackboards. I got back this morning, Alex.'

'When was the last time you saw Naomi?' I asked Mary Ellen as we crossed onto a pretty street called Wannamaker Drive. It felt all wrong to be talking to Naomi's friend like a homicide detective, but I had to do it.

The question had stung Mary Ellen. She took a deep breath before she answered me. 'Six days ago, Alex. We drove down to Chapel Hill together. We were doing work there for Habitat for Humanity.'

Habitat for Humanity was a community-service group that rebuilt houses for the poor. Naomi hadn't mentioned that she did volunteer work for them. 'Did you see Naomi after that?' I asked.

Mary Ellen shook her head. The gold dancing bells around her neck jangled softly. I suddenly got the feeling that she didn't want to look at me.

'That was the last time, I'm afraid. I was the one who went to the police. I found out they have a twenty-four-hour rule on most disappearances. Naomi was gone almost two and a half days before they put out any all-points bulletins. Do you know why?' she asked.

I shook my head, but didn't want to make a big deal out of it in front of Mary Ellen. I still didn't know exactly why there was such a band of secrecy surrounding the case. I'd put in calls to Detective Nick Ruskin that morning, but he hadn't returned any of them.

'Do you think Naomi's disappearance has anything to do with the other women who have disappeared lately?' Mary Ellen asked. Her blue eyes were pierced with pain.

'There could be a connection. There was no physical evidence at the Sarah Duke Gardens, though. Honestly, there's very little to go on. Mary Ellen.' If Naomi was abducted at a public garden right on the campus, there were no witnesses. She had been seen in the gardens half an hour before she missed a class in Contracts. Casanova was scarily good at what he did. He was like a ghost.

We finished our walk, ending up full circle where we had begun. The dormitory house was set back twenty to thirty yards from a graveled path. It had high white columns, and the large veranda was crowded with shiny white wicker rockers and tables. The antebellum period, one of my favorites.

'Alex, Naomi and I really haven't been as close lately,'

Mary Ellen suddenly confided in me. 'I'm sorry. I thought you should know that.'

Mary Ellen was crying as she leaned in and kissed me on the cheek. Then she ran up the polished whitewashed stairs and disappeared inside.

Another troubling mystery to solve.

22

Casanova watched Dr Alex Cross. His quick, sharp mind was whizzing about like a sophisticated computer – possibly the fastest computer in the whole Research Triangle.

Look at Cross, he muttered. *Visiting Naomi's old friend! There's nothing to be found there, Doctor. You're not even warm yet. You're getting colder, actually.*

He followed Alex Cross at a safe distance as he walked across the Duke campus. He had read extensively about Cross. He knew all about the psychologist and detective who'd made his reputation tracking down a kidnapper-killer in Washington. The so-called crime of the century, which was a lot of media hype and horseshit.

So who's better at this game? he wanted to shout out to Dr Cross. *I know who you are. You don't know dogshit about me. You never will.*

Cross stopped walking. He took a pad from the back pocket of his trousers and made a note.

What's this, Doctor? Had a thought of some consequence? I rather doubt that. I honestly do.

The FBI, the local police, they've all been trailing me for months. I suppose they make notes, too, but none of them has a clue . . .

Casanova watched Alex Cross continue to walk along the campus until he finally disappeared from sight. The idea that Cross would actually track and capture him was unthinkable. It simply wasn't going to happen.

He started to laugh, and had to catch himself since the Duke campus was fairly crowded on a Sunday afternoon.

No one has a clue, Dr Cross. Don't you get it? . . . That's the clue!

23

I was a street detective again.

I spent most of Monday morning interviewing people who knew Kate McTiernan. Casanova's latest victim was a first-year intern who'd been abducted from her apartment on the outskirts of Chapel Hill.

I was attempting to put together a psych profile of Casanova, but there wasn't enough information. Period. The FBI wasn't helping. Nick Ruskin still hadn't returned my phone calls.

A professor at North Carolina med school told me that Kate McTiernan was one of the most conscientious students she'd taught in twenty years. Another professor at the school said that her commitment and intelligence were indeed high, but 'her temperament is the truly extraordinary thing about Kate.'

It was unanimous in that regard. Even competing interns at the hospital agreed that Kate McTiernan was something else. 'She's the least narcissistic woman I've ever met,' one of the woman interns told me. 'Kate's totally driven, but she knows it and she can laugh at herself,' said another. 'She's a really cool person. This is such a sad, numbing thing for everyone at the hospital.' 'She's a brain, who happens to be built like a brick shithouse.'

I called Peter McGrath, a history professor, and he reluctantly agreed to see me. Kate McTiernan had dated him for almost four months, but their relationship had ended abruptly. Professor McGrath was tall, athletic-looking, a bit imperious.

'I could say that I fucked up royally by losing her,' McGrath admitted to me. 'And I did. But I couldn't have held on to the Katester. She's probably the strongest-willed person, man or woman, that I've ever met. God, I can't believe this has happened to Kate.'

His face was pale, and he was obviously shaken up by her disappearance. At least he appeared to be.

I ended up eating by myself in a noisy bar in the college town of Chapel Hill. There were hordes of university students, and a busy pool table, but I sat alone with my beers, a greasy, rubbery cheeseburger, and my early thoughts on Casanova.

The long day had drained me. I missed Sampson, my kids, my home in D.C. A comfortable world without any monsters. Scootchie was still missing, though. So were several other young women in the Southeast.

My thoughts kept drifting back to Kate McTiernan, and what I'd heard about her today.

This is the way cases got solved – at least it was the way I had always solved them. Data got collected. Data ran loose in the brain. Eventually, connections were made.

Casanova doesn't just take physically beautiful women, I suddenly realized in the bar. *He takes the most extraordinary women he can find. He's taking only the heartbreakers . . .*

the women that everybody wants but nobody ever seems to get.

He's collecting them somewhere out there.

Why extraordinary women? I wondered.

There was one possible answer. *Because he believes he's extraordinary, too.*

24

I almost went back to see Mary Ellen Klouk again, but I changed my mind and returned to the Washington Duke Inn. A couple of messages were waiting for me.

The first was from a friend in the Washington PD. He was processing information I needed for a meaningful profile on Casanova. I'd brought a laptop with me and I hoped I would be in business soon.

A reporter by the name of Mike Hart had called four times. I recognized his name, and I knew his newspaper – a tabloid out of Florida called the *National Star*. The reporter's nickname was No-Heart Hart. I didn't return No-Heart's calls. I'd been featured on the front page of the *Star* once, and once was enough for this lifetime.

Detective Nick Ruskin had finally returned one of my calls. He left a short message. *Nothing new on our end. Will let you know.* I found that hard to believe. I didn't trust Detective Ruskin or his faithful sidekick Davey Sikes.

I drifted off to a restless sleep in a cozy armchair in my room and had the most vivid, nightmarish dreams. A monster right out of an Edvard Munch painting was chasing Naomi. I was powerless to help her; all I could do was watch the macabre scene in horror. Not much need for a trained psychotherapist to interpret that one.

I woke up sensing that someone was in the hotel room with me.

I quietly placed my hand on the butt of my revolver and stayed very still. My heart was pounding. How could someone have gotten into the room?

I stood up slowly, but stayed low in a shooting crouch. I peered around as best I could in the semidarkness.

The chintz window drapes weren't completely drawn, so there was enough light from outside for me to make out shapes. Shadows of tree leaves danced on the hotel room wall. Nothing else seemed to be moving.

I checked the bathroom, Glock pistol first. Then the closets. I began to feel a little silly stalking the hotel room with my gun drawn, but I had definitely heard a noise!

I finally spotted a piece of paper under the door, but I waited a few seconds before I flipped on the light. Just to be sure.

A black-and-white photograph was staring up at me. Instant associations and connections jumped to mind. It was a colonial British postcard, probably from the early 1900s. At that time the postcards had been collected by Westerners as pseudoart, but mostly as soft pornography. They had been a racy turn-on for male collectors in the early part of the century.

I bent down to get a better look at the old-fashioned photo.

The card showed an odalisque smoking a Turkish cigarette, in a startling acrobatic posture. The woman was dark, young, and beautiful; probably in her mid-teens. She was naked to the waist, and her full breasts hung upside down in the posed photograph.

I flipped the card over with a pencil.

There was a printed caption near where a stamp could be placed: *Odalisques with great beauty and high intelligence were carefully trained to be concubines. They learned to dance quite beautifully, to play musical instruments, and to write exquisitely lyrical poetry. They were the most valuable part of the harem, perhaps the emperor's greatest treasure.*

The caption was signed in ink with a printed name. *Giovanni Giacomo Casanova de Seingalt.*

He knew that I was here in Durham. He knew who I was.

Casanova had left a calling card.

25

I'm alive.

Kate McTiernan slowly forced open her eyes inside a dimly lit room . . . *somewhere.*

For a couple of blinks of her eyes, she believed she was in a hotel that she couldn't for the life of her remember checking into. A really weird hotel in an even weirder Jim Jarmusch art movie. It didn't matter, though. At least she wasn't dead.

Suddenly, she remembered being shot point-blank in the chest. She remembered the intruder. Tall . . . long hair . . . gentle, conversational voice . . . *sixth-degree animal.*

She tried to get up, but thought better of it immediately. 'Whoa there,' she said out loud. Her throat was dry, and her voice sounded raspy as it echoed unpleasantly inside her head. Her tongue felt as if it needed a shave.

I'm in hell. In a circle from Dante's Inferno, with a very low number, she thought, and she began to shiver. Everything about the moment was terrifying, but it was so horrible, and so unexpected, she couldn't orient herself to it.

Her joints were stiff and painful; she ached all over. She doubted that she could press a hundred pounds right now. Her head felt huge, bloated like aging fruit, and it hurt, but she could vividly remember the attacker. He was tall, maybe six two, youngish, extremely powerful, articulate. The images were hazy, but she was absolutely certain they were true.

She remembered something else about the monstrous attack in her apartment. He'd used a stun gun, or something like it, to immobilize her. He'd also used chloroform, or maybe it was halothane. That could account for her bruising headache.

The lights had purposely been left on in the room. She noticed they were coming from modern-looking dimmers built into the ceiling. The ceiling was low, possibly under seven feet.

The room looked as if it had recently been built, or remodeled. It was actually decorated tastefully, the way she might have done her own apartment if she had the money and time . . . A real brass bed. Antique white dresser with brass handles. A dressing table with a silver brush, comb, mirror. There were colorful scarves tied on the bedposts, just the way she did them at home. That struck her as strange. Very odd.

There were no windows in the room. The only way out appeared to be through a heavy wooden door.

'Nice decor,' Kate muttered softly. 'Early psycho. No, it's late psycho.'

The door to a small closet was open halfway and she could see inside. What she saw made her feel physically ill.

He'd brought her clothes to this horrible place, this bizarre prison cell. All of her clothes were here.

Using her remaining strength, Kate McTiernan forced herself to sit upright in the bed. The effort made her heart race, and the pounding in her chest frightened her. Her arms and legs felt as if heavy weights were tied to them.

She concentrated hard, trying to focus her eyes on the incredible scene. She continued to stare into the closet.

Those weren't actually her clothes, she realized. He'd gone out and bought clothes *just like hers*! Exactly to her taste and style. The clothes displayed in the closet were brand-new. She could see some of the store tags dangling from the blouses and skirts. The Limited. The Gap *in Chapel Hill*. Stores she actually shopped in herself.

Her eyes darted to the top of the antique white dresser across the room. Her perfume was there, too. Obsession. Safari. Opium.

He'd bought all of it for her, hadn't he?

Next to the bed was a copy of *All the Pretty Horses*, the same book she had bought on Franklin Street in Chapel Hill.

He knows everything about me!

26

Dr Kate McTiernan slept. Awoke. Slept some more. She made a joke of it. Called herself 'lazybones.' She *never* slept in. Not since before med school, anyway.

She was beginning to feel more clearheaded and alert, more in command of herself, except that she had lost track of time. She didn't know if it was morning, noon, or night. Or even which day it was.

The man, whoever the bastard was, had been inside the mysterious, despicable room while she slept. The thought made her physically ill. There was *a note* propped on the bedside table, where she was sure to *see* it.

The note was handwritten. *Dear Dr Kate*, it said. Her hands were trembling as she read her own name.

I wanted you to read this, so that you understand me better, and also the rules of the house. This is probably the most important letter you'll ever receive, so read it carefully. And please take it very seriously.

No, I am not crazy or out of control. Actually, I'm

quite the opposite. Apply your obviously high intelligence to the concept that I'm relatively sane, and that I know exactly what I want. Most people don't know what they want.

Do you, Kate? We'll talk about that later. It's a subject worthy of much lively and interesting discussion. Do you know what you want? Are you getting it? Why not? For the good of society? Whose society? Whose life are we living, anyway?

I won't pretend that you are happy to be here, so no false-sounding welcomes. No cellophaned basket of fresh fruit and champagne. As you will soon see, or have already, I've tried to make your stay as comfortable as possible. Which brings up an important point, perhaps the most important point of this first attempt at communication between us.

Your stay will be temporary. You will leave – if, Big If – you listen to what I tell you . . . so listen carefully, Kate.

Are you listening now? Please listen, Kate. Chase away the justifiable anger and the white noise in your head. I am not crazy or out of control.

That's the whole point: I am in control! See the distinction? Of course you do. I know how very bright you are. National merit scholar and all that.

It is important that you know how special you are to me. That's why you are completely safe here. It is also why you'll leave, eventually.

I picked you from thousands and thousands of women at my disposal, so to speak. I know, you're saying 'lucky me.' I know how funny and cynical you can be. I even know that laughter has gotten you through difficult times. I'm beginning to know you better than anyone has ever known you. Almost as well as you know yourself, Kate.

Now for the bad parts. And Kate, these next points are as important as any of the good news I've stated above.

These are the house rules, and they are to be strictly observed:

1. The most important rule: You must never try to escape – or you will be executed within hours, however painful that would be for both of us. Believe me, there is precedent for this. There can be no reprieve following an escape attempt.

2. Just for you, Kate, a special rule: You must never try to use your karate skills on me. (I almost brought your gi, your crisp white karate suit, but why encourage you to temptation.)

3. You must never call out for help – I'll know if you do – and you will be punished with facial and genital disfigurement.

You want to know more – you want to know everything at once. But it doesn't work that way. Don't bother trying to figure out where you are. You won't guess, and will only give yourself an unnecessary headache.

That's all for now. I've given you more than enough to think about. You are totally safe here. I love you more than you can imagine. I can't wait for us to talk, really talk.

Casanova

And you are hopelessly out of your mind! Kate McTiernan thought as she paced the eleven-by-fifteen-foot room. Her claustrophobic prison. Her hell on this earth.

Her body felt as if it were floating, as if warm viscous fluid were flowing over her. She wondered if she'd suffered a head injury during the attack.

She had only one thought: *how to escape.* She began to analyze her situation in every possible way. She reversed the conventional assumptions, and broke down each to its component parts.

There was a single, double-locked, thick wooden door.

There was no way out other than through that door.

No! That was the conventional assumption. There had to be another way.

She remembered a problem-solution puzzle from some heretofore useless undergrad logics course she had taken. It began with ten matchsticks arranged as Roman numerals in a math equation:

$$X\ 1+1 = X$$

The problem was how to correct the equation without touching any of the matches. Without adding new matches. Without taking away any matches.

No easy way out.

No apparent solution.

The problem had been unsolvable to many students, but she had figured it out relatively quickly. A solution was there, where none seemed to be. She solved it by reversing the conventional assumptions. She turned the page upside down.

$$X = 1+1\ X$$

But she couldn't turn this prison room upside down. Or could she? Kate McTiernan examined every single floorboard and each two-by-four in the wall. The wood smelled new. Maybe he was a builder, a contractor, or perhaps an architect?

No way out.

No apparent solution.

She couldn't, *wouldn't* accept that answer.

She thought about seducing him – if she could force herself to do it. No. He was too clever. He would know. Worse than that, she would know.

There had to be a way. She would find it.

Kate stared down at the note on the bedside table.

You must never try to escape – or you will be executed within hours.

27

The following afternoon I visited the Sarah Duke Gardens, the place where Naomi had been abducted six days ago. I needed to go there, to visit the scene, to think about my niece, to grieve in private.

There were more than fifty acres of exquisitely landscaped woodland gardens adjacent to the Duke University Medical Center, literally miles of allees. Casanova couldn't have hoped for a better site for his kidnapping. He had been thorough. Perfect, so far. How was that possible?

I talked to staff members and also to a few students who had been there the day Naomi disappeared. The picturesque gardens were officially open from early morning until dusk. Naomi had last been seen at around four o'clock. Casanova had taken her in broad daylight. I couldn't figure out how he'd done it. Not yet. Neither could the Durham police or the FBI.

I walked around the woods and gardens for almost two hours. I was overwhelmed by the thought that Scootchie had been taken *right here*.

A spot called the Terraces was particularly beautiful. Visitors could enter through a wisteria-covered pergola. Lovely wooden stairways led down to an irregular-shaped fishpond with a rock garden stacked directly behind. Visually, the Terraces were horizontal bands of rock, accented by stripes of the most beautiful color. Tulips, azaleas, camellias, irises, and peonies were in bloom.

I knew instinctively that this was a place that Scootchie would love.

I knelt near a visually striking patch of bright red and yellow tulips. I was wearing a gray suit with an open-necked white shirt. The ground was soft and stained my trousers, but it didn't matter. I bowed my head low. Finally, I wept for Scootchie.

28

Tick-cock. Tick-cock.

Kate McTiernan thought that she'd heard something. She was probably imagining it. You could definitely get a little buggy in here.

There it was again. The slightest creak in the floorboards. The door opened and he walked into the room without saying a word.

There he was! Casanova. He had on another mask. He looked like some kind of dark god – slender and athletic. Was that his fantasy image of himself?

Physically, he would be considered a hunk at the university or even as a cadaver in an autopsy room, which was preferable to her.

She noted his clothes: tight, faded blue jeans, black cowboy boots edged with soil, no shirt. He was definitely a hardbody, proud of his rippling chest. She was trying to remember everything – for the time when she escaped.

'I read all your rules,' Kate said, trying to act as calm as possible. Her body was shivering, though. 'They're very thorough, very clear.'

'Thank you. No one likes rules, least of all me. But they're necessary sometimes.'

The mask hid his face, and it held Kate's attention. She couldn't take her eyes away from it. It reminded her of the elaborate, decorative masks from Venice. It was handpainted, ritualistic in its artistic detail, and weirdly beautiful. *Was he trying to be seductive?* Kate wondered. *Was that it?*

'Why do you wear the mask?' she said. She kept her voice subservient, curious, but not demanding.

'As I said in my note, one day you'll go free. You'll be released. It's all in my plan for you. I couldn't bear to see you hurt.'

'If I'm good. If I obey.'

'Yes. If you're good. I won't be that hard, Kate. I like you so much.'

She wanted to hit him, to go after him. *Not yet*, she warned herself. *Not until you're sure. You'll only get one try at him.*

He seemed to read her mind. He was very quick, very bright.

'No karate,' he said, and she sensed that he was smiling behind the mask. 'Please remember that, Kate. I've actually seen you perform at your dojo. I've watched you. You're very quick and you're strong. So am I. I'm no stranger to martial arts.'

'That wasn't what I was thinking about.' Kate frowned and looked up at the ceiling. She rolled back her eyes. She thought it was pretty fair acting under the pressure circumstances. No threat to Emma Thompson or Holly Hunter, but decent.

'I'm sorry then. I apologize,' he said. 'I shouldn't put words in your mouth. I won't do it again. That's a promise.'

110

He seemed almost sane at times, and that terrified her more than anything else so far. It was as if they were having a nice normal chat in a nice normal house, not in his house of horrors.

Kate looked at his hands. The fingers were long, and might even be considered elegant. An architect's? A doctor's hands? An artist's? Certainly not a workingman's hands.

'Well, what do you have in mind for me?' Kate decided on the direct approach. 'Why am I here? Why this room, the clothes? All my things?'

His voice remained gentle and calm. He was actually trying to seduce her. 'Oh, I guess I want to fall in love, to stay in love for a while. I want to feel real romance every day that I possibly can. I want to feel something special in my life. I want to experience intimacy with another person. I'm not that different from everyone else. Except that I act instead of day-dream.'

'Don't you feel *anything*?' she asked. She feigned concern for him. She knew that sociopaths couldn't feel emotion, at least that was her understanding.

He shrugged. She sensed that he was smiling again, laughing at her. 'Sometimes I feel a great deal. I think that I'm too sensitive. May I tell you how beautiful you are?'

'Under the present circumstances, I wish you wouldn't.'

He laughed a nice laugh and shrugged his shoulders again. 'Okay. That's settled then, isn't it? No sweet talk for the two of us. Not for now, anyway. Bear in mind, I can be romantic. I actually prefer it that way.'

She wasn't prepared for his sudden movement, his quickness. The stun gun appeared and hit her with a vicious jolt. She recognized the gun's crackling sound, smelled the ozone. Kate fell back hard against the bedroom wall and cracked her head. The impact shook the whole house – *wherever* she was being kept.

'Oh, Jee-sus no,' Kate moaned softly.

He was all over her. Flailing arms and legs, all of his weight pressing down on her. He was going to kill her now. Oh God, she didn't want to die like this, to have her life end in this way. It was so pointless, absurd, sad.

She felt a fierce and explosive rage swelling up in her. With a desperate effort she managed to kick out one leg, but she couldn't move her arms. Her chest was on fire. She could feel him ripping off her blouse, touching her all over. He was aroused. She could feel him rubbing against her.

'No, please no,' she moaned. Her own voice sounded very far away.

He was kneading her breasts with both hands. She could taste blood, and feel its warmth trickle from the corner of her mouth. Kate finally began to cry. She was choking, and she could hardly breathe.

'I tried to be nice,' he said through tightly gritted teeth.

He stopped suddenly. He got up and unzipped his blue jeans and yanked them down around his ankles. He didn't bother to take them off.

Kate stared up at him. His penis was large. Fully erect, and bright with pulsing blood and thick veins. He threw himself down on her and rubbed it against her body, moving it slowly against her breasts, her throat, and then her mouth and eyes.

Kate began to drift in and out of consciousness, in and out of reality. She tried to hold on to each thought that came to her. She needed to feel some control, even if it was only over her thoughts.

'Keep your eyes open,' he warned her in a deep growl.

'Look at me, Kate. Your eyes are so beautiful. You're the most beautiful woman I've ever seen. Do you know that? Do you know how desirable you are?'

He was in a trance now. It seemed like it to Kate. His powerful body danced, snaked, writhed, as he thrust himself in and out of her. He sat up and he played with her breasts again. He caressed her hair, different parts of her face. His touch became gentle after a while. That made it even worse for her. She felt such humiliation and horrible shame. She hated him.

'I love you so much, Kate. I love you more than I'm capable of saying. I've never felt this way before. I promise you I haven't. Never like this.'

He wasn't going to kill her, Kate realized. He was going to let her live. He was going to come back again and again, whenever he wanted her. The horror was overwhelming, and Kate finally passed out. She let her spirit fall far away.

She didn't feel it when he gave her the softest kiss goodbye. 'I love you, sweet Kate. And I'm truly sorry about this. I do feel . . . *everything*.'

29

I received an urgent phone call from a law student and class-mate of Naomi's. She said her name was Florence Campbell and that she had to talk to me as soon as possible. '*I really must talk with you, Dr Cross. It's imperative,*' she said.

I met her on the Duke campus near the Bryan University Center. Florence turned out to be a black woman in her early twenties. We walked among the magnolias and well-kept Gothic-style school buildings. Neither of us looked as if we particularly belonged in the setting.

Florence was tall and gawky and somewhat mystifying at first. She had a stiff, high hairstyle that made me think of Nefertiti. Her appearance was decidedly odd, or maybe old-fashioned, and it struck me that people like her might still exist in rural Mississippi or Alabama. Florence had done her undergraduate work at Mississippi State University, which was about as far away from Duke University as you could get.

'I'm very, very sorry, Dr Cross,' she said as we sat on a stone-and-wood bench with student memorabilia etched into its rails. 'I apologize to you and your family.'

'You apologize about what, Florence?' I asked her. I didn't understand what she meant.

'I didn't make the effort to talk to you when you came to campus yesterday. No one had made it clear that Naomi might actually have been kidnapped. The Durham police certainly didn't. They were just rude. They didn't seem to think Naomi was in any real trouble.'

'Why do you think that is?' I asked Florence a question that was bouncing around inside my own head.

She stared deeply into my eyes. 'Because Naomi's an Afro-American woman. The Durham police, the FBI, they don't care about us as much as they do about the white women.'

'Do you believe that?' I asked her.

Florence Campbell rolled her eyes. 'It's the truth, so why wouldn't I believe it? Frantz Fanon argued that racist super-structures are permanently embedded in the psychology, economy, and culture of our society. I believe *that*, too.'

Florence was a very serious woman. She had a copy of Albert Murray's *The Omni-Americans* under her arm. I was beginning to like her style. It was time to find out what secrets she knew about Naomi.

'Tell me what's going on around here, Florence. Don't edit your thoughts because I'm Naomi's uncle, or because I'm a police detective. I need somebody to help me out. I am resisting a *superstructure* down here in Durham.'

Florence smiled. She pulled a tangle of hair away from her face. She was part Immanuel Kant, part Prissy from *Gone With the Wind*. 'Here's what I know so far, Dr Cross. This is why some girls in the dorm were upset with Naomi.'

She took a sip of the magnolia-fragrant air. 'It started with a man named Seth Samuel Taylor. He's a social worker in the projects of Durham. I introduced Naomi to Seth. He's

115

my cousin.' Florence suddenly looked a little uncertain as she talked.

'I don't see a problem so far,' I told her.

'Seth Samuel and Naomi fell in love around December of last year,' she went on. 'Naomi was walking around with a starry-night look in her eyes, and that's not like her, as you know. He came to the dorm at first, but then she started staying at Seth's apartment in Durham.'

I was a little surprised that Naomi had fallen in love and hadn't mentioned it to Cilla. Why didn't she tell any of us about it? I still didn't understand the problem with the other girls at the dorm.

'I'm pretty sure Naomi wasn't the first coed to fall in love at Duke. Or to have a man over for tea and crumpets and whatever,' I said.

'She wasn't just having a man over for whatever, she was having a black man over for *whatever*. Seth would show up from the projects in his dusty overalls and dusty workboots, and his leather engineering jacket. Naomi started to wear an old sharecropper's straw hat around campus. Sometimes, Seth wore a hard hat with "Slave Labor" written on it. He *dared* to be a little caustic and ironic about the sisters' social activity, and, heaven forbid, their social awareness. He scolded the black housekeepers when they tried to do their jobs.'

'What do *you* think about your cousin Seth?' I asked Florence.

'Seth has a definite chip on his shoulder. He's angry about racial injustice, to the point where it gets in the way of his ideas sometimes. Other than that, he's really great. He's a doer, not afraid to get his hands dirty. If he wasn't my *distant* cousin . . . ' Florence said with a wink.

I had to smile at Florence's sneaky sense of humor. She was a little Mississippi-gawky, but she was a neat lady. I was even starting to like her high hairstyle.

'You and Naomi were fast friends?' I asked her.

'We weren't at first. I think we both felt we were competing for Law Review. Probably only one black woman could make it, you understand. But as our first year wore on, we got very close. I love Naomi. She's the greatest.'

I suddenly wondered if Naomi's disappearance might be connected to her boyfriend, and maybe had nothing to do with the killer loose in North Carolina.

'He's a real good person. Don't go hurting him,' Florence warned me. 'Don't even think about it.'

I nodded. 'I'll only break *one* of his legs.'

'He's strong as an ox,' she came back at me.

'I *am* an ox,' I told Florence Campbell, imparting a little secret of my own.

30

I stared into the dark eyes of Seth Samuel Taylor. He stared back. I kept on staring. His eyes looked like jet black marbles set in almonds.

Naomi's boyfriend was tall, very muscular, and working-man-hard. He reminded me more of a young lion than an ox. He looked disconsolate, and it was hard for me to question him. I had the premonition that Naomi was gone forever.

Seth Taylor hadn't shaved, and I could tell that he hadn't slept in days. I don't think he had changed his clothes, either. He had on a badly wrinkled blue plaid shirt over a T-shirt, and holey 501s. He still wore his dusty workboots. Either he was very upset, or Seth Taylor was a shrewd actor.

I put out my hand, and his handshake was powerful. I felt as if I had put it into a carpenter's vise.

'You look like shit' were Seth Taylor's first words to me. Digital Underground was blaring out the 'Humpty Dance' somewhere in the neighborhood. Just like it was D.C., only a little behind the times.

'You do, too.'

'Well, fuck y'all,' he said. It was a familiar greeting on the streets, and we both knew it and laughed.

Seth's smile was warm, and somewhat contagious. He had an overconfident air about him, but it wasn't too obnoxious, Nothing I hadn't seen before.

I could see that his broad nose had been broken a few times, but he was still good-looking in a rough-hewn sort of way. His presence dominated a room as Naomi's did. The detective in me wondered about Seth Taylor.

Seth lived in an old working-class area north of downtown Durham. At one time, the neighborhood had been filled with tobacco-factory workers. His apartment was a duplex in an old shingled house that had been converted into two apartments. Posters of Arrested Development and Ice-T were up on the hallway walls. One poster read: *Not since slavery has so much ongoing catastrophe been visited on black males.*

The living room was filled with his friends and neighborhood folks. Sad Smokey Robinson songs played from a blaster. The friends were there to help in the search for Naomi. Finally, maybe I had some allies in the South.

Everyone at the apartment was anxious to talk to me about Naomi. None of them had any suspicions about Seth Samuel.

I was struck in particular by a woman with wise, sensitive eyes and skin the color of coffee with cream. Keesha Bowie was in her early thirties, a postal worker in Durham. Naomi and Seth had apparently talked her into going back to college to get her degree in psychology. She and I hit it off right away.

'Naomi is educated, so articulate, but you already know that.' Keesha took me aside and talked seriously to me. 'But Naomi never ever uses her abilities or her education to belittle someone else, or make herself seem superior. That struck every one of us when we met her. She's so down-to-earth, Alex. She doesn't have a phony bone inside her. That this could happen to her is the saddest thing.'

I talked with Keesha some more, and I liked her very much. She was smart and pretty, but this wasn't the time for any of that stuff. I looked for Seth and found him off by himself on the second floor. The bedroom window was open, and he was sitting outside on the gently sloping roof. Robert Johnson was singing his haunting blues somewhere in the dark.

'Mind if I come out and join you? This old roof hold us both?' I said from the window.

Seth smiled. 'If it doesn't and we both crash through to the front porch, it'll be a good story for everybody. Worth the fall and the broken neck. C'mon out, you got a mind to.' He spoke in a sweet, almost musical, drawl. I could see why Naomi would like him.

I climbed out and sat with Seth Samuel in the darkness settling over Durham. We heard a smaller-town version of the police sirens and excited shouts of the inner city.

'We used to sit out here,' Seth muttered in a low voice. 'Naomi and I.'

'You okay?' I asked him.

'Nah. Never been any worse in my life. You?'

'Never worse.'

'After you called,' Seth said, 'I was thinking about this visit, about this talk that we'd eventually have. I tried to think the way that you might be thinking. You know, like a police *detective*. Please, don't have any more thoughts that there's some chance that I could have anything to do with Naomi's disappearance. Don't waste time on that.'

I looked over at Seth Samuel. He was hunched over, and his head rested on his chest. Even in the dark I could see that his eyes were shiny-wet. His grief was a palpable thing. I wanted to tell him that we were going to find her and that everything would work out, but I knew no such thing.

We finally held on to each other. We were both missing Naomi in our own way, mourning together, on the dark roof.

31

A friend of mine from the FBI finally returned one of my phone calls that night. I was doing some reading when he called: *The Diagnostic and Statistical Manual of Mental Disorders.* I was working on Casanova's profile and still not getting very far.

I had originally met Special Agent Kyle Craig during the long, difficult manhunt for the serial kidnapper Gary Soneji. Kyle had always been a straight shooter. He wasn't territorial like most FBI agents, and not too uptight by Bureau standards, either. Sometimes I thought that he didn't *belong* in the FBI. He was too much of a human being.

'Thanks for finally returning my calls, stranger,' I said over the phone. 'Where are you working out of these days?'

Kyle surprised me with his answer. 'I'm here in Durham, Alex. To be a little more precise, I'm in the lobby of your hotel. C'mon down for a drink or three in the infamous Bull Durham Room. I need to talk to you. I've got a special message for you from J. Edgar himself.'

'I'll be right down. I've been wondering what the Hoove's been up to since he faked his own death.'

Kyle was seated at a table for two beside a large bay window. The window faced directly onto the putting green of the university golf course. A lanky man who looked like a school-boy was teaching a Duke coed how to putt in the dark. The jock was standing behind his lady, showing her his best putt-putt moves.

Kyle was watching the lesson of the links with obvious amusement. I watched Kyle with obvious amusement. He turned as if he could sense my presence.

'Man, you have a nose for bad trouble,' he said by way of a greeting. 'I was sorry to hear that your niece is missing. It's good to see you, in spite of the particularly vile and shitty circumstances.'

I sat down across from the agent, and we started to talk shop. As always, he was extremely upbeat and positive without sounding naïve. It's a gift he has. Some people feel that Kyle could wind up at the top of the Bureau, and that it would be the best thing that ever happened.

'First, the honorable Ronald Burns appears in Durham. Now you show up. What gives?' I asked Kyle.

'Tell me what *you* have so far,' he said. 'I'll try to reciprocate as much as I can.'

'I'm doing psych profiles on the murdered women,' I told Kyle. 'The so-called *rejects*. In two of the cases, the rejected women had very strong personalities. They probably gave him a lot of trouble. That could be why he killed them, to get rid of them. The exception was Bette Anne Ryerson. She was a mother, in therapy, and she might have had a nervous breakdown.'

Kyle massaged his scalp with one hand. He was also

shaking his head. 'You've been given no information, no help whatsoever. But *zip-a-dee-doo-dah*' – he smiled at me –'you're still a half-step ahead of our people. I haven't heard that theory about the 'rejects.' It's pretty good, Alex, *especially* if he's a control freak.'

'He could definitely be a control freak, Kyle. There has to be a damn good reason why he got rid of those three women. Now, I thought you were going to tell me some things I didn't know.'

'Maybe, if you pass a few more simple tests, that is. What else have you figured out?'

I bad-eyed Kyle while I slowly sipped my beer. 'You know, I thought you were all right, but you're just another FBI prick.'

'*I was programmed at Quantico*,' Kyle said in a passable computer voice. 'Have you done a psych profile on Casanova?'

'I'm working on it.' I told him what he already knew. 'As much as I can with virtually no information available.'

Kyle beckoned with the cupped fingers of his right hand. He wanted it all, and then *maybe* he'd share something with me.

'He has to be someone who blends into the community well,' I said. 'No one's even come close to catching him. He's probably driven by the same obsessive sexual fantasies that he's had since he was a boy. He could have been the victim of abuse, maybe incest. Maybe he was a Peeping Tom, a rapist, or a date rapist. Now he's a very fancy collector of extremely beautiful women; he seems to choose only the extraordinary ones. He's *researching* them, Kyle. I'm almost sure of it. He's lonely. Maybe he wants the perfect woman.'

Kyle shook his head back and forth. 'You are so goddamn crazy, man. You *think* like him!'

'Not funny.' I grabbed Kyle's cheek between my thumb and forefinger. 'Now you tell me something *I* don't know.'

Kyle pulled away from my cheekhold. 'Let me run a deal by you, Alex. This is a *good* deal, so don't get cynical on me.'

I raised my hand high in the air for the table waitress. 'Check! *Separate* checks, please.'

'No, no. Wait. This is a good deal, Alex. I hate to say, "Trust me," but trust me. Just to prove my truthfulness, I simply can't tell you everything right now. I'll admit that the case is definitely bigger than anything you've seen so far. You're right about Burns. The deputy director wasn't down here by accident.'

'I figured Burns wasn't here to see the azaleas.' I felt like yelling at Kyle inside the quiet hotel bar. 'Okay, tell me one thing I don't know already.'

'I can't tell you any more than I already have.'

'*Damn* you, Kyle. You haven't told me a goddamn thing.' I raised my voice. 'What's the deal you have for me?'

He put up a hand. He wanted me calm for this. 'Listen. As you know, or suspect, this is already a four-star, multi-jurisdictional nightmare, and it hasn't really heated up yet. Believe me on that. Nobody's getting anything done, Alex. Here's what I'd like you to consider.'

My eyes rolled back. 'I'm glad I'm sitting down for this,' I said.

'This is an excellent offer for a man in your position to consider. Since you're already outside the multijurisdictional mess, and therefore immune to it, why don't you keep it that way. Stay on the outside, and work *directly* with me.'

'Work with the Federal Bureau?' I choked on my beer. 'Collaborate with the Feebies?'

'I can give you access to all the information we get, as soon as we get it. I'll give you everything you need in terms of resources and information and all of our current data.'

'And *you* don't have to share anything I come up with? Not even with the local or state police?' I said.

Kyle had become his intense self again. 'Look, Alex, this investigation is large and expensive, but it's getting nowhere. Officers are falling over one another while women all over the South, including your niece, are disappearing right under our noses.'

'I understand the problem, Kyle. Let me think about your solution. Give me a little space on this one.'

Kyle and I talked some more about his offer, and I was able to pin him down on a few specifics. Basically I was sold, though. Working with Kyle would give me access to a firstrate support team, and I'd have clout whenever I needed it. I wouldn't be alone anymore. We ordered burgers and more beers, and continued to talk and put the final touches on my deal with the Devil. For the first time since I'd come South, I was feeling a little hopeful.

'I do have something else to share with you,' I finally told him. 'He dropped me a note last night. It was a nice note, thoughtful, welcoming me to the area.'

'We know.' Kyle grinned like the grown-up Andy Hardy that he is. 'It was a postcard, actually. It showed an odalisque, a love slave from a harem.'

32

By the time I got back to my room it was a little late, but I called Nana and the kids, anyway. I always call home when I'm away, twice every day, morning and night. I hadn't missed yet, and didn't plan to start that night.

'Are you listening to Nana and being a good girl for a change?' I asked Jannie when she came on the phone.

'I'm always a good girl!' Jannie squealed with little-girl glee. She loves talking to me. I feel the same way about her. Amazing, we were still madly in love after five years together.

I closed my eyes and visualized my girl. I could just see her puffing out her little chest, making her face look defiant, but smiling pointy crooked teeth at the same time. Once, Naomi had been a sweet little girl like that. I remembered everything about those times. I chased away the thought, the vivid portrait of Scootchie.

'Well, how about your big brother? Damon says he's being especially good, too. He says Nana's called you "the holy terror" today. Is that so?'

'Unh-uh, Daddy. That's what Nana called him. Damon's the holy terror in *this house*. I'm Nana's angel all the time. I'm Nana Mama's good girl angel. You can axt her.'

'Uh-huh. That's good to hear,' I told my little spin-doctor. 'Did you pull Damon's hair just a tiny bit at Roy Rogers junkfood restaurant today?'

'*Not* junk food, pally-wally! *He* pulled *my* hair first. Damon almost pulled my hair out, like I was Baby Clare without her hair now.'

Baby Clare had been Jannie's main doll since she was two years old. The doll was 'her baby,' absolutely sacred to Jannie. Sacred to all of us. Once we had left Baby Clare at Williamsburg during a day trip, and we had to drive all the way back. Magically, Clare was waiting for us at the front-gate office, having a nice chat with the security guard.

'I couldn't pull Damon's hair, anyway. He's almost *bald*, Daddy. Nana got him his summer haircut. Wait'll you see my bald brother. He's a *pool* ball!'

I could hear her laughing. I could *see* Jannie laughing. In the background, Damon wanted the phone back. He wanted his rebuttal about the state of his haircut.

After I finished with the kids, I talked to Nana.

'How are *you* holding up, Alex?' She went right to the point, as she always does. She would have made an outstanding detective, or anything else she wanted to be. 'Alex, I asked how you're doing?'

'I'm doing just fine and dandy. Love my work,' I told her. 'How are you, old woman?'

'Never mind that. I could watch these children in my sleep. You don't sound good to me. You're not sleeping, and you haven't made a lot of progress, have you?'

Man, she was tough when she wanted to be. 'It's not going as well as I would have hoped,' I told her. 'Something good might have just happened tonight.'

'I know,' Nana said, 'that's why you're calling up so late. But you can't share the good news with your grandmother. You're afraid I might call the *Washington Post.*'

We'd had this discussion before on cases I was working on. She always wants inside information, and I can't give it up.

'I love you,' I finally said to her. 'That's the best I can do right now.'

'And I love you, Alex Cross. That's the best I can do.'

She *had* to have the final word.

After I finished with Nana and the kids, I lay in the dark on the unmade, unwelcoming hotel bed. I didn't want maids or anyone else in the room, but the *Do Not Disturb* tag hadn't deterred the FBI.

A bottle of beer sat upright on my chest. I slowed my breathing, let the bottle balance there. I've never liked hotel rooms, not even on a vacation.

I started thinking about Naomi again. When she was a little girl like Jannie, she used to ride up on my shoulders, so she could see 'far, far away in the Big People's World.' I remembered that Naomi thought Christmas was 'Kissmass,' so she would kiss everybody during the holidays.

Finally, I let my mind settle on the monster who had taken Scootchie away from us. The monster was winning so far. He seemed invincible, uncatchable; he didn't make any mistakes, and didn't leave any clues. He was very sure of himself . . . he even left me a cute little postcard for sport. What should that tell me?

He might have read my book about Gary Soneji, I thought. He just might have read my book. Had he taken Naomi to challenge me? Maybe to prove how good he was.

I didn't like that thought very much.

33

I'm alive, but I'm in hell!

Kate McTiernan tucked her legs close against her chest and shivered. She was certain that she'd been drugged. Severe tremors, accompanied by gnawing nausea, swept over her in powerful waves *that would not stop* no matter what she tried.

She didn't know how long she had been asleep on the cold floor, or what time it was now. Was he watching her? Was there a peephole hidden in the walls? Kate could almost *feel* his eyes crawling all over her.

She remembered every gruesome and hideous detail of the rape. The *feel* of it was so vivid. The thought of being touched by him was repulsive, and the most horrifying images snapped at her.

Anger, guilt, violation all fused in her mind. Adrenaline surged powerfully through her body. 'Hail Mary, full of grace . . . the Lord is with thee.' She thought she had forgotten how to pray. She hoped that God hadn't forgotten her.

Kate's head was spinning. He was definitely trying to break her will, break her resistance. That was his plan, wasn't it?

She had to think, make herself *think*. Everything in the room was out of focus. *The drugs*! Kate tried to figure what he might be using. *What* drug? Which one? . . .

Perhaps it was Forane, a strong muscle relaxant that was used prior to anesthesia. It came in a one-hundred-milliliter bottle. It could be sprayed directly into a victim's face, or poured over a cloth and held to someone's face. She tried to remember the drug's aftereffects. Shivering and nausea. Dry throat. Decrease in intellectual functioning for a day or two. She had those symptoms! All of them!

He's a doctor! The thought struck her like a low punch. It made perfect sense to her. Who else would have access to a drug like Forane?

At the dojo in Chapel Hill, a discipline was taught to help students control their emotions. You had to sit in front of a blank dojo wall, and remain sitting no matter how much you wanted, or thought you *needed*, to move.

Kate's body was drenched with perspiration, but she was determined. She would never let him break her will. She could be unbelievably strong when she needed to be. That was how she'd gotten through medical school on no money and against all odds.

She sat in a lotus position for more than an hour in 'her prison room.' She breathed quietly and concentrated on clearing her mind of the pain, the nausea, and the rape. She focused on what she had to do next.

One simple concept.

Escape.

34

Kate rose slowly to her feet after the hour of meditation. She was still woozy, but she felt a little better, more in control. She decided to search for his peephole. It had to be there, hidden somewhere in the natural wood walls.

The bedroom was exactly twelve by fifteen. She'd measured it several times. In a tiny alcove the size of a closet, there was the equivalent of an outhouse.

Kate carefully looked for even the tiniest slit in the wall, but she saw nothing. The toilet in the alcove seemed to empty directly into the ground. There was no plumbing, at least not in this part of the building. *Where am I being kept? Where am I?*

Her eyes watered from the acrid odor as she knelt over the black wooden seat and squinted into the dark hole. She had learned to put up with the overpowering smell, and only a single dry heave came this time.

The opening looked as if it dropped about ten or twelve feet. *Dropped to what?* Kate wondered.

It looked very narrow, and she didn't think she could

squeeze through it, not even if she took off all of her clothes. *Maybe she could, though. Never say never.*

She heard his voice directly behind her. Her heart dropped and she felt faint.

There he was! No shirt again. Rippling muscles everywhere, but especially around his stomach and thighs. He was wearing another mask. An angry-looking one. Crimson and bone-white swatches against a shiny black background. Was he angry today? Were the masks like mood rings for him?

'Not one of your better ideas, Katie. It's been tried by someone slimmer than you are,' he said in a singsongy voice. 'I won't go down there to help you back up. Very shitty way to die. Think it through.'

Kate struggled to her feet and began to retch. She did her best to do it convincingly. 'I'm sick. I thought I was going to throw up,' she said to Casanova.

'I definitely believe you do feel sick,' he said. 'That will pass. But it *isn't* the real reason you were kneeling over the toilet. Tell the truth, and shame the devil.'

'What do you *want* from me?' Kate asked. He sounded different today . . . maybe the drugs were distorting her hearing. She studied the mask. It seemed to turn him into another person. Another kind of creep. Was he a split personality?

'I want to be in love. I want to make love to you again. I want you to get beautiful for me. Maybe one of the lovely dresses from Neiman Marcus. Nylons and high heels.'

Kate was terrified and disgusted, but trying not to show it. She had to do something, say something, that would keep him away from her for now.

'I'm not in the mood, honey,' Kate shot back an answer. 'I don't feel up to getting dressed.' She couldn't keep the sarcasm completely out of her voice. 'I have a headache. What kind of day is it, anyway? I haven't been outside yet.'

He laughed. An almost-normal laugh; a nice-enough laugh from behind his nasty mask. 'Sunny Carolina blue skies, Kate. Temperature in the high seventies. One of the ten best days of the year.'

With one hand, he suddenly yanked her to her feet. He pulled her arm hard – as if he were trying to tear it from its socket. Kate yelled as violent pain shot up her arm. It exploded in the soft space, the hollow behind her eyes.

In a fury, in panic, she reached out and pulled down on the mask.

'Stupid! *Stupid*!' he yelled into her face. 'And you're *not* a stupid woman!'

Kate saw the stun gun in his hand and realized she had made a terrible mistake. He leveled it at her chest and shot her.

She tried to keep standing, willed herself to stay up, but her body didn't work anymore, and she slumped to the floor.

He was going crazy now. She stared at him in muted horror as he raised his boot and began to kick out at her. A *tooth* spun in slow motion, spun over and over on its trail across the wooden floor.

The revolving tooth fascinated her. It took her a moment to realize that it was *her tooth*.

She could taste blood, and feel her lips swelling.

There was a hollow ringing in Kate's ears, and she knew she was slipping into unconsciousness. She clung to what she had seen behind the mask.

Casanova knew she had seen a part of his face.

A smooth pink cheek; no beard or mustache visible.

His left eye – *blue*.

35

Naomi Cross was trembling as she pressed herself hard against the bolted door that sealed off her room. Somewhere in the house of horror a woman was screaming.

The sound was muffled by the walls, by the soundproofing he'd built into the house, but it was still terrifying. Naomi realized that she was biting down on her hand. Hard. She felt sure he was killing someone. It wouldn't be the first time.

The screams stopped.

Naomi pressed harder against the door, straining to hear some sound.

'Oh, no, please,' she whispered, 'don't let her be dead.'

Naomi listened to the electric silence for a long time. Finally, she moved away from the door. There was nothing she could do for the poor woman. Nothing anyone could do.

Naomi knew she had to be very good right now. If she broke any of his rules, he would beat her. She couldn't let that happen.

He seemed to know everything about her. What clothes she liked to wear, all her underwear sizes, her favorite colors, even the shades she preferred. He knew about Alex, and Seth Samuel, and even about her friend Mary Ellen Klouk. 'The tall, pretty blonde thing,' he called her. *Thing*.

Casanova was very kinky; he was into play-acting and fantasy psychodramas. He loved to talk to her about pornographic acts: sex with prepubescent girls and animals; nightmarish sadism; masochism; gynecocracy; enema torture. He talked about everything so casually. At times he would even be poetic, in a sick way. He quoted from Jean Genet, John Rechy, Durrell, de Sade. He was well read, probably well educated.

'You're smart enough to understand me when I talk,' he had told Naomi on one of his visits. 'That's why I picked you, sweet darling.'

Naomi was startled by the sound of more screaming. She ran to the door and placed her cheek against the cool thick wood. *Was it the same woman, or was he killing someone else?* she wondered.

'Somebody please help me!' she heard. The woman was screaming at the top of her voice. She was breaking the house rules.

'Somebody help! I'm being held captive in here. Somebody help . . . my name is Kate . . . Kate McTiernan. Somebody help!'

Naomi shut her eyes. This was so bad. The woman had to stop. But over and over again the calls for help were repeated. That meant Casanova wasn't in the house. He must have gone out.

'Somebody please help me. My name is Kate McTiernan. I'm a doctor from the University of North Carolina hospital.' The screams continued . . . ten times, twenty times. Not in panic, Naomi began to realize. In rage!

137

He couldn't be in the house. He wouldn't let her go on this long. Naomi finally summoned up her courage and shouted as loud as she could. '*Stop* it! You must *stop* calling for help. He'll kill you! Shut up! *That's all I'm going to say!*'

There was silence . . . blessed silence, finally. Naomi thought she could *hear* the tension all around her. She certainly *felt* it.

Kate McTiernan didn't stop for long. 'What's your name? How long have you been here? Please, talk to me . . . hey, I'm talking to *you!*' she shouted.

Naomi wouldn't answer her. What was wrong with the woman? Had she lost it after the last beating?

Kate McTiernan called out again. 'Listen, we can help each other. I'm sure we can. Do you know where you're being kept?'

The woman was definitely brave . . . but she was being foolish, too. Her voice was strong, but it was beginning to sound hoarse. *Kate.*

'Please talk to me. He isn't here now, or he would have come with his stun gun. *You know I'm right!* He won't know if you talk to me. Please . . . I have to hear your voice again.'

'Please. For two minutes. That's all. I promise you. *Two minutes.* Please. Just *one* minute.'

Naomi still refused to answer her. He could have come back by now. He might be in the house, listening to them. Even watching them through the walls.

Kate McTiernan was back on the air. 'All right, thirty seconds. Then we'll stop. Okay? I promise I'll stop . . . *otherwise*, I'll keep this up until he does come back . . .'

Oh, God, please, stop talking, a voice inside Naomi was screaming. *Stop it, right now.*

'He'll kill me,' shouted Kate. 'But he's going to do that,

anyway! I saw part of his face. *Where are you from?* How long have you been here?'

Naomi felt as if she were suffocating. She couldn't breathe, but she stayed at the door and listened to every word the woman had to say. She wanted to talk to her so badly.

'He may have used a drug called Forane. Hospitals use it. *He might be a doctor.* Please. What do we have to fear – except torture and death?'

Naomi smiled. Kate McTiernan had guts, and also a sense of humor. Just hearing another voice was so unbelievably good.

The words tumbled out of Naomi's mouth, almost against her will. 'My name is Naomi Cross. I've been here for eight days, I *think*. He hides behind the walls. He watches all the time. I don't think he ever sleeps. He raped me,' she said in a clear voice. It was the first time she had said the words out loud. *He raped me.*

Kate answered right back. 'He raped me, too, Naomi. I know how you feel, terribly bad . . . *dirty* all over. It's so good to hear your voice, Naomi. I don't feel so alone anymore.'

'Me, too, Kate. Now please *shut up.*'

Downstairs in her room, Kate McTiernan felt so tired now. Tired, but hopeful. She was slumped against one of the walls when she heard the voices around her.

'Maria Jane Capaldi. I think I've been here about a month.'

'My name is Kristen Miles. Hello.'

'Melissa Stanfield. I'm a student nurse. I've been here nine weeks.'

'Christa Akers, North Carolina State. Two months in hell.'

There were at least six of them.

PART TWO

Hide and Seek

36

A twenty-nine-year-old *Los Angeles Times* reporter named Beth Lieberman stared at the tiny, blurred green letters on her computer terminal. She watched with tired eyes as one of the biggest stories at the *Times* in years continued to unfold. This was definitely the most important story of her career, but she almost didn't care anymore.

'This is so crazy and sick . . . *feet*. Jesus Christ,' Beth Lieberman groaned softly under her breath. '*Feet.*'

The sixth 'diary' installment sent to her by the Gentleman Caller had arrived at her West Los Angeles apartment early that morning. As had been the case with the previous diary entries, the killer supplied the precise location of a murdered woman's body before starting into his obsessive, pyschopathic message for her.

Beth Lieberman had immediately called the FBI from her home, and then she drove quickly to the offices of the *Times* on South Spring Street. By the time she arrived, the Federal Bureau had verified the latest murder.

The Gentleman had left his signature: fresh flowers.

The body of a fourteen-year-old Japanese girl had been found in Pasadena. As was the case with the five other women, Sunny Ozawa had disappeared without a trace two nights ago. It was as if she'd been sucked up into the damp, muggy smog.

To date, Sunny Ozawa was the Gentleman's youngest reported victim. He'd arranged pink and white peonies on her lower torso. *Flowers, of course, remind me of a woman's labia*, he'd written in one of the diary entries. *The isomorphism is obvious, no?*

At quarter to seven in the morning, the *Times* offices were deserted and eerie. *Nobody should be up this early except head-bangers who haven't been to bed yet*, Lieberman thought. The low hum from the central air conditioning, mingling with the faint roar of traffic outside, was annoying to her.

'Why feet?' the reporter muttered.

She sat before her computer, almost comatose, and wished she had never written an article about mail-order pornography in California. That was how the Gentleman claimed he had 'discovered' her; how he had chosen her to be his 'liaison with the other citizens of the City of Angels.' He proclaimed that they were on the same 'wavelength.'

Following endless administrative meetings at the highest levels, the *Los Angeles Times* had decided to publish the killer's diary entries. There was no doubt that they had actually been written by the Gentleman Caller.

He knew where the murder victims' bodies were before the police did. He also threatened 'special bonus kills' if his diary wasn't published for everyone in Los Angeles to read over breakfast. 'I am the latest, and I'm by far the greatest,' the Gentleman had written in one diary entry. Who could argue with that? Beth wondered. Richard Ramirez? Caryl Chessman? Charles Manson?

Beth Lieberman's job right now was to be his contact. She also got to make the first edit of the Gentleman's words. Therewas no way the intense, graphic diary entries could run intact. They were filled with obscene pornography and the most brutally violent descriptions of the murders he had committed.

Lieberman could almost hear the madman's voice as she typed the latest entry on her word processor. The Gentleman Caller was speaking to her again, or *through* her:

Let me tell you about Sunny, as much as I know about Sunny, anyway. Listen to me, dear reader. Be there with me. She had small, delicate, clever feet. That's what I remember best; that's what I will always remember about my beautiful Sunny night.

Beth Lieberman had to shut her eyes. She didn't want to listen to this shit. One thing was certain: the Gentleman Caller had definitely given Beth Lieberman her first break at the *Times*. Her byline appeared on each of the widely read front-page features. The murderer had made her a star, too.

Listen to me. Be there with me.

Think about fetishism, and all its amazing possibilities to liberate the psyche. Don't be a snob. Open up your mind. Open your mind right now! Fetishism holds a fascinating array of diverse pleasures that you may be missing out on.

Let us not become too sentimental about 'young' Sunny. Sunny Ozawa was into the games of the night. She told me that, in confidence of course. I had picked her up at the Monkey Bar. We'd gone to my place, my hideaway, where we began to experiment, to play the night away.

She asked me if I'd ever done it with a Japanese woman before. I told her that I hadn't, but I'd always wanted to. Sunny told me that I was 'quite the gentleman.' I was honored.

This night, it seemed to me that nothing was so libertine as to focus on a woman's feet, to caress them as I made love to Sunny. I'm talking about sunbrowned feet covered in luxurious nylon and semipricey high-heeled pumps from Saks. I'm talking about clever little feet. Very sophisticated communicators.

Listen. To really appreciate the very erotic mime show of a beautiful woman's feet, the woman should be on her back while the man stands. That's how it was with Sunny and me earlier tonight.

I lifted up her slender legs and watched closely where they joined together in such a way that the vulva puckered from her buttocks. I kissed the top of her stockings repeatedly. I fixated on her well-formed ankle, the lovely lines leading to her shiny black pump.

I concentrated all my attention on that flirtatious pump as our fevered action set her foot into rapid motion. Her little feet were talking to me now. An absolutely manic excitement rose in my chest. It felt as if there were live birds tweeting and twittering in there.

Beth Lieberman stopped typing and closed her eyes again. Tight! She had to stop the images that were flashing out at her. He had murdered the young girl that he was talking about so blithely.

Soon the FBI and the Los Angeles police would come storming into the relatively sedate offices of the *Times*. They would ask the usual battery of questions. They had no answers yet themselves. No significant leads so far. They said that the Gentleman committed 'perfect crimes.'

The FBI agents would want to talk for hours about the gruesome details of the murder scene. *The feet*! The Gentleman had cut off Sunny Ozawa's feet with some kind of razor-sharp knife. Both her feet were missing from the crime scene in Pasadena.

Brutality was his trademark, but that was the only consistent pattern so far. He had mutilated genitalia in the past. He had sodomized one victim, then cauterized her. He had cut open a woman investment banker's chest and removed her heart. Was he experimenting? He was no gentleman once he selected his victim. *He was a Jekyll and Hyde in the 1990s.*

Beth Lieberman finally opened her eyes and saw a tall, slender man standing very close to her in the newsroom. She sighed loudly and she held back a frown.

It was Kyle Craig, the special investigator from the FBI.

Kyle Craig knew *something* that she desperately needed to know, but he wouldn't tell her squat. He knew why the deputy director of the FBI had flown to Los Angeles the previous week. He knew secrets that she needed to know.

'Hello, Ms Lieberman. What do you have for me?' he asked.

37

Tick-cock, dickory dock.

This was the way he hunted for the women. This was how it really happened, time after time. There was never any danger for him personally. He fit in wherever he chose to hunt. He did his best to avoid any kind of complication or human error. He had a passion for orderliness and, most of all, perfection.

That afternoon, he waited patiently in a crowded arcade of a trendy shopping mall in Raleigh, North Carolina. He watched attractive women enter and leave the local Victoria's Secret across a long marble transverse. Most of the women were well dressed. A copy of *Time* magazine and also *USA Today* were folded on the marble bench beside him. The newspaper headline read: *Gentleman Calls for 6th Time in LA*.

He was thinking to himself that the 'Gentleman' was zooming out of control in southern California. He was taking gruesome souvenirs, doing two women a week sometimes, playing stupid mind games with the *Los Angeles Times*, the LAPD, and the FBI. He was going to get caught.

148

Casanova's blue eyes moved back across the crowded shopping mall. He was a handsome man, as the original Casanova had been. Nature had equipped the eighteenth-century adventurer with beauty, sensuality, and great enthusiasm for women – and so it was with him as well.

Now where was the lovely Anna? She had slipped into Victoria's Secret – to buy something campy for her boyfriend, no doubt. Anna Miller and Chris Chapin had been in law school together at North Carolina State. Now Chris was an associate in a law firm. They liked to dress in each other's clothes. Cross-dress to get their kicks. He knew all about them.

He had watched Anna whenever he could for almost two weeks. She was a startling, dark-haired twenty-three-year-old beauty, maybe not another Dr Kate McTiernan, but close enough.

He watched Anna finally leave Victoria's Secret and walk almost directly toward him. The *click* of her high heels made her sound so wonderfully haughty. She *knew* she was an extraordinary young beauty. That was the very best thing about her. Her supreme confidence nearly matched his own.

She had such a nicely arrogant, long-legged stride. Perfect slender lines up and down her body. Legs wrapped in dark nylons; heels for her part-time job in Raleigh as a paralegal. Sculptured breasts that he wanted to caress. He could see the subtle lines of her underwear under a clinging tan skirt. Why was she so provocative? Because she *could* be.

She seemed intelligent, too. Promising, anyway. She had just missed Law Review. Anna was warm, sweet, nice to be around. A keeper. Her lover called her 'Anna Banana.' He loved the sweet, stupid intimacy of the nickname.

All he had to do was take her. It was that easy.

Another very attractive woman suddenly broke into his field of vision. She smiled at him, and he smiled back. He stood up and stretched, then walked toward her. She had store packages and bags piled high in both arms.

'Hi there, beautiful,' he said when he got close. 'Can I take some of those? Ease your heavy load, sweet darlin'?'

'You're such a sweet, handsome thing yourself,' the woman said to him. 'But then you always were. Always the romantic, too.'

Casanova kissed his wife on the cheek and helped her with the packages. She was an elegant-looking woman, self-possessed. She had on jeans, a loose-fitting workshirt, a brown tweed jacket. She wore clothes well. She was effective in many ways. He had picked her with the greatest care.

As he took some bags, he held the nicest, warmest thought: *They couldn't catch me in a thousand years. They wouldn't know where to start to look. They couldn't possibly see past this wonderful, wonderful disguise, this mask of sanity. I am above suspicion.*

'I saw you watching the young chippie. Nice legs,' his wife said with a knowing smile and a roll of her eyes. 'Just as long as all you do is watch.'

'You caught me,' Casanova said to his wife. 'But her legs aren't as nice as yours.'

He smiled in his easy and charming way. Even as he did so, a name exploded inside his brain. *Anna Miller*. He had to have her.

38

This was harder than hard.

I slapped on a happy, make-believe smile as I barged through my own front door back home in Washington. A day off from the chase was necessary. More important, I had promised the family a meeting, a report on Naomi's situation. I was also missing my kids and Nana. I felt as if I were home on leave from a war.

The last thing I wanted Nana and the kids to know was how anxious I was about Scootchie.

'No luck yet,' I told Nana as I stooped and kissed her cheek. 'We're making a little progress, though.' I stepped away from her before she could cross-examine me.

Standing in the living room, I launched into my best working-father lounge act. I sang 'Daddy's Home, Daddy's Home.' Not Shep and the Limelites' version; my own original tune. I scooped up Jannie and Damon in my arms.

'Damon, you got bigger and stronger and you're handsome as a prince of Morocco!' I told my son. 'Jannie, you got bigger and stronger and beautiful as a princess!' I told my daughter.

'So did you, Daddy!' The kids squealed the same kind of sweet nonsense right back at me.

I threatened to scoop up my grandmother, too, but Nana Mama made a serious-looking cross with her fingers to ward me off. Our family sign. 'You just stay away from me, Alex,' she said. She was smiling, *and* issuing a baleful stare. She can do that. 'Decades of practice,' she likes to say. '*Centuries*,' I always come back at her.

I gave Nana another big kiss. Then I more or less 'palmed' the kids. I held them out the way big men can hold basketballs as if they were nothing but an extension of their arms.

'Have you two been good little rapscallions?' I began my interrogation techniques with my very own repeat offenders. 'Clean your rooms, do your chores, eat your brussels sprouts?'

'*Yes, Daddy!*' they shouted in unison. 'We been good as gold,' Jannie added as convincing detail.

'You lyin' to me? Brussels sprouts? Broccoli, too? You wouldn't lie so brazenly to your daddy? I called home at ten-thirty the other night, both of your were still up. And *you say to me* that you've been good. Good as *gold!*'

'Nana let us watch pro *hoops*!' Damon howled with laughter and undisguised glee. That young con man can get away with anything, which worries me sometimes. He is a natural mimic, but also an ingenious creator of his own original material. At this point, his humor level is about that of the TV hit *In Living Color*.

I finally reached into my travel satchel for their cache of presents. 'Well, in that case, I've brought y'all something from my trip down South. I say y'all now. I learned it in North Carolina.'

'Y'all,' Jannie said back at me. She giggled wildly and did an impromptu dance turn. She was like the cutest puppy kept in the house for an afternoon. Then you come home and she's all over you like sticky flypaper. Just like Naomi was when she was a little girl.

I pulled out Duke University NCAA champion basketball T-shirts for Jannie and Damon. The trick with those two is they have to get the same thing. Same exact design. Same exact color. That will last for another couple of years, and then neither one of them will be caught dead in anything vaguely associated with the other.

'Thank you, y'all,' the kids said one after the other. I could feel their love – it was so good to be home. On leave, or otherwise. Safe and sound for a few hours.

I turned to Nana. 'You probably thought I forgot all about you,' I said to her.

'You will never forget me, Alex.' Nana Mama squinted her brown eyes hard at me.

'You got that right, old woman.' I grinned.

'I surely do.' She *had* to have the last word.

I took a beautifully wrapped package from my duffel bag of wonders and surprises. Nana unwrapped it, and she found the most handsome handmade sweater that I had ever seen anywhere. It had been created in Hillsborough, North Carolina, by eighty- and ninety-year-old women who still worked for a living.

For once, Nana Mama had nothing to say. No smart comebacks. I helped her on with the hand-knitted sweater, and she wore it for the rest of the day. She looked proud, happy, and beautiful, and I loved seeing her like that.

'This is the nicest gift,' she finally said with a tiny crack in her voice, 'other than you being home, Alex. I know you're supposed to be a tough hombre, but I worried about you down there in North Carolina.'

Nana Mama knew enough not to ask too much about Scootchie yet. She also knew exactly what my silence meant.

39

In the late afternoon, thirty or so of my very closest friends and relatives swarmed through the house on Fifth Street. The investigation in North Carolina was the topic of discussion. This was natural even though they knew I would have told them if I had any good news to report. I made up hopeful leads that just weren't there. It was the best I could do for them.

Sampson and I finally got together on the back porch after we'd had a little too much imported beer and rare beefsteaks. Sampson needed to listen; I needed some cop talk with my friend and partner.

I told him everything that had happened so far in North Carolina. He understood the difficulty of the investigation and manhunt. He'd been there with me before, on cases without a single clue.

'At first, they shut me out completely. Wouldn't listen to squat from me. Lately, it's been a little better,' I said to him. 'Detectives Ruskin and Sikes dutifully check in and keep me up to date. Ruskin does, anyway. Occasionally, he even tries to be helpful. Kyle Craig is on the case, too. The FBI still won't tell me what they know.'

'Any guesses, Alex?' Sampson wanted to know. He was intense as he listened and occasionally made a point.

'Maybe one of the kidnapped women is connected to somebody important. Maybe the number of victims is a lot higher than they're letting on. Maybe the killer is connected to somebody with power or influence.'

'You *don't* have to go back down there,' Sampson said after he'd heard all the details. 'Sounds like they've got enough 'professionals' on the case. Don't start on one of your vendettas, Alex.'

'It's already started,' I told him. 'I think Casanova's enjoying the fact that he has us stumped with his perfect crimes. I think he likes it that *I'm* stumped and frustrated, too. There's something else, but I can't figure it out yet. I think he's in heat now.'

'Mmm, hmm. Well it sounds to me like *you're* in heat, too. Back the hell off him, Alex. Don't play Sherlock fuckin' Holmes with this kinky madman.'

I didn't say anything. I just shook my head, my very *hard* head.

'What if you can't get him,' Sampson finally said. 'What if you can't solve this case? You have to think about that, Sugar.'

That was the one possibility I *wouldn't* consider.

40

When Kate McTiernan woke up, she knew immediately that something was very wrong, that her impossible situation had gotten even worse.

She didn't know what time it was, what day it was, where she was being held. Her vision was blurred. Her pulse was jumpy. All her vital signs seemed off kilter.

She had gone from extreme feelings of detachment, to depression, to panic, in just the few moments she had been conscious. What had he given her? What drug would produce these symptoms? If she could solve that puzzle, it would prove she was still sane, at least still competent to think things through clearly.

Maybe he'd given her Klonopin, Kate considered.

Ironically, Klonopin was usually prescribed as an anti-anxiety medication. But if he started her at a high-enough dosage, say five to ten milligrams, she would experience approximately the same side effects she was feeling now.

Or maybe he'd used Marinol capsules? They were prescribed for treatment of nausea during chemotherapy. Kate knew Marinol was a real beaut! If he put her on, say two hundred milligrams a day, she'd be bouncing off the walls. Cottonmouth. Disorientation. Periods of manic depression. A dosage of fifteen hundred to two thousand milligrams would be lethal.

He had taken away her escape plan with the powerful drugs. She couldn't fight him like this. Her karate training was useless. Casanova had seen to that.

'You fucker,' Kate said out loud. She almost never swore. 'You motherfucker,' she whispered between clenched teeth.

She didn't want to die. She was only thirty-one years old. She was finally trained to be a doctor, a good one, she hoped. *Why me? Don't let this happen. This man, this awful maniac, is going to kill me for no good reason*!

Shivers as cold as icicles ran up and down her spine. She felt as if she were going to throw up, or maybe even pass out. *Orthostatic hypotension*, she thought. It was the medical term for fainting when you get up fast from a bed or chair.

She couldn't defend herself against him! He'd wanted her powerless, and he'd apparently succeeded. More than anything else that finally got to her, and she started to cry. *That* made her even angrier.

I don't want to die.

I don't want to die.

How do I stop it from happening?

How do I stop Casanova?

The house was so very quiet again. She didn't think he was there. She desperately needed to talk to somebody. To the other women prisoners. She had to work herself up to it again.

He *could* be hiding in the house. Waiting. Watching her right at this second.

'Hello out there,' she finally called, surprised at the raspiness of her own voice.

'This is Kate McTiernan. Please listen. He's given me a lot of drugs. I think he's going to kill me soon. He told me that he was. I'm very afraid . . . I don't want to die.'

Kate repeated the same message once more, word for word. She repeated it again.

There was silence; no response from anybody. The other women were afraid, too. They were right to be petrified. Then a voice came floating down from somewhere above her. The voice of an angel.

Kate's heart jumped. She remembered the voice. She listened closely to every word from *her brave friend*.

'This is Naomi. Maybe we can help each other somehow. Every so often he gets us together, Kate. You're still on probation. He kept each of us in the downstairs room at first. Please *don't fight him!* We can't talk anymore. It's too dangerous. You're not going to die, Kate.'

Another woman called out. 'Please be brave, Kate. Be strong for all of us. Just don't be *too* strong.'

Then the women's voices stopped, and it became very quiet again, very lonely, in her room.

The drug, whatever he had pumped into her, was working full blast now. Kate McTiernan felt as if she were going mad.

41

Casanova was going to kill her, wasn't he? It was going to happen soon.

In the terrible silence and loneliness, Kate felt the overwhelming need to pray, to talk to God. God would still hear her in this grotesquely evil place, wouldn't He?

I'm sorry if I only partially believed in You for the last few years before this. I don't know if I'm agnostic, but at least I'm honest. I have a pretty good sense of humor. Even when humor is inappropriate.

I know this isn't 'Let's Make a Deal,' but if You can get me out of this one, I'll be eternally grateful.

Sorry about that. I keep saying this can't happen to me, but it's happening. Please help me. This is not one of Your better ideas . . .

She was praying so hard, concentrating, that she didn't hear him at the door. He was always so quiet, anyway. A phantom. A ghost.

'You *don't listen* a whit, do you? You just *don't learn!*' Casanova said to her.

He held a hospital syringe in one hand. He had on a mauve-colored mask smeared with thick white and blue paint. It was the most gruesome and upsetting mask he'd worn so far. The masks *did* match his moods, didn't they?

Kate tried to say *don't hurt me*, but nothing came out. Only a little *pff* sound escaped from her lips.

He was going to kill her.

She could barely stand, or even sit, but she gave him what she thought was a faint smile.

'Hi . . . good to see you.' She got that much out. Had she made *any* sense? she wondered. She didn't know for sure.

He said something back to her, *something important*, but she had no idea what it was. The mysterious words echoed inside her brain . . . meaningless mumbo jumbo. She *tried* to listen to what he was saying. She tried so hard . . .

'*Dr Kate . . . talked to the others . . . broke house rules!*

'*Best girl, the best! . . . Could have been . . . so smart that you're stupid!*

Kate nodded her head as if she understood what he'd just told her, followed his words and logic perfectly. He obviously knew she had talked to the others. Was he saying that she was so smart that she was stupid? That was true enough. You got that right, pal.

'I wanted . . . talk,' she managed. Her tongue felt as if it were enclosed in a woolen mitten. What she had wanted to say was *Let's talk. Let's talk this all out. We need to talk.*

He wasn't much into talking on this visit, though. He seemed *inside* of himself. Very distant. The Iceman. Something especially inhuman about him. That hideous mask. Today, his persona was Death.

He was less than ten feet away, armed with the stun gun *and* a syringe. *Doctor*, her brain screamed. He's a doctor, isn't he?

161

'Don't want to die. Be good,' she managed to say with great effort. 'Get dressed up . . . high heels . . .'

'Should have thought of that earlier, Dr Kate, and you shouldn't have broken the rules of my house every chance you got. You were a mistake on my part. I don't usually make mistakes.'

She knew that the electric shocks from the gun would immobilize her. She tried to concentrate on what she could do to save herself.

She was on full automatic pilot now. All learned reflexes. *One straight, true kick*, she thought. But that seemed impossible right now. She reached deep inside herself, anyway. *Total concentration*. All of her years of karate practice channeled into one slender chance to save her life.

One last chance.

She'd been told a thousand times in the dojo to focus on a single target, and then use the enemy's force and energy *against him*. Total focus. As much as she could right now.

He came toward her and raised the stun gun to his chest. He was moving very purposefully.

Kate rasped out '*kee-ai*!' or something like that. The best she could manage right then. She kicked out with all of her remaining strength. She aimed for his kidneys. The blow could incapacitate him. She wanted to kill him.

Kate missed the kick of her life, but something happened. She did connect solidly with bone and flesh.

Not the kidney, not even close to her intended target. The kick had slammed into his hip, or his upper thigh. No matter – it had hurt him.

Casanova yelped in pain. He sounded like a dog clipped by a speeding car. She could tell that he was surprised, too. He took a sudden stutter-step backward.

Then Jack and the Goddamn Beanstalk Giant toppled over hard. Kate McTiernan wanted to scream for joy.

She had hurt him.

Casanova was down.

42

I was back in the South, back on this ugly homicide and kidnapping investigation. Sampson had been right – this time it was personal. It was also an impossible case, the kind that can go on for years.

Everything was being done that could be done. There were eleven suspects currently under surveillance in Durham, Chapel Hill, and Raleigh. Among them were assorted deviates, but also university professors, doctors, and even a retired cop in Raleigh. On account of the 'perfect' crimes, all area policemen had been checked by the Bureau.

I didn't concern myself with these suspects. I was to look where no one else was looking. That was the deal I had made with Kyle Craig and the FBI. I was the designated hitter.

There were several ongoing cases across the country at that time. I read hundreds of detailed FBI briefs on all of them. A killer of gay men in Austin, Texas. A repeat killer of elderly women in Ann Arbor and Kalamazoo, Michigan. Pattern killers in Chicago, North Palm Beach, Long Island, Oakland, and Berkeley.

I read until my eyes burned and my insides felt even worse.

There was a nasty case that was grabbing national headlines – the Gentleman Caller in Los Angeles. I pulled up the killer's 'diaries' on Nexus. They had been running in the *Los Angeles Times* since the beginning of the year.

I began to read the L.A. killer's diaries. I short-circuited as I read the next-to-last diary entry from the *Times*. It took my breath away. I almost didn't believe what I'd just read on the computer.

I backed the story up on the screen. I reread the entry one more time, very slowly, word for word.

It was a tale about a young woman who was being held 'captive' by the Gentleman Caller in California.

The young woman's name: Naomi C. Her occupation: Second-year law student.

Description: Black, very attractive. Twenty-two years old.

Naomi was twenty-two . . . a second-year law student . . . How could a savage, recreational killer in Los Angeles know anything about Naomi Cross?

43

I immediately called the reporter at the paper whose byline appeared on the diary stories. Her name was Beth Lieberman. She answered her own phone at the *Los Angeles Times*.

'My name is Alex Cross. I'm a homicide detective involved with the Casanova murders in North Carolina,' I told her. My heart was pounding as I tried to quickly explain my situation.

'I know exactly who you are, Dr Cross,' Beth Lieberman cut me off. 'You're writing a book about this. So am I. For obvious reasons, I don't think I have anything to say to you. My own book proposal is circulating around New York right now.

'Writing a book? Who told you that? I'm not writing any book.' My voice level was rising in spite of my better instincts. 'I'm *investigating* a spree of kidnappings and murders in North Carolina. That's what I'm doing.'

'The chief of detectives in D.C. says otherwise, Dr Cross. I called *him* when I read you were involved with the Casanova case.'

The Jefe strikes again, I thought. My old boss in D.C., George Pittman, was a complete asshole, who also wasn't a fan of mine. 'I wrote a book about Gary Soneji,' I said. 'Past tense. I needed to get it out of my system. Trust me, I'm—'
  'History!'
Beth Lieberman hung up on me. Bang!
'Son of a bitch,' I muttered into the dead receiver in my hand. I dialed the paper again. This time I got a secretary on the line. 'I'm sorry, Ms Lieberman has left for the day,' she said in a staccato cadence.
  I was a little hot. 'She must have left in the *ten seconds* it just took me to get reconnected. Please put Ms Lieberman back on the phone. I know she's there. Put her on now.'
  The secretary also hung up on me.
  'You're a son of a bitch, too!' I said to the dead phone line. 'Dammit all to hell.'
  I was getting noncooperation in two cities on the same case now. The infuriating part was that I thought I might be onto something. Was there some kind of bizarre connection between Casanova and the killer on the West Coast? *How could the Gentleman Caller possibly know about Naomi? Did he know about me as well?*
  It was just a hunch so far, but much too good to brush aside. I called the editor in chief at the *Los Angeles Times*. It was easier to get through to the big man than it was to his reporter. The editor's assistant was a male. His phone voice was crisp, efficient, but as pleasant as Sunday brunch at the Ritz-Carlton in D.C.
  I told him that I was Dr Alex Cross, that I'd been involved in the Gary Soneji investigation, and that I had some important information on the Gentleman Caller case. Two-thirds of that was absolutely true.

'I'll tell Mr Hills,' the assistant informed me, still sounding as if he were pleased as punch to hear from me. I was thinking it would be nifty to have an assistant like that.

It didn't take long for the editor in chief to come on the phone himself. 'Alex Cross,' he said, 'Dan Hills. I read about you during the Soneji manhunt. Glad to take your call, especially if you have something for us on this messy affair.'

As I talked to Dan Hills, I pictured a big man in his late forties. Tough enough, but California-dapper at the same time. Pin-striped shirt with the sleeves rolled to the elbow. Hand-painted tie. Stanford all the way. He asked me to call him Dan. Okay, I could do that. He seemed like a nice guy. Probably had a Pulitzer or two.

I told him about Naomi, and my involvement with the Casanova case in North Carolina. I also told him about the Naomi entry in the L.A. diaries.

'I'm sorry about your niece's disappearance,' Dan Hills said. 'I can imagine what you're going through.' There was a pause over the line. I was afraid that Dan was about to be either politically or socially correct with me. 'Beth Lieberman is a good young reporter,' he went on. 'She's tough, but she's professional. This is a big story for her, and for us as well.'

'Listen,' I cut off Hills – I had to. 'Naomi wrote me a letter almost every week that she was in school. I saved those letters, all of them. I helped to bring her up. We're close. *That* means a lot to me.'

'I hear you. I'll see what I can do. No promises, though.'

'No promises, Dan.'

Good to his word, Dan Hills called me back at the FBI offices within the hour. 'Well, we had a meeting of the minds out here,' he told me. 'I talked to Beth. As you can imagine, this puts both of us in a tough spot.'

'I understand what you're telling me,' I said. I was cushioning myself for a soft blow, but I got something else.

'There are mentions of Casanova in the unedited versions of the diaries that the Gentleman sent her. It sounds like the two of them *could be* talking, even sharing exploits. Almost as if they're friends. It seems like they're communicating for some reason.'

Bingo!

The monsters were communicating.

Now I thought I knew what the FBI had been keeping secret, what they were afraid would come out in the open.

There were coast-to-coast serial killers.

44

Run! Go! Just run your butt off! Get the hell out of here now!

Kate McTiernan staggered and weaved out through the heavy wooden door he had left open behind him.

She didn't know how badly Casanova was hurt. Escape was her only thought. *Go now! Get away from him while you can.*

Her mind was playing tricks on her. Confusing images came and went, without making the proper connections. The drug, whatever it was, was taking its full toll. She was disoriented.

Kate touched her face, and realized her cheeks were wet. Was she crying? She couldn't even tell that for sure.

She was barely able to climb a steep wooden stairway outside her door. Was it heading to another floor? Had she just come up these stairs? *She couldn't remember. She couldn't remember anything.*

She was hopelessly bewildered and confused now. Had she really knocked Casanova down, or was she hallucinating?

Was he coming after her? Was he racing up the stairs behind her right now? Blood was roaring in her ears. She felt dizzy enough to fall down.

Naomi, Melissa Stanfield, Christa Akers. Where were they being held?

Kate was having tremendous difficulty navigating her way through the house. She weaved like a drunken person down the long hallway. What kind of strange structure was she in? It *looked* like a house. The walls were new, freshly built, but what kind of house was this?

'Naomi!' she called out, but her voice barely made a sound. She couldn't concentrate, couldn't focus for more than a few seconds. *Who was Naomi?* She couldn't remember exactly.

She stopped and pulled hard on a doorknob. The door wouldn't open for her. Why was the door locked? What on earth was she looking for? What was she doing here? The drugs wouldn't allow her to think in straight lines.

I'm going into shock, trauma, she thought. She felt so cold and numb now. Everything that could gallop was galloping out of control inside her head.

He's coming to kill me. He's coming from behind!

Escape! she commanded herself. Find the way out. Focus on that! Bring back help.

She came to another flight of wooden stairs that looked ancient, almost from another era. Dirt was caked on the stairway. Soil. Little rocks and glass fragments. These were really old stairs. Not like the new wood inside.

Kate couldn't keep her balance any longer. She pitched forward suddenly and almost hit her chin on the second stair. She kept crawling, scrabbling, up the stairs. She was on her knees. Climbing stairs. Toward what? An attic? Where would she end up? Would he be there, waiting for her with the paralyzing stun gun and the syringe?

Suddenly she was *outside!* She was actually out of the house! She had made it somehow.

Kate McTiernan was half blinded by the streaming bands of sunlight, but the world had never looked so beautiful. She breathed in the sweet smell of the gums of trees: oaks, sycamores, towering Carolina pines, with no limbs except at the very top. Kate looked at the woods and the sky, high, high above, and she cried. Tears washed down her face.

Kate stared up at the tall, tall pines. Scuppernongs reached from treetop to treetop. She'd grown up in woods like these.

Escape; she suddenly thought of Casanova again. Kate tried to run a few steps. She fell again. She did the hands-and-knees waltz. She lurched back to her feet. *Run! Get away from here!*

Kate turned around in a full, sweeping circle. She kept on turning – once, twice, three times – until she almost fell again.

No, no, no! The voice inside her head was loud, screaming at her. She couldn't believe her eyes, couldn't trust any of her senses.

This was the weirdest, craziest thing yet. It was the scariest daydream. There was no house! There was no house anywhere Kate looked as she whirled and turned in circles under the towering pines.

The house, wherever she had been kept, had completely *disappeared.*

45

Run! Move your damn legs fast, one after the other. Faster! Faster than that, girl. Run away from him.

She tried to concentrate on finding her way out of the dark, dense forest. The tall Carolina pines were like umbrellas that filtered light onto the hardwoods that grew beneath them. There wasn't enough light for the young saplings, and they stood like upright tree skeletons.

He would be coming after her now. He *had* to try to catch her, and he'd *kill* her if he did. She was pretty sure she hadn't hurt him very badly, though God knows she had tried.

Kate settled into a herky-jerky rhythm of running and stumbling forward. The forest floor was soft and spongy, a carpet of pine straw and leaves. Long spindly briar brambles grew straight up from the ground, reaching for the sunlight. She felt like a bramble herself.

Have to rest . . . hide . . . let the drugs wear off, Kate mumbled to herself. *Then go get help . . . logical thing to do. Get the police.*

Then she heard him crashing about behind her. He

screamed out her name. 'Kate! Kate! Stop right now!' His voice echoed loudly through the forest.

His bravado had to mean that nobody was around for miles; nobody to help her in the godforsaken woods. She was on her own out here.

'Kate! I'm going to get you! It's inevitable, so stop running!'

She climbed a steep, rocky hill that seemed like Mount Everest in her exhausted state. A black snake was sunning itself on a smooth patch of rock. The snake looked *like a fallen tree limb*, and Kate almost stooped to pick it up. She thought she could use it as a support. The startled black snake slithered away, and she was afraid she was hallucinating again.

'Kate! Kate! You're doomed! I'm so angry now!'

She went down hard in a mesh of honeysuckle and pointy rocks. Excruciating pain shot through her left leg, but she pushed herself up again. *Ignore the blood. Ignore the pain. Keep going.*

You have to get away. You have to bring help. Just keep running. You're smarter, faster, more resourceful than you think you are. You're going to make it!

She heard him pounding up the steep hill – the mountainside – whatever she had just climbed herself. He was very close.

'I'm right here, Kate! Hey, Katie, I'm coming up behind you! Here I am!'

Kate finally turned around. Curiosity and terror got the best of her.

He was climbing easily. She could see his white flannel shirt flashing through the almost-black trees below, and his long blonde hair. Casanova! He was still wearing his mask. The stun gun, or *some kind of gun*, was in his hand.

He was laughing loudly. Why was he laughing now?

Kate stopped running. All hope of getting away suddenly left her. She experienced a jolting moment of shock and disbelief; she cried out in anguish. She was going to die right here, she knew.

Kate whispered, 'God's will.' That was all there was now, nothing else.

The top of the steep hill ended abruptly in a canyon. Steep, sheer rock dropped at least a hundred feet. Only a few bare scrub pines grew out of the rock. There was nowhere to hide, and nowhere to run. Kate thought it was such a sad, lonely place to die.

'Poor Katie!' Casanova screamed. 'Poor *baby*!'

She turned to see him again. There he was! Forty yards, thirty, then twenty yards away. Casanova *watched* her as he climbed up the steep hillside. He never took his eyes off her. The painted black mask seemed immobile, fixed on her.

Kate turned away from him, turned her back on the death mask. She peered down at the steep valley of rocks and trees. *It must be a hundred feet, maybe more than that*, she thought. The dizziness she felt was almost as terrifying as the deadly alternative rushing up behind her.

She heard him scream her name. 'Kate, no!'

She didn't look behind her again.

Kate McTiernan jumped.

She tucked in her knees and held on to them. *Just your regular swimming-hole cannonball leap*, she thought to herself.

There was a stream down below. The silver-blue ribbon of water was coming at her unbelievably fast. The roar was getting louder in her ears.

She had no idea how deep it was, but how deep could a

175

small stream like that be? Two feet? Maybe four feet? Ten feet deep if this was the luckiest few seconds of her life, which she sincerely doubted.

'Kate!' She heard his screams from high above. 'You're *dead*!'

She saw tiny whitecaps – which meant rocks beneath the rippling water. *Oh, dear God, I don't want to die.*

Kate hit a wall of freezing cold water – *hard*.

She hit bottom so quickly it was as if there hadn't been *any* water in the fast-running stream. Kate felt shooting pain, terrible pain, everywhere. She swallowed water. She realized she was going to drown. She was going to die, anyway. She had no strength left – *God's will be done.*

46

Durham homicide detective Nick Ruskin called and informed me that they had just found another woman, and that it wasn't Naomi. A thirty-one-year-old intern from Chapel Hill had been fished out of the Wykagil River by two young boys playing hooky for the day and caught by cruel fate instead.

Ruskin's flashy green Saab Turbo picked me up in front of the Washington Duke Inn. He and Davey Sikes were trying to be more cooperative lately. Sikes was taking a day off, his first in a month, according to his detective partner.

Ruskin actually seemed glad to see me. He hopped out of the car in front of the hotel and pumped my hand as if we were friends. As always, Ruskin was dressed for success. Black Armani rip-off sportcoat. Black pocket T-shirt.

Things were picking up a little for me in the new South. I got the feeling that Ruskin knew I had connections with the FBI, and that he wanted to use them, too. Detective Nick Ruskin was definitely a mover and shaker. This was a career-making case for him.

'Our first big break,' Ruskin said to me.

'What do you know about the intern so far?' I asked en route to the University of North Carolina Hospital.

'She's hanging in there. Apparently, she came down the Wykagil like a slippery fish. They're saying it's a miracle. Not even a major broken bone. But she's in shock, or something worse. She can't talk, or she won't talk. The docs are using words like catatonic and post-traumatic shock. Who knows at this point? At least she's alive.'

Ruskin had a lot of enthusiasm, and he could also be charismatic. He definitely wanted to use my connections. Maybe I could use his.

'Nobody knows how she got into the river. Or how she got away from him,' Ruskin told me as we entered the college town of Chapel Hill. The thought of Casanova stalking female students here was terrifying. The town was so pretty and seemed so vulnerable.

'Or whether she actually was with Casanova,' I added a thought. 'We don't know that for sure.'

'We don't know shit from Shinola, do we?' Nick Ruskin complained as he turned down a side street marked HOSPITAL. 'I'll tell you one thing, though, this story is about to go public in a big way. The circus just came to town. See, up ahead.'

Ruskin had that right. The scene outside North Carolina University Hospital was already media bedlam. Television and press reporters were camped out in the parking lot, the front lobby, and all over the serene, sloping green lawns of the university.

Photographers snapped my picture, as well as Nick Ruskin's, when we arrived. Ruskin was still the local star detective. People seemed to like him. I was becoming a minor celebrity, at least a curiosity, in the case. My involvement in the Gary Soneji kidnapping had already been broadcast by the local wags. I was Dr Detective Cross, an expert on human monsters from up North.

'Tell us what's going on,' a woman reporter called out. 'Give us a break, Nick. What's the real story with Kate McTiernan?'

'If we're lucky, maybe she can tell us.' Ruskin smiled at the reporter, but he kept on walking until we were safely inside the hospital.

Ruskin and I were far from first in line, but we were allowed to see the intern later that night. Kyle Craig pulled the necessary strings for me. A determination had been made that Katelya McTiernan wasn't psychotic, but that she was suffering from post-traumatic stress syndrome. It seemed a reasonable diagnosis.

There was absolutely nothing that I could do that night. Anyway, I stayed after Nick Ruskin left, and I read all the medical charts, the nursing notes, and write-ups. I perused the local police reports describing how she had been found by two twelve-year-old boys who had skipped school to fish and smoke cigarettes down by the riverside.

I suspected I knew *why* Nick Ruskin had called me, too. Ruskin was smart. He understood that Kate McTiernan's current state might involve me in the case as a psychologist, especially since I had dealt with this kind of post-stress trauma before.

Katelya McTiernan. Survivor. But just barely. I stood beside her bed for a full thirty minutes that first night. Her IV was hooked up to a drip monitor. The bed's siderails were up high and tight around her. There were already flowers in the room. I remembered a sad, powerful Sylvia Plath poem called 'Tulips.' It was about Plath's decidedly unsentimental reaction to flowers sent to her hospital room after a suicide attempt.

I tried to recall what Kate McTiernan had looked like before she got the black eyes. I'd seen photos. A lot of ugly swelling made her face look as if she were wearing goggles or a gas mask. There was more nasty swelling surrounding her jaw. According to the hospital write-up, she'd lost a tooth, too. Apparently, it had been knocked out at least two days before she was found in the river. He'd beaten her. Casanova. The self-proclaimed *Lover*.

I felt bad for the young intern. I wanted to tell her it would be all right somehow.

I rested my hand lightly on hers, and repeated the same sentences over and over. 'You're among friends now, Kate. You're in a hospital in Chapel Hill. You're safe now, Kate.'

I didn't know if the badly injured woman could hear me, or even understand me. I just wanted to say something consoling to her before I left for the night.

And as I stood there watching the young woman, the image of Naomi's face flashed before me. I couldn't imagine her dead. *Is Naomi all right, Kate McTiernan? Have you seen Naomi Cross?* I wanted to ask, but she couldn't have answered, anyway.

'You're safe now, Kate. Sleep easy, sleep well. You're safe now.'

Kate McTiernan couldn't say a word about what had happened. She had lived through a horrifying nightmare that was worse than anything I could imagine.

She had seen Casanova, and he had left her speechless.

47

Tick-cock.

A young lawyer named Chris Chapin had brought home a bottle of Chardonnay de Beaulieu, and he and his fiancée, Anna Miller, were drinking the California wine in bed. It was finally the weekend. Life was good again for Chris and Anna.

'Thank God this godawful workweek is over,' sandy haired twenty-four-year-old Chris exclaimed. He was an associate at a prestigious law office in Raleigh. Not exactly Mitch McDeere in *The Firm* – no German-made convertible to sign on – but a good start on his lawyering career.

'Unfortunately, I have a paper on contracts due Monday.' Anna grimaced. She was in her third year of law school. 'Plus, it's for the sadist Stacklum.'

'Not tonight, Anna Banana. Screw Stacklum. Better still, screw me.'

'Thank you for bringing home the vino.' Anna finally smiled. Her white teeth were dazzling.

Chris and Anna were good for each other. Everyone said so, all their lawyer pals. They complemented each other, had pretty much the same worldview, and, most of all, were smart enough not to try to change each other. Chris was obsessive about his job. Okay, fine. Anna needed to go antiquing at least twice a month. She spent her own money as if there were no tomorrow. That was okay, too.

'I think this wine needs to breathe a little while longer,' Anna said with an impish grin. 'Uhm, while we're waiting.' She slipped down the straps of a white lace demibra. She'd purchased the bra and matching lace strip at Victoria's Secret in the mall.

'Yep. *Thank God*, it's the weekend,' said Chris Chapin.

The two of them fell into an all-purpose embrace, playfully undressing each other, kissing, caressing, losing themselves in the sexy moment.

In the middle of their lovemaking, Anna Miller had a strange feeling.

She sensed that someone else was in the bedroom. She pulled away from Chris.

Someone was standing at the foot of the bed!

He was wearing a grimly painted mask. Red and yellow dragons. Fierce ones. Angry and grotesque figures that appeared to be clawing at one another.

'Who the hell are you? *What* are you?' Chris said in a frightened voice. He searched for the ball bat they kept under the bed and found the bat handle. 'Hey, I asked you a fucking question.'

The intruder growled like a wild animal.

'Well here's a fucking answer.' Casanova's right arm came up holding a Luger. He fired once, and a large red hole opened in Chris Chapin's forehead. The young lawyer's naked body slammed back against the bed's headboard. The ball bat in his hand dropped to the floor.

Casanova moved quickly. He whipped out a second gun, and shot Anna in the chest with his stunner.

'I'm sorry about this,' he whispered softly as he carried her from the bed. 'I'm so sorry. But I promise, I'll make it up to you.'

Anna Miller was Casanova's next great love.

48

A dizzying medical mystery began the following morning. Everyone at North Carolina University Hospital was baffled, especially me.

Kate McTiernan had begun to talk very early that morning. I wasn't there, but apparently Kyle Craig was in her room at daybreak. Unfortunately, our valuable witness was making no sense to anyone.

The highly intelligent intern raved incoherently throughout most of the morning. She seemed to be psychotic at times, and almost as if she were speaking in tongues. She experienced tremors, convulsions, and signs of abdominal and muscle cramps, according to the hospital write-up reports.

I visited with her late that afternoon. There was still concern that she had suffered brain damage. Most of the time I was in her room, she was quiet and unresponsive. Once, when she tried to speak, only a terrifying scream came out.

The doctor in charge came by the room while I was in there. We had already talked a couple of times that day. Dr

Maria Ruocco wasn't interested in withholding important information about her patient from me. She was extremely helpful and nice, in fact. Dr Ruocco said she wanted to help catch whoever, or *whatever*, had done this to the young intern.

I suspected that Kate McTiernan believed she was still being held captive. As I watched her struggle against unseen forces, I sensed that she was a terrific fighter. I found myself rooting for her in the hospital room.

I volunteered to sit with Kate McTiernan for long stretches. Nobody fought me for hospital-surveillance duty. Maybe she would say something, though. A phrase, or even a single word, might become an important clue in the hunt for Casanova. All we needed was one clue to mobilize everything.

'You're safe now, Kate,' I whispered every so often. She didn't seem to hear me, but I kept it up, anyway.

I got an idea, an irresistible notion, around nine-thirty that night. The team of doctors assigned to Kate McTiernan had already left for the day. I needed to tell someone, so I called the FBI and persuaded them to let me call Dr Maria Ruocco at her home near Raleigh.

'Alex, are you still there at the hospital?' Dr Ruocco asked when she got on the phone. She seemed more surprised than angry about the nocturnal call to her house. I had already spoken with her at great length during the day. We had both gone to Johns Hopkins and we talked a little about our backgrounds. She was very interested in the Soneji case and had read my book.

'I was sitting here obsessing as usual. I was trying to figure out how he kept his victims subdued.' I began to tell Maria Ruocco my theory, and what I had already done about it. 'I figured he might drug them, and maybe he used something sophisticated. I called your lab for the results from Kate McTiernan's toxic screen. They found *Marinol* in her urine.'

'Marinol?' Dr Ruocco sounded surprised, just as I had been at first. 'Hmmp. How the hell did he get Marinol to give her? That's a real bolt out of the blue. What a clever idea, though. It's almost brilliant. Marinol is a good choice if he wanted to keep her submissive.'

'Wouldn't that account for her psychotic episodes today?' I said. 'Tremors, convulsions, hallucinations – the whole package fits if you think about it.'

'You could be right, Alex. Marinol! Jesus. The symptoms of Marinol withdrawal could mimic the most severe D.T.s. But how would he know so much about Marinol and how to use it? I don't believe a layman would come up with that.'

I had been wondering the same thing. 'Maybe he's been in chemotherapy? He could have been been ill with cancer. Perhaps he had to take Marinol. Maybe he's disfigured in some way.'

'Maybe he's a *doctor*? Or a pharmacist?' Dr Ruocco offered up another guess. I had thought of those possibilities as well. He could even be a doctor working at University Hospital.

'Listen, our favorite intern might be able to tell us something about him that can help us stop him. Can we do anything to get her through this withdrawal a little faster?'

'I'll be there in about twenty minutes. Less than that,' Maria Ruocco said. 'Let's see what we can do to help the poor girl out of her bad-dream state. I think we'd both like to talk to Kate McTiernan.'

49

Half an hour later, Dr Maria Ruocco was with me in Dr Kate McTiernan's room. I hadn't told the Durham police, or the FBI, what I had discovered. I wanted to talk to the intern first. This could be a break in the case, the biggest so far.

Maria Ruocco examined her important patient for nearly an hour. She was a no-nonsense, but user-friendly, doctor. She was very attractive, ash blonde, probably in her late thirties. A little bit of a Southern belle, but pretty terrific, anyway. I wondered if Casanova had ever stalked Dr Ruocco.

'The poor kid is really going through it,' she said to me. 'She had nearly enough Marinol in her system to kill her.'

'I wonder if that was the original idea,' I said. 'She might have been one of his rejects. Dammit, I want to talk to her.'

Kate McTiernan seemed to be asleep. A restless sleep, but sleep. The instant Dr Ruocco's hands touched her, though, she moaned. Her bruised face twisted into a stark, fearful mask. It was almost as if we were watching her back in captivity. The terror was palpable, scary.

Dr Ruocco was extremely gentle, but the soft moans and

groans continued. Then Kate McTiernan finally spoke without opening her eyes.

'Don't touch me! Don't! Don't *you dare* touch me, you fucker!' she shouted. Her eyes still didn't open. She was squeezing them very tightly, in fact. 'Leave me alone, you son of a bitch!'

'These young doctors.' Dr Ruocco made a joke of it. She was a cool head under pressure. 'Incredibly disrespectful as a group. And the goddamn *language*.'

Watching Kate McTiernan now was like seeing someone being physically tortured. I thought of Naomi again. Was she in North Carolina? Or in California somehow? Was the same thing happening to her? I chased the disturbing image out of my head. One problem at a time.

It took another half hour for Dr Ruocco to treat Kate McTiernan. She put her on an IV dose of Librium. Then she reconnected the heart monitor Kate was on because of her injuries. When she had finished, the intern drifted off into an even deeper sleep. She wasn't going to tell us any of her secrets tonight.

'I like your work,' I whispered to Dr Ruocco. 'You did good.'

Maria Ruocco motioned for me to step outside with her. The hospital corridor was in semidarkness; it was very quiet, and as eerie as hospitals can be at night. I had the recurring thought that Casanova could be a doctor at University Hospital. He might even be inside the hospital now, even at this late hour.

'We've done everything we can do for her right now, Alex. Let the Librium do its job. I count three FBI agents, plus two of Durham's finest, guarding young Dr McTiernan from the bogeyman for tonight. Why don't you go back to your hotel. Get some sleep yourself. How about a little Valium for you, kind sir?'

I told Maria Ruocco that I preferred to sleep at the hospital. 'I don't think Casanova will come after her here, but there's no way to tell. He just might.' Especially if Casanova was a local physician, I was thinking, but I didn't mention that to Maria. 'Besides, I feel a connection to Kate in there. I have from the first time I saw her. Maybe she knew Naomi.'

Dr Maria Ruocco stared up at me. I had at least a foot in height on her. She spoke with a total deadpan look on her face. 'You *appear* sane, you *sound* sane at times, but you're certifiable,' she said and smiled. Her bright blue eyes twinkled playfully.

'Plus, I'm armed and dangerous,' I said.

'Good night, Dr Cross,' Maria Ruocco said and she blew me a feathery kiss.

'Good night, Dr Ruocco. And thank you.' I sailed a kiss back at her as she walked down the corridor.

I slept restlessly on two uncomfortable club chairs pulled together inside Kate McTiernan's room. I kept my revolver cradled in my lap. Pleasant dreams, I'm sure.

50

'Who are you? *who the hell are you, mister?*'

A loud, high-pitched voice woke me up. It was close by. Almost in my face. I remembered immediately that I was at the University of North Carolina Hospital. I remembered *exactly* where I was in the hospital. I was with Kate McTiernan, our prize witness.

'I'm a policeman,' I said in a soft and hopefully reassuring voice to the traumatized intern. 'My name is Alex Cross. You're in North Carolina University Hospital. Everything is okay now.'

At first, Kate McTiernan looked as if she might cry, then she seemed to take hold of herself. Watching her grab control like that helped me understand how she had survived both Casanova and the river. This was a very strong-willed woman I had been watching over.

'I'm in the hospital?' Her words were slightly slurred, but at least she was coherent.

'Yes, that's right,' I said holding up one hand, palm facing out. 'You're safe now. Let me run and get a doctor. Please, I'll be right back.'

The slight slurring continued, but Dr McTiernan was focused, scarily so.

'Hold on a minute. I *am* a doctor. Let me get my bearings before we invite company in to visit. Just let me collect my thoughts. You're a policeman?'

I nodded. I wanted to make this as easy for her as I possibly could. I wanted to hug her, hold her hand, do something supportive and yet not threatening, after what she'd been through the past few days. I also wanted to ask her about a hundred important questions.

Kate McTiernan looked away from me. 'I think he drugged me. Or maybe all that was a dream?'

'No, it wasn't a dream. He used a powerful drug called Marinol.' I told her what we knew so far. I was being so careful not to push Kate the wrong way.

'I must have been really tripping.' She tried to whistle, and made a funny sound. I could see where she was missing a tooth. Her mouth was probably dry; her lips were swollen, especially the upper lip.

Odd as it seemed, I found myself smiling. 'You were probably on the planet Weirdness for a while. It's nice to have you back.'

'It's really nice to be back,' she said in a whisper. Tears welled up in her eyes. 'Sorry,' she said. 'I tried so hard not to cry in that horrible place. I didn't want him to see any weakness he could exploit. I want to cry now. I think I will.'

'Oh, please, you just cry your eyes out,' I whispered, too. I could barely talk or keep back tears myself. My chest felt tight. I went over to the hospital bed, and I lightly held Kate's hand as she wept.

'You don't sound like you're from the South,' Kate

191

McTiernan finally spoke again. She was grabbing control of herself. It amazed me she could do that.

'I'm from Washington, D.C., actually. My niece disappeared from Duke Law School ten days ago. That's why I'm down here in North Carolina. I'm a detective.'

She seemed to see me for the first time. She also appeared to be remembering something important. 'There were other women at the house where I was kept prisoner. We weren't supposed to talk. All communication was strictly forbidden by Casanova, but I broke the rules. I talked to a woman named Naomi—'

I stopped her, cut her off there. 'My niece's name is Naomi Cross,' I said. 'She's alive? She's all right?' My heart felt as if it were going to implode. 'Tell me what you remember, Kate. Please.'

Kate McTiernan grew more intense. 'I talked to a Naomi. I don't remember a last name. I also talked to a Kristen. The drugs. Oh, God, was it your niece? . . . Everything is so hazy and dark right now. I'm sorry . . .' Kate's voice trailed off as if someone had let the air out of her.

I gently squeezed her hand. 'No, no. You just gave me more hope than I've had since I came down here.'

Kate McTiernan's eyes were fixed and solemn, staring into mine. She seemed to be looking back at something horrifying that she wanted to forget. 'I don't remember a lot of it right now. I think Marinol has that side effect . . . I remember that he was going to give me another injection. I kicked him, hurt him enough to get away. At least *I think* that's what happened . . .

'There were thick, thick woods. Carolina pines, hanging moss everywhere . . . I remember, I swear to God . . . the house . . . wherever we were being kept, it disappeared.

The house where we were being held captive just *disappeared* on me.'

Kate McTiernan slowly shook her head of long brown hair back and forth. Her eyes were wide with astonishment. She seemed amazed at her own story. 'That's what I remember. How could that be? How could a house disappear?'

I could tell that she was reliving her very recent, terrifying past. I was right there with her. I was the first one to hear the story of her escape, the only one so far to hear our witness speak.

51

Casanova was still disturbed and highly agitated about the loss of Dr Kate McTiernan. He was restless and had been wide-awake for hours. He rolled over and over in bed. This was no good. This was dangerous. He had made his first mistake.

Then someone whispered in the darkness.

'Are you all right? Are you okay?'

The woman's voice startled him at first. He *had been* Casanova. Now he seamlessly switched over to his other persona: *the good husband.*

He reached out and gently rubbed his wife's bare shoulder. 'I'm okay. No problem. Just a little trouble sleeping tonight.'

'I noticed. How could I not? The human Mexican jumping bean strikes again.' There was a smile in her sleepy voice. She was a good person, and she loved him.

'Sorry,' Casanova whispered, and kissed his wife's shoulder. He stroked her hair as he thought about Kate McTiernan. Kate had much longer brown hair.

He kept stroking his wife's hair, but he drifted back into

his own tortured thoughts again. He really didn't have anyone to talk to, did he? Not anymore. Not around here in North Carolina certainly, not even in the highfalutin Research Triangle belt.

He finally climbed out of bed and trudged downstairs. He shuffled into his den and quietly shut and locked the door.

He looked at his wristwatch. It was 3:00 A.M. That would make it twelve out in Los Angeles. He made the call.

Actually, Casanova *did* have someone to talk to. One person in the world.

'It's me,' he said, when he heard the familiar voice on the line. 'I'm feeling a little crazy tonight. I thought of you, of course.'

'Are you implying that I lead a wanton and half-mad life?' the Gentleman Caller asked with a chuckle.

'That goes without saying.' Casanova was feeling better already. There *was* someone he could talk to and share secrets with. 'I took another one yesterday. Let me tell you about Anna Miller. She's exquisite, my friend.'

52

Casanova had struck again.

Another student, a bright beautiful woman named Anna Miller, had been abducted from a garden apartment she shared with her lawyer-boyfriend near the State University of North Carolina in Raleigh. The boyfriend had been murdered in their bed, which was a new twist for Casanova. He left no note, and no other clues at the crime scene. After a mistake, he was showing us he was letter-perfect again.

I spent several hours with Kate McTiernan at the University of North Carolina hospital. We got along well; I felt that we were becoming friends. She wanted to help me with the psychological profile on Casanova. She was telling me everything that she knew about Casanova and his women captives.

As far as she could tell, there had been six women held as hostages, including herself. It was possible that there were more than six.

Casanova was extremely well organized, according to Kate. He was capable of planning weeks and weeks ahead, of studying his prey in amazing detail.

He seemed to have 'built' the house of horrors by himself. He had installed plumbing, a special sound system, and air conditioning, apparently for the comfort of his women captives. Kate had only seen the house in a drugged state, though, and she couldn't describe it very well.

Casanova could be a control freak who was violently jealous and extremely possessive. He was sexually active and capable of several erections in a night. He was obsessed with sex and the male sexual urge.

He could be thoughtful in his way. He could also be 'romantic,' his own word. He loved to cuddle and kiss and talk to the women for hours. He said that he loved them.

In midweek, the FBI and the Durham police finally agreed on a secure place in the hospital for Kate McTiernan to meet with the press for the first time. The news conference was held in a wide entrance corridor on her floor.

The all-white hallway was jam-packed to the glowing red exit signs with reporters clutching their notepads, and TV people with minicams hoisted on their shoulders. Policemen with automatic weapons were also present. Just in case. Homicide detectives Nick Ruskin and Davey Sikes stayed close to Kate during the course of the TV taping.

Kate McTiernan was well on her way to becoming a national figure. Now the general public would get to actually meet the woman who had escaped from the house of horrors. I felt sure that Casanova would be watching, too. I hoped he wasn't right there in the hospital with us.

A male nurse, who was clearly a bodybuilder, pushed Kate into the noisy, crowded hallway. The hospital wanted her in a wheelchair. She had on baggy UNC sweatpants and a simple white cotton T-shirt. Her long brown hair was full and shiny. The bruising and swelling around her face was down a lot. 'I almost *look* like my old self,' she had told me. 'But I don't *feel* like my old self, Alex. Not inside.'

When the nurse wheeled the bulky chair almost up to a stand of microphones, Kate surprised everyone. She slowly stood up and walked the rest of the way.

'Hello, I'm Kate McTiernan. Obviously,' she said to the assembled reporters who now pushed in even closer to the prime witness. 'I have a very brief statement to make, then I'll get out of everybody's hair.' Her voice was strong and vibrant. She was very much in control of herself, or so it seemed to all of us watching and listening.

Her light touch and subtle humor drew smiles and laughter from the crowd. One or two of the reporters tried to ask questions, but the noise level had risen and it was hard to hear them. Cameras flashed and buzzed up and down the packed hospital corridor.

Kate stopped speaking, and it became relatively quiet again. At first everyone thought the press conference was too much for her to handle. A nearby doctor stepped forward, but she waved him away.

'I'm fine. I'm really okay, thanks. If I'm woozy or anything, I'll sit right down in the chair like a model patient. I promise you I will. No false bravado from me.'

She was *definitely* in control of this moment. She was older than most medical students or interns, and in fact she looked like a doctor.

She peered around the room – she was *curious*, it seemed. Maybe a little amazed. Finally, she apologized for the momentary lapse. 'I was just gathering my thoughts . . . What I would like to do is tell you what I can about what happened to me – and I will tell you everything I can – but that will be it for today. I won't answer any questions from the press. I'd like you all to respect that. Is that a fair deal?'

She was poised and impressive in front of the TV cameras. Kate McTiernan was surprisingly relaxed under the circumstances, as if she could have done this for a living. I'd found her to be very self-assured and confident whenever she needed to be. At other times, she could be as vulnerable and afraid as the rest of us.

'First, I would like to say something to all the families and friends who have someone missing. Please, don't give up hope. The man known as Casanova strikes only if his explicit commands are disobeyed. I broke his rules, and I was badly beaten. But I did manage to escape. There are other women where I was kept captive. My thoughts are with them in ways you can't imagine. I believe in my heart that they are still alive and safe.'

The reporters pressed in closer and closer to Kate McTiernan. Even in her battered condition she was magnetic, her strength shone through. The TV cameras liked her. So would the public, I knew.

For the next few moments, she did everything she could possibly do to allay the fears of the families of the missing women. She stressed again that she had been hurt only because she broke the house rules set down by Casanova. I thought that maybe she was sending a message to him, too. *Blame me, not the other women.*

As I watched Kate speak, I asked myself some questions: *Does he take only extraordinary women? Not just beauties, but women who are special in every way? What did that mean? What was Casanova really up to? What game was he playing?*

My suspicion was that the killer was obsessed with physical

beauty, but that he couldn't bear to be around women who weren't as smart as he was. I sensed that he craved intimacy also.

Finally, Kate stopped speaking. Tears were shining in her eyes, like perfect glass drops. 'I'm through now,' she said in a soft voice. 'Thank you for taking this message out to the families of the missing women. I hope that it helped a little bit. Please, no more questions for now. I still can't remember everything that happened to me. I've told you what I can.'

At first there was an unnatural silence. There wasn't a single question. She had been clear about that. Then the reporters and the hospital personnel began to clap. They knew, just as Casanova knew, that Kate McTiernan was an extraordinary woman.

I had one fear. Was Casanova there clapping, too?

53

At 4:00 A.M., Casanova packed a spanking-new, green-and-gray Lands' End knapsack with necessary food and supplies. He headed out to his hideaway for a morning of long-awaited pleasures. He actually had a favorite catchphrase for his forbidden games: *Kiss the girls.*

He fantasized about Anna Miller, his newest captive, on the car drive there, and then as he hiked through thick woods. He visualized over and over what he was going to do to Anna today. He remembered something, a quite wonderful and appropriate line, out of F. Scott Fitzgerald: *The kiss originated when the first male reptile licked the first female, implying in a complimentary way that she was as succulent as the small reptile he had for dinner the night before.* It was all biological, wasn't it? *Tick-cock.*

When he finally arrived at the hideaway, he turned on the Stones full volume. The incomparable *Beggar's Banquet* album. He needed to hear loud, antisocial rock music today. Mick Jagger was fifty, right? He was only thirty-six himself. This was *his* moment.

He posed naked in front of a floor-length mirror and admired his slender, well-muscled physique. He combed out his hair. Then he slipped into a shimmery hand-painted silk robe that he'd bought once upon a time in Bangkok. He left it open to expose himself.

He selected a different costume mask, a beautiful one from Venice, originally purchased for just such a special occasion. A moment of mystery and love. At last he was ready to see Anna Miller.

Anna was so haughty. Absolutely untouchable. Exquisite physically. He needed to break her quickly.

Nothing could match this physical and emotional feeling: adrenaline pumping, heart beating loudly, total exhilaration in every part of his body. He brought warm milk in a glass pitcher. Also a small wicker basket with a special surprise for Anna.

In truth, it was something he'd been planning for Dr Kate. He'd wanted to share this moment with her.

He had put on the loud rock 'n' roll so that Anna would know it was time to get ready. It was a signal. He was certainly ready for her. Pitcher full of warm milk. Long rubber tubing with a nozzle. Cuddly present in the wicker basket. Let the games begin.

54

Casanova couldn't take his eyes off Anna Miller. The air around him seemed to roar. Everything was charged with high expectations. He was feeling more than a little out of control. Not like himself. More like the Gentleman Caller.

He looked down on his art – his creation. He held a thought: *Anna has never looked like this for anyone else.*

Anna Miller lay on the bare wooden floor of the downstairs bedroom. She was naked, except for her jewelry, which he wanted her to wear. Her arms were bound with leather behind her back. A comfortable pillow was propped underneath her buttocks.

Anna's perfect legs hung from a rope tied to a ceiling beam. This was how he wanted her; this was exactly the way he'd imagined her so many times.

You can do anything that you want to do, he thought.

And so, he did.

Most of the warm milk was already inside her. He'd used the rubber hose and nozzle to do that.

She reminded him a little of Annette Bening, he was

thinking, except that she was his now. She wasn't a flickering image on some Cineplex movie screen. She would help him get over Kate McTiernan, and the sooner the better.

Anna wasn't so haughty anymore; she wasn't supremely untouchable, either. He was always curious about how much it took to break someone's will. Not so much, usually. Not in this age of cowards and spoiled brats.

'Please take it away. Don't do this to me. I've been good, haven't I?' Anna pleaded convincingly. She had such a beautiful and interesting face – in happiness – and especially in sorrow.

Her cheeks rose sharply whenever she spoke. He memorized the look, everything he could about this special moment. Details to dream about later on. Like the exact tilting angle of her derriere.

'It can't harm you, Anna,' he told her truthfully. 'Its mouth is sewn shut. I sewed it myself. The snake is harmless. I would never hurt you.'

'You're sick and vile,' Anna suddenly snapped at him. 'You're a sadist!'

He merely nodded. He had wanted to see the real Anna, and there she was: another snapping dragon.

Casanova watched the milk as it slowly dripped from her anus. So did the small black snake. The sweet fragrance of the milk drew it forward across the wooden two-by-fours of the bedroom floor. It was quite magnificent to observe. This truly was an image for beauty and the beast.

The cautiously alert black snake paused, then suddenly jutted its head forward. The head smoothly slid inside Anna Miller. The black snake cleverly gathered itself in folds and slid farther inside.

Casanova closely watched Anna's beautiful eyes widen.

How many other men had ever seen this, or felt anything like what he was experiencing now? How many of those men were still alive?

He had first heard of this sexual practice for enlarging the anus on his trips to Thailand and Cambodia. Now he'd performed the ceremony himself. It made him feel so much better – about the loss of Kate, about other losses.

That was the exquisite and surprising beauty of the games he chose to play at his hideaway. He loved them. He couldn't possibly stop himself.

And neither could anyone else. Not the police, not the FBI, and *not* Dr Alex Cross.

55

Kate still couldn't remember much from the actual day of her escape from hell. She agreed to be hypnotized, at least to let me try, though she thought her natural defenses might be too strong. We decided to do it late at night in the hospital, when she was already tired and might be more susceptible.

Hypnotism can be a relatively simple process. First, I asked Kate to close her eyes, then to breathe slowly and evenly. Maybe I would finally meet Casanova tonight. Maybe through Kate's eyes I'd see how he worked.

'In with the good air, out with the bad,' Kate said, keeping her good humor most of the time. 'Something like that. Right, Dr Cross?'

'Clear your mind as much as you can, Kate,' I said.

'I don't know about the wisdom of that.' She smiled. 'There's an awful lot bumping around in there right now. Rather like an old, old attic filled with unopened dressers and portmanteaus.' Her voice was beginning to sound a little sleepy. That was a hopeful sign.

'Now just count back slowly from a hundred. Begin whenever you feel like it,' I told her.

She went under easily. That probably meant that she trusted me somewhat. With the trust came responsibility on my part.

Kate was vulnerable now. I didn't want to hurt her under any circumstances. For the first few minutes, we talked as we often did when she was fully conscious and awake. We had enjoyed talking to each other from the start.

'Can you remember being kept in the house with Casanova?' I finally asked her a leading question.

'Yes, I remember quite a lot now. I remember the night he came into my apartment. I can see him carrying me through some kind of woods, to wherever I was kept. He carried me like my weight was nothing.'

'Tell me about the woods you went through, Kate.' This was our first dramatic moment. She was actually with Casanova again. In his power. A captive. I suddenly realized how quiet the hospital was all around us.

'It was too dark, really. The woods were very thick, very creepy. He had a flashlight with him, kept it on a string or rope around his neck . . . He's *unbelievably* strong. I thought of him as an animal, physically. He compared himself to Heathcliff from *Wuthering Heights*. He has a very romantic view of himself and what he's doing. That night . . . he whispered to me as if we were already lovers. He told me he loved me. He sounded . . . *sincere.*'

'What else do you remember about him, Kate? Anything you recall is helpful. Take your time.'

She turned her head, as if she were looking at someone off to my right. 'He always wore a different mask. He wore a reconstructive mask one time. That was the scariest one. They're called "death masks" because hospitals and morgues

207

sometimes use them to help identify accident victims who are unrecognizable.'

'That's interesting about the death masks. Please go on, Kate. You're being incredibly helpful.'

'I know that they can make them right from a human skull, pretty much any skull. They'll take a photo of it . . . cover the photo with tracing paper . . . draw the features. Then they build an actual mask from the drawing. There was a death mask in the movie *Gorky Park*. They aren't usually meant to be worn. I wondered how he'd gotten it.'

Okay, Kate, I was thinking to myself, *now keep going about Casanova*. 'What happened on the day that you escaped?' I asked her, leading her just a little.

For the first time, she seemed uncomfortable with a question. Her eyes opened for a split second, as if she were in a light sleep and I had woken her, jarred her. Her eyes shut again. Her right foot was tapping very rapidly.

'I don't remember very much about that day, Alex. I think I was drugged out of my mind, off the planet.'

'That's okay. Anything you remember is very good for me to know. You're doing beautifully. You told me once that you kicked him. Did you kick Casanova?'

'I kicked him. About three-quarters speed. He yelled out in pain, and he went down.'

There was another long pause. Suddenly, Kate started to cry. Tears welled up in her eyes, and then she was sobbing very, very hard.

Her face was wet with perspiration as well. I felt that I should bring her out of the hypnosis. I didn't understand what had just happened, and it scared me a little.

I tried to keep my own voice very calm. 'What's the matter, Kate? What's wrong? Are you okay?'

'I left those other women there. I couldn't find them at first. Then I was so unbelievably confused. I left the others.'

Her eyes opened and they were filled with fear, but also tears. She had brought herself out. She was strong like that. 'What made me so afraid?' she asked me. 'What just happened?'

'I don't know for sure,' I told Kate. We would talk about it later, but not right now.

She averted her eyes from mine. It wasn't like her. 'Can I be alone?' she whispered then. 'Can I just be alone now? Thank you.'

I left the hospital room feeling almost as if I had betrayed Kate. But I didn't know if there was anything that I could have done differently. This was a multiple-homicide investigation. Nothing was working so far. How could that be?

56

Kate was released from University Hospital later that week. She had asked if we could talk for a while each day. I readily agreed.

'This isn't therapy in any way, shape, or form,' she told me. She just wanted to vent with somebody about some difficult subjects. Partly because of Naomi, we had formed a quick, strong bond.

There was no further information, no more clues about Casanova's link with the Gentleman Caller in Los Angeles. Beth Lieberman, the reporter at the *Los Angeles Times*, refused to talk to me. She was peddling her hot literary property in New York.

I wanted to fly out to L.A. to see Lieberman, but Kyle Craig asked me not to. He assured me that I knew everything the *Times* reporter had on the case. I needed to trust someone; I trusted Kyle.

On a Monday afternoon, Kate and I went for a walk in the woods surrounding the Wykagil River, where she'd been found by the two boys. It was still unspoken, but we seemed to be in this thing together now. Certainly no one knew more about Casanova than she did. If she could remember anything more it would be so useful. The smallest detail could be a clue that might open up everything.

Kate became quiet and unusually subdued as we entered the dark, brooding woods east of the Wykagil River. The human monster could be lurking out here, maybe prowling in the woods right now. Maybe he was watching us.

'I used to love walking in woods like these. Blackberry brambles and sweet sassafras. Cardinals and blue jays feeding everywhere. It reminds me of when I was growing up,' Kate told me as we walked. 'My sisters and I used to go swimming every single day in a stream like this one. We swam nekkid, which was forbidden by my father. Anything my father strictly forbade, we tried to do.'

'All that swimming experience came in handy,' I said. 'Maybe it helped get you safely down the Wykagil.'

Kate shook her head. 'No, that was just pure stubbornness. I *vowed* I wasn't going to die that day. Couldn't give him the satisfaction.'

I was keeping my own discomfort about being in the woods to myself. Some of my uneasiness had to do with the unfortunate history of these woods and the surrounding farmlands. Tobacco farms had been spotted all through here once upon a time. Slave farms. *The blood and bones of my ancestors.* The extraordinary kidnapping and subjugation of more than four million Africans who were originally brought to America. They had been *abducted*. Against their will.

'I don't remember any of this terrain, Alex,' Kate said. I had strapped on a shoulder holster before we left the car. Kate winced and shook her head at the sight of the gun. But she didn't protest beyond the baleful look. She sensed that I was the dragonslayer. She knew there was a real dragon out here. She'd met him.

'I remember I ran away, escaped into woods just like these. Tall Carolina pines. Not much light getting through, eerie as a bat cave. I remember clearly when the house disappeared on me. I can't remember too much else. I'm blocking it. I don't even know how I got into the river.'

We were about two miles from where we'd left the car. Now we hiked north, staying close to the river Kate had floated down on her miraculous, 'stubborn' escape. Every tree and bush reached out relentlessly toward the diminishing sunlight.

'This reminds me of the Bacchae,' Kate said. Her upper lip curled in an ironic smile. 'The triumph of dark, chaotic barbarism over civilized human reason.' It felt as if we were moving against a high, relentless tide of vegetation.

I knew she was trying to talk about Casanova and the terrifying house where he kept the other women. She was trying to understand him better. We both were.

'He's refusing to be civilized, or repressed,' I said. 'He does whatever he wants. He's the ultimate pleasure seeker, I suppose. A hedonist for the times.'

'I wish you could hear him talk. He's very bright, Alex.'

'So are we,' I reminded her. 'He'll make a mistake, I promise.'

I was getting to know Kate very well by now. She was getting to know me. We had talked about my wife, Maria, who was killed in a senseless drive-by shooting in Washington, D.C. I told her about my kids, Jannie and Damon. She was a good listener; she had excellent bedside-manner potential. Dr Kate was going to be a special kind of doctor.

By three that afternoon, we must have walked four or five

miles. I felt grungy and a little achy. Kate didn't complain, but she must have been hurting. Thank God the karate kept her in great shape. We hadn't found any sign of where she had run during her escape. None of the landmarks we passed looked familiar to her. There was no disappearing house. No Casanova. No outstanding clues in the deep, dark woods. Nothing to go on.

'How the hell did he get so good at this?' I muttered as we tramped back to the car.

'Practice,' Kate said with a grimace. 'Practice, practice, practice.'

57

The two of us stopped to eat at Spanky's on Franklin Street in Chapel Hill. We were bushed, famished, and most of all thirsty. Everybody knew Kate at the popular bar and restaurant, and they made a nice fuss over her when we walked in. A muscular, blonde-haired bartender named Hack started a big round of applause.

A waitress and friend of Kate's gave us a table of honor at a front window on Franklin Street. The woman was a doctoral candidate in philosophy, Kate told me. Verda, the waitress-philosopher of Chapel Hill.

'How do you like being a celebrity?' I kidded Kate once we were seated.

'Hate it. *Hate it*,' she said with her teeth clenched tightly. 'Listen, Alex, can we get blotto drunk tonight?' Kate suddenly asked. 'I'd like a tequila, a mug of beer, and some brandy,' she told Verda. The waitress-philosopher grimaced and wrinkled her nose at the order.

'I'll have the same,' I said. 'When in collegeville.'

'This definitely *isn't* therapy,' Kate said to me as soon as Verda departed. 'We're just going to bullshit some tonight.'

'That sounds like therapy,' I said to her.

'If it is, then we're *both* on the couch.'

We talked about a lot of unrelated things for the first hour or so: cars, rural versus big-city hospitals, the UNC-Duke rivalry, Southern gothic literature, slavery, childrearing, doctors' salaries and the health-care crisis, rock 'n' roll lyrics versus blues lyrics, a book we'd both enjoyed called *The English Patient*. We had been able to talk to each other right from the beginning. Almost from that first moment at University Hospital, there had been some kind of bright sparks between us.

After the first blitzkrieg round of drinks, we settled into slow-sipping – beer in my case, the house wine in Kate's. We got a little buzzed, but nothing too disastrous. Kate was right about one thing. We definitely needed some kind of release from the stress of the Casanova case.

Around our third hour in the bar, Kate told a true story about herself that was almost as shocking to me as her abduction. Her brown eyes were wide as she spun her tale. Her eyes sparkled in the bar's low light. 'Let me tell you this one time now. Southerners love to tell a story, Alex. We're the last safekeepers of America's sacred oral history.'

'Tell me the story, Kate. I love to listen to stories. So much so that I made it my job.'

Kate put her hand on top of mine. She took a deep breath. Her voice got soft, very quiet. 'Once upon a time, there was the McTiernan family of Birch. This was a happy group of campers, Alex. Tight-knit, especially the girls: Susanne, Marjorie, Kristin, Carole Anne, and Kate. Kristin and I were the youngest *goils* – twins. Then there was Mary, our mother, and Martin, our father. I'm not going to say too much about Martin. My mother made him leave when I was four. He was very domineering and could be as mean as a stepped-on copperhead sometimes. To hell with him. I'm way past my father by now.'

Kate went on for a bit, but then she stopped and looked deeply into my eyes. 'Did anybody ever tell you what a terrific, *terrific* listener you are? You make it seem like you're interested in everything I have to say. That makes me want to talk to you. I have *never* told this whole story to anyone, Alex.'

'Well, I am interested in what you have to say. It makes me feel good that you're sharing this with me, that you trust me enough.'

'I trust you. It's not a very happy story, so I must trust you a lot.'

'I have that sense,' I told Kate. It struck me again how very beautiful her face was. Her eyes were very large and lovely. Her lips weren't too full, or too thin. I kept being reminded why Casanova had chosen her.

'My sisters, my mother, they were so great when I was growing up. I was their little slave, *and* I was their pet. There wasn't much money coming into the house, so there was always too much to do. We canned our own veggies, jelly, and fruit. We took in washing and ironing. Did our own carpentry, plumbing, auto repair. We were lucky: we liked one another. We were always laughing and singing the latest hit song off the radio. We read a lot, and we'd talk about everything from abortion rights to recipes. A sense of humor was mandatory in our house. "*Don't be so serious*" was the famous line there.'

Finally, Kate told me what had happened to the McTiernan family. Her story; her secret came out in an agitated burst that darkened her face.

'Marjorie got sick first. She was diagnosed with ovarian cancer. Margie died when she was twenty-six. She already had three kids. Then, in order, Susanne, my twin Kristin, and my mother died. All of breast or ovarian cancer. That left Carole Anne, me, and my father. Carole Anne and I joke that we inherited my father's snarly mean streak, so we're destined to die of nasty heart attacks.'

Kate suddenly swung her head down and to one side. Then she looked back up at me. 'I was going to say, I don't know why I told you that. But I do know. I like you. I want to be your friend. I want you to be my friend. Is that possible?'

I started to say something about how I felt, but Kate stopped me. She put the tips of her fingers on my lips. 'Don't be sentimental right now. Don't ask me any more about my sisters right now. Tell me something you don't ever tell other people. Tell me quick now. before you change your mind. Tell me one of your big secrets, Alex.'

I didn't think about what I was going to say. I just let it come out. It seemed fair after what Kate had told me. Besides, I wanted to share something with her; I wanted to confide in Kate, at least see if I could.

'I've been screwed-up ever since my wife, Maria, died,' I told Kate McTiernan, one of my secrets, one of the things I keep bottled inside. 'I put on clothes every morning, and a sociable face, and my six-gun some days . . . but I feel hollow most of the time. I got into a relationship after Maria, and it didn't work out. It failed in a spectacular fashion. Now I'm not ready to be with anyone again. I don't know if I ever will be.'

Kate peered into my eyes. 'Oh, Alex, you're wrong. You are so ready,' she told me without any doubt in her eyes or her voice.

Sparks.

Friends.

'I'd like us to be friends, too,' I finally told her. It was something I rarely said, and never this quickly.

As I stared across the table at Kate, stared over the glowing wick of a dwindling candle. I was reminded of Casanova again. If nothing else, he was a very good judge of a woman's beauty and character. He was just about perfect.

58

The harem cautiously shuffled toward a large living area at the end of a winding hallway inside the mysterious, loathsome house. The place had two floors. On the lower one, there was only a single room. Upstairs, there were as many as ten.

Naomi Cross walked cautiously among the women. They had been told to go to the common room. Since she had been there, the number of captives had ranged from six to eight. Sometimes a girl left, or *disappeared*, but there always seemed to be a new one to take her place.

Casanova was waiting for them in the living room. He had on another of his masks. This one was handpainted with white and bright green streaks. Festive. *A party face.* He wore a gold silk robe and was naked underneath it.

The room was large and tastefully furnished. The floor was covered with an oriental rug. The walls were off-white and freshly painted.

'Come in, come in ladies. Don't be shy. Don't be bashful,' he said from the back of the room. He had a stun gun and a pistol and struck a dashing pose.

Naomi imagined that he was smiling behind the mask. More than anything she wanted to see his face, just once, and then obliterate it forever, shatter it into tiny pieces, grind the pieces into nothing.

Naomi felt her heart skip as she entered the large, attractive sitting room. Her violin was on a table near Casanova. He had taken her violin and brought it to this awful place.

Casanova was waltzing around the low-ceilinged room like the host at a sophisticated costume party. He knew how to be classy, even gallant. He carried himself with confidence.

He lit a woman's cigarette with a gold lighter. He stopped to talk with each of his girls. He touched a bare shoulder, a cheek, caressed someone's long blonde hair.

The women all looked stunning. They wore their own beautiful clothes, and had carefully applied makeup. The scents of their perfumes filled the room. If only they could rush him all at once, Naomi thought to herself. There had to be a way to take Casanova down.

'As some of you may have already guessed,' he raised his voice, 'we have a nice surprise for tonight's festivities. A little night music.'

He pointed to Naomi, and beckoned her to come forward. He was always careful when he brought them together like this. He had his gun in hand, holding it casually.

'Please play something for us,' he said to Naomi. 'Anything that you'd like. Naomi plays the violin, and very beautifully I might add. Don't be shy, dear.'

Naomi couldn't take her eyes off Casanova. His robe was open so that they could see his nakedness. Sometimes he had one of them play an instrument, or sing, or read poetry, or just talk about their lives before hell. Tonight it was Naomi's turn.

Naomi knew that she had no choice. She was determined to be brave, to look confident.

She picked up the violin, her precious instrument, and so many painful memories swept over her. *Brave . . . confident . . .* she repeated inside her head. She'd been doing that since she was a young girl.

As a young black woman she had learned the art of acting poised. She needed all the poise she could muster now.

'I'm going to try to play Bach's sonata number one,' she quietly announced. 'This is the adagio, the first movement. It's very beautiful. I hope I can do it justice.'

Naomi shut her eyes as she brought the violin up to her shoulder. She opened her eyes again as she placed her chin on the rest and slowly began to tune the instrument.

Brave . . . confident, she reminded herself.

Then she began to play. It was far from perfect, but it did come from her heart. Naomi's style had always been personal. She concentrated more on making music than on her technique. She wanted to cry, but she held back the tears, held everything inside. Her feelings came out only in the music, the beautiful Bach sonata.

'Brava! Brava!' Casanova shouted as she finished.

The women clapped. That was permitted by Casanova. Naomi stared out at their beautiful faces. She could feel their shared pain. She wished that she could talk to them. But when he brought them together, it was only to show off his power, his absolute control over them.

Casanova's hand moved and lightly touched Naomi's arm. It was hot, and she felt as if she'd been burned.

'You'll stay with me tonight,' he said in the softest voice.

221

'That was so beautiful, Naomi. *You* are so beautiful, the most beautiful one here. Do you know that, sweetheart? Of course you do.'

Brave, strong, confident, Naomi told herself. She was a Cross. She wouldn't let him see her fear. She would find a way to beat him.

59

Kate and I were working at her apartment in Chapel Hill. We'd been talking about the disappearing house again, still trying to figure out that mind-bending mystery. At a little past eight the front doorbell rang, Kate went to see who it was.

I could see her talking to someone, but I couldn't tell who. My hand went for my revolver, touched the handle. She let the visitor come inside.

It was Kyle Craig. I was immediately struck by the drawn and somber look on his face. Something must have happened.

'Kyle says he has something you're going to want to see,' Kate said as she led the FBI man into the living room.

'I tracked you down, Alex. It wasn't too hard,' Kyle said. He sat on the sofa arm next to me. He looked as if he needed to sit down.

'I told the hotel desk and the operator where I'd be until nine or so.'

'Like I said, it wasn't hard. Check out the look on Alex's

face, Kate. Now you see why he's still a detective. He's hooked on The Job, wants to solve all the great puzzles, even the not-so-great ones.'

I smiled, and shook my head. Kyle was partly right. 'I love my work, *mostly* because I get to spend time with sophisticated and high-minded individuals like yourself. What's happened, Kyle? Tell me right now.'

'The Gentleman made a personal call on Beth Lieberman. She's dead. He cut off her fingers, Alex. After he killed her, he torched her studio apartment in West Los Angeles. He set half her building on fire.'

Beth Lieberman hadn't exactly endeared herself to me, but I was shocked and saddened to hear about her murder. I'd taken Kyle's word that she had nothing worth traveling to Los Angeles for. 'Maybe he knew there was something in her apartment that needed to be torched. Maybe she actually had something important.'

Kyle glanced over at Kate again. 'You see how good he is? He's a machine. She *did* have something incriminating,' he said to both of us. 'Only she had it on her computer at the *Times*. So now we have it.'

Kyle handed me a long, curling fax. He pointed to some copy at the very bottom of the sheet. The fax was from the FBI's office in Los Angeles.

I glanced down the page and read the entry that was underscored.

Possible Casanova!!! it said. *Very possible suspect.*

Dr William Rudolph. First-class creep.

Home: the Beverly Comstock. Work: Cedars-Sinai Medical Center.

Los Angeles.

'We've finally got our break. We've got a first-class lead,

anyway,' Kyle said. 'The Gentleman could be this doctor. This creep, as she calls him.'

Kate looked at me, then at Kyle. She had told both of us that Casanova might be a doctor.

'Anything else in Lieberman's notes?' I asked Kyle.

'Not that we've been able to find so far,' Kyle said. 'Unfortunately, we can't ask Ms Lieberman about Dr William Rudolph, or why she made the note in her computer. Let me tell you two new theories that are making the rounds with our profilers out on the West Coast,' Kyle went on. 'Are you ready for a little outrageous mind trip, my friend? Some profiler speculation?'

'I'm ready. Let's hear the latest and greatest theories from FBI West.'

'The first theory is that he's sending the diary entries *to himself*. That he's Casanova *and* the Gentleman Caller. He could be *both* killers, Alex. They each specialize in "perfect" crimes. There are other similarities, too. Maybe he's a split personality. FBI West, as you call it, would like Dr McTiernan to fly out to Los Angeles right away. They'd like to talk to her.'

I didn't like the first West Coast theory too much myself, but I couldn't completely discount it. 'What's the other theory from the wild, wild West?' I asked Kyle.

'The other theory,' he said, 'is that there are two men. But that they aren't just communicating, they're *competing*. This could be a scary competition, Alex. This could all be a scary game they've invented.'

PART THREE

The Gentleman Caller

60

He had been a Southern gentleman.

A gentleman scholar.

Now he was the very finest gentleman in Los Angeles. Always a gentleman, though. A hearts-and-flowers kind of guy.

An orangish-red sun had begun its long, slow shimmy and slide toward the Pacific Ocean. Dr William Rudolph thought it looked visually stunning as he strolled at a leisurely pace along Melrose Avenue in Los Angeles.

The Gentleman Caller was 'shopping' that afternoon, absorbing all the sights and sounds, the hectic flash-and-cash of his surroundings.

The street scene reminded him of something one of the hard-boiled detective writers, maybe Raymond Chandler, had written: '*California, the department store.*' The description still worked pretty damn well.

Most of the attractive women he observed were in their early and mid-twenties. They had just come from the stultifying workaday world of the ad agencies, money managers, and law firms in the entertainment district around Century Boulevard. Several of them wore high heels, platforms, clinging spandex miniskirts, here and there a form-fitting Rollo suit.

He listened to the casually sexy rustle of crushed silk, the martial *click-click* of designer shoes, the sultry *scuff* of cowboy boots that cost more than Wyatt Earp had earned in a lifetime.

He was getting hot and a little frenzied. *Nicely* frenzied. Life in California was good. It *was* the department store of his dreams.

This was the best part: the foreplay before he made his final selection. The Los Angeles police were still stumped and baffled by him. Maybe one day they would figure it all out, but probably not. He was simply too good at this. He *was* Jekyll and Hyde for this age.

As he strolled between La Brea and Fairfax, he breathed in the scents of musk and heavy floral perfumes, of chamomile- and lemon-scented hair. The leather handbags and skirts also had a distinct scent.

It was all a big tease, but he *adored* it. It was so ironic that these lovely California foxes were teasing and provoking *him* of all people.

He was the small, adorable, fluffy-haired boy loose in the candy store, wasn't he? Now which forbidden sweets should he choose this afternoon?

That little twit in red heels, no stockings? That poor man's Juliette Binoche? The provocateuse in the French-vanilla-and-black harlequin-print suit?

Several of the women actually gave Dr Will Rudolph approving glances as they wandered in and out of their favorite shops. Exit I, Leathers and Treasures, La Luz de Jesus.

He was strikingly handsome, even by strict Hollywood standards. He resembled the singer Bono from the Irish rock group U2. Actually, he looked the way Bono would if he had chosen to become a successful doctor in Dublin or Cork, or right here in Los Angeles.

And that was one of the Gentleman's most private secrets: *The women almost always chose him.*

Will Rudolph wandered into Nativity, which was one of the currently hot A-rated shops on Melrose. Nativity was the place to buy a designer bustier, a mink-lined leather jacket, an 'antique' Hamilton wristwatch.

As he watched the supple young bodies in the busy store, he was thinking of Hollywood's A parties, its A restaurants, even its A stores. The city was completely hung up on its own pecking order.

He understood status perfectly! Yes, he did. *Dr Will Rudolph was the most powerful man in Los Angeles.*

He reveled in the secure feeling it gave him, the reassuring front-page news stories that told him he truly existed, that he wasn't a twisted figment of his own imagination. The Gentleman was in control of an entire city, and an influential city at that.

He strolled near an irresistible blonde woman all decked-out in twentysomething finery.

She was idly looking at Incan jewelry, seemingly bored with the whole deal: her *life*. She was by far the most striking woman inside Nativity, but that wasn't what attracted him to her.

She was absolutely *untouchable*. She sent off a clear signal, even in a pricey store filled mostly with other attractive twentysomething females. *I'm untouchable. Don't even think about it. You're unworthy, no matter who you are.*

He felt thunder roar through his chest. He wanted to scream out inside the loud, crowded boutique:

I can have you. I can!

You have no idea – but I'm the Gentleman Caller.

The blonde woman had a full and arrogant mouth. She understood that no lipstick or eyeshadow was necessary for her. She was slender and narrow-waisted. Elegant in her own southern California way. She wore a faded cotton vest, wrap skirt, and colorblocked moccasins. Her tan was even and perfect, healthy-looking.

She finally glanced his way. *A glancing blow*, Dr Will Rudolph thought.

Lord, what eyes. He wanted them all to himself. He wanted to roll them through his fingers, carry them around for a good-luck charm.

What *she* saw was a tall and slender, interesting-looking man in his early thirties. He had broad shoulders, and a build like an athlete, or even a dancer. His sun-lightened brown curls were tied back in a ponytail. He had Irish-boy blue eyes. Will Rudolph also wore a slightly wrinkled white medical jacket over his very traditional Oxford blue shirt and hospital-approved striped rep's tie. He had on expensive Dr Martens boots – indestructible footwear. He seemed *so sure* of himself.

She spoke first. *She chose him, didn't she?* Her blue eyes were calm and deep, untroubled, very sexy in their confidence. She played with one of her gold-plated earrings. 'Was it something I didn't say?'

He started to laugh, genuinely delighted that she had an adult sense of humor about the dating charade. *This was going to be a fun night*, he thought. He knew it.

'I'm sorry. I usually don't stare. At least I never get caught blatantly doing it,' he said. He couldn't stop laughing for a moment. He had an easy laugh, a pleasant laugh. It was a modern tool of the trade, especially in Hollywood, New York, Paris: his favorite haunts.

'At least you're honest about it,' she said. She was laughing now, too, and a gold-link necklace jangled against her chest. He ached to reach out and rip it off, to run his tongue over her breasts.

She was doomed now, if that was his desire, his wish, his slightest whim. Should he go on? Perhaps look a little further?

The blood in his head was roaring, swirling with tremendous force. He had to decide. He looked into the untroubled blue eyes of the blonde woman again, and saw the answer.

'I don't know about you,' he said, trying to sound calm, 'but I think I've found what I like very much in here.'

'Yes, I think I may have found what I need, too,' she said after a pause. Then *she* laughed. 'Where are you from? You're not from around here, are you?'

'Originally from North Carolina.' He held the bell-jangling door open for her, and they left the antique-clothing store together. 'I've worked on losing my accent.'

'You've succeeded,' she said.

She was wonderfully impressed with herself, not the least bit self-conscious. She had an aura of self-confidence and competency – which he would absolutely shatter. Oh, God, he wanted this one so badly.

61

'Here we go, action fans. He's leaving Nativity with the blonde girl. They're out on Melrose Avenue.'

We were using binoculars to watch the incredible encounter through Nativity's decorative front window. The FBI also had directional microphones on Dr Will Rudolph, as well as on the blonde woman in the trendy shop.

It was an FBI-only stakeout. They hadn't even clued in the LAPD. Nada. It was pretty typical Bureau tactics, only I was on their side this time, compliments of Kyle Craig. The FBI had wanted to talk to Kate in Los Angeles. Kyle arranged for me to come after I *beat on him* about the deal we'd made, and how this could be the most important break we'd had on the *Casanova* investigation.

It was just past five-thirty; noisy, chaotic rush hour on a California-gorgeous, sunny day. Temperature in the mid-seventies. Heartbeats rising toward at least a thousand inside our car.

We were finally closing in on one of the monsters, at least we hoped so. Dr Will Rudolph struck me as a modern-day vampire. He had spent the afternoon casually roaming among the stylish shops: Ecru, Grau, Mark Fox. Even the girls idling in front of Johnny Rocket's fifties-style burger stand were potential targets of his. He was definitely a hunter today. He was girl-watching. Was he the Gentleman Caller, though?

I was working closely with two senior FBI agents in an anonymous-looking minivan parked on a side street off Melrose Avenue. Our radio was hooked to the state-of-the-art directional mikes that were in two of the other five cars trailing the man believed to be the Gentleman. It was almost show-time.

'I think I may have found what I need, too,' we heard the blonde woman say. She reminded me of the beautiful students Casanova had abducted in the South. *Could he be one and the same monster? A coast-to-coast killer? Maybe a split personality?*

FBI experts here on the West Coast believed they had the answer. In their view, the same creep did the so-called 'perfect crimes' on both coasts. A victim had never been kidnapped or killed on the same day. Unfortunately, there were at least a dozen theories about the Gentleman Caller and Casanova that I was aware of. I still wasn't convinced by any of them.

'How long have you been in Hollywood?' we heard the blonde woman ask Rudolph. Her voice sounded alluring and sexy. She was obviously flirting with him.

'Long enough to meet you.' He was soft-spoken and courteous so far. His right hand rested lightly under her left elbow. The Gentleman?

He didn't look like a killer, but he *did* resemble the Casanova that Kate McTiernan had described. He was a hunk physically, clearly attractive to women, and he was a doctor.

His eyes were *blue* – the color Kate had seen behind Casanova's mask.

'Cockfucker looks like he could have any girl he wanted,' one of the FBI agents turned to me and said.

'Not to do what he wants to do to them,' I said.

'You got a point there.'

The agent, John Asaro, was Mexican-American. He was balding, but with a compensating bushy mustache. He was probably in his late forties. The other agent was Raymond Cosgrove. Both of them were good men, high-level Bureau professionals. Kyle Craig was taking care of me so far.

I couldn't take my eyes off Rudolph and the blonde woman. She was pointing toward a shiny black Mercedes convertible with its tan top down. More expensive shops stood out in the background: I.a. Eyeworks, Gallay Melrose. Another garish store sign, eight-foot-high cowboy boots, framed her wind-blown hair.

We listened as they talked on the crowded street. The directional mikes picked up everything. No one in the surveillance car was making a sound.

'That's my car over there, sport. The red-haired lady in the passenger seat – she's my sweetie. Did you really think you could pick me up just like *that*?' The blonde woman snapped her fingers and the colorful bracelets on her arm rattled in Rudolph's face. 'Kiss off, Dr Kildare.'

John Asaro groaned out loud. 'Christ, she shot him down! *She* set *him* up. Isn't that beautiful! Only in L.A.'

Raymond Cosgrove pounded the dash with the thick heel of his hand. 'Son of a bitch! She's walking away. Go back to him, sweetheart! Tell him you were only kidding!'

We'd had him, or were very close to it. It made me

physically sick to think that he was getting away. We had to *catch him* at something, or an arrest wouldn't hold up.

The blonde woman crossed Melrose and slid into the sleek black Mercedes. Her friend had short red hair, and her silver bangle earrings caught the late-day sunlight. The woman leaned in and gave her sweetie a kiss.

As Dr Will Rudolph watched them, he didn't appear at all upset. He stood on the sidewalk with his hands stuffed into the pockets of his white jacket, looking cool and relaxed. Neutral. As if nothing had happened. Were we seeing the Gentleman Caller's mask?

The two lovers in the convertible waved as the Mercedes roared past, and he gave them a smile, a shrug of the shoulders, a cool nod of his head.

We could hear him hiss through the directional mikes. 'Ciao, ladies. I'd like to cut you both into pieces and feed you to the gulls at Venice Beach. And I *do* have your license plate number, you silly twats.'

62

We trailed Dr Will Rudolph to his luxury penthouse apartment at the Beverly Comstock. The FBI knew where he lived. They hadn't shared that information with the LAPD, either. The tension and disappointment were heavy inside our car. The FBI was playing a dangerous game of freeze-out with the Los Angeles police.

I finally left the stakeout at around eleven o'clock. Rudolph had been inside for more than four hours. A loud, unidentifiable buzzing noise in my head wouldn't go away. I was still moving on Eastern time. It was 2:00 A.M. for me, and I needed to get some sleep soon.

The FBI agents promised to call right away if anything broke, or if Dr Rudolph went out hunting again that night. It had to have been a bad scene for him on Melrose, and I thought that he might go after someone else soon.

If he was actually the Gentleman Caller.

I was driven to the Holiday Inn at Sunset and Sepulveda. Kate McTiernan was staying there, too. The FBI had flown her to California because Kate knew more about Casanova than anyone they had assigned to the case. She had been kidnapped by the creep and had lived to tell about it. Kate might be able to identify the killer if he and Casanova were the same person. She had spent most of the day being interviewed at the FBI offices in downtown Los Angeles.

Her room was several doors down from mine at the hotel. I only had to knock once before she opened a white door with a black 26 on the knocker.

'I couldn't sleep. I was up waiting,' she said. 'What happened? Tell me everything.'

I guess I wasn't in a great mood after the failed bust. 'Unfortunately, nothing happened,' I told her the bottom line.

Kate nodded, waiting for more. She had on a light blue tank top, khaki shorts, and yellow flip-flops. She was wide awake and revved up. I was glad to see her, even at half-past two on a shitty morning.

I finally came in and we talked about the FBI stakeout on Melrose Avenue. I told Kate how close we might have come to getting Dr Will Rudolph. I remembered everything he'd said, every gesture. 'He sounded like a gentleman. He acted like a gentleman, too . . . right up until the blonde woman made him angry.'

'What does he look like?' Kate asked. She was eager to help. I couldn't blame her. The FBI had flown her to Los Angeles, then stuck her in a hotel room for most of the day and night.

'I know how you feel, Kate. I've talked to the FBI, and you're going to ride with me tomorrow. You're going to see him, probably in the morning. I don't want to set up any bias in your mind. Is that okay?'

Kate nodded, but I could tell her feelings were hurt. She definitely wasn't happy about her level of involvement so far.

'I'm sorry. I don't want to act like a tough detective, a controlling bastard,' I finally said. 'Let's not fight about it.'

'Well, you were distant. Anyway, you're forgiven. I guess we better get some sleep. Tomorrow's another day. Big day maybe?'

'Yeah, tomorrow could be a big day. I really am sorry, Kate.'

'I know you are.' She finally smiled. 'You really are forgiven. Sweet dreams. Tomorrow we nail Beavis. Then we get Butt-Head.'

I finally went off to my room. I hit the bed and thought about Kyle Craig for a while. He'd been able to sell my unorthodox style to his confrères for one reason: it had worked before. I already had one monster's scalp on my belt. I hadn't played according to the rules to get it. Kyle understood and respected results. In general, so did the Bureau. They were certainly playing according to their own rules here in Los Angeles.

My last semiconscious thought was of Kate in those khaki shorts. Take your breath away. I had a passing thought that she might come down the hall and *knock, knock, knock* on my door. We were in Hollywood, after all. Wasn't that the way it happened in the movies?

But Kate didn't come knocking on my hotel door. So much for Clint Eastwood and Rene Russo fantasies.

63

This was going to be a big day in Tinseltown. The manhunt of manhunts was playing in Beverly Hills. Just like the day they finally caught the killer-strangler Richard Ramirez out here.

Today we get Beavis.

It was a few minutes past eight in the morning. Kate and I were sitting in an arctic-blue Taurus parked half a block from Cedars-Sinai Medical Center in Los Angeles. There was an electrical sound in the air, as if the city were being run on a single, huge generator. A play on an old line ran through my head: *Hell is a city much like Los Angeles.*

I was nervous and tense; my body felt numb, and my stomach was queasy. The burnout factor. Not enough sleep. Too much stress for too long a stretch. Chasing monsters from sea to shining sea.

'That's Dr Will Rudolph climbing out of the BMW,' I said to Kate. I was so wound up, I felt as if strong hands were squeezing me.

'Good-looking,' Kate muttered. 'Real sure of himself, too. The way he moves. *Doctor* Rudolph.'

Kate didn't say another word as she intently watched Rudolph. Was he the Gentleman Caller? Was he also Casanova? Or were we being set up for some sick, psychopathic reason that I didn't understand yet?

The morning's temperature hovered in the low sixties. The air had a crisp snap, like fall in the Northeast. Kate had on an old college sweatsuit, high-topped running shoes, dime-store sunglasses. Her long brown hair was bunched back in a ponytail. Sensible stakeout attire and grooming.

'Alex, the FBI's all around him now?' she asked me without looking away from the binoculars. 'They're here right now? That scum can't possibly get away?'

I nodded. 'If he does anything, *anything* that shows us he's the Gentleman, they'll grab him. They want this arrest for themselves.'

But the FBI was also giving me whatever rope I needed. Kyle Craig had kept his promise. So far, anyway.

Kate and I watched as Dr Will Rudolph slid out of the BMW coupe, which he'd just parked in a private lot on the west side of the hospital. He wore a European-style charcoal-gray suit. It was cut well and looked expensive. It probably cost as much as my house in D.C. His brown hair was held back in a fashionable ponytail. He had on dark glasses with round tortoiseshell frames.

A doctor in an exclusive Beverly Hills hospital. Smug as hell. *The goddamn Gentleman Caller who was setting this city on fire?*

I ached to run across the parking lot and hit him, take him down right now. I ground my teeth until my jaw was stiff. Kate wouldn't take her eyes away from Dr Will

Rudolph. Was he Casanova, too? Were they one and the same monster? Was that it?

We both watched Rudolph as he crossed the hospital lot. His stride was long and quick and buoyant. Nothing bothering him today. Finally, he disappeared inside a gray metal side door of the hospital.

'A *doctor*.' Kate said and shook her head back and forth. 'This is so weird, Alex. I'm shaking on the *inside*.'

The static on the car radio startled us, but we could hear agent John Asaro's deep, raspy voice.

'Alex, did you guys see him? Get a good look? What does Ms McTiernan think? What's the verdict on our Dr Squirrel?'

I looked across the front seat at Kate. She looked all of her thirty-one years right now. Not quite so confident and assured, a little gray around the gills. The prime witness. She understood the deadly seriousness of the moment perfectly.

'I don't think he's Casanova,' Kate finally said. She shook her head. 'He's not the same physical type. He's thinner . . . *carries* himself differently. I'm not a hundred percent sure, but I don't think it's him, goddammit.' She sounded a little disappointed.

Kate continued to shake her head. 'I'm almost sure he isn't Casanova, Alex. There must be two of them. Two Mr Squirrels.' Her brown eyes were intense, as she looked at me.

So there *were* two of them. Were they competing? What the hell was their coast-to-coast game all about?

64

Small talk, surveillance talk; it was familiar territory for me. Sampson and I had a saying about surveillance back in D.C.: *They* do the crime; *we* do the time.

'How much could he make with a successful Beverly Hills medical practice? Ballpark number, Kate,' I asked my partner. We were still watching the doctors' private parking lot of Cedars-Sinai. There was nothing to do but eyeball Rudolph's spiffy new BMW and wait, and talk like old friends on a front stoop in D.C.

'He probably charges about a hundred and fifty to two a visit. He could gross five or six hundred thousand a year. Then there are surgery fees, Alex. That's if he has a conscience about the prices he charges, and we *know* he doesn't have a conscience.'

I shook my head in disbelief as I rubbed my palm over my chin. 'I have to get back into private practice. Baby needs new shoes.'

Kate smiled. 'You miss them, don't you, Alex? You talk about your kids a lot. Damon and Jannie. Poolball-head and Velcro.'

I smiled back. Kate knew my nicknames for the kids by now. 'Yeah, I do. They're my babies, my little pals.'

Kate laughed some more. I liked to make her laugh. I thought of the bittersweet stories she'd told me about her sisters, especially her twin, Kristin. Laughter is good medicine.

The black BMW coupe just sat there, shining brightly and expensively in the California sunlight. *Surveillance sucks*, I thought, *no matter where you have to do it. Even in sunny L.A.*

Kyle Craig had gotten me a lot of rope here in Los Angeles. Certainly much more than I'd had in the South. He'd gotten rope for Kate, too. There was something in it for him, though. The old quid pro quo. Kyle wanted me to interview the Gentleman Caller once he was caught, and he expected me to report everything to him. I suspected that Kyle himself hoped to bag Casanova.

'Do you really think the two of them are competing?' Kate asked me after a while.

'It makes psychological sense out of some things for me,' I told her. 'They might feel a need to 'one up' each other. The Gentleman's diaries could be his way of saying: See, I'm better than you. I'm more famous. Anyway, I haven't decided yet. Sharing their exploits is probably more for thrill purposes than intimacy, though. They *both* like to get turned on.'

Kate stared into my eyes. 'Alex, doesn't it make you feel creepy as hell trying to figure this out?'

I smiled. 'That's why I want to catch Butt-Head and Beavis. So the creepiness will finally stop.'

Kate and I waited at the hospital until Rudolph finally reappeared. It was nearly two in the afternoon. He drove straight to his office on North Bedford, west of Rodeo Drive. Rudolph saw patients there. Mostly women patients.

Dr Rudolph was a plastic surgeon. As such, he could *create* and *sculpt*. Women *depended* on him. And . . . his patients all *chose* him.

We followed Rudolph home at around seven. Five or six hundred thousand a year, I was thinking. It was more than I could make in a decade. Was it the money he needed to be the Gentleman Caller? Was Casanova wealthy, too? Was he a doctor also? Was that how they committed their perfect crimes?

These questions were rolling around in my head.

I fingered an index card in my trouser pocket. I had begun to keep a 'short list' on both Casanova and the Gentleman. I would add or subtract what I considered key attributes to the profile. I carried the card with me at all times.

CASANOVA
collector
harem
artist, organized
different masks . . . To
    represent moods or
    personas?
doctor?
claims to 'love' victims
gaining a taste for violence
knows about me
competing with Gary
    Soneji?
competing with the L.A.
    Gentleman?

GENTLEMAN
gives out flowers – sexual?
extremely violent and
    dangerous
takes beautiful young
    women of all types
extremely organized
not artistic in terms of his
    killing
doctor
cold and impersonal as a
    killer . . . a butcher
craves recognition and fame –
possibly wealthy –
penthouse apartment
graduated Duke Medical
    School, 1986
raised in North Carolina

I thought some more about the connection between Rudolph and Casanova as Kate and I twiddled our thumbs outside the apartment. A relevant psychological condition had occurred to me. It was called twinning, and it could be a key. Twinning just might explain the bizarre relationship between the monsters. Twinning was caused by an urge to bond, usually between two lonely people. Once they 'twin,' the two become a 'whole'; they become dependent on each other, often obsessively so. Sometimes the 'twins' become highly competitive.

Twinning was like an addiction to *couple*. To belong to a *secret club*. Just two people and no passwords. In its negative form, it was the fusing of two people for their own individual needs, which weren't mutually healthy.

I ran it by Kate. She was a twin, too.

'Quite often, there's a dominant figure in a twinning relationship,' I said. 'Was that true of you and your sister?'

'I probably was with Kristin,' Kate said. 'I got the good grades in school. I was a little pushy sometimes. She even called me "Push" in high school. Worse names than that, too.'

'The dominant twin can act in a male role-model behavior structure,' I said to Kate. The two of us were talking doctor to doctor. 'The dominant figure might *not* be the more skillful at manipulation, though.'

'As you could imagine, I've read a little about the phenomenon,' Kate said and smiled. 'Twinning creates a uniquely powerful structure within which the bonded pair can operate in complex ways. Something like that?'

'That's correct, Dr McTiernan. In the case of Casanova and the Gentleman, each would have his own bodyguard-cum-supportive person. That could be why they *achieve* so well. Perfect crimes. They each have a built-in, and very effective, emotional support system.'

The question ringing loudly in my mind was – *how had they originally met?* Was it at Duke? Had Casanova been a student there, too? It made some sense. It also reminded me of the Leopold-Loeb case in Chicago. *Two very smart boys, special boys, committing forbidden acts together. Sharing evil thoughts and dirty secrets because they were lonely and had no one else to talk to . . . twinning at its most destructive.*

Was that the beginning of the solution to this puzzle? I wondered. Were the Gentleman and Casanova twinning? Were they actually working together? What was their nasty little game all about? What game were they playing?

'Let's go smash in his picture windows with a tire iron,' Kate said. She was feeling it, too. We were both ready to rumble.

We wanted to take down this grown-up Leopold and Loeb.

65

Eight o'clock came and went on the surveillance watch. Maybe Dr Will Rudolph wasn't the Gentleman Caller. The *Los Angeles Times* reporter Beth Lieberman could have been wrong. There was no way to ask her about it now.

Kate and I had been gabbing about the Lakers without Magic Johnson and Kareem, about Aaron Neville's latest album, Hillary and Bill Clinton's life together, the merits of Johns Hopkins versus University of North Carolina medical school.

Strange sparks were still flying between us. I'd had some unofficial therapy sessions with Kate McTiernan and I had hypnotized her once. I also understood that I was afraid of any kind of fire starting between us. What was wrong with me? It was time to start my life again, to get over the loss of my wife, Maria. I thought I had something good with a woman named Jezzie Flanagan, but she had left an emptiness in me that I could barely get over.

Kate and I finally began to cover subjects a little closer to the heart. She asked why I was shying away from relationships (*because my wife had died; because my last relationship had imploded; because of my two kids*). I asked her why she was wary of meaningful relationships (*she was afraid she was going to die of ovarian or breast cancer like her sisters; she was afraid her lovers might die, or leave her – that she would keep on losing people*).

'We're quite the pair.' I finally shook my head and smiled.

'Maybe we're both terrified of losing someone again,' Kate said. 'Maybe it's better to love and lose than be afraid.'

Before we could really get into that thorny subject, Dr Will Rudolph finally reappeared. I looked at the time on the dashboard clock. It was 10:20.

Rudolph was decked out in all-black party clothes. Form-fitting blazer, turtleneck, clinging slacks, snazzy cowboy boots. He got into a white Range Rover this time instead of the BMW sedan. He looked freshly showered. Probably had taken a nap. I envied him that.

'Black on black for the good doctor,' Kate said with a tight smile. 'Dressed to kill?'

'Maybe he has a dinner date,' I said. 'Now there's a scary idea. He sups with the women, then kills them.'

'That could get him inside their apartments at least. What a terrible creep. *Two* unbelievable creeps on the loose.'

I started up our car and we followed Rudolph. I didn't see any FBI coverage, but I was sure they were there.

The Bureau still hadn't brought in the LAPD on this. It was a dangerous game, but not an unusual one for the FBI. They considered themselves the best policemen for any job, and the ultimate authority. They had decided this was an interstate crime spree, so it was theirs to solve. Somebody at the Bureau had a hard-on for this case.

'Vampires always hunt at night, huh,' Kate said as we

headed south through L.A. 'That's what this feels like, Alex. Bram Stoker's *The Gentleman Caller*. A real-life horror story.'

I knew what Kate was feeling. I felt it too. 'He is a monster. Only he's created himself. So has Casanova. It's another similarity they share. Bram Stoker, Mary Shelley, they wrote only about human monsters roaming the earth. Now we have sickos living out their elaborate fantasies. What a country.'

'Love it or leave it, bub,' Kate said with a drawl and a wink.

I had done enough surveillance early in my career to get reasonably good at it. I figured I had earned a graduate degree in tracking during the Soneji/Murphy manhunt. So far, I'd noticed that the West Coast FBI was good, too.

Agents Asaro and Cosgrove checked in on the radio as soon as we started to move again. They were in charge of the tracking unit on Will Rudolph. *We still didn't know if he was the Gentleman.* We had no proof. We couldn't move on Dr Rudolph yet.

We followed the Range Rover west through Los Angeles. Rudolph finally turned onto Sunset Drive and took it all the way to the Pacific Coast Highway. Then he headed north on U.S. Highway 1. I noticed that he was careful to keep the Range Rover at the speed limit inside L.A. But once he hit the open road, he started to fly.

'Where the heck is he going? My heart's in my throat,' Kate finally admitted.

'We'll be okay. It seems scary chasing him at night,' I said. It did feel as if we were alone with him. Where the hell was he going? Was he hunting? If his pattern held, he was due for another killing soon. He had to be in heat.

It turned out to be a very long ride. We watched the stars brighten the coastal California night. Six hours later, we were still tacking on Highway 1. The Range Rover finally pulled off at a quaint, wooden signpost that read Big Sur State Park, among other things.

As if to validate that we were really in Big Sur, we passed an antique van with a bumper sticker: VISUALIZE INDUS-TRIAL COLLAPSE.

'Visualize Dr Will Rudolph having a massive stroke,' Kate growled softly.

I checked my watch as we left the main highway. 'It's past three. Getting late for him to get into any serious trouble tonight.' I hoped that was the case.

'If there was ever any doubt, this may *prove* he's a blood-sucking vampire,' Kate muttered. Her arms were crossed tightly across her chest and had been for most of the long ride. 'He's going off to sleep in his favorite coffin.'

'Right. That's when we drive a wooden stake through his heart,' I told her. We were both a little groggy. I had taken a pill during the ride. Kate declined. She said she knew too much about drugs and was leery of most of them.

We passed a complex of directional signs: Point Sur, Pfeiffer Beach, Big Sur Lodge, Ventana, the Esalen Institute. Will Rudolph headed in the direction of Big Sur Lodge, Sycamore Canyon, Bottchers Gap Campgrounds.

'I was hoping he would go to Esalen,' Kate quipped. 'Learn to meditate, deal with his inner turmoil.'

'What in *hell* is he up to tonight?' I wondered out loud. What were he and Casanova doing? So far it was impossible to figure out. 'His *hideaway* might be up here in the woods, Kate,' I offered a thought. 'Maybe he has a house of horror just like Casanova's.'

Twinning, I thought again. It made a lot of sense. They would be providing support systems for each other. Parallel tracks for the two monsters. Where did they meet, though? Did the two of them ever hunt together? I suspected that they had.

The white Range Rover was winding along a hilly and rather rambunctious side road that branched east from the ocean. Ancient, somber redwoods flashed on either side of the narrow ribbon of highway. A pale full moon seemed to be moving directly above the Rover, following it.

I let him get a safe distance ahead – so that he was actually out of our sight. The huge fir trees seemed to float past our car on either road shoulder. Dark shadows in real life. A bright yellow sign in the headlights read: *Impassable in wet weather*.

'*He's right there, Alex.*' Kate's warning came a little too late. '*He's stopped*!'

The Gentleman's hooded eyes glared at our car as we passed him and the Range Rover.

He had seen us.

66

Dr Will Rudolph had turned into a rutted, dirt-and-gravel driveway hidden from the main road. He was stooped down inside the Rover, and was gathering an armful of who-knew-what from the backseat. He stared up at our passing car with a cold, questioning look in his eyes.

I kept speeding along on the blacktop road that was accentuated by overhanging, gnarled black branches. A few hundred yards farther, just around a curve, I eased over onto the narrow shoulder. I stopped in front of a dented metal road sign that promised more dangerous twists and turns in the road up ahead.

'He's stopped at a cabin,' I said into the FBI car's two-way radio. 'He's on foot, out of the Rover.'

'We saw that. We've got him, Alex.' John Asaro's voice came back over the two-way radio. 'We're on the other side of the cabin now. Looks dark inside. He's turning on lights. *El pais grande del sur*. That's what the Spanish called this place way back when. Beautiful spot to catch this fucker.'

Kate and I got out of the car. She looked a little pale,

understandably so. The temperature was probably in the forties, maybe even the thirties, and the mountain air was bracing. But Kate wasn't shivering just from the damp cold.

'We're going to get him soon,' I said to her. 'He's starting to make mistakes.'

'It could be another house of horror. You were right,' she said in a low voice. Her eyes stared straight ahead. I hadn't seen her this unsettled since I'd first met her in the hospital. 'It *feels* like it, Alex . . . feels almost the same. Feels creepy. I'm not being very brave, am I?'

'Believe me, Kate. I'm not feeling particularly brave right now, either.'

The thick coastal fog seemed to roll on forever. My stomach felt icy and sour. We had to get moving.

Kate and I went into the dark screen of woods, heading toward the cabin. The north wind whistled and howled loudly through the towering redwood and fir trees. I had no idea what to expect from here on.

'Shit,' Kate whispered her summation of the night's experience. 'I'm not kidding, Alex.'

'You've got that right.'

El pais grande del sur at three o'clock in the morning. Rudolph had come to a lonely outpost on the edge of the earth. Casanova had a house in the South, in the deep woods, too. A 'disappearing' house where he kept a collection of young women.

I thought of the spooky diaries in the *Los Angeles Times*. Could Naomi have been moved out here for some crazy, psychopathic reason? Maybe she was being kept in the cabin, or somewhere nearby?

I stopped walking suddenly. I could hear wind chimes, which sounded particularly creepy under the circumstances.

Up ahead, a small cabin was visible. It was pink, with white doors and white window trim. It looked like a pleasant-enough summer place.

'He left a light for us,' Kate whispered behind me. 'I remember that Casanova used to play loud rock 'n' roll music when he was in the house.'

I could tell it was painful for her to be thinking about her captivity again, to be reliving it. 'You see any similarities to this cabin?' I asked her. I was trying to be very still inside, trying to get ready for the Gentleman.

'No. I only saw the *inside* of the other place, Alex. Let's hope it won't disappear on us.'

'I'm hoping for a lot of things right now. I'll put that on the list.'

The cabin was an A-frame, and probably built to be a vacation home or weekend retreat. There were three or four bedrooms from the look of it.

I took out my Glock as we got closer. The Glock was the weapon of choice these days in the inner city; it weighed a little over a pound when loaded and was easily concealed. It would probably work fine in *el pais grande del sur*, too.

Kate kept behind me as we moved toward a clearing in the trees that served as a backyard. There were actually two lights glittering and drawing bugs to the house. One was the frontporch lamp. The second was in the back of the cabin. I made my way toward the second, dimmer light in back. I gestured for Kate to stay back, which she did.

This could be the Gentleman Caller, I warned myself. *Take it very slow. This could also be a trap. Anything could happen here. There's no predicting from here on.*

I could see into a rear bedroom window. I was less than ten steps away from the cabin walls, and probably the mass murderer who was terrifying the West Coast. *Then I saw him.*

Dr Will Rudolph was pacing around the small wood-paneled room and he was talking to himself. He appeared to be highly agitated. He was hugging himself with both arms. As I moved closer, I could see that he was perspiring heavily. Not in good shape at all. The scene reminded me of 'quiet rooms' in mental hospitals, where patients sometimes go to act out their problems and volatile emotions.

Rudolph suddenly screamed at someone . . . *but there was no one else in the room.*

His face and his neck were bright crimson red as he screamed again and again . . . *at absolutely no one!*

He was screaming at the top of his lungs. His veins looked ready to burst.

Seeing him like this chilled me, and I slowly backed away from the cabin.

I could still hear his voice, hear the words ringing in my ears: '*Goddamn* you, Casanova! Kiss the girls! *Kiss the fucking girls yourself from now on!*'

67

'What the hell is Cross doing?' Agent John Asaro asked his partner. They were in the thick woods on the other side of the cabin at Big Sur. The cabin reminded Asaro of The Band's first album, *Music from Big Pink*. He half expected flower children and hippies to step out of the fog.

'Maybe Cross is a peeping Tom, Johnny. What do I know? He's a guru, a squirrel profiler. He's Kyle Craig's boy,' Ray Cosgrove said with a shrug.

'So that means he can do whatever he wants to do?'

'Probably.' Cosgrove shrugged a second time. He had seen far too many crazy situations, too many 'special accommodations,' in his Bureau career to let this one bother him.

'First of all,' Cosgrove said, 'whether we like it or not, he has Washington's blessing.'

'I hate Washington with a freaking passion that just won't quit,' Asaro said.

'Everybody hates Washington, Johnny. Second, Cross strikes me as a pro at least. He's not just some glory hound. Third,' the older, more experienced partner continued, 'and most important, what we have on Dr Rudolph is hardly conclusive evidence that he's our squirrel. Otherwise, we would have called in the LAPD, army, navy, and marines.'

'Maybe the late Ms Lieberman made a mistake when she logged his name into her computer?'

'She definitely made some kind of mistake somewhere, Johnny. *Maybe* her hunch was all wrong.'

'Maybe Will Rudolph was an ex-boyfriend of hers? She was just doodling his name on her PC?'

'Doubtful. But a possibility,' Cosgrove said.

'So we watch Dr Rudolph, and we watch Dr Cross watch Dr Rudolph?' Agent Asaro said.

'You got it, partner.'

'Maybe Dr Cross and Dr McTiernan will provide us with a little entertainment at least.'

'Hey, you never know about these things,' Raymond Cosgrove said. He was smiling now. He thought this whole thing was probably a wild goose chase, but it wouldn't be his first one. This was a huge, nasty case no matter what. It was interstate now, and every possible lead was being chased down with a vengeance. A coast-to-coast serial squirrel connection!

So he and his partner, and two other FBI agents, were going to hang around in the dark woods of Big Sur all night and into the morning, if need be. They would dutifully watch the summer cabin of a plastic surgeon from L.A., who maybe was a real bad killer, but maybe was just a plastic surgeon from L.A.

They would watch Alex Cross and Dr McTiernan, and speculate about the two of them. Cosgrove wasn't really in the mood for any of this. On the other hand, it was a big case. And if he did happen to catch the Gentleman Caller, he might just become a glory hound himself. He wanted Al Pacino to play him in the movie. Pacino did Spanish guys, right?

68

Kate and I moved back a safe distance from the cabin. We ducked behind a stand of thick fir trees.

'I heard him scream,' Kate said when we got into the deeper woods. 'What did you see back there, Alex?'

'I saw the devil.' I told her the truth. 'I saw an absolutely crazy and evil man talking to himself. If he isn't the Gentleman, he does a great imitation.'

The two of us took shifts watching Rudolph's hideaway over the next several hours. That way, we both got some rest. Around six in the morning I met with the FBI team, and they gave me a pocket-sized walkie-talkie in case we needed to talk in a hurry. I still wondered how much they'd told me of what they knew.

When Dr Will Rudolph eventually made another appearance outside, it was past one o'clock on Saturday afternoon. The silver-blue nimbus of sea mist had finally burned off. Scrub jays swooped and hollered overhead. Under different circumstances, it would have been a nice setting for a weekend in the mountains.

Dr Rudolph cleaned up in a whitewashed outdoor shower behind the house. He was muscular, with a washboard stomach, and looked agile and fit. He was extremely handsome. He cavorted and danced around in the nude. His bearing seemed a little formal. *The Gentleman.*

'He's so unbelievably sure of himself, Alex,' Kate said as we watched Rudolph from the woods. 'Just look at him.'

Everything seemed very odd and ritualistic. Was the dance part of his act? His pattern?

When he finished his shower, he walked across the back-yard to a small wildflower garden. He picked about a dozen flowers and brought them into the house. *The Gentleman had his flowers! What now?*

At four in the afternoon, Rudolph came out the back screen door of the cabin again. He was dressed in tight black jeans, a plain white pocket T, black leather sandals. He hopped in the Range Rover and drove toward Highway 1.

About two miles south on the coast road, he pulled into a restaurant and café called Nepenthe. Kate and I waited on the sandy road shoulder, then we followed the Range Rover into a large, crowded parking lot. Jimi Hendrix's 'Electric Ladyland' was playing loudly from speakers hidden in the trees.

'Maybe he's just your average horny Los Angeles doctor,' Kate said as we finally entered the parking area and searched for a space.

'No. He's the Gentleman, all right. He's our California butcher boy.' I was sure of it after watching him the night before, and now today.

Nepenthe was busy, filled mostly with good-looking people in their twenties and thirties, but also a sprinkling of aging hippies, some of whom were sixty or more. Stonewashed jeans, the latest West Coast swimsuit creations, colorful flip-flops, expensive hiking boots were everywhere.

So were a lot of attractive women, I noticed. All ages, all sizes, all ethnic castes. *Kiss the girls.*

I had heard of Nepenthe, actually. It had been hot and famous in the sixties, but, even before that, Orson Welles had bought the desirable, breathtakingly beautiful property for Rita Hayworth.

Kate and I watched how Dr Rudolph operated at the bar. He was polite. A smile for the bartender. Shared laughter. He looked around and seriously checked out several attractive women. Apparently they weren't attractive enough, though.

He ventured out onto a large fieldstone terrace overlooking the Pacific. Rock music from the seventies and eighties was playing from an expensive sound system. The Grateful Dead. The Doors. The Eagles. This was Hotel California.

'It's a beautiful spot for it, Alex. Whatever in hell he's up to.'

'He's up to six. He's looking for victim number seven,' I said.

Far below, on an inaccessible beach, we could see sea lions, brown pelicans, cormorants. I wished that Damon and Jannie were here to see them, and I wished the circumstances of my being here were completely different.

Out on the terrace, I took Kate's hand. 'Makes us look like we belong,' I said and winked at her.

'Maybe we do.' Kate gave an exaggerated wink back.

We watched Rudolph approach a striking blonde woman. She was the Gentleman's type. In her early twenties. Shapely. Beautiful face. She was also Casanova's type, I couldn't help thinking.

Her wavy, sunbleached hair fell to her tiny waist. She wore

a red-and-yellow flowered dress from Putumayo's that flowed down to a pair of black European workboots. She flowed when she moved as well. She was drinking champagne by the glass.

I hadn't spotted agents Cosgrove or Asaro yet, which was making me a little nervous, a little nuts.

'She's beautiful, isn't she? She's just perfect,' Kate whispered at my side. 'We can't let him hurt her, Alex. We can't let anything happen to that poor woman.'

'We won't,' I said, 'but we have to catch him in the act, nail him for kidnapping, if nothing else. We need evidence that he is the Gentleman Caller.'

I finally spotted John Asaro at the crowded main bar. He had on a bright yellow Nike T-shirt and fit in okay. I didn't spot Ray Cosgrove or any of the other agents – which was actually a good sign.

Rudolph and the young blonde woman seemed to have hit it off immediately. She appeared to be gregarious and fun-loving. She had perfect white teeth and her smile was dazzling. She couldn't help but make an impression across the crowded room. My brain was sliding into overload. *We were watching the Gentleman Caller at work, weren't we?*

'He's hunting . . . and just like that' – Kate snapped her fingers – 'he picks them up. Gets almost any woman he wants. That's how he does it. So simple . . .

'It's the way he looks that gets them, Alex,' Kate continued. 'He has a rebellious look about him *and* he's very handsome. That combination is irresistible to some women. She let him think it was his line of small talk that won her over, but it's because he's such a hunk.'

'So, she just picked *him* up?' I asked. 'Our killer hunk?'

Kate nodded. She wouldn't take her eyes off the two of them. 'She just picked up the Gentleman Caller. He wanted her to, of course. I'll bet that's how he gets them, and why he never gets caught.'

'It's not how Casanova works, though. Is it?'

'Maybe Casanova isn't good-looking.' Kate turned and looked at me. 'That might explain the masks he wears. Maybe he's ugly, or disfigured, and ashamed of how he looks.'

I had another thought, another theory, about Casanova and his masks, but I didn't want to say anything just yet.

The Gentleman and his new girlfriend ordered ambrosiaburgers, the house specialty. So did Kate and I. When in paradise . . . They hung around the café until around seven o'clock and then got up to leave.

Kate and I rose from our table, too. Actually, I was half enjoying myself, considering the eerie circumstances. We had a table that overlooked the water. Down below, the Pacific crashed against a black wall of slippery rocks, and we could hear sea lions barking loudly.

I noted that there was no touching between the two of them as they walked out to the parking lot. It suggested to me that one of them was secretly shy.

Dr Will Rudolph politely held open the door of his Range Rover, and the blonde woman was laughing as she hopped in. He performed a tiny, elegant bow at the car door. *The Gentleman.*

She chose him, I was thinking. *It wasn't kidnapping yet. She was still making choices for herself.*

We had nothing to go after him for, nothing to hold him on. Perfect crimes.

On both coasts.

69

We trailed the Range Rover at a discreet distance, straight back to the cabin. I parked about a quarter of a mile up the road. My heart was hammering hard and loud. This was the moment of truth, the real deal was going down now.

Kate and I ran back through the woods and found a safe spot that was well hidden from view. It was less than fifty yards from Dr Rudolph's hideaway, and we could still hear the musical tinkle of the wind chimes as they moved gently. The cold, damp sea mist was inching in, and I could feel a chill right up through my shoes.

The Gentleman Caller was inside that cabin up ahead. Getting ready to do what?

My stomach felt hollow and incredibly tight. I wanted to move on him in the worst way. I didn't want to think about how many times Dr Will Rudolph had done this before. Taken a young woman somewhere. Mutilated her. Taken home feet, eyes, fingers, a human heart. Souvenirs of his kill.

I glanced at my wristwatch. Rudolph had been inside the

cabin for only a few minutes with the blonde woman from Nepenthe. I'd seen movement in the woods on the other side of the house. The FBI was there. It was getting hairy.

'Alex, what if he kills her?' Kate asked. She stood close to me, and I could feel the heat from her body. She knew what it felt like to be a captive in a house of horror. She understood the danger better than anyone.

'He doesn't grab his victims and kill them immediately. The Gentleman Caller has his routine,' I said to Kate. 'He's kept every one of the victims for a day. He likes to play. He won't break away from the pattern.'

I believed that, but I didn't know it for certain. Maybe Dr Rudolph knew we were outside . . . maybe he wanted to get caught. Maybe, maybe, maybe.

I remembered stalking the madman Gary Soneji/Murphy. It was hard not to rush the cabin. Take our chances right now. We might find physical evidence of other murders inside. Maybe the missing body parts were kept here. Maybe he did the actual killing here in Big Sur. Or maybe he was planning another kind of surprise for us. The drama was unfolding less than fifty yards away.

'I'm going to try to get in a little closer,' I finally said to Kate. 'I have to see what's happening in there.'

'I'm glad you said that,' Kate whispered.

The talk was cut short. A bloodcurdling scream came from the cabin. 'Help! Help me! *Somebody* help me!' the blonde woman screamed.

I ran at full speed for the closest door into the cabin. So did at least five men in dark blue Windbreakers from the other side of the house. I spotted Asaro and Cosgrove among them.

FBI, the Windbreakers read. Rain-slicker yellow on navy blue.

All hell was breaking loose in Big Sur. We were about to meet the Gentleman.

70

I got there first, at least I think I did. I threw myself hard against the cabin's wood-plank back door. It wouldn't give. On the second try the frame splintered, and the door burst open with a wounded grunt. I charged into the cabin with my pistol drawn.

I could see across the small kitchen, and all the way down a narrow hallway that led into a bedroom. The blonde woman from Nepenthe was naked, and curled sideways on an antique brass bed. Wildflowers had been thrown around her body. Her wrists were pinioned with handcuffs near the small of her back. She was in pain, but at least she was still alive. The Gentleman Caller wasn't there.

From outside the cabin I heard a loud bark, the harsh sound of gunfire. At least half a dozen shots were fired in rapid succession, like a string of powerful firecrackers. 'Jesus, don't kill him!' I shouted as I ran from the cabin.

Complete chaos reigned in the woods! The Range Rover was already backing wildly from the driveway when I came out. Two of the FBI men were down on the ground. One was agent Ray Cosgrove. The others had opened fire on the Range Rover.

A side window exploded. Jagged holes opened in the Range Rover's sheet metal. The off-road vehicle swerved sideways, its wheels spinning in the dirt and gravel.

'Don't kill him!' I yelled again. No one even looked at me in the wild confusion of the moment.

I sprinted through the side woods, hoping to cut off Rudolph if he headed west, back toward Highway I. I got there just as the Range Rover made a shrieking, skidding turn out onto the road. A gunshot blew out another side window. Great! The FBI was shooting at both of us now.

I grabbed the passenger side door and yanked hard at the handle. It was locked. Rudolph tried to accelerate, but I held on tightly. The Rover fishtailed, still caught in a swale of driveway gravel. That gave me time to grab the roof rack with my free hand. I pulled myself onto the roof.

Rudolph finally got the Rover onto the concrete roadway and accelerated. He floored the vehicle for seventy yards. *Then he hit the brakes hard*!

I was thinking ahead – that far ahead, anyway. My face was pressed tightly against the sheet metal, which was still warm from sitting in the sun at Nepenthe. My arms and legs were splayed out against the roof rack. I was wedged like a Samsonite all-nighter on the roof.

I wasn't coming off there, not if I could help it. He had killed at least half a dozen women around Los Angeles, and I had to find out if Naomi was still alive. He knew Casanova, and he knew about Scootchie.

Rudolph floored the Range Rover again, and the engine roared through its gears as he tried to shake me loose. He was weaving all over the road.

Trees and ancient telephone poles zoomed past me in blurry, fast motion. The rushing pines, redwoods, and mountain vines were like the changing patterns in a kaleidoscope. A lot of the foliage was brownish-gray, prickly as vineyards in the Napa Valley. It was a strange perspective on the world.

I wasn't exactly enjoying the scenery from my perch on the Range Rover. It took all of my strength to concentrate on hugging the roof.

Rudolph drove very fast along the winding narrow road, doing seventy or eighty where fifty was dangerous.

The FBI agents, what was left of them, hadn't been able to catch up. How could they? They'd had to run back to their cars. They would be several minutes behind us.

Other cars passed us as we got closer to the Pacific Coast Highway. Drivers gave us the strangest looks. I wondered what Rudolph was thinking as he drove. He wasn't trying to throw me off anymore. What options did he still have? In particular – what was he planning as his next move?

We were both temporarily in check. Somebody had to lose very big, and very soon, though. Will Rudolph had always been too clever to be caught. He wouldn't expect to be stopped now. But how would he get out of this one?

I heard the noisy diesel chug of a VW van. I *saw* the *rear end* of the van coming fast. We passed it as if it were standing still.

There was a flow of traffic against us as we approached the ocean road. Mostly kids out for an early evening spin. Some of them pointed at the Range Rover and thought it was a big joke. Just some major asshole from the Sur pulling a stunt, right? Some aging merry prankster high on tequila, or maybe even twenty-year-old acid. A crazed man hanging onto the roof of a Range Rover doing seventy miles an hour in what amounted to a very scenic parking lot.

What was his next goddamn move?

Rudolph didn't bother to slow down on the curvy, extremely populated, blacktop road. The motorists headed in the opposite direction blared their horns angrily. No one did anything to stop us. What could they do? What could I do now? *Hang on as tightly as I could, and pray!*

71

A bright flash of grayish-blue ocean broke through the scrim of fir and redwood branches. I heard rock music blasting from the slow-moving parade of cars up ahead. A collage of music was in the air: Pop 40 rap, West Coast grunge bands, acid rock from thirty years ago.

Another splash of Pacific blue hit me right in the eye. The setting sun was casting its golden glow on the spreading firs. Wheeling terns and gulls passed slowly over the trees. Then I saw the full expanse of the Pacific Coast Highway up ahead.

What the hell was he doing? He couldn't drive back to Los Angeles like this. Or was he crazy enough to try? Eventually he'd have to stop for gas. What would he do then?

Traffic on the highway was light heading north, but heavy moving south. The Range Rover was still doing sixty or better – careening faster than anyone ought to drive on the curvy side highway, especially as it merged into the busier coast road.

Rudolph didn't slow down as he approached the crowded

highway! I could see family station wagons, convertibles, four-wheel-drive vehicles. Just another crazy Saturday night on the northern California shoreline, but it was about to get a whole lot crazier.

We were fifty yards from the highway now. He was going as fast as ever, if not faster. My arms were stiff and numb. My throat was dry from exhaust fumes. I didn't know how much longer I could hold on. Then suddenly, I thought I knew what he was going to do.

'You son of a bitch!' I yelled, just to yell. I wedged my body even tighter against the straining metal roof rails.

Rudolph had created an impromptu escape plan. He was only ten to fifteen yards from the highway traffic, no more than that.

Just as the Rover reached the sharp turn onto the Pacific Coast Highway, he braked hard. The loud screech of radial tires was terrifying, especially from where I was listening.

A bearded face in a passing multicolored minivan yelled out. 'Slow down, you asshole!' *Which asshole?* I wondered. *This* asshole definitely wanted to slow down.

The top-heavy Range Rover held its path for a few yards, then it started to fishtail right, then left, then right again.

It was total bedlam now. Horns were blowing everywhere at once on the busy highway. Drivers and passengers couldn't believe what they were seeing, what was bearing down on them from the side road.

Rudolph was doing everything *wrong* at the wheel on purpose. He *wanted* the Rover to spin out.

Its tires still squealing like animals being slaughtered, the Range Rover slid left until it was facing south, but it was actually traveling west into traffic. Then the Rover's tail end swerved all the way around.

We were going to hit the traffic *moving backward*! We were going to crash. I was sure we would both be killed. Images of Damon and Jannie flashed before me.

I couldn't guess how fast we were going when we broadsided a silver-blue minivan. I didn't even try to hang on to the roof rack. I concentrated on relaxing my body, preparing for a bonebreaking, possibly deadly, impact in the next few seconds.

I yelled, but the sound of my voice was lost in the high-pitched screeching crash, the blaring car horns, the screaming spectators.

I barely missed the lineup of northbound traffic as I jetted off the roof. More horns blared. I was flying through the air with the greatest of ease. The sea wind both cooled and stung my face. It was going to be a crash landing.

I flew into the smoky blue mist that was settling between the Pacific Ocean and the Pacific Coast Highway. I hit the thick branches of a fir tree. As I fell through scraping, scratching tree branches, I knew the Gentleman Caller was going to escape.

72

Skip forward. Cut forward. Spin, fall head over heels forward!

I was badly shaken and bruised from the car crash and fall, but apparently there were no broken bones. A crackerjack EMS team looked me over at the accident site on Highway 1. They wanted to check me into a nearby hospital for tests and observation, but I had other plans for the night.

The Gentleman was running loose. He had commandeered a car heading north. The car had already been found, but not Dr Rudolph. At least not so far.

When she arrived at the bad scene at the highway, Kate went ballistic. She wanted me to go to the local hospital, too. Agent Cosgrove of the FBI was already there as a patient. We had a heated discussion, but eventually Kate and I caught the last AirWest shuttle out of Monterey. We were headed back to L.A.

I had spoken to Kyle Craig twice already. FBI teams were camped out at Rudolph's apartment in Los Angeles, but nobody expected the Gentleman to return there. They were searching the place now. I wanted to be there with them. I needed to see exactly how he lived.

On the flight, Kate continued to show concern about my physical condition. She had already developed a top-notch bedside manner, warm and empathetic, but also surprisingly firm with a stubborn patient like myself.

Kate talked to me with her hand cupped lightly under my chin. She was intense. 'Alex, you *have* to go to a hospital as soon as we get to Los Angeles. I'm serious. As you might be able to tell, this isn't my usual humor-in-the-face-of-adversity approach. You're going to a hospital as soon as we land. *Hey*! Are you even listening to me?'

'I'm listening to you, Kate. I also happen to agree with what you're saying. Basically, that is.'

'Alex, that's no answer. That's crap.'

I knew Kate was right, but we didn't have time for a hospital check-in tonight. Dr Will Rudolph's trail was still warm, and maybe we could pick up his scent and nab him in the next few hours. It was a slim chance, but by tomorrow the Gentleman's trail could be stone-cold.

'You could be bleeding internally, and you wouldn't even know it,' Kate continued to make her case. 'You could die right here in this airplane seat.'

'I've got some nasty body bruises and contusions, and I ache all over. I've got the makings of some first-class scabs up and down my right side, where I made my first couple of bounces. I've got to see his apartment before they take it apart, Kate. I have to see how that bastard lives.'

'Half a million or more a year? Trust me. He lives very well,' Kate came back at me. 'You, on the other hand, could be in bad shape. Human beings don't *bounce*.'

'Ahh, well, black human beings do. We've had to learn

that special knack for survival. We hit the ground, we bounce right back.'

Kate didn't laugh at my joke. She folded her arms across her chest and peered out the tiny plane's window. She was angry with me for the second time in hours. That must mean she cared.

She knew she was right and she wasn't backing down. I liked the fact that she was concerned for me. *We were actually friends.* What a fantastic concept for men and women in the nineties. Kate McTiernan and I had become friends during both our times of need. We were in the process of compiling that all-important dossier of shared experiences now. It was some kind of dossier so far.

'I like it that we're pals,' I finally told Kate in a low, conspiratorial voice. I wasn't afraid to say cute, dumb things to her, almost the way I talked to my kids.

She didn't turn away from the window as she spoke. Still pissed off at me. Good for her. I probably deserved it. 'If you were really my damn friend, you'd listen to me when I'm worried sick and frightened for you. You were in an automobile accident a few hours ago. You fell about thirty yards down a pretty steep ravine, *pal.*'

'I hit a tree first.'

She finally turned back to me and pointed a finger at my heart, like a stake. 'Big deal. *Alex*, I'm worried about your stubborn black ass. I'm worried so much my stomach hurts.'

'That's the nicest thing anybody's said to me in months,' I told her. 'Once when I was shot, Sampson showed some genuine concern. It lasted about a minute and a half.'

Her brown eyes held on to mine and wouldn't let go, wouldn't lighten up. 'I let you help me in North Carolina. I let you *hypnotize* me, for God's sake. Why won't you let me help you here? Let me help, Alex.'

'I'm working up to it,' I told her. That was true enough. 'Macho policemen have a tough field to hoe. We abhor being helped. We're classic enablers. Most of the time, we like it like that, too.'

'Oh, cut the psychobabble, *Doctor*! It's self-serving and doesn't reflect you at your best.'

'I'm not at my best. I was just in a terrible accident.'

It went on like that between us for the remainder of the shuttle flight to Los Angeles. Toward the end of the ride, I catnapped peacefully on Kate's shoulder. No complications, No unnecessary baggage. Very, very nice.

73

Unfortunately, the California night was still young and probably extremely dangerous for everyone involved. When we arrived at Rudolph's penthouse apartment at the Beverly Comstock, the LAPD was everywhere. So was the Federal Bureau of Investigation. It was police bedlam.

We could see the flashing crimson and blue emergency lights from several blocks away. The local police were justifiably angry for being kept out of the chase by the FBI. It was a very nasty, very political, very sensitive mess. This wasn't the first time the FBI had been high-handed with a local police agency. It had happened to me back in Washington. Plenty of times.

The Los Angeles press posse was there, too, and in full force. Newspaper, local TV, radio, even a few film producers were on the scene. I wasn't happy that many of the reporters knew Kate and me by sight.

They called out to us as we hurried through police lines and barricades. 'Kate, give us a few minutes.' 'Give us a break!' 'Dr Cross, is Rudolph the Gentleman Caller?' 'What went wrong up in Big Sur?' 'Is this the killer's apartment?'

'No comment right now,' I said, trying to keep my head down, eyes down.

'From either one of us,' Kate added.

The police and FBI let us inside the Gentleman Caller's apartment. Technical people were busy in every room of the expensive-looking penthouse. Somehow, the Los Angeles detectives seemed smarter, slicker, richer than cops in other cities.

The rooms were sparsely decorated, almost as if no one lived there. The furniture was mostly leather but with lots of chrome and marble touches. All angles – no curves. The art on the wall was modern and vaguely depressing. Jackson Pollock and Mark Rothko look-alikes, that sort of thing. It looked like a museum – but one with a lot of mirrors and shiny surfaces.

There were several interesting touches, possible clues about the Gentleman Caller.

I noted everything. Recording. Remembering.

His dining-room hutch held sterling silver, bone china, real stoneware, expensive linen napkins. *The Gentleman knew how to set his table.*

On top of his desk were formal writing paper and envelopes with elegant silver trim. *Always the Gentleman.*

A copy of Hugh Johnson's *Pocket Encyclopedia of Wine* was sitting out on the kitchen table.

Among his dozen expensive suits were two tuxedos. The suit closet was small, narrow, and oh-so-neat. It was less a closet than a shrine for his clothes.

Our strange, strange Gentleman.

I came over to Kate after an hour or so of touring the Gentleman's place. I had read the local detectives' reports. I'd talked to most of the techs, but so far they had nothing.

280

That didn't seem possible to any of us. The newest laser equipment was being brought from downtown Los Angeles. Rudolph had to have left clues somewhere. But he hadn't! So far, that was his closest parallel to Casanova.

'How are *you* doing?' I asked Kate. 'I'm afraid I've been lost in my own world for the last hour.'

We were at a window overlooking Wilshire Boulevard and also the Los Angeles Country Club. Lots of shimmering car and building lights surrounding an eighteen-hole expanse of darkness. A disturbing Calvin Klein billboard was brightly lit up down on the street. It showed a naked model on a couch. She looked to be about fourteen. *Obsession* the ad proclaimed. *For men.*

'I've got my second or third wind,' Kate said. '*All* the world's a hideous nightmare suddenly, Alex. Have they found anything at all?'

I shook my head as I looked at the two of us in the dark, reflective window. 'It's maddening. Rudolph commits "perfect crimes," too. The techies might eventually match fiber from his clothes to one or more of the crime scenes, but Rudolph is unbelievably careful. I think he has a knowledge of forensic evidence.'

'There's enough written about it these days, isn't there? Most doctors are pretty good at absorbing technical information, Alex.'

I nodded at the truth of her statement. I'd thought the same thing. Kate had the makings of a detective. She looked tired. I wondered if I looked as exhausted as I felt.

'Don't even say it.' I dialed up a smile. 'I'm *not* going to a hospital now. I think we're done here for the night, though. We lost him, goddammit, we lost them both.'

74

We left Will Rudolph's penthouse apartment at just past two in the morning. That made it 5:00 A.M. our time. I was reeling. So was Kate. We called ourselves 'the bruise brothers.' We were both out of it.

Grogginess, exhaustion, possible internal injuries, they were one and the same. If I had ever felt this badly before, I couldn't remember the time, and didn't want to. We collapsed into the first of our rooms when we reached the Holiday Inn on Sunset.

'Are you all right? You don't look so good to me.' Not unexpectedly, Kate resumed her advertisement for the McTiernan Medical Group. She was a compelling spokeswoman, actually. She had a way of crinkling her forehead that made her look thoughtful and wise, and highly professional.

'I'm not dying, I'm just dead tired.' I groaned and slowly lowered myself onto the edge of the comfy bed. 'Just another tough day at the office.'

'You're *so damn stubborn*, Alex. Always the macho big-city detective. All right, I'm going to examine you myself.

Don't try to stop me or I'll break your arm, which I'm entirely capable of doing.'

Kate pulled a stethoscope and sphygmomanometer out of one of her travel bags. She wasn't taking 'no,' 'absolutely not,' or 'no way' as an answer.

I sighed. 'I'm not having a physical exam now, and especially here,' I told her with as much resolve as I could muster under the circumstances.

'I've seen it all before.' Kate rolled her eyes and frowned. Then she smiled. No, actually she laughed. A doctor with a smile and a nice sense of humor. Imagine that.

'Take your shirt off, Detective Cross,' Kate said to me. 'Make my day. My night, anyway.'

I started to pull my shirt over my head. I half moaned, half yelled. Just taking the shirt off hurt like hell. Maybe I *was* seriously hurt.

'Oh, you're just *fine* and *dandy*,' Dr McTiernan pronounced with a wicked chuckle. 'Can't even get your shirt off.'

She bent in close, extremely close, and listened to my breathing with the stethoscope. I could hear her breathing without the help of any machine. I liked the sound of her heartbeat up close like this.

Kate probed my shoulder blade. Then she moved my arm back and forth, and it hurt. Maybe I was banged up a lot worse than I thought. More likely, she wasn't using her gentlest touch while she examined me.

She poked my abdomen and ribs next. I saw stars, but not a peep came from me in protest.

'That hurt at all?' she asked. Doctor-to-patient talk. Detached, professional.

'No. Maybe. Yes, a little. Okay, quite a lot. Ow! That wasn't so bad. *Ow!*'

'Getting hit by a train isn't the way to keep the average human body in excellent running shape,' she said. She touched my ribs again, gentler this time.

'That wasn't my plan,' I said, offering the only defense I had.

'What *was* your plan?'

'My fleeting thought up at Big Sur was that maybe he knew where Naomi was, and I couldn't let him get away. My ultimate plan was to find Naomi. It still is.'

Kate used both her hands to feel my rib cage. She applied pressure, but nothing too extreme. She asked me if it hurt to take a breath.

'To tell the truth, I kind of like this part,' I told her. 'You have a nice touch.'

'Uh-huh. Now the trousers, Alex. You can keep your drawers on if it makes you feel better.' A little of her drawl was creeping into her speech.

'My *drawers*?' I grinned.

'Your bikini underwear from *Gentlemen's Quarterly*. Whatever you're wearing today. Let's see the goodies, Alex. I'd like to see a little skin.'

'You don't have to show such obvious damn glee about this.' I was very much awake all of a sudden. I did like the way Kate touched me, though. I liked it a lot, in fact. Different kinds of sparks were starting to fly.

I pulled off my pants. I *could not* get to my socks, not even close.

'Mmm. Not so bad, actually,' she offered her opinion of something or other. I began to feel hot, uncomfortably warm, in the hotel room. Under these circumstances, anyway.

Kate applied gentle pressure against my hips, then against my pelvis. She asked me to slowly raise my feet off the bed, one at a time, while she kept her hands firmly on my hip joints. Very carefully, she felt my legs from my groin area, all the way down to my feet. I mostly liked that, too.

'Lots of abrasions,' she said. 'I wish I had some bacitracin ointment on hand. It's an antibiotic.'

'I was just thinking the same thing.'

Finally, Kate stopped all the probing and poking and pulled away from me. She frowned and wrinkled her nose, nibbled her upper lip. She looked smart, academic, professional as the surgeon general.

'Blood pressure's a little high, borderline, but I don't think anything's broken,' she pronounced. 'I don't like the discoloration on your abdomen and your left hip, though. Tomorrow you'll feel sore and stiff, and we have to go over to Cedars-Sinai and get a few X rays taken. Do we have a deal?'

Actually, I felt a little better after Kate examined me and pronounced that I wouldn't die suddenly during the night. 'Yes. It wouldn't be a complete day without one of our deals. Thank you for the examination, Doctor . . . thank you, Kate,' I said.

'You're quite welcome. It was an honor.' She finally smiled. 'You look a little like Muhammad Ali, you know. The Great One.'

So I have been told. 'In his prime,' I joked. 'I do dance like a butterfly.'

'I'll bet. I sting like a bee.' She winked and crinkled her nose again. A nice tic of hers.

Kate lay back on the bed. I stayed there beside her. Close, but not close enough to touch. We were at least a foot apart. Very strange, but nice strange. I missed her touch already.

We were quiet for the next minute or so. I glanced over at her. Maybe it was more than a glance. Kate had on a black skirt with black tights, a red peasant blouse. The bruises on her face had faded. I wondered about the rest of her. I held in a sigh.

'I'm *not* Nanu the ice queen,' she said softly. 'Trust me, I'm normal as they come. Frisky, fun, a little crazy. At least I was a month ago.'

I was surprised that Kate thought I might be feeling that way about her. She was the opposite, warm and compassionate. 'I think you're great, Kate. Truth be told, I like you an awful lot.' There, it was out. Probably an understatement at that.

We kissed gently. Just the briefest kiss. There was something right about it. I liked the feel of Kate's lips, her mouth on mine. We kissed again, maybe to prove that the first one hadn't been a mistake, or maybe to prove that it had been.

I felt as if I could kiss Kate all night, but we both gently pulled away. This *was* probably more than either of us could handle right now.

'Don't you admire my self-control?' Kate smiled and said.

'Yes and no,' I told her.

I pulled on my hair shirt again. It took some effort, and produced hellacious pain. I *would* definitely go for X rays tomorrow. Kate started to cry and buried her face in the pillow. I turned toward her and put my hand on her shoulder.

'You okay? Hey?'

'I'm sorry. Shoot,' she whispered, trying to stop the tears. 'I just . . . I know I don't seem like it most of the time, but I'm freaking out, Alex. I've *been* freaking out. I've seen so many horrible things. Is this case as bad as your last one – the child kidnapping in D.C.?' she asked me.

I held Kate very gently in my arms. I hadn't seen her quite

so vulnerable, so open about it, anyway. Everything suddenly became more relaxed between us.

I whispered into her hair. 'This case is as bad as anything I've seen. It's actually worse because of Naomi, and because of what happened to you. I want him more than I wanted Gary Soneji. I want both of these monsters.'

'When I was a very little girl back home,' Kate said, still in a whisper, 'I was just learning to talk. I was probably four months old.' She smiled at the exaggeration. 'No, I was around two. When I would get cold, and I wanted to be held, I'd combine the two ideas. I used to say, "Cold me." It meant "Hold me, I'm cold." Friends can do that. Cold me, Alex.'

'Friends should,' I whispered back.

We cuddled on top of the covers and kissed a little more, until we both finally fell asleep. Merciful sleep.

I was the one who woke up first. It was 5:11 A.M. on the hotel room clock.

'You awake? Kate?' I whispered.

'Mmm hmmm. I'm awake *now*.'

'We're going back to the Gentleman's apartment,' I told her.

I called ahead and talked to the FBI agent in charge. I told him where to look, and what to look for.

75

Dr Will Rudolph's once orderly and pristine penthouse apartment had ceased to exist as such. The three-bedroom penthouse looked like a state-of-the-art crime lab. It was a little past six when Kate and I arrived back there. I was pumped about my hunch.

'Did you dream about the Gentleman?' Kate wanted to know. 'Your hunch?'

'Uh huh. I was processing information. It's all processed now.'

A half-dozen or so FBI techies and LAPD homicide detectives were still on the scene. The latest Pearl Jam played from somebody's radio. The lead singer seemed to be in terrible pain. Dr Rudolph's wide-screen Mitsubishi TV was on, but with the sound turned off. One of the techies was eating an egg sandwich off greasy paper.

I went searching for an agent named Phil Becton, the FBI's suspect profiler. The Man. He had been called down from Seattle to gather all the available information on Rudolph, then match it against known data on other psychopaths. A profiler, if he or she is good, is actually invaluable in an investigation of this kind. I'd heard from Kyle Craig that Becton was 'spooky good.' He had been a sociology professor at Stanford before he joined the Bureau.

'You fully awake? Ready for this?' Becton asked when I finally located him in the master bedroom. He was at least six four, with another three inches of wiry red hair. Plastic evidence pouches and manila evidence envelopes were spread all around the bedroom. Becton wore one pair of eyeglasses, and had another pair on a chain around his neck.

'I'm not sure if I'm awake,' I told Becton. 'This is Dr Kate McTiernan.'

'Nice to meet you.' Becton shook hands with her, studying Kate's face at the same time. She was data for him. He seemed a weird man, perfect for his job.

'See there,' he said, pointing across the bedroom. The FBI had already taken apart the Gentleman's clothes closet. 'You were right on the money. We found a fake wall that Dr Rudolph Hess built behind his skinny clothes closet. There's about a foot and a half of extra space in there.'

The clothes closet for his suits had been too skinny and peculiar. I'd made the connection in that strange region of the edge of sleep. The closet had to be his hiding spot. It was a shrine, but not to his expensive suits.

'That's where he kept his souvenirs?' I made an educated guess.

'You got it. Little waist-high refrigerator-freezer back there. It's where he kept the body parts he collected.' Becton pointed to the sealed containers. 'Sunny Ozawa's feet. Fingers. Two ears with different earrings, two separate victims.'

'What else was in his collection?' I asked Phil Becton. I

wasn't in a hurry to look at feet, ears, fingers. His trophies from the murders of young girls around L.A.

'Well, as you'd expect from reading the murder-scene briefs, he likes to collect their underwear as well. Freshly worn panties, bras, pantyhose, a woman's T-shirt that says Dazed and Confused and still smells of Opium perfume. He likes to keep photographs, a few locks of auburn hair. He's so *neat*. He kept each specimen in its own plastic bag. One through thirty-one. He's labeled them with numbers.'

'Preserve the smells,' I muttered. 'The sandwich bags.'

Becton nodded, and he also grinned like a gawky, goofy teenager. Kate looked at the two of us as if we were both a little nuts, which we were.

'There's something else I think you should see, though. This, you're going to appreciate. Come over to my office.'

On a plain wooden table next to the bed were some of the Gentleman's treasures and souvenirs. Most of the paraphernalia had already been marked. It takes an organized task force to catch an organized killer.

'Spooky good' Phil Becton emptied out one of the five-by-seven-inch envelopes so I could see the contents. A single photograph fell out of the envelope. It was of a young male, probably in his early twenties. The condition of the photo, as well as the male's clothing, suggested it had been taken years earlier. Eight to ten years was my quick guess.

The hair on my neck was starting to rise. I cleared my throat. 'Who's this supposed to be?'

'Do you know this man, Dr McTiernan?' Phil Becton turned to Kate. 'Ever see this man before?'

'I . . . don't know,' Kate answered Phil Becton. She swallowed hard. The Gentleman's bedroom was quiet. Outside on the streets of Los Angeles, the orangish-red glow of morning had fallen over the city.

Becton handed me metal tweezers that he kept handy in his breast pocket. 'Flip it over for *all the vital stats*. Just like those Topps baseball cards we used to collect as kids. At least we did in Portland.'

I figured that Becton had collected a lot more than baseball cards in his life and times. I carefully turned over the photo.

A neatly handwritten legend was on the back. It reminded me of the way Nana Mama identified every single old photo in our house. 'Sometimes you forget who people are, Alex. Even people in photographs with you,' she told me. 'You don't believe me, but you'll see as time passes you by.'

I didn't think that Will Rudolph was likely to forget the person in the picture, but he had handwritten a legend all the same. My head was spinning a little. We finally had an unbelievable break in the case. I was holding it right under my nose with crime-scene tweezers.

Dr Wick Sachs, the handwriting on the photo read.

A doctor, I thought. *Another doctor. Imagine that.*

Durham, North Carolina, the legend continued.

He was from the Research Triangle area. He was from the South.

Casanova, Rudolph had written.

PART FOUR

Twinning

76

Naomi Cross was awakened by rock music blaring from the wall speakers. She recognized the Black Crowes. The overhead lights flashed on and off. She jumped out of bed and quickly pulled on wrinkled jeans and a turtleneck and ran to the door of her room.

The loud music and boldly flashing lights signaled a meeting. *Something terrible has happened*, she thought. Her heart was in free fall.

Casanova kicked open the door. He had on tight jeans, engineering boots, a black leather jacket. His mask was painted with chalky streaks that resembled lightning. He was in a frenzy. Naomi had never seen him look this angry.

'Living room! Now!' he shouted as he grabbed her arm and yanked her out of the room.

The floor of the narrow corridor felt damp and cold under Naomi's bare feet. She had forgotten to put on her sandals. It was too late to go back for them.

She fell in step with a young woman. The two of them walked nearly parallel to each other. Naomi was surprised when the woman quickly turned her head and stared at her. The eyes were large and deep green. Naomi had given her the name *Green Eyes*.

'I'm Kristen Miles.' The woman spoke in a hurried whisper. 'We have to do something to help ourselves. We have to take a chance. And *soon*.'

Naomi said nothing in response, but she reached out and lightly grazed the back of Green Eyes' hand.

Contact was forbidden, but just to touch another human inside the horrifying prison was necessary now. Naomi looked into the woman's eyes and saw only defiance. No fear. That made her feel so good. Both of them had kept themselves together – somehow.

The captive women in the hallway glanced furtively at Naomi as they shuffled in silence toward the living room in the strange house. Their eyes were dark and hollow. Some of them didn't wear makeup anymore and their appearance frightened Naomi. It was getting worse every day, ever since Kate McTiernan had managed to escape somehow.

Casanova had brought a new girl to the house. Anna Miller. Anna was breaking the house rules, just as Kate McTiernan had done. Naomi had heard the woman's cries for help and Casanova might have heard them, too. It was difficult to figure out when he would be away. He kept very odd hours.

Lately, Casanova was leaving them without any contact for longer and longer periods. He wasn't going to let them go. That was one of his lies. Naomi knew it was getting dangerous for all the women.

Naomi sensed something desperate in the air. She could

hear cries of alarm up ahead, and she tried to calm her own mounting fears and panic. She had lived in the projects of Washington. She'd seen horror before. Two of her friends had been murdered by the time she was sixteen.

Then she heard him. His voice was strange and high-pitched. He was a madman. 'Come right in, ladies. Don't be shy. Don't stop in the doorway! Come in, come in. Join the party, the *swinging* soirée.'

Casanova was yelling above the testosterone rock 'n' roll that blared through the halls. Naomi closed her eyes for a brief moment. She tried to collect herself. *I don't want to see this, whatever it is, but I have to.*

She finally entered the room. Her body began to shake. What she saw was worse than anything she remembered from the projects. She had to push her fist into her mouth to keep from screaming out.

A long, slender body twirled in lazy circles from the ceiling beams. The woman was naked except for silver-blue stockings running up her long legs. A blue high-heeled shoe dangled from one foot. The other shoe had dropped to the floor and lay on its side.

The girl's lips were already purplish-blue, and her tongue protruded sideways from them. The eyes were stretched wide with terror and pain. *It must be Anna*, Naomi thought. A girl had been calling out for help. She'd broken the house rules. She said her name was Anna Miller. *Poor Anna. Whoever you were before he kidnapped you.*

Casanova turned off the music and spoke calmly from behind his mask; he talked as if nothing much had happened. 'Her name is Anna Miller, and she did this to herself. Do you all understand what I'm saying? She was plotting through the walls, talking about escaping. There is no escape from here!'

Naomi shuddered. *No, there is no escape from hell*, she thought. She looked at Green Eyes and nodded her head. Yes, they had to take a chance, and soon.

77

The gentleman stopped to play the game in Stoneman Lake, Arizona. It was a beautiful morning for it. It was crisp and cool and the smell of a wood fire was in the air.

He was parked in woods among the boulders, just off the rural road. No one could see him. He sat there and thought about the way this should go down as he watched a cozy, white-shingled family house through hooded lids. He could actually feel the beast taking over. The transformation. The strange *passion* that accompanied it. *Jekyll and Hyde*.

He saw a man leave the house and get into a silver Ford Aerostar. The husband seemed in a hurry, probably late for work. The wife was alone now, maybe still in bed. Her name was Juliette Montgomery.

At a little past eight, he carried an empty gas container up to the house. If anybody happened to see him, no problem. He needed fuel for his rented car.

No one saw him. Probably nobody around for miles.

The Gentleman climbed the front porch steps. He paused for a moment, then gently turned the doorknob. He found it amazing that people didn't lock their doors in Stoneman Lake.

God, he loved this . . . lived for it . . . his times as Mr Hyde.

Juliette was making breakfast for herself. He could hear her half humming, half singing as he made his way across the living room. The aroma and the crackling sound of bacon frying made him think of his family's house in Asheville.

His father had been the original gentleman. Army colonel and proud and arrogant about it. Inflexible asshole who was never pleased about anything his son did. Big fan of the thick leather belt to instill discipline. Liked to scream at the top of his lungs as he beat the shit out of him. Raised the perfect son. High school standout scholar and athlete. Phi Beta Kappa undergrad. High honors in Duke medical school. Human monster.

He watched Juliette Montgomery from the doorway that led into her spotlessly clean kitchen. The window shades were up and the room was flooded with sunlight. She was still singing . . . an old Jimi Hendrix song called 'Castles Made of Sand.' Unexpected tune from the pretty lady.

He loved watching her like this – when she thought she was alone. Singing something she'd probably be embarrassed to in front of him. Carefully laying out her three strips of bacon on a paper towel that came close to matching the beige-and-brown kitchen wallpaper.

Juliette wore a sheer white cottony negligee that fluttered around her thighs as she moved between the stove and table. She was in her mid-twenties. Long dancer's legs. Nicely tanned. Bare feet on the kitchen linoleum. Auburn hair she'd bothered to brush before coming down to make her breakfast.

A set of knives in a butcher-block holder sat on the counter. He took out the cleaver. The knife made a soft ringing noise as it lightly struck a stainless steel pot on the counter.

She turned at the sound. Very lovely in profile. Freshly scrubbed, radiant. Juliette liked herself, too. He could tell that she did.

'Who are you? What are you doing in my house?'

The words came out in small gasps. Her face was as pale as her negligee.

Now move fast, he told himself.

He grabbed Juliette and held the cleaver up high. Shades of Hitchcock's *Psycho* and also *Frenzy*. High-concept melodrama.

'Don't make me hurt you. It's all in your control,' he said softly.

She stopped the scream before it got out of her mouth, but *the scream was in her eyes*. He loved the look on Juliette's face. Lived for it.

'I won't hurt you as long as you don't do anything to hurt me. Are we all right so far? Are we clear as a bell?'

She nodded her head curtly. A couple of nods. Her blue-green eyes were tilted up strangely. She was afraid to move her head too much for fear he'd slash her.

She sighed. Amazing. She seemed to trust him a little. His voice had that effect on people. His style and fine manners. Mr Hyde. *The Gentleman Caller*.

She was looking deeply into his eyes, searching for some explanation. He had seen that questioning look so many times before. Why? it said.

'I'm going to take your panties off now. No doubt this has been done for you before, so there's no reason to panic.

You have the softest, nicest skin. I mean that,' said the Gentleman.

The cleaver slashed quickly.

'I like you, Juliette, I really do . . . as much as I'm able to like anyone,' the Gentleman said in his softest voice.

78

Kate McTiernan was home again. Home again, home again, jiggitty-jig. First thing she did was to call her sister Carole Anne, who lived far away in Maine now. Then she called a few close friends in Chapel Hill. She reassured them that she was perfectly all right.

That was total bullshit, of course. She knew that she wasn't anything close to all right, but why cause them to worry? It wasn't Kate's way to inconvenience other people with her unsolvable problems.

Alex didn't want her to go back to her house, but she had to. This was *where she lived*. She tried to calm herself a little, to slow down the big bad world in her head, at least. She drank wine and watched late-night TV. She hadn't done that in years. Centuries!

She was missing Alex Cross already, and more than she wanted to admit to herself. Staying home and watching TV was a good test, but she was failing miserably. She was such a schlump sometimes.

She had developed – *what?* – a schoolgirl *crush* on Alex? He was strong, smart, funny, kind. He loved children, and was even in touch with the child in himself. He had a sculpted body, fabulous bone structure, a sensational torso, also. Yes, she had a crush on Alex Cross.

Understandable; nice. Only maybe it was more than a crush. Kate wanted to call Alex at his hotel in Durham. She picked up the phone a couple of times. *No!* She wouldn't let herself do it. Nothing was going to happen between her and Alex Cross.

She was an intern, and she wasn't getting any younger. He lived in Washington with his two children and his grandmother. Besides, they were *too much* alike, and it wouldn't work out. He was a willful black man; she was an extremely willful white woman. He was a homicide detective . . . but he was also sensitive and sexy and generous. She didn't care whether he was black, green, or purple. He made her laugh; he made her as happy as a clam in deep wet sand.

But nothing was going to happen between her and Alex.

She would just sit here in her scary apartment. Drink her cheap Pinot Noir. Watch her bad, semiromantic Hollywood movie. Be afraid. Be a little horny. Let it get worse. That's what she would do, dammit. Build her character.

She had to admit she was frightened to be in her own house, though. She hated that feeling. She wanted all of this shitty madness to stop, but it wouldn't. Not even close. There were still two horrifying monsters on the loose out there.

She kept hearing creepy noises all around her in the house. Old creaking wood. Banging shutters. Wind chimes she had put on an old elm tree outside. The chimes reminded her of the cabin in Big Sur. They had to come down tomorrow – if not sooner.

Kate finally fell asleep with the wineglass, which was really an old Flintstones jelly glass, balanced in her lap. The glass was a holy relic from the house in West Virginia. She and her sisters used to fight over it sometimes at breakfast.

The glass tipped and spilled onto her bedcovers. It didn't matter. Kate was dead to the world. For one night at least.

She didn't usually drink much. The Pinot Noir hit her like the freight trains that used to rumble through Birch when she was a kid. She woke at 3:00 A.M. with a throbbing headache, and hurried into her bathroom, where she got sick.

Images of *Psycho* flashed through her mind as she bent over the sink. She thought of Casanova in the house again. He was in the bathroom, wasn't he? *No – of course no one was there . . . please, make this stop. Make this end . . . right . . . now!*

She went back to bed and crawled under the covers. She heard the wind rattling the shutters. Heard those stupid chimes. She thought about death – her mother, Susanne, Marjorie, Kristin. All gone now. Kate McTiernan pulled the blanket over her head. She felt like a little girl again, afraid of the bogeyman. Okay, she could handle that.

Trouble was, she could *see* Casanova and the horrifying death mask whenever she closed her eyes. She held a secret thought buried in the center of her chest: *He was coming for her again, wasn't he?*

At seven in the morning her phone rang. It was Alex.

'Kate, I was in his house,' he said.

79

Around ten the night we returned from California, I drove to the Hope Valley residential area of Durham. I went alone to see Casanova. Doctor Detective Cross was back in the saddle again.

There were three clues that I considered essential to solving the case. I reviewed them again as I drove. There was the simple fact that they both committed 'perfect crimes.' There was the aspect of twinning, the codependence of Casanova and the Gentleman. There was the mystery of the disappearing house.

Something had to come from one, or all, of those bits of information. Maybe something was about to happen in the Hope Valley suburb of Durham. I hoped so.

I drove slowly along Old Chapel Hill Road until I reached a formal, white-brick, portal-type entrance into the upscale Hope Valley estates. I got the feeling that I wasn't supposed to intrude beyond the gate, that just maybe I was the first black man not in workingman's overalls to pass through here.

I knew I was taking a chance, but I had to see where Dr Wick Sachs lived. I needed to *feel* things about him, needed to know him better, and in a big hurry.

The streets of Hope Valley didn't run in straight lines. The road I was on didn't have curbs or gutters, and there were not many streetlamps. The neighborhood was unpleasantly hilly, and as I drove I began to have the sense of being lost, of moving in a great looping circle. The houses were mostly up-scale Southern Gothic, old and expensive. The notion of the killer next door had never been more powerful.

Dr Wick Sachs lived in a stately red-brick house set back on one of the highest hills.

The shutters were painted white, matching the gutters. The house looked too expensive for a university professor, even one at Duke, the 'Harvard of the South.'

The windows were all dark and looked as shiny as slate. The only lights came from a single brass carriage lamp dangling over the front door.

I already knew that Wick Sachs had a wife and two small children. His wife was a registered nurse at Duke University Hospital. The FBI had checked her credentials. She had an excellent reputation, and everyone spoke very highly of her. The Sachses' daughter, Faye Anne, was seven; and their son, Nathan, was ten.

I figured that the FBI was probably watching me as I drove up to the Sachses' house, but I didn't much care. I wondered if Kyle Craig was with them . . . he was deeply involved in the grisly case, almost as much as I was. Kyle had also gone to Duke. Was this case personal for him, too? How personal?

My eyes very slowly ran up and down the front of the house, then along the well-tended grounds. Everything was extremely orderly, actually quite beautiful, perfect as could be.

I had already learned that human monsters can live anywhere; that some of the clever ones chose ordinary all-American-looking houses. Just like the house I was examining now. The monsters are literally everywhere. There is an epidemic running out of control in America, and the statistics are frightening. We have nearly seventy-five percent of the human hunters. Europe has almost all the rest, led by England, Germany, and France. Mass murderers are changing the face of modern homicide investigations in every American city, village, and town.

I studied everything I could about the house's exterior. The southeast side had what was known as a 'Florida room.' There was a patio, which was living-room size. The lawn was fescue, and it was extremely well kept. There was no moss, no crabgrass, no weeds.

The cobbled-brick walkway from the driveway was carefully edged, and not a single stray blade of grass peeked through the stones. The bricks of the walk perfectly matched the bricks of the house.

Perfect.

Meticulous.

As I sat in the car, my head was pounding from too much tension and stress. I kept the motor running, in case the family Sachs suddenly came home.

I knew what I wanted to do, what I had to do, what I'd been planning to do for the last few hours. *I needed to break into his house.* I wondered if the FBI would try to stop me, but I didn't think they would. I believed that maybe they actually wanted me to break inside and look around. We knew very little about Dr Wick Sachs. I still wasn't officially involved in the Casanova manhunt, and I could try things that the others couldn't. I was supposed to be the 'loose cannon.' That was my deal with Kyle Craig.

Scootchie was out there someplace, at least I prayed that she was still alive. I hoped that all the missing women were alive. *His harem. His odalisques. His collection of beautiful, special women.*

I shut off the motor and took a deep breath before I climbed out of the car.

I walked quickly across the springy lawn in a crouch. I remembered something that Satchel Paige used to say: 'Keep the juices flowing by jangling around gently as you move.' I was *jangling*.

Shaped boxwoods and azaleas ran along the front of the house. A child's red bike with silver streamers on the handle-bars lay on its side near the porch.

Nice, I was thinking as I hurried along. *Too nice.*

Casanova's child's bike.

Casanova's respectable house in the suburbs.

Casanova's fake, perfect life. His perfect disguise. His big, ugly joke on all of us. Right in the city of Durham. His middle finger extended to the world.

I carefully made my way around to the patio, which was built with white tile. It was bordered with the same brick as the house and the front walk. I noticed that creeping tendrils had invaded the red-brick walls. Maybe he wasn't so perfect, after all.

I quickly crossed the patio, moving toward the Florida room. There was no turning back now. I'd done a little breaking and entering in the name of duty before this. That didn't make it right, just easier.

I broke a small windowpane in a door and let myself in.

Nothing. Not a sound. I didn't think that Wick Sachs would have any use for an alarm system. I seriously doubted that he wanted the Durham police to investigate a breaking and entering.

The first thing I noticed was the familiar cloying smell of lemon furniture polish. Respectability. Civility. Order. It was all a façade, a perfectly designed *mask*.

I was inside the monster's house.

80

The house was as neat and orderly as the outside grounds. Maybe even more so. *Nice, nice, much too nice.*

I was nervous and afraid, but that didn't matter anymore. I was used to living with the feelings of fear and uncertainty. Carefully, I roamed from room to room. Nothing seemed out of place, even with two small children living there. *Strange, strange, very strange.*

The house reminded me a little of Rudolph's apartment in Los Angeles. It was as if no one really lived there. *Who are you? Show me who you really are, fucker. This house isn't the real you, is it? Does anyone know you without your masks? The Gentleman does, doesn't he?*

The kitchen was right out of *Country Living* magazine. Antiques and other beautiful 'things' were in almost every room.

In a small study, the professor's notes and papers were strewn everywhere, covering every available surface. *He's supposed to be very orderly and neat*, I thought, and stored the conflicting data. *Who was he?*

I was searching for something specific, but I didn't know exactly where to look. Down in the basement I saw a heavy oak door. It was unlocked. It led into a small furnace room. I searched the room carefully. On the far side of the furnace room, I found another wooden door. It looked like a door to a closet, to some small, insignificant space.

The second door was closed with a hook, which I removed as quietly as I could. I wondered if there could be more rooms in here? Maybe an underground space? Maybe the house of horror? Or a tunnel?

I pushed open the wooden door. Pitch-blackness. I switched on the lights, and entered a single room that must have been twenty-five by forty. My heart skipped a beat. My knees got weak and I felt a little sick.

There were no women in here, no harem, but I had found Wick Sachs's fantasy room. It was right in his house. Hidden in a secret corner of his basement. The room didn't fit in with the design of the rest of the house. *He had built this room specially for himself. He liked to build things, to be creative, didn't he?*

The special room was laid out like a library. There was a heavy oak desk, and two red leather club chairs were on either side of it. The four walls of bookcases were filled with books and magazines from floor to ceiling. My blood pressure must have soared fifty points. I tried to be still inside, but I couldn't.

This was a collection of pornography and erotica, the most extraordinary I had ever seen or even heard described. There were at least a thousand books in the room. I read titles as I quickly roamed from wall to wall, shelf to shelf.

Strangest Sex Acts in Modes of Love of All Races –
Illustrated Cherries. Printed for the Erotica Biblion Society
of New York Humiliations of Anastasia and Pearl
The Harem Omnibus: a reader
Until She Screams
The Hymen. A Medico-Legal Study in Rape

I concentrated and tried to focus on what I needed to do here. First, I tried to quiet the roaring noise in my head.

I wanted to leave Wick Sachs a sign that I had been here; that I knew about his dirty little secret place; that he had no more secrets. I wanted him to experience the same kind of pressure, stress, and fear that all of us were going through. I wanted to hurt Dr Wick Sachs. I hated him beyond anything I could have imagined.

On the desk was a copy of a pamphlet from a supplier of erotic books and magazines: *Nicholas J. Soberhagen, 1115 Victory Boulevard, Staten Island, N.Y. By Appointment.* I made a quick note. I wanted to hurt Nicholas Soberhagen, too.

Sachs, or someone else, had checked off several books on the pamphlet's pages. I leafed quickly through it, reading with an ear cocked for sounds of a car on the street. Time was short now.

The Special Orders of St Theresa. Not to be missed! This reprint of an extremely rare original edition was issued in the 1880s. Here are actual recollections on the proper use of the rod at a Spanish nunnery outside Madrid.

The Lovemaster. Lively sexual adventures of a dancer in Berlin; the various sex manias she encounters. For every serious collector!

Release. An interpretive first novel based on the actual and imagined life of the French serial murderer, Gilles de Rais.

I scanned the rows of wooden shelves directly behind the work desk. How long should I push my luck inside the house? It was getting late for Sachs and his family to be out. I stopped at a shelf behind his chair.

My heart tightened when I saw several books on Casanova! I read the titles under my breath.

Memoirs by Casanova
Casanova. 102 Erotic Engravings
The Most Wonderful Nights of Love of Casanova

I thought of the two small children who lived in this house, Nathan and Faye Anne, and I felt badly for them. Their father, Dr Wick Sachs, had his delirious, evil fantasies in this room. Stimulated by his dirty books, his collection of erotica, he decided which fantasy to act out in real life, didn't he? I could feel Sachs's presence in this room. I was getting to know him, finally.

Was it possible that he kept the women somewhere nearby? Somewhere in town, where we would never expect to look? Was that why none of the searches had uncovered the house of horror? Was it somewhere right in suburban, highly respectable Durham?

Was Naomi close by, waiting for someone to find her? The longer she was kept, the more dangerous her situation would become.

I heard a noise upstairs, and listened closely, but there was no other sound. It might have been an electrical appliance, or just the wind, or a loose part in my skull.

It was past time to get out of the house. I hurried upstairs and back out across the patio. I had been tempted to draw *a cross* on the pamphlet on Sachs's desk, to leave my mark. I resisted the impulse. He knew who I was. He had contacted me as soon as I arrived in Durham. But I was the one in heat now!

I was back in my hotel room at a little past midnight. I felt empty and numb. Adrenaline was pumping through my body at a furious rate.

The phone rang almost as soon as I walked in the door. A nasty, insistent hotel phone ring that demanded to be picked up.

'Who the *hell*?' I muttered. I was half crazed by now. I wanted to race out into the Southern night, to search helter-skelter for Naomi. I wanted to grab Dr Wick Sachs and beat the truth out of him. *Whatever it takes*.

'Yes. Who is this?' I spoke a little too loudly into the phone.

It was Kyle Craig.

'Well?' he began. 'What did you find out?'

81

Morning had broken again; nothing had really changed about the ghoulish investigation. Kate was still my partner in crime. That was her choice, but I approved. She knew Casanova better than the rest of us combined.

She and I spied on the big, beautiful Sachs house from the triangle of dense fir woods off Old Chapel Hill Road. We had already seen Wick Sachs once that morning. Our lucky day.

The Beast was up bright and early. He was tall and professorial-looking, with sandy blonde hair brushed straight back and horn-rimmed glasses. He appeared to have a very good build.

He had ventured out to the porch at around seven to pick up the Durham paper. The headline read: *Casanova Watch Continues*. The local newspaper editors could have had no idea, no clue, how accurate those words were.

Sachs glanced at the front page, then casually folded it under his arm. Nothing of interest for him today. Another hohum day at the serial-killer office.

At a little before eight, he came out with his children in tow. He had a big toothy smile turned on for the kids. The good father was taking them to school.

His little boy and girl were outfitted as if they belonged in the front window of Gap For Kids or Esprit. They looked like adorable little dolls. The FBI would follow Sachs and the children to the school.

'Isn't this a little unusual, Alex? Two surveillance jobs in a row like this?' Kate asked me. She was analytical and her mind never stopped working all the angles. She was as obsessive about the case as I was. That morning she was dressed down as usual. Tatty jeans, a navy blue T-shirt, sneakers. Her beauty shone through, anyway. She couldn't hide it.

'Investigations of repeat killers are almost always unusual. This one is stranger than most,' I admitted. I talked about the twinning angle again. Two badly twisted men with no one to talk to, to share with. No one to understand, until they met each other. Then a powerful connection between the two killers. Kate was a twin, but she'd experienced a benign form of twinning. With Casanova and the Gentleman, it was something else.

Wick Sachs came right back from the drop-off at school. We could hear him whistling cheerfully as he strolled to his perfect house. Kate and I had talked about the fact that he was a doctor after all, though a doctor of philosophy.

Nothing much happened for the next few hours. There was no sign of Sachs, or his wife, the lovely Mrs Casanova.

Wick Sachs left the house on the hill again at eleven. He was blowing off his teaching classes today. He had already missed his ten o'clock tutorial, according to the schedule I had from Dean Lowell. Why was that? What slick game was he playing now?

There were two cars in the circular driveway. He chose the burgundy one, a Jaguar XJS convertible with a tan top, twelve-cylinder engine. The other car was a black Mercedes sedan. Not too shabby on a professor's salary.

He was heading out now, hitting the road. Was he going to visit his girls?

82

We followed Wick Sachs's sporty Jaguar onto Old Chapel Hill Road. We eased through Hope Valley, passing very substantial houses that had been built in the twenties and thirties. Sachs didn't seem to be in a hurry.

So far, this was his game. We didn't know the rules, or even what game he was playing.

Casanova.

The Beast of the Southeast.

Kyle Craig was still working on a financial investigation of Sachs with Internal Revenue. Kyle also had half-a-dozen agents filling in all the dots that might connect Sachs and Will Rudolph in the past. The two had definitely been class-mates at Duke. High honor students. Phi Beta Kappa. They had known each other but weren't close friends in school, at least they didn't seem to have been. Actually, Kyle had been at Duke then, too, in the Law School. Phi Beta himself.

When had the actual twinning taken place? How had the strong, freakish bond occurred? Something wasn't making sense to me about Rudolph and Sachs yet.

'What if he lets that XJS out?' Kate said as we discreetly followed the monster to what we hoped was his lair in the woods, his harem, his 'disappearing house.' We were tailing Sachs in my old Porsche.

'I doubt he wants to draw a lot of attention to himself,' I told her. Although the XJS and the Mercedes kind of worked against that theory. 'Besides, a Jaguar isn't much of a test for a Porsche.'

'Even a Porsche from another century?' Kate asked.

'Ho,' I answered her, 'ho.'

Sachs drove down Interstate 85, then turned onto 40. He got off at the exit for Chapel Hill. We followed him for another two miles through town. He finally stopped and parked near the University of North Carolina campus on Franklin Street.

'All of this is making me feel so weird, Alex. A professor at Duke University. A wife and two beautiful children,' Kate said. 'The night he grabbed me, he probably followed me off the campus. He watched me. I think he chose me *right here*.'

I glanced over at Kate. 'You okay?' I asked her. 'Tell me if you're not up to this.'

Kate looked at me. Her eyes were intense, troubled. 'Let's get this the hell over with. Let's get him today. Deal?'

'Deal,' I agreed.

'We've got you, Butt-Head,' Kate muttered into the car windshield.

The quaint and pretty Chapel Hill street was already busy at quarter to twelve. College kids and profs were sliding in and out of the Carolina Coffee Shop, Peppers Pizza, the newly rebuilt Intimate Bookstore. All the favorite Franklin Street haunts were doing a pretty good business. The college-town atmosphere was appealing; it took me back to my days at Johns Hopkins. Cresmont Avenue in Baltimore.

Kate and I were able to follow Wick Sachs from about a block and a half away. It would be easy for him to lose us now, I knew. Would he run to the house in the woods? Would he go to see his girls? Was Naomi still there?

He could easily duck into the Record Bar, or into Spanky's restaurant on the corner. Come out a side door and disappear. A game of cat and mouse had begun. His game; his rules. Always his rules, so far.

'He seems too smug, too self-satisfied,' I said as we tailed along at a reasonable distance. He hadn't even turned to see if he was being followed. He looked like a tweedy, jaunty prof on a lunchtime errand. Maybe that was all this was.

'You still okay?' I checked on Kate again.

She was watching Sachs like a scrapyard dog with a grudge to settle. I remembered that she took karate lessons somewhere near here in Chapel Hill. 'Mmm, hmm. Lot of bad memories stirred up, though. Scene of the crime and all that,' Kate muttered.

Wick Sachs finally stopped in front of the nicely retro Varsity Theatre in downtown Chapel Hill. He stood next to a community billboard covered with all sorts of handwritten notices and posters, mostly aimed at university students and faculty members.

'Why would that scum be going to a movie?' Kate whispered, sounding more incensed than ever.

'Maybe because he likes to escape, as in *sublimate*. This is the secret life of Wick Sachs. We're watching it.'

'I'd kind of like to go after him right now. Rumble,' Kate said.

'Yeah, me too. Me too, Kate.'

I had noticed the cluttered community billboard on one

of my walks here before. There were several notices about missing persons in the Chapel Hill area. *Missing students.* All of them were women. It struck me that this was a cruel plague that had come to the community, and no one had been able to do anything to stop it. No one had the cure.

Wick Sachs seemed to be waiting for something or somebody. 'Who the hell is he going to meet here in Chapel Hill?' I muttered.

'Will Rudolph,' Kate said without missing a beat. 'His old school chum. His best friend.'

I'd thought about Rudolph coming back to North Carolina, actually. Twinning could be an almost physical addiction. In its negative form, it was based on codependency or enabling behavior. The two of them abducted beautiful women, and then tortured or killed them. Was that their shared secret? Or was there even more to it than that?

'He looks like Casanova would look without the mask,' Kate said. We had slipped inside a small cutesie-pie shop called School Kids. 'He has the same color hair. But why wouldn't he disguise his hair?' she muttered. 'Why only a mask?'

'Maybe the mask isn't a disguise at all? It might mean something different in his private fantasy world,' I suggested. 'It's possible that Casanova is his real persona. The mask, the whole human-sacrifice aura, the symbolism – all of that would be very important for him.'

Sachs was still waiting in front of the community billboard. Waiting for what? I had a gut feeling that something wasn't right with this picture. I sneaked a peek at him through the binoculars.

His face was unconcerned, almost serene. A day in the park for the vampire Lestat. I wondered if he might be high on some kind of drug. He certainly knew about sophisticated tranquilizers.

Behind him on the community board were all sorts of messages. I could read them with the binoculars.

Missing – Carolyn Eileen Devito
Missing – Robin Schwartz
Missing – Susan Pyle
Women for Jim Hunt for Governor
Women for Lt. Governor Laurie Garnier
The Mind Sirens at the Cave

All of a sudden, I had a possible answer. *Messages*!

Casanova was sending out a cruel message for us – for anyone who was watching him, anyone who dared to follow him.

I slammed my hand down hard against the dusty window-sill inside the small store.

'The son of a bitch is playing mind games!' I nearly shouted in the crowded shop where we were watching Wick Sachs. The elderly shopkeeper eyed me as if I were dangerous. I was dangerous.

'What's wrong?' Kate was suddenly peering over my shoulder, leaning her body against me, trying to see whatever it was that I saw up the street.

'It's the *poster* behind him. He's been standing under it for the past ten minutes. That's his message, Kate, to whoever's following him. That bright orange-and-yellow poster says it all.'

I handed her the binoculars. One poster on the bulletin board was larger and more prominent than the others. Kate read it out loud.

'Women and children are starving . . . as you walk by with loose change in your pocket. Please change your behavior now! You can actually save lives.'

83

'Oh, Jesus, Alex,' Kate spoke in a tense whisper. 'If he can't go out to the house they'll starve, and if he's followed he won't go out to the house. That's what he's telling us! Women are starving . . . change your behavior now.'

I wanted to take out Wick Sachs right there. I knew there was nothing we could do to him. Nothing legal, anyway. Nothing sane.

'Alex, look.' Kate sounded an alarm. She handed me the glasses.

A woman had come up to Sachs. I squinted through the binoculars. The noonday sun was bright off shiny glass-and-metal surfaces up and down Franklin Street.

The woman was slender and attractive, but she was older than the women who had been abducted. She had on a black silky blouse, tight black leather slacks, black shoes. She was carrying a briefcase loaded with books and papers.

'She doesn't seem to fit his mold, his pattern,' I said to Kate. 'She looks in her late thirties.'

'I know her. I know who she is, Alex,' Kate whispered.

I looked at her. 'Who, for God's sake, Kate?'

'She's a professor in the English Department. Her name is Suzanne Wellsley. Some of the students call her "Runaround Sue." There's a joke about Suzanne Wellsley throwing her underwear against the wall, and it sticks.'

'They could tell the same joke about Dr Sachs,' I said. He had a nasty reputation as a rake on campus. He'd had the bad rep for years, but no disciplinary action was ever taken. More perfect crimes?

He and Ms Suzanne Wellsley kissed in front of the 'hunger' billboard. A tongue kiss, I could see as I watched through the binoculars. A very hot embrace, too, with no apparent concern about the public venue.

I had second thoughts about the 'message.' Maybe it was just a coincidence, only I didn't believe in coincidences anymore. Maybe Suzanne Wellsley was involved with the 'house' that Sachs kept. There could be others, too. Maybe this whole thing involved some kind of adult sex cult. I knew they existed; even in our nation's capital they existed and flourished.

The two of them walked casually a short way down crowded Franklin Street. In no apparent hurry. They were headed in our direction. Then they stopped at the Varsity Theatre ticket booth. They were holding hands. Cute as could be.

'Damn him. He *knows* he's being watched,' I said. 'What is his game?'

'She's looking this way. Maybe she knows, too. Hello, Suzanne. What the hell are you up to, dragon lady?'

They bought movie tickets, like any normal couple, and went inside. The theatre marquee advertised '*Roberto Benigni is Johnny Stecchino – riotous comedy.*' I wondered how Sachs could be in the mood for an Italian comedy. Was Casanova that cool? Yes, he probably was. Especially if this was all part of some plan of his.

'Is the movie marquee a message, too? What is he telling us, Alex?'

'That this is all a "riotous comedy" for him? It just might be,' I said.

'He does have a sense of humor, Alex. I can vouch for that. He was capable of laughing at his own bad jokes.'

I called Kyle Craig from a pay phone in a nearby Ben & Jerry's Ice Cream. I told him about the *woman and children are starving* poster. He allowed that it could be a message for us. Anything was possible with Casanova.

When I came out of the store, Sachs and Suzanne Wellsley were still inside the Varsity Theatre, presumably laughing riotously at the Italian actor Roberto Benigni. Or perhaps Sachs was laughing at us? *Women and children are starving.*

Just past two-thirty, Sachs and Dr Wellsley came out of the Varsity Theatre. They strolled back to the corner of Franklin and Columbus. The half-block walk seemed to take ten minutes. They ducked inside the ever-popular Spanky's, where they had a late lunch.

'Isn't this sweet. Young love,' Kate said with a hiss in her voice. 'Damn him. And damn her, too. Damn Spanky's for giving them food and grog.'

They sat near the front window inside the restaurant. On purpose? They held hands at their table and kissed a few times. Casanova the Lover? A lunchtime tryst with another professor? None of it made any sense yet.

At three-thirty they left Spanky's restaurant and walked the half-block back to the message board. They kissed again, but this time with more restraint, and finally parted. Sachs drove back to his house in Hope Valley. Wick Sachs was definitely playing with us. His own game, for his own private pleasure.

Rat and cat.

84

Kate and I decided to have a late supper at a place called Frog and the Redneck in downtown Durham. She said we had to have a couple of hours' break from the action. I knew she was right.

Kate wanted to go home first, and asked me to call for her in a couple of hours. I wasn't prepared for the Kate who opened the door of her apartment. It wasn't Kate's usual *bas couture* look. She had on a beige linen sheath with a flowered blouse worn as a jacket. Her long brown hair was tied back with a bright yellow scarf.

'My Sunday-go-to-eatin' clothes,' Kate said with a conspiratorial wink. 'Except I can never afford to go out to eat on my post-med-school budget. Occasionally KFC or Arby's.'

'You have a hot date tonight?' I asked her in my usual kidding tone. I wondered who was kidding whom, though.

She casually took my arm in the crook of hers. 'As a matter of fact, maybe I do. You look nice tonight. Very dashing, very cool.'

I had abandoned my usual *bas couture* look, too. I'd decided on dashing and cool instead.

I don't remember much about the car ride to the Durham restaurant, except that we talked all the way. We never had any trouble talking. I don't exactly remember the meal, except that it was very good regional/continental grub. I have the recollection of Muscovy duck, of blueberries and plums in whipped cream.

What I remember most clearly is Kate sitting with one arm propped on the table, her face resting easily on the back of her hand. A very nice picture-portrait. I remember Kate taking off the yellow scarf at one point during dinner. 'Too much,' she said and grinned.

'I have a new pet theory, theory du jour, about the two of us. I think it's right. Do you want to hear it?' she asked me. She was in a good mood, in spite of the harrowing and frustrating investigation. We both were.

'Nah,' said the wiseguy in me, the part afraid of too much in the way of emotions. Lately, anyway

Kate wisely ignored me and went on with her theory. 'I'll start . . . Alex, we're both really, really afraid of attachments right now in our lives. That's obvious. We're both *too* afraid, I think.' She was carefully leading the way. She sensed this was difficult territory for me, and she was right.

I sighed. I didn't know if I wanted to get into any of this right now, but I plunged ahead. 'Kate, I haven't told you much about Maria . . . We were very much in love when she died. It was like that between us for six years. This isn't selective memory on my part. I used to tell myself, "God I'm unbelievably lucky I found this person." Maria felt the same way.' I smiled. 'Or so she told me. So yes, I *am* afraid of attachments. Mostly I'm afraid of losing someone I love that much again.'

'I'm afraid of losing someone else, too. Alex.' Kate said in a soft voice. I could barely hear her words. Sometimes she seemed shy, and it was touching. 'There's a magical line in *The Pawnbroker*, magical to me, anyway. "Everything I loved was taken away from me, and I did not die."'

I took her hand and kissed it lightly. I felt an overwhelming tenderness toward Kate at that moment. 'I know the line,' I said.

I could see anxiety in her dark brown eyes. Maybe we both needed to take this thing forward, whatever was beginning to happen between us, whatever the risks might be.

'Can I tell you something else? One more true confession that doesn't come easily? This is a bad one,' she said.

'I want to hear it. Of course I do. Anything you want to tell me.'

'I'm afraid I'm going to die just like my sisters, that I'll get cancer, too. At my age, I'm a medical time bomb. Oh, Alex, I'm afraid to get close to someone, and then get sick on them.' Kate let out a long, deep breath. It was obviously a hard thing for her to say.

We held hands for a long time in the restaurant. We sipped port wine. We were both a little quiet, letting powerful new feelings wash over us, getting used to them.

After dinner we went back to her apartment in Chapel Hill. The first thing I did was to check around for uninvited houseguests. I had tried to talk her into a hotel room during the car ride, but, as usual, Kate said no. I remained paranoid about Casanova and his games.

'You're so damn stubborn,' I told her as we both checked all the doors and windows.

'Fiercely independent is a much better description,' Kate countered. 'It comes with the black belt in karate. Second degree. Watch yourself.'

'I am.' I laughed. 'I've also got eighty pounds on you.'

Kate shook her head. 'Won't be enough.'

'You're probably right.' I laughed out loud.

No one was hiding in the apartment on Old Ladies Lane. No one was there except the two of us. Maybe that was the scariest thing of all.

'Please don't run off now. Stay for a while. Unless you want to or have to,' Kate said to me. I was still standing in her kitchen. My hands were awkwardly jammed into my pockets.

'I've got nowhere I'd rather be,' I told her. I was feeling a little nervous and keyed up.

'I have a bottle of Château de la Chaize. I think that's the name. It only cost nine bucks, but it's decent wine. I bought it just for tonight, even though I didn't know it at the time.' Kate smiled, 'Three months ago when I made the purchase.'

We sat on Kate's couch in the living room. The place was neat but still funky. There were black-and-white photos on the walls of her sisters and her mother. Happier times for Kate. There was an amazing picture of her in her pink uniform at the Big Top Truck Stop, where she worked to pay her way through school. The waitressing job was part of the reason medical school had meant so much to her.

Maybe the wine made me tell Kate more about Jezzie Flanagan than I wanted to. It had been my only attempt at a serious attachment since Maria's death. Kate told me about her friend, Peter McGrath. History professor at the University of North Carolina. As she talked about Peter, I had the disturbing thought that maybe he was one suspect we had glossed over too quickly.

I couldn't leave the case alone, not even for one night. Maybe I was just trying to escape into my work again. Still, I made a mental note to check out Dr Peter McGrath a little more carefully.

Kate leaned in close to me on the couch. We kissed. Our mouths made a perfect fit. We had both done this before, kissed, but maybe never as well.

'Will you stay tonight? Please stay,' Kate whispered. 'Just this one night, Alex. We don't have to be scared about this, do we?'

'No, we don't have to be scared.' I whispered back. I felt like a schoolboy. Maybe that was okay, though.

I didn't know exactly what to do next, how to touch Kate, what to say, what *not* to do. I listened to the soft hum of her breathing. I let everything take its natural course.

We kissed again, as gently as I ever remember kissing anyone. We *were* both needy. But we were so vulnerable at that moment.

Kate and I went to her room. We held each other for a long time. We talked in whispers. We slept together. We didn't make love that night.

We were best friends. We didn't want to ruin it.

85

Naomi thought that she was finally losing the last pieces of her sanity. She had just *seen Alex kill Casanova*, even though she knew it hadn't really happened. She'd seen the shooting with her own eyes. She was hallucinating, and she couldn't stop the waves of delusion anymore.

She talked to herself sometimes. The sound of her own voice was comforting.

Naomi became quiet and thoughtful as she sat on an armchair in the darkened prison cell. Her violin was there, but she hadn't played it in days. She was afraid for a whole new reason now. *Maybe he wasn't coming back again.*

Maybe Casanova had been caught, and he wouldn't tell the police where he kept his captives. That was his ultimate leverage, wasn't it? That was his diabolical secret. His final edge and bargaining chip.

Maybe he'd already been killed in a shootout. How could the police hope to find her and the others if he was dead? *Something's happened*, she thought. *He hasn't been here in the last two days. Something has changed.*

She desperately wanted to see sunny blue skies, grass, the Gothic spires of the university, the layered terraces at the Sarah Duke Gardens, even the Potomac River in all of its muddy-gray glory back home in Washington.

She finally got up from the easy chair beside her bed. Very, very slowly, Naomi shuffled across the bare wooden floor, and stood by the locked door with her cheek pressed against the cool wood.

Should I do this crazy thing? she wondered. *Do I sign my own death warrant?*

Naomi could barely catch her breath. She listened for sounds in the mysterious house, any tiny, insignificant sound at all. The rooms had been soundproofed – but if you made enough noise, some sound carried through the eerie building.

She went over what she wanted to say, exactly what she would say.

My name is Naomi Cross. Where are you, Kristen? Green Eyes? I've decided that you're right. We have to do something . . . We have to do something together . . . He's not coming back.

Naomi had thought this moment through clearly, intelligently, she hoped – but she *couldn't say* the words out loud. She understood that plotting against him could mean her death.

Kristen Miles had called out to her a few times during the past twenty-four hours, but Naomi hadn't answered back. It was forbidden to talk, and she had seen his warning to them. The hanged woman a few days before. Poor Anna Miller. Another law student.

She couldn't hear anything, right now. White noise, that was all. The static of silence. The gentle hum of eternity. There was never even the sound of a car. Not a single backfire or a distant horn. Not even the boom of an airplane passing overhead.

Naomi had decided they must be underground, at least a couple of levels down into the earth. Had he built this underground complex, this sinplex? Had he thought it all through, dreamed about it, and then done it in some burst of psychopathic fury and energy? She thought that he had indeed.

She was getting herself ready to break the silence. She *had* to talk to Kristen, to Green Eyes. Her mouth was so dry. It felt like cotton wool. Naomi finally licked her lips.

'I would kill for a Coke, I would kill him for a Coke,' she whispered to herself. 'I *could* kill him given the chance.'

I could kill Casanova. I could commit a murder. I'm that far gone, aren't I? she thought and had to stifle a sob.

Naomi finally called out in a loud, strong voice. 'Kristen, can you hear me? Kristen? It's Naomi Cross!'

She was shivering, and warm tears streamed down her cheeks. She'd gone against him and his shitty, sacred rules.

Green Eyes called back immediately. The other woman's voice sounded so good. 'I can hear you, Naomi! I think I'm only a few doors away from you. I hear you fine. Keep talking. I'm sure he's not here, Naomi.'

Naomi didn't think anymore about what she was doing. Maybe he wasn't there; maybe he was. It didn't matter now.

'He's going to kill us,' she called back. 'Something's different about him! He's going to kill us for sure. If we're going to do anything, we have to do it the first chance we get.'

'Naomi's right!' Kristen's voice was slightly muffled, as if she were talking from the bottom of a well. 'Do you all hear Naomi? Of course you do!'

'I have one idea for everyone to consider.' Naomi spoke

even more loudly this time. She wanted to keep this communication going now. They all had to hear her, all the trapped women. 'The next time he gets us together – we have to go for it. If we rush him all at once, he might hurt some of us. But he can't stop all of us! What do you think?'

Just then the heavy wooden door to Naomi's room opened a crack. Light streamed in.

Naomi watched in stark horror as the door swung open. She couldn't move, couldn't speak a word.

Her heart beat painfully in her chest, *pounding*, and she couldn't get a breath. She felt as if she were about to die. He'd been there, waiting, listening all this time.

The door opened all the way.

'Hello, my name is Will Rudolph,' the tall, good-looking man in the doorway said in a pleasant voice. 'I like your plan very much, but I don't think it will work. Let me tell you why.'

86

I was at Raleigh-Durham International Airport at a little before nine on Wednesday morning. The cavalry was arriving. Fresh troops were here. Team Sampson was back in town.

In contrast to the creeping terror and paranoia that were present everywhere on the streets of Durham and Chapel Hill, the early-morning businesspeople at the airport seemed oblivious to harm in their dark, pressed suits, their floral print dresses from Neiman Marcus and Dillard. I liked that. Good for them. Denial is an approach.

I finally saw Sampson loping through the USAir gate with long, determined strides. I waved my local newspaper at him. It was characteristic of me to wave and for Man Mountain not to. He gave me a city-cool head nod, though. Bad to the bone. Just what the doctor ordered.

I brought Sampson up to speed while we drove from the airport to Chapel Hill.

I needed to check out the Wykagil River area. It was just another hunch of mine, but it could lead to something . . . like the location of the 'disappearing house.' I had enlisted

338

the help of Dr Louis Freed, a mentor and former teacher of Seth Samuel's. Dr Freed was a noted black historian on the Civil War, a period I was also interested in. Slaves and the Civil War in North Carolina . . . In particular, the Underground Railroad that had been used for slaves escaping to the North.

As we entered Chapel Hill, Sampson got to see for himself what the abductions and grisly murders had done to the once-peaceful college town. The nightmarish scene reminded me of a couple of my subway trips in New York City. It also reminded me a little of home, our nation's capital. The people of Chapel Hill now hurried along the picturesque streets with their heads down. They no longer made eye contact with one another, especially with strangers. Trust had been replaced by fear and terror. The sweet small-townness had vanished.

'You think Casanova is enjoying this *Invasion of the Body Snatchers* aura?' Sampson asked as we cruised the side streets bordering the University of North Carolina campus, former home base of Michael Jordan and too many other pro-basketball stars to mention.

'I think he's learned to enjoy being a local celebrity, yes. He likes to play the game. He's especially proud of his handi-work – his art.'

'Doesn't he want a larger venue? Larger canvas, so to speak?' Sampson asked as we climbed the gentle hills the college town had apparently been named for.

'I don't know about that yet. He might be a very territorial rec killer. Some recs are strictly territorial: Richard Ramirez, the Son of Sam, the Green River killer.'

I then told Sampson about my theory on twinning. The more I thought about it, the sounder it got for me. Even the FBI was starting to believe in it a little. 'The two of them have to be sharing some big secret. That they abduct beautiful women is only part of it. One of them thinks of himself as a "lover" and artist. The other is a brutal killer, much more typical of serial-killer cases. They complete each other, they correct each other's weaknesses. Together, I think they're virtually unstoppable. More importantly, I think they do, too.'

'Which one is the leader?' Sampson asked a very good question. It was completely intuitive on his part. The way he always solves problems.

'I think it's Casanova. He's definitely the more imaginative of the two. He's the one who hasn't made any major mistakes yet, either. But the Gentleman isn't really comfortable being a follower. He probably moved to California to see if he could succeed on his own. And he couldn't.'

'Is Casanova this kinky-assed college professor? Dr Wick Sachs? The pornography professor you told me about? Is he our man, Sugar?'

I peered across the front seat at Sampson. We were into the real deal now. Cop shop talk. 'Sometimes, I think it's Sachs, and that he's so goddamn clever and smart he can *let us know who he is*. He enjoys watching us squirm. That could be the ultimate power game for him.'

Sampson nodded – *one* nod. 'And other times, Dr Freud, what is your alternative thought process on Dr Sachs?'

'Other times, I wonder if Sachs has been set up. Casanova is very bright, and he's been extremely careful. He seems to send out misinformation that has everyone chasing his own tail. Even Kyle Craig's getting uptight and crazy.'

Sampson finally showed his large, very white teeth. Maybe it was a smile, or maybe he was going to bite me. 'Looks like I'm here just in the motherfucking nick of time.'

As I slowed for a stop sign on the side street, a man with

340

a gun suddenly moved away from a parked car and toward us. There was nothing I could do to stop him, nothing Sampson could do.

The gunman pointed a Smith and Wesson right into my face, up against my cheekbone.

Endgame! I thought.

Tilt!

'Chapel Hill police,' the man shouted into the open window. 'Get the hell out of the car. Assume the position!'

87

'You got here *just* in the nick of time,' I muttered to Sampson under my breath. We climbed out of the car very slowly and carefully.

'Looks like it,' he said. 'Be cool now. Don't get us shot or beat up, Alex. I wouldn't appreciate the irony.'

I thought I knew what was happening, and it made me incredibly angry. Sampson and I were 'suspects.' Why were we suspects? Because we were a couple of black males riding on the side streets of Chapel Hill at ten o'clock in the goddamn morning.

I could tell that Sampson was furious, too, but he was angry in his own way. He was smiling thinly and shaking his head back and forth. 'This is rich,' he said. 'This is the best yet.'

Another Chapel Hill detective appeared to assist his partner. They were tough-looking studs, in their late twenties. Longish hair. Full mustaches. Hard, muscular bodies from workout central. Nick Ruskin and Davey Sikes in training.

'You think this is funny?' The second officer's voice was disembodied, so low I could barely hear the words. 'You think

342

you're a laugh riot, Home?' he asked Sampson. He had a lead sap out and was holding it close to his hip, ready to strike.

'Best I could come up,' Sampson said, keeping his smile turned on low. He wasn't afraid of saps.

My scalp was crawling and sweat dribbled slowly down my back. I couldn't remember being rousted recently, and I didn't like it one bit. Everything bad I had felt since I'd been here fell into place. Not that rousting black males is peculiar to North Carolina or the South anymore.

I started to tell the cops who we were. 'My name is—'

'Shut the fuck up, asshole!' One of them popped me in the small of the back before I could finish. Not hard enough to leave a bruise, but it stung like a good rabbit punch. It hurt in a couple of ways, actually.

'This one looks fucked up to me. Eyes are bloodshot,' the low-voiced patrolman said to his partner. 'This one is high.' He was talking about me.

'I'm Alex Cross. I'm a police detective, you *motherfucker!*' I suddenly yelled at him. 'I'm part of the Casanova investigation. Call detectives Ruskin and Sikes right now! Call Kyle Craig from the FBI!'

At the same time, I spun around fast and hit the closest one in the throat. He dropped to the ground like a stone. His partner jumped forward, but Sampson had him on the sidewalk before he could do anything too dumb. I took away the first stud's revolver easier than I could disarm a fourteen-year-old hugger-mugger in D.C.

'*Assume the position*?' Sampson said to his 'suspect.' There was no merriment in his deep voice. 'How many brothers you pull that shit on? How many young men you call "homes" and humiliate like that? – like you might fuckin' understand what their life is about. Makes me *sick*.'

'You know damn well the serial killer Casanova isn't a black man,' I said to the two disarmed Chapel Hill cops. 'You haven't heard the last of this particular incident, gentlemen. Believe me on that one.'

'There been a lot of robberies in this neighborhood,' the deep-voiced one said. He was contrite all of a sudden, doing the Corporate America step'n'fetchit, the old two-step back-step.

'Save the sorry bullshit!' Sampson said, jabbing out with his own gun, letting the two detectives feel a little humiliation of their own.

Sampson and I got back into our car. We kept the detectives' guns. Souvenirs of our day. Let them explain it to their bosses back at police headquarters.

'Son of a bitch!' Sampson said as we pulled away. I hit the steering wheel with the heel of my palm. I hit it a second time. The bad scene had shaken me more than I had realized, or maybe I was just too ragged and frayed right then.

'On the other hand,' Sampson said, 'we did take those boys down like *snap*. Little bullshit racism gets my adrenaline flowing, blood boiling. Gets the demons going. That's good. I have the proper *edge* now.'

'It's nice to see your ugly face again,' I said to Sampson. I had to smile, finally. We both did. Then we were both laughing out loud in the car.

'Nice to see you, too, Brown Sugar. You'll be happy to know you've still got your looks. Strain's not showing too bad. Let's go to work. You know, I pity that poor psycho if we catch him today – which is likely, I might add.'

Sampson and I were twinning, too. It felt as good as ever.

88

Sampson and I found Dean Browning Lowell working out at the new faculty gym in Allen Hall on the Duke campus. The gym was filled with the latest and greatest muscle-building and toning equipment: shiny new rowing machines, Stair-Masters, treadmills, Gravitrons.

Dean Lowell was working with free weights. We needed to talk to him about Wick Sachs, doctor of pornography.

Sampson and I watched Browning Lowell do a tough set of lateral raises, then some leg curls and presses. It was an impressive workout, even by the standards of two dedicated gym rats like ourselves. Lowell was quite a physical specimen.

'So this is what an Olympian god looks like up close,' I said as we finally strolled across the gym floor toward him. Whitney Houston was playing from speakers in the gym's walls. Whitney was getting all the professor types pumped up to the max.

'You're walkin' with an Olympian god,' Sampson reminded me.

'It's easy to forget in the presence of the great, yet humble, ones,' I said and grinned.

Dean Lowell looked up as he heard our street shoes tattooing on the gymnasium floor. His smile was friendly and welcoming. That nice guy Browning Lowell. Actually, he did seem like a nice man. He went out of his way to create that impression.

I needed as much insider's detail as I could get from him in a hurry. Somewhere in North Carolina there had to be a missing puzzle piece that would begin to make sense out of all this murder and intrigue. I introduced Sampson and we skipped the polite small talk. I asked Lowell what he knew about Wick Sachs.

The dean was extremely cooperative, as he'd been on our first meeting. 'Sachs is our campus skell, has been for a decade. Every university seems to have at least one,' Dean Lowell said and frowned deeply. I noticed that even his frown lines had muscles.

'Sachs is widely known as "Doctor Dirt." He's got tenure, though, and he's never been caught at anything completely untoward. I guess I should give Dr Sachs the benefit of the doubt, but I won't.'

'You ever hear about an exotic book and film collection that he owns, keeps at his house? Pornography masquerading as erotica?' Sampson decided to ask my next question for me.

Lowell stopped his vigorous exercises. He looked at both of us for a long moment before he spoke again. 'Is Dr Sachs a serious suspect in the disappearances of these young women?'

'There are a lot of suspects, Dean Lowell. I can't say any more than that right now.' I told him the truth.

Lowell nodded. 'I respect your judgment, Alex. Let me tell you some things about Sachs that might be important,' he said. He had stopped exercising by now. He began toweling off his thick neck and shoulders. His body looked like polished rock.

Lowell continued to talk as he dried himself meticulously. 'Let me start at the beginning: There was an infamous murder of a young couple here a while back. This was in nineteen eighty-one. Wick Sachs was an undergrad at the time, a liberal arts student, very brilliant mind. I was in the graduate school then. When I became dean, I learned that Sachs had actually been one of the suspects in the murder investigation, but he was definitely cleared. There wasn't any evidence that he was involved in any way. I don't know every detail, but you can check it for yourself with the Durham police. It was in the spring of 'eighty-one. The murdered students were Roe Tierney and Tom Hutchinson. It was a huge scandal, I remember. In those days, a single murder case could still actually shock a community. Thing is, the case was never solved.'

'Why didn't you bring this up before?' I asked Lowell.

'The FBI knew all about it, Alex. I told them myself. I know that they talked to Dr Sachs several weeks ago. It was my impression that he wasn't under suspicion, and that they had decided there was no connection with the earlier murder case. I'm absolutely sure of it.'

'Fair enough,' I said to the dean. I asked him for another big favor. Could he dredge up everything on Dr Sachs that the FBI had originally requested? I also wanted to see the Duke yearbooks from the time when Sachs and Will Rudolph had both been students. I needed to do some important homework on the class of '81.

Around seven that night, Sampson and I met with the Durham police again. Detectives Ruskin and Sikes showed up, among others. They were feeling heavy-duty pressure, too.

They pulled us aside before the update on the Casanova investigation. The stress had gotten to them, cooled their jets a little.

'Listen, you two have worked big, bad cases like this before,' Ruskin said. As usual, he was doing most of the talking. Davey Sikes didn't seem to like us any better now than he had the first day we met.

'I know that my partner and I got a little territorial at first. I want you to know, though, all we want to do is *stop the killing now.*'

Sikes nodded his large, blocklike head. 'We want to nail Sachs. Trouble is, our brass has us chasing our tails as usual.'

Ruskin smiled, and finally so did I. We all understood departmental politics. I still didn't trust the Durham homicide detectives. I was certain they wanted to use Sampson and me or at least keep us out of the way.

Also, I had the feeling they were still holding evidence back.

The Durham homicide detectives told us they were mired in an investigation of medical doctors in the Research Triangle, doctors with any kind of criminal record or associations. Wick Sachs was the chief suspect, but not the only one.

There was still a strong chance that Casanova would turn out to be someone we hadn't even heard of. That was the way it often worked with repeat-killer cases. He was out there – but we might have no idea who he really was. That was the scariest part of all, the most frustrating, too.

Nick Ruskin and Sikes took Sampson and me over to the suspects board that had been put up. There were seventeen names on it at this point. Five were doctors. Kate had originally believed that Casanova was a doctor, and Kyle Craig did, too.

I read off the doctors' names.

Dr Stefan Romm
Dr Francis Constantini
Dr Richard Dilallo
Dr Miguel Fesco
Dr Kelly Clark

I wondered again if several people could somehow be involved with the house of horror. Or was Wick Sachs our man? Was he Casanova?

'You're the big guru.' Davey Sikes was suddenly leaning over my shoulder. 'Who is he, my man? Help us local yokels out. Catch the bogeyman, Dr Cross.'

89

Late that night, Casanova was on the move again. He was hunting again. He had missed the thrill these last few days, but this was going to be an important night.

He easily penetrated the security of the sprawling Duke University Medical Center complex through a little-used gray-metal door in the private parking area reserved for doctors. On the way to his appointed destination, he passed several chirping nurses and serious-faced young doctors. Some of the doctors and nurses nodded, and even smiled at him.

As always, Casanova fit in perfectly with the surroundings. He could go anywhere – and he usually did.

As he hurried down the sterile white hospital corridors, his head was busy figuring out complicated, important calculations about his future. He'd had a hugely successful run here in the Research Triangle area and the Southeast, but it was definitely drawing to an end. Starting tonight.

Alex Cross and the other dreary plodders were getting too close to him. Even the Durham police were becoming dangerous. He *was* a 'territorial rec.' He knew their inadequate terminology for him. Eventually, someone would find the house. Or worse, someone would probably find him through dumb luck.

Yes, it was time to move on. *Maybe he and Will Rudolph should go to New York City*, he thought. *Or sunny Florida, which had drawn Ted Bundy? Arizona might be pleasant. Spend the fall season in Tempe or Tucson . . . bustling college towns filled to bursting with prey. Or maybe they could settle in near one of the huge campuses in Texas. Austin was supposed to be nice. Or Urbana, Illinois? Madison, Wisconsin? Columbus, Ohio?*

He was leaning toward Europe actually, either London, Munich, or Paris. His version of the grand tour. Maybe that was the right concept for the times. A truly grand tour for the whiz kids. Who needed to go watch *Dracula* when there were real monsters roaming the countryside day and night?

Casanova wondered if anyone had managed to follow him into the Medical Center maze. How about Alex Cross? It was a possibility. Dr Cross had relatively impressive staying power. He had bested that unimaginative child molester, that garden-variety psycho killer, up in D.C. Cross had to be eliminated before he and Will Rudolph left the area for bigger and better things. Otherwise, Cross would follow them to hell and back.

Casanova passed into Building Two of the Byzantine hospital maze. This was the way to the hospital morgue and maintenance, so the foot traffic was usually lighter.

He peered down the long, off-white corridor behind him. *No followers.* No one willing to lead in this gutless, witless age, either.

Maybe they *didn't* know about him yet. Maybe they hadn't figured anything out. But they would eventually. There *were*

351

clues. It could all be traced back to Roe Tierney and Tom Hutchinson. The unsolved golden couple murder. The very beginning for him and Will Rudolph. God, he was glad his friend was back. Rudolph always made him feel better when he was around. Rudolph truly *understood* desire, and ultimately, freedom. Rudolph understood *him* as no one else ever had.

Casanova began to jog down a brightly polished corridor in Building Two of the Medical Center.

As he quickened his pace, the sound of his slapping footsteps echoed in the empty halls. In a few minutes he was in Building Four, all the way over on the northwest side of the hospital.

He looked back one more time.

Nobody had followed. Nobody had guessed right yet. Maybe they never would.

Casanova came out into the brightly lit, almost orangish, parking area. A black Jeep was parked close to the building, and he nonchalantly climbed inside.

The vehicle had MD plates, state of North Carolina. Yet another of his *masks*.

He was feeling strong and sure of himself again. He felt wonderfully free and alive tonight. This was exhilarating; it could be one of his finest hours, actually. He felt as if he could fly through the silky black night.

He took off to claim his victim.

Dr Kate McTiernan was next *again*.

He missed her so much.

He loved her.

90

The gentleman caller was on the move. Dr Will Rudolph passed inexorably through the night toward his unsuspecting prey. His juices were surging. *Sloshing.* He was going to make a house call, as an outstanding doctor should, at least a doctor who really cared.

Casanova didn't want him out roaming the streets of Durham or Chapel Hill. He'd *forbidden* it, in fact. Understandable enough, admirable, but not possible. They were working together again. Besides, the danger was minimal at night and the rewards far exceeded the risks.

This next scene in the drama had to be done just right, and he was the one to do it. Will Rudolph was certain of that. He had no emotional baggage. No Achilles' heel. Casanova did . . . Her name was Kate McTiernan.

In a strange way, he thought, she had become his competition. Casanova had bonded with her in a special way. She was very close to the 'lover' he claimed to be obsessively searching for. As such, she was dangerous to his own special relationship with Casanova.

As he drove into Chapel Hill, he thought about his 'friend.' Something was different and even more satisfying between them now. Being torn apart for almost a year made him appreciate the strange relationship. It was more powerful than ever. There was no one else he could talk to, not one person.

How very sad, Rudolph thought.

How droll.

During his year in California, Will Rudolph had remembered all too well the searing loneliness he had experienced as a boy. He'd grown up at Fort Bragg, North Carolina, then in Asheville. He was a bird colonel's boy, an army brat, a true son of the South. Right from the beginning, he had been clever enough to keep up a façade: honor student; polite, helpful, social graces to beat all. The perfect gentleman. No one had guessed the truth about his desires and needs . . . which was exactly why the loneliness had been so unbearable.

He knew when the loneliness had ended. Exactly when and where. He remembered the first dizzying meeting with Casanova. It had taken place right on the Duke campus, and it was a dangerous meeting for both of them.

The Gentleman remembered the scene so well. He had a small room, like any other student on campus. Casanova had shown up one night well past midnight, closer to two. Scared the shit out of him.

He seemed so sure of himself when Rudolph opened the door and saw him there. There was a theatrical suspense movie called *Rope*. The scene reminded him of the movie.

'You going to invite me in? I don't think you want what I have to say broadcast out here in a public hallway.'

Rudolph had let him in. Shut the door. His heart was thundering.

'What do you want? It's almost two in the morning. Christ.'

The smile again. So cocksure. *Knowing*. 'You killed Roe Tierney and Thomas Hutchinson. You were stalking her for over a year. You have a loving remembrance of Roe right here in this room. Her tongue, I believe.'

It was the most dramatic moment of Will Rudolph's life. Someone actually knew who he was. Someone had found him out.

'Don't be frightened. I also know there's no way they'll ever *prove* you committed the murders. You committed perfect crimes. Well, *near perfect*. Congratulations.'

Acting as well as he could under the circumstances, Rudolph had laughed in his accuser's face. 'You're completely out of your mind. I'd like you to leave now. That's the craziest thing I've ever heard.'

'Yes, it is,' the accuser said, 'but you've been waiting to hear it all your life . . . Let me tell you something else you've wanted to hear. I *understand* what you did and why. I've done it myself. I'm a lot like you, Will.'

Rudolph had felt a powerful connection immediately. The first real human connection of his life. Perhaps that was what love was? Did ordinary people feel so much more than he did? Or were they deluding themselves? Creating grandiose romantic fantasies around the mundane exchange of seminal fluids?

He was at his final destination before he knew it. He stopped the car under a towering, old elm and switched off the headlamps. Two black men were standing on the porch of Kate McTiernan's house.

One of them was Alex Cross.

91

At a little past ten, Sampson and I rode down a dark, winding street on the outskirts of Chapel Hill. It had been a long day in the tank for both of us.

I'd taken Sampson to meet Seth Samuel Taylor earlier that evening. We had also spoken to one of Seth's former teachers, Dr Louis Freed. I gave Dr Freed my theory about the 'disappearing house'; he agreed to help me with some important research for the investigation on where it might be located.

I hadn't told Sampson too much about Kate McTiernan yet. It was time for them to meet, though. I didn't know exactly what our friendship was about, and neither did Kate. Maybe Sampson could add a few thoughts after he saw her. I was sure he would.

'You working late hours like this every night?' Sampson wanted to know as we eased down Kate's street, Old Ladies Lane, as she called it.

'Until I find Scootchie, or admit that I can't,' I told him. 'Then I plan to take a whole night off.'

Sampson chortled. 'You devil, you.'

We hopped out of the car and went to the door. I rang the bell. 'No key?' Sampson deadpanned.

Kate flipped on the outdoor light for us. I wondered why she didn't keep it on all the time. Because she would save five cents a month if she didn't use the light? Because the light would attract bugs? Because she was stubborn, and maybe wanted another shot at Casanova? That was more like it, knowing Kate the way I was starting to. She wanted Casanova as badly as I did.

She came to the door in an old gray sweatshirt, tattered, holey jeans, bare feet with playfully red toenails. Her dark hair was bobbed at shoulder length, and she looked beautiful. No getting away from that.

'It's like a damn bughouse out here,' Kate commented as she looked around her porch.

She hugged me and gave me a kiss on the cheek. I had a thought about the two of us holding each other the night before. Where was this going? I wondered. Did it have to be going anywhere?

'Hi, John Sampson,' she greeted him with a pumping handshake. 'I know a few things about you, ever since you two met when you were ten. You can fill me in on the rest over a cold beer or two. Tell your side.' She smiled then. It always felt good to be on the other side of one of her smiles.

'So you're the famous Kate.' Sampson held on to her hand, and stared into the deep pools of her brown eyes. 'I hear you worked your way through medical school at a truck stop, or some such apocryphal nonsense. Second degree black belt, too. A Nidan.' He started to smile and bowed respectfully.

Kate grinned at Sampson as she bowed back. 'Come in out of the eternal bugs and the infernal heat. Looks like Alex has been talking behind our backs. We'll get him for that. Let's both gang up on him.'

'That's Kate,' I said to Sampson as I followed him inside. 'What do you think?'

He looked back at me. 'She likes you for some strange reason. She even likes me, which makes a lot more sense.'

We sat in her kitchen and the talk was easy and comfortable, the way it usually was around her. Sampson and I drank beer, and Kate had several iced teas. I could tell that Kate and Sampson liked each other fine. There was nothing not to like about either of them. They were both independent spirits, very smart, generous.

I filled her in on our latest day of detective work, our disappointing meeting with Ruskin and Sikes, and she told us about her day at the hospital, even some verbatims from her offservice notes.

'Sounds like you have an eidetic memory to go along with the black belt,' Sampson said with a raised eyebrow about the size of a boomerang. 'No wonder Dr Alex is so impressed with you.'

'You are?' Kate gave me a look. 'Well, you never told *me* that.'

'Kate, believe it or not, is not self-centered enough,' I told Sampson. 'Rare, rare disease in our quarter-century. It's because she doesn't watch much TV. She reads too many books instead.'

'It's not polite to analyze your friends in front of your other friends,' Kate said to me with a little slap on the arm.

We talked about the case some more. About Dr Wick Sachs and his head-games. About harems. The masks. The 'disappearing' house. My newest theory involving Dr Louis Freed.

'I was doing some light reading before you got here,' Kate told us. 'An essay on the male sexual urge, the natural beauty and power of it. It's about modern men trying to distance themselves from their mothers, from the smothering cosmological mom. It proposes that many men want the freedom to assert their masculine identities, but contemporary society continually frustrates that. Comments, gentlemen?'

'Men will be men.' Sampson showed his big white teeth. 'Good case in point. We're still lions and tigers at heart. Never met a cosmological mom, so I won't comment on that part of your essay.'

'What do you think, Alex?' Kate asked me. 'Are you a lion or a tiger?'

'I've never liked certain things about most men,' I said. 'We *are* incredibly repressed. Monochromatic because of it. Insecure, defensive. Rudolph and Sachs are asserting their masculinity to the extreme. They refuse to be repressed by society's mores or laws.'

'Ba dum bun.' Sampson did a talk-show drumbeat for me.

'They think they're smarter than everyone else,' Kate said. 'At least Casanova does. He laughs at all of us. He's a nasty son of a bitch.'

'And that's why I'm here,' Sampson told her, 'to catch him, and put him in a cage, and lock the cage on a far mountaintop. And by the way, he'd be stone dead in the cage, anyway.'

The time passed like that, flashed by real quickly. Finally, it was getting late and we had to leave. I tried to talk Kate into staying at a hotel for the night. We had been over this subject repeatedly, and her answer was always the same.

'Thanks for the concern, but no thanks,' she said as she brought us out onto the porch. 'I can't let him chase me out of my own house. That will not happen. He comes back, we tangle.'

'Alex is right about the hotel,' Sampson said to her in the gentle voice he reserves for friends. There it was – a double recommendation from two of the sharpest cops around.

Kate shook her head, and I knew there was no sense in arguing with her anymore. 'Absolutely not. I'll be just fine, I promise,' she said.

I didn't ask Kate if I could stay, but I wanted to. I didn't know if Kate even wanted me to stay. It was a little complicated with Sampson there. I suppose I could have given him my car to drive back, but it was already after one-thirty. We all needed to get some sleep, anyway. Sampson and I finally left.

'*Very* nice. *Very* interesting woman. *Very* smart. Not your type,' Sampson said as we pulled away from the house. From him, it was a rare, rave review. '*My* type,' he added.

When we reached the end of the block, I turned and looked back at the house. It was cooler now, in the low seventies, and Kate had already turned off the porch light and gone in. She was stubborn, but she was smart. It had gotten her through med school. It had gotten her past the deaths of people she loved. She would be okay; she always had been.

I called Kyle Craig when I got back to the hotel, though. 'How's our man Sachs?' I asked him.

'He's just fine. He's all tucked in for the night. Not to worry.'

92

After the good ship Alex and Sampson left, Kate carefully checked and *double-checked* all the doors and windows to her apartment. They were securely locked. She had liked Sampson right away. He was huge and scary, nice and scary, sweet and scary. Alex had brought his closest friend to see her, and she liked that.

As she did her rounds, her safety check of home sweet home, she ruminated about a new life, far away from Chapel Hill, far away from everything terrifying and bad that had happened here. *Hell, I'm living a Hitchcock movie*, she thought, *if Alfred Hitchcock had stayed alive long enough to see and react to the madness and horror of the 1990s.*

Exhausted, she finally climbed into bed. *Yuk.* She felt stale bread or cake crumbs against her legs. She hadn't made the bed that morning.

She wasn't accomplishing much lately, and that made her angry, too. She'd been on a proper schedule to complete her intern year this spring. Now she didn't know if she'd make it by the end of summer.

Kate pulled the covers up under her chin – in early June. She was getting *soooo* buggy. Her anxiety wasn't going to stop while the monster Casanova was on the loose out there, she knew. She thought about killing him. Her first and only violent fantasy. She imagined going to Wick Sachs's house. An eye for an eye. She remembered the appropriate passage from the Book of Exodus. Eidetic memory, right.

She really wished that Alex had stayed, but she didn't want to embarrass him in front of Sampson. She wanted to talk to Alex the way they always did, and she wished he was with her now. She wanted to be in his arms tonight. Maybe more than just in Alex's arms. Maybe she was ready for more. *One night at a time.*

She wasn't sure what she believed in anymore, or if she believed in anything at all. She was praying lately, so maybe she did believe. Rote prayers, but prayers all the same. *Our Father who art . . . Hail Mary full of . . .* She wondered if a lot of people did the same thing. 'I do love the idea of you, God,' she finally whispered. 'Please love the idea of me back.'

She couldn't stop obsessing about Casanova, about Dr Wick Sachs, about the mysterious, disappearing house of horror, and the poor women still trapped there. But she was so used to the continuous, terrifying nightmares that she finally drifted off to sleep, anyway.

Kate never heard him come into the house.

93

Tick-cock. Tick-cock.

Tickory, dickory, cock.

Kate finally heard a noise. A floorboard creaked on the right side of the bedroom.

Tiny, tiny sound . . . but unmistakable.

That wasn't her imagination, wasn't a dream. She sensed that he was there in her bedroom again.

Let it be a crazy thought; let it be a scene in a nightmare; let this whole past month be a nightmare I'm having.

Oh Jesus, oh God, no! she thought.

He was in her room. He'd come back! This was so bad that she couldn't make herself believe it was happening.

Kate held her breath until her chest ached and threatened to cave in. She never *really* believed he would come back.

Now she realized that was a terrible mistake. The worst of her life, but not the last one she was allowed, she hoped.

Who was this extraordinary madman? Did he hate her so much that he would risk everything? Or did he think he loved her so much, the sick, pathetic bastard?

She sat tensely on the edge of the bed and listened intently for another sound. She was ready to spring at him. There it was again . . . *a tiny creak*. It was coming from the right side of the room.

Finally, she could see the full, dark silhouette of his body. She gulped in air greedily and almost gagged.

There he was, goddamn him to hell.

A powerful, hateful energy, like currents of electricity, surged between them. Their eyes finally met. Even in the darkness his eyes seemed to burn through her. She remembered his eyes so well.

Kate tried to roll away from him, from his first strike.

The blow came fast and hard. He hadn't lost his quickness. Excruciating pain ripped through her shoulder and down her left side.

Karate training kept her moving somehow. Sheer stubbornness. A will to live that was becoming her trademark. She was off the bed. Up on her feet. Ready for him.

'Mistake,' she whispered. 'Yours, this time.'

She saw the outline of a body again. This time against the moonlight streaming in a bedroom window. Fear and loathing gripped Kate. Her heart felt as if it might stop, just pack it in on her.

She fired a powerful kick. Hit him hard in the face and heard the *crunch* of bone. It was horrifying yet wonderful to hear.

A high-pitched voice shrieked out in pain. She'd hurt him!

Now do it again, Kate. She bobbed, moved, kicked hard at the dark, shifting body, striking the stomach area. Again he grunted in pain.

'How do you like it?' Kate screamed at him. 'How do *you* like it?'

She had him, and Kate vowed that she wasn't going to lose this time. She was going to capture. Casanova all by herself. He was ripe for the catching. First, she was going to hurt him, though.

She punched him again. Short, compact, lightning fast, and powerful. Satisfying beyond anything she could imagine. He was staggering, moaning out loud.

His head snapped back hard. His hair flew out. She wanted him *down* on the floor. Maybe unconscious. Then she would turn on a light. Then she just might kick him while he was down.

'That was a love tap,' she told him. 'Just a start.'

She watched him stumble in front of her. He was going down.

Woof – something, someone, struck her square in the back. The blow knocked all the breath out of her.

She couldn't believe she'd been blindsided. Pain rushed through her body as if she'd been shot.

Woof.

It happened again.

There were *two* of them in her bedroom.

94

Kate was in shocking pain, but she stayed on her feet, and finally she saw the second man in her bedroom. He swung hard and struck her in the forehead. She heard a metallic *ring*, and felt herself falling, toppling. Felt herself *vaporizing*, actually. Then her body bounced off the wooden floorboards.

Two voices were floating above her. Two monsters inside her bedroom. Stereo nightmares.

'You shouldn't be here.' She recognized Casanova's voice. He was talking to the second intruder. The demon behind door number two. Dr Will Rudolph?

'Yes, I'm the one who *should* be here. I'm not involved with this stupid bitch, am I? I couldn't care less about her. Think it through. Be smart.'

'All right, all right, Will. What do you want to do with her?' Casanova spoke again. 'This is your show. Isn't that what you want?'

'Personally, I'd like to eat her, a nibble at a time,' said Dr Will Rudolph. 'Is that too extreme?'

They kept laughing like two buddies talking at a sports bar. Kate felt herself fading away from the scene. *She was leaving. Where was she going?*

Will Rudolph said that he bought her *flowers*. They both began to laugh at the joke. They were hunting together again. No one could stop them. Kate could smell their body odor, a strong male musk that seemed to combine into an overpowering presence.

She stayed conscious for a long time. She fought with all her strength. She was stubborn, willful, proud as hell. The light finally went out for her like a tube in an old-fashioned TV set. A blurry picture, then a small dot of light, then blackness. It was that simple, that prosaic.

They turned on the bedroom lights when they were finished, so that all of Kate McTiernan's admirers could have a last good look at her.

Murdered *beyond* cold blood.

95

My arms and legs were shaking uncontrollably as I tried to drive the five miles or so from Durham to Chapel Hill. Even my teeth were chattering, hitting together hard.

I finally had to pull off Chapel Hill-Durham Boulevard, or I thought I would probably crash the car.

I sat slumped in the front seat with the car headlamps shining across dancing dust motes and light-crazed insects that hovered in the early-morning air.

I took deep breath after deep breath, trying to suck in some sanity. It was past five in the morning, and the birds were already singing away. I put my hands over my ears to shut out their songs. Sampson was still asleep back at the hotel. I'd forgotten that he was there.

Kate had never been afraid of Casanova. She trusted in her ability to take care of herself, even after her abduction.

I knew that it was irrational and crazy to blame myself, but I did. Somewhere, at some time during the past few years, I had stopped behaving like a professional police detective. There was some good in that, but, in a way, it was bad.

There was too much pain on The Job, if you let yourself feel it. That was the surest, fastest way to burnout.

I eventually eased the car back onto the road. About fifteen minutes later, I was at the familiar clapboard house in Chapel Hill.

'Old Ladies Lane,' Kate had dubbed the street. I could see her face, her sweet, easy smile, her enthusiasm and conviction about things that mattered to her. I could still hear her voice.

Sampson and I had been at this house less than three hours ago. My eyes were tearing, my brain screaming. I was losing control.

I remembered one of the last things she'd said to me. I could hear Kate's voice. 'He comes back, we tangle.'

Black-and-white police cruisers, somber-looking EMS vans, and TV trucks were already parked everywhere on the narrow two-lane blacktop street. They were filling every available space. I was sick to death of the sight of crime scenes. It looked as if half the town of Chapel Hill was congregated outside Kate's apartment.

In the early-morning light all the faces looked pale and grim. They were shocked and angry. This was supposed to be a gentle college town, liberal-thinking, a safe haven from the whirling chaos and madness of the rest of the world. That was why most people chose to live here, but it wasn't like that anymore. Casanova had changed that forever.

I fumbled on a pair of dusty and stained sunglasses that had been sitting on the dash of the car for months. They were Sampson's shades, originally. He'd given them to Damon, so he could look as tough as Sampson whenever I gave him any trouble. I needed to look tough right now.

96

I began to walk toward Kate's house on unsure, rubbery legs. Maybe I looked like the toughest motherfucker around, but my heart was heavy and incredibly fragile.

News photographers snapped my picture again and again. The camera flashes sounded like hollow, muffled gunshots. Reporters approached, but I waved them off.

'Keep back, man,' I finally warned a couple of them. Serious warning. 'This is not the time. *Not now!*'

But I noticed that even the reporters and cameramen looked dazed and confused and shocked.

Both the FBI and the Durham PD were at the scene of the unspeakable, cowardly attack. I saw a lot of local policemen. Nick Ruskin and Davey Sikes had come down from Durham. Sikes gave me the evil eye – like what did I think I was doing here?

Kyle Craig was already at the scene. He had personally called me at the hotel to give me the terrible news.

Kyle came up to me and he put his arm around my shoulder, spoke to me in a low whisper. 'She's very bad, Alex, but she's hanging in somehow. She must want to live very, very much. They should be bringing her out any minute now. Stay out here with me. Don't go inside. Trust me on this, will you?'

I listened to Kyle's words and I was afraid I was going to break down in front of all the cameras, all the strangers, and the few people I knew. My head, my heart – it was all whirling chaos. I finally went inside the house, and I looked at as much as I could bear.

He had come into her bedroom again . . . he had been right there.

Something was wrong, though . . . something didn't track in straight lines for me. Something . . . what was wrong here?

The emergency team from Duke Medical Center put Kate on a stretcher, the kind used for broken backs and severe head injuries. I don't think I've ever seen anyone carried so delicately, under any tragic circumstances. The doctors looked ashen as they began to carry her out of the house. The crowd became suddenly hushed when the EMS crew appeared outside.

'They're bringing her to the Duke Medical Center. You'll get some arguments from the university people, but that's the best facility in the state,' Kyle told me. He was trying to be reassuring in his soothing, mechanical-man way. Actually, he was surprisingly good at it.

Something was wrong . . . something was all out of kilter . . . Think. Focus your thoughts somehow. This could be important . . . but I couldn't think in straight lines. Not yet, I couldn't.

'What about Wick Sachs?' I asked Kyle.

'He got home before ten o'clock. He's there now . . . We don't know that he didn't go out for sure, I suppose. He *could* have slipped out past us somehow. Maybe he has a way out of the house. I don't think so, though.'

I moved away from Kyle Craig and went over to one of the white-coated Duke University doctors near the ambulance. Camera flashes were erupting everywhere around us. Hundreds of 'memorable' pictures were being taken by the night-crawlers at the crime scene.

'Can I ride with her?'

The EMS doctor very gently shook his head at me. 'No, sir,' he said. He seemed to be talking in slow motion. 'No, sir, only the family can ride in the ambulance. I'm sorry, Dr Cross.'

'I'm her family tonight,' I said. I pushed past him and climbed into the rear of the ambulance. He didn't try to stop me. He couldn't have, anyway.

I felt numb all over. Kate lay amid the solemn monitoring and resuscitation equipment in the close quarters of the rescue ambulance. I was afraid that she had died as I was getting into the ambulance, or when they were carrying her outside.

I sat beside Kate and held just the tips of her fingers. 'It's Alex. I'm here for you,' I whispered to her. 'Be strong right now. You're so strong, anyway. Be strong now.'

The same doctor who had told me I couldn't get into the ambulance came in and sat next to me. He felt obliged to tell me the rules, but he didn't care to enforce them. His name tag said Dr B. Stringer, Duke University EMS Team. I owed him a big favor.

'Can you tell me anything about Kate's chances?' I asked as the emergency ambulance slowly pulled away from the nightmare scene in Chapel Hill.

'That's a tough question, I'm afraid. She's alive, and that's a miracle in itself,' he spoke in a low, respectful voice. 'There are multiple fractures and contusions, some with open gashes in them. Both cheekbones are fractured. She may have a sprained neck. She must have played dead on him. Somehow, she had the presence of mind to trick him.'

Kate's face was swollen badly and cut. She was almost unrecognizable. I knew the same was true all over her body. I clung gently to Kate's hand as the ambulance sped toward Duke Medical Center. *She had the presence of mind to trick him?* That was Kate, all right. I wondered, though.

I held on to another mind-blowing thought. It had hit me hard outside the house. *I thought I knew what had been wrong in Kate's bedroom.*

Will Rudolph had been in the bedroom, hadn't he? The Gentleman Caller had been there for the attack. He had to be the one. It was his style. Extreme, graphic violence. *Rage*.

There was little evidence of Casanova. No artistic touches. There was such extraordinary violence, though . . . *They were twinning! Two monsters bonding to make one*. Perhaps Rudolph resented Kate because Casanova had loved her. Maybe she had come between them in his twisted perception. Maybe they had left Kate alive on purpose – so she could be a vegetable for the rest of her life.

They were working together now, weren't they? There were two of them to catch, to stop.

97

The FBI and Durham police decided to bring Dr Wick Sachs in for questioning early the next morning. This was a big deal; a pivotal decision in the case.

A special investigator was flown down from Virginia to do the delicate interrogation. He was one of the FBI's best, a man named James Heekin. He questioned Sachs throughout most of the morning.

I sat with Sampson, Kyle Craig, and detectives Nick Ruskin and Davey Sikes. We watched the interrogation through a two-way mirror inside Durham Police Headquarters. I felt like a starving man with his nose pressed against the window of an expensive restaurant. But there was no food being served inside.

The FBI interrogator was good, very patient, and as crafty as a star district attorney. But so was Wick Sachs. He was articulate; extremely cool under verbal fire; even smug.

'This fucker is going down,' Davey Sikes finally said inside the quiet observation room. It was good to see that he and Ruskin cared at least. In a way, I could empathize with them

374

in their role as local detectives: they had been on the outside looking in for most of the frustrating investigation.

'What do you have on Sachs? Tell me if you're holding anything back,' I said to Nick Ruskin at the coffee machine.

'We brought him in because our chief of police is an asshole,' Ruskin told me. 'We don't have anything on Sachs yet.' I wondered if I could believe Ruskin, or anyone else connected with this case.

After nearly two hours of tense parrying back and forth, Agent Heekin's interrogation had established little more than that Sachs was a collector of erotica, and that he'd been promiscuous with consenting students and professors over the last eleven years at the university.

As much as I had wanted to bust Sachs, I couldn't really understand why he'd been brought in at this time. Why now?

'We found out where his money comes from.' Kyle told me part of the answer that morning. 'Sachs is the owner of an escort service working out of Raleigh and Durham. The service is called Kissmet. Interesting name. They advertise "lingerie modeling" in the Yellow Pages. At the least, Dr Sachs will have some serious problems with Internal Revenue. Washington decided we should apply pressure now. They're afraid he's going to run soon.'

'I don't agree with your people in Washington,' I told Kyle. I knew that some agents called headquarters up there Disneyland East. I could see why. They could be risking the investigation right now, and by remote control.

'Who does agree with Washington?' Kyle said and shrugged his wide, bony shoulders. It was his way of admitting that he wasn't in full control anymore. The case was too big now. 'By the way, how is Kate McTiernan doing?' he asked.

I had already been on the phone three times with Duke

Medical Center that morning. They had a number for me at the Durham station, in case Kate's condition changed. 'She's listed as grave, but she's still hanging in there,' I told Kyle.

I got the chance to talk to Wick Sachs just before eleven o'clock that morning. It was Kyle's concession to me.

I tried to put Kate out of my mind before I had to be in the same room with Sachs. Anger thundered and roared inside my body all the same. I didn't know if I could control myself. I wasn't even sure if I wanted to anymore.

'Let me do this one, Alex. Let me go in there with him.' Sampson held my arm before I went inside. I broke away from him and went to meet Dr Wick Sachs.

'I'm going to do him.'

98

'Hello, Dr Sachs.'

The lighting in the small, impersonal interrogation room was even brighter and harsher than it had looked from behind the two-way mirror. Sachs was red-eyed, and I could tell he was as tense as I was. His skin looked stretched taut over his skull. But he was as confident and smug with me as he'd been with James Heckin of the FBI.

Was I looking into the eyes of Casanova? I wondered. *Could he possibly be the human monster?*

'My name is Alex Cross,' I said as I slumped down on a shopworn metal chair. 'Naomi Cross is my niece.'

Sachs spoke through gritted teeth. He had a mild drawl. According to Kate, Casanova had no noticeable accent.

'*I know who the hell you are.* I *read* the newspapers, Dr Cross. I don't know your niece. I *read* that she was abducted.'

I nodded. 'If you read the papers, you must also be aware of the handiwork of the scum who calls himself Casanova.'

Sachs smirked, at least it looked like that to me. His blue eyes were filled with contempt. It was easy to see why he was widely disliked at the university. His blonde hair was slicked back, not a strand out of place. His horn-rimmed glasses helped make him seem officious and condescending.

'There is no record of violence anywhere in my past. I could never commit those horrifying murders. I can't even kill palmetto bugs in my house. My aversion to violence is well documented.'

I'll bet it is, I thought. *All of your clever fronts and façades are neatly, perfectly in place, aren't they? Your devoted wife, the nurse. Your two children. Your well-documented 'aversion to violence.'*

I rubbed my face with both my hands. It took all of my strength to keep from hitting him. He remained haughty and unapproachable.

I leaned across the table and spoke in a whisper. 'I looked through your erotic book collection. I was there in your basement, Dr Sachs. The collection's *full* of perverse, sexual *violence* The physical degradation of men, women, and children. That might not constitute a "record of violence," but it gives me some subtle hints about your true character.'

Sachs dismissed what I said with a wave of his hand. 'I'm a noted philosopher *and* sociologist. Yes, I study *eroticism* – just as you study the criminal mind. I don't suffer from libertine dementia, *Dr* Cross. My erotic collection is the key to my understanding the fantasy life of Western culture, the escalating war between men and women.' His voice level went up. 'I also don't have to explain any of my private affairs to you. I've broken no laws. I'm here voluntarily. You, on the other hand, entered my house without a search warrant.'

I tried to keep Sachs off balance by asking him about something else. 'Why do you think you're so successful with young women? We already know about your sexual conquests of students at the university. Eighteen-, nineteen-, twenty-year-olds. Beautiful young women; your own students, in some cases. There's a record of that, certainly.'

For a moment his anger surfaced. Then he caught himself and did something odd, and maybe very revealing. Sachs showed his need to exert power and control, to be the star of the show, even to me. Insignificant as I was to him.

'Why am I successful with women, Dr Cross?' Sachs smiled and he let his tongue play between his teeth. The message was subtle, but also clear. Sachs was telling me that he knew how to sexually control most women.

He continued to smile. An obscene smile from an obscene man. 'Many women want to be freed from their sexual inhibitions, especially young women, the modern women on campuses. I free them. I free as many women as I possibly can.'

That did it. I was across the table in a second. Sachs's chair tumbled over backwards. I landed heavily on top of him. He grunted in pain.

I pressed my body down hard on his. My arms and legs were shaking. I held back from actually throwing a punch. *He was absolutely powerless to stop me*, I realized. *He didn't know how to fight back. He wasn't very strong or athletic.*

Nick Ruskin and Davey Sikes were inside the interrogation room in a flash, and Kyle and Sampson were right behind them. They jammed into the room and tried to pull me off Sachs.

Actually, I pulled myself away from Wick Sachs. I didn't hurt him, never intended to. I whispered to Sampson. 'He isn't physically strong. Casanova is. He isn't the monster. *He isn't Casanova.*'

99

That night, Sampson and I had dinner together at a pretty good spot in Durham. Ironically, it was called Nana's.

Neither of us was especially hungry. The overly large steaks with shallots and mountains of garlic mashed potatoes went to waste. It was late in the game with Casanova, and we seemed to be falling all the way back to square one.

We talked about Kate. I had been told by hospital officials that her condition was still poor. *If* she lived, the doctors believed that she had little chance of full recovery, of ever being a doctor again.

'You two were more than, you know, good friends?' Sampson finally asked. He was gentle with his probing, the way he can be when he wants to.

I shook my head. 'No, we were friends, John. I could talk to her about anything, and in ways I'd mostly forgotten. I've never been so comfortable with a woman so quickly, except maybe for Maria.'

Sampson nodded a lot, and mostly listened to me air it all out. He knew who I was, past and present.

My beeper sounded while we were still pushing around the generous portions of food on our plates. I called Kyle Craig from a phone downstairs in the restaurant. I reached him in his car. He was on his way to Hope Valley.

'We're about to arrest Wick Sachs for the Casanova murders,' he said. I almost dropped the receiver. 'You're about to *what*?' I shouted into the phone. I couldn't believe what I had just heard.

'When the hell is this going to happen?' I asked. 'When was the decision made? *Who* made it?'

Kyle kept his cool as always. The Iceman. 'We're going into the house in the next couple of minutes. This time it's the Durham police chief's game. Something was found in the house. *Physical evidence*. It will be a joint arrest, the Bureau in cooperation with the Durham PD. I wanted you to know, Alex.'

'He's not Casanova,' I said to Kyle. 'Don't take him down. Don't arrest Wick Sachs.' The level of my voice was high. The pay phone was in a narrow corridor of the restaurant, and people were filing in and out of the nearby restrooms. I was drawing stares, both angry and fearful looks.

'It's a done deal,' Kyle said. 'I'm sorry about it myself.' Then he hung up the car phone on me. End of discussion.

Sampson and I rushed to Sachs's house in the Durham suburbs. Man Mountain was quiet at first, then he asked the sixty-four-thousand-dollar question: 'Could they have enough to convict, without you knowing anything?' It was a tough question for me. His meaning: How out of the loop was I?

'I don't think Kyle has enough for an arrest now. He would have told me. The Durham PD? I don't know what the hell they're up to. Ruskin and Sikes have been off doing their own thing. We've been in their position ourselves.'

When we arrived in Hope Valley, I found out that we weren't the only ones who had been called to the arrest scene. The quiet suburban street was blocked off. Several TV station trucks and minivans were already there. Police cruisers and FBI sedans were parked everywhere.

'This is *really* fucked up. Looks like a block party.' Sampson said as we got out of the car. 'Worst I've seen, I think. Worst screwup.'

'It has been from the beginning,' I agreed. '*A multijuris-dictional nightmare.*' I was shaking like a wino in winter on a D.C. street. I had taken one body blow after another. Nothing completely made sense to me anymore. How out of the loop was I?

Kyle Craig saw me coming. He walked up to me and firmly grabbed my arm. I had the feeling he was ready to body-block me if necessary.

'I know how damn upset you are. So am I' were his first words. He seemed apologetic, but Kyle also appeared angry as hell. 'This wasn't our doing, Alex. Durham blindsided us this time. The chief of police made the decision himself. There's political pressure right up to the statehouse on this thing. Something smells so bad I want to put a handkerchief over my nose and mouth.'

'What the hell did they find in the house?' I asked Kyle. 'What physical evidence? Not the dirty books?'

Kyle shook his head. 'Women's underwear. He had a large cache of clothes hidden in the house. There was a University of North Carolina T-shirt that belonged to Kate McTiernan. Casanova apparently kept souvenirs, too. Just like the Gentleman in L.A.'

'He wouldn't do that. He's different from the Gentleman,' I said to Kyle. 'He has the girls and plenty of their clothes

383

at his hideaway. He's careful, and obsessive about it. Kyle, this is fucking crazy. This isn't the answer. This is a huge mess-up.'

'You don't know that for sure,' Kyle said. 'Good theories aren't going to stop this from happening.'

'How about good logic and a little common sense?'

'That won't work, either, I'm afraid.'

We started to walk toward the back porch of the Sachs house. TV cameras whirred into action, shooting anything that moved. It was a full-scale, three-ring media circus; a disaster of the highest order in progress.

'They searched the house sometime late this afternoon,' Kyle told me as we walked. 'Brought dogs in. Special dogs from Georgia.'

'Why the hell would they do that? Why suddenly search the Sachs house now? Goddammit.'

'They received a tip, and they had reason to believe it. That's what I'm getting from them. I'm on the outside, too, Alex. I don't like it any more than you do.'

I could barely see two feet ahead of me. My vision was tunneled. Stress will do that. Anger, too.

I wanted to shout, to scream out, at somebody. I wanted to punch out lights on the Sachses' veranda-style porch. 'Did they tell you *anything* about this anonymous tipster? Jesus Christ, Kyle. Goddammit to hell! An anonymous tip. Awhh *goddammit!*'

Wick Sachs was being held hostage inside his own beautiful house. The Durham police apparently wanted this historic moment recorded on local and national TV. This was it for them. North Carolina law-enforcement hall-of-fame time.

They had the wrong man, and they wanted to show him off to the world.

100

I recognized the Durham chief of police right away. He was in his early forties and looked like an ex-pro quarterback. Chief Robby Hatfield was around six two, square-jawed, powerfully built. I had a wild, paranoid thought that maybe he was Casanova. He looked the part, anyway. He even fit the psych profile of Casanova.

Detectives Sikes and Ruskin were flanking the prisoner, Dr Wick Sachs. I recognized a couple of other Durham detectives. They all appeared nervous as hell but jubilant, and mostly relieved. Sachs looked as if he'd taken a shower in his clothes. He looked guilty.

Are you Casanova? Are you the Beast after all? If so, what the hell are you pulling now? I wanted to ask Sachs a hundred questions, but couldn't.

Nick Ruskin and Davey Sikes joked around some with their brother officers in the crowded foyer. The two detectives reminded me of a few professional jocks I'd known around D.C. Most of them liked the spotlight; some of them lived for it. Most of the Durham police force seemed to operate like that, too.

Ruskin's hair was shiny and slicked back, combed back tight against his skull. He was ready for the spotlight, I could see. Davey Sikes looked ready, too. *You two bozos should be checking your list of doctor suspects*, I wanted to tell them. *This thing isn't over! It's just starting now. The real Casanova is cheering for you right now. Maybe he's watching from the crowd.*

I made my way up closer to Wick Sachs. I needed to see everything here, just as it was. Feel it. Watch and listen to it. Understand it, somehow.

Sachs's wife and the two beautiful children were being kept in the dining room off the vestibule. They looked hurt, very sad, and confused. They knew something was wrong here, too. The Sachs family didn't look guilty.

Chief Robby Hatfield and Davey Sikes finally saw me. Sikes reminded me of the chief's favorite bird dog. He was 'pointing' at me now.

'Dr Cross, thank you for your help on all this.' Chief Hatfield was magnanimous in his moment of triumph. I had forgotten that I was the one here who'd brought back the photo of Sachs from the Gentleman's apartment in Los Angeles. Such great detective work . . . such a convenient goddamn clue to discover.

This was all wrong. It just felt wrong and it smelled wrong. This was a setup of the first order, and it was working perfectly. Casanova was escaping; he was getting away right now. He would never be caught.

The Durham chief of police finally put out his hand. I took the chief's hand and squeezed it tight, held on to it.

I think he was afraid I was going to walk out into the

camera lights with him. Robby Hatfield had seemed like a hands-off administrator up until now. He and his star detectives were about to parade Wick Sachs outside. It would be a big dazzling moment under a full moon and the blazing klieg lights. All that was missing were the baying bloodhounds.

'I know I helped find him, but Wick Sachs didn't do it,' I told Hatfield straight to his face. 'You're arresting the wrong man. Let me tell you why. Give me ten minutes right now.'

He smiled at me, and it seemed like a goddamn condescending smile. It was almost as if he were stoned on the moment. Chief Hatfield pulled away from me and walked outside.

He walked out in front of the bright TV camera lights, playing his part beautifully. He was so taken with himself that he almost forgot about Sachs.

Whoever called about the women's underwear is Casanova, I was thinking to myself. I was getting closer in my mind to who that might be. *Casanova did this. Casanova is behind it, anyway.*

Dr Wick Sachs passed by me as they led him outside. He was dressed in a white cotton shirt and black trousers. All of his fine clothes were drenched through with his sweat. I imagined he was swimming in his shoes, too: gold-buckled black loafers. His hands were cuffed behind his back. All of his arrogance was long gone.

'I didn't do anything,' he said to me in the softest, choking voice. His eyes were pleading. He couldn't believe this, either. Then he said the most pathetic thing of all. 'I don't hurt women. I love them.'

I was struck with a mad, absolutely dizzying, thought on the Sachs porch. I felt as if I were in the middle of a somersault, and then I just stopped. Time stopped. *This is Casanova!* I suddenly understood.

Wick Sachs was the original model used for Casanova, anyway. That was the monsters' plan from the start: they had a fall guy for their perfect murders and de Sade-like adventures.

Dr Wick Sachs was actually Casanova, but he wasn't one of the monsters. Casanova was a front, too. He knew nothing about the real 'collector.' He was another victim.

101

'I'm the gentleman caller,' Will Rudolph announced with a polite, theatrical bow. He was wearing a dinner jacket, black tie, dress shirt. His hair was tied in a tight ponytail. He'd bought white roses for the special occasion.

'And you know who I am, ladies. You all look so very lovely,' Casanova spoke at his side. He was a striking contrast to his partner. Tight black jeans. Black cowboy boots. No shirt. His stomach washboard-hard. He had on a black fright mask with thick, handpainted median-gray streaks.

The killers introduced themselves as the women filed into the living room at the hideaway. They lined up in front of a long table.

This was to be a special celebration, they had been informed earlier in the day. 'The mad dog Casanova has finally been caught,' Casanova told them. 'It's all over the news. Turned out that he was some crazed college professor. Who can you trust these days?'

The women had been asked to wear serious party clothes, whatever they would choose for a special night out. Gowns with plunging necklines, high-heeled evening shoes with sheer stockings, and perhaps pearls or long earrings. No other jewelry. They were to look 'elegant.'

'Only seven pretty ladies here now,' Rudolph noted as he and Casanova watched the women enter the living room and form a receiving line. 'You're too picky, you know. The original Casanova was a voracious lover who wasn't choosy at all.'

'You have to admit that the seven are extraordinary,' Casanova said to his friend. 'My collection is a masterpiece, the best in the world.'

'I quite agree with you,' said the Gentleman. 'They look like paintings. Shall we begin?'

They had agreed to play an old favorite game. 'Lucky seven.' At other times it had been 'lucky four,' 'lucky eleven,' 'lucky two.' It was the Gentleman's game, actually. This was his night. Perhaps the final night at the house for the two of them.

They calmly walked down the receiving line. They talked with Melissa Stanfield first. Melissa wore a red silk sheath. Her long blonde hair was pinned back on one side. She reminded Casanova of a young Grace Kelly.

'Have you been saving yourself for me?' the Gentleman asked.

Melissa's smile was demure. 'I've been saving my heart for someone.'

Will Rudolph smiled at the clever answer. He ran the back of his hand across her cheek. He let his hand slowly track down her throat and over her firm breasts. She submitted without showing fear or revulsion. That was one of the rules when the games were played.

'You're very, very good at our little game,' he said. 'You're a worthy player, Melissa.'

390

Naomi Cross was next in the line. She had on an ivory cocktail dress. Very chic. She would have been the belle at some Washington law firm's ball. The scent of her perfume made Casanova feel a little giddy. He had been tempted to declare her off-limits to the Gentleman. He wasn't fond of her uncle, Alex Cross, after all.

'We might come back to visit with Naomi,' the Gentleman said. He lightly kissed her hand. '*Enchanté.*'

Rudolph nodded, then stopped at the sixth woman in the receiving line. He turned his head and checked out the final girl, then his eyes returned to number six.

'You're very special,' he spoke softly, almost shyly. 'Extraordinary, actually.'

'This is Christa,' Casanova said with a knowing smile.

'Christa is my date for tonight,' the Gentleman exclaimed in an enthusiastic voice. He'd made his choice. Casanova had given him a present – to do with as he pleased.

Christa Akers tried to smile. That was the house rule. But she couldn't. That was what the Gentleman especially liked about her: *the delicious fear in her eyes.*

He was ready to play *kiss the girls*.

One last time.

PART FIVE

Kiss the Girls

102

The morning after the arrest of Dr Wick Sachs, Casanova strolled the corridors of the Duke Medical Center. He calmly turned into Kate McTiernan's private room.

He could go anywhere now. He was free again.

'Hello, my darling. How goes the wars?' he whispered to Kate.

She was all by her lonesome, though there was still a Durham policeman stationed on the floor. Casanova sat on the straight-backed chair beside her bed. He looked at the sad physical wreck that had once been such an outstanding beauty.

He wasn't even angry with Kate anymore. There wasn't much to be angry with now, was there? *The lights are still on*, he thought as he stared into the vacant brown eyes, *but there's nobody home, is there, Katie?*

He enjoyed being in her hospital room – it got his juices going, turned him on, moved his spirit toward great things. Actually, just sitting beside Kate McTiernan's bed made him feel at peace.

That was important now. There were decisions to be made. How, exactly, to handle the situation with Dr Wick Sachs? Did more tinder need to be thrown on that fire? Or would that be overkill, and therefore dangerous in itself?

Another tricky decision would have to be made soon. Did he and Rudolph still have to leave the Research Triangle area? He didn't want to – this was home – but maybe it had to be. And how about Will Rudolph? He had clearly been emotionally disturbed in California. He had been taking Valium, Halcion, and Xanax – that Casanova *knew* of. Sooner or later he was going to blow it for both of them, wasn't he? On the other hand, it had been so unbearably lonely when Rudolph was away. He'd felt cut in half.

Casanova heard a noise behind him at the hospital room door. He turned – *and smiled at the man.*

'I was just leaving, Alex,' he said, and got up from the chair. 'No change here. What a damn shame.'

Alex Cross let Casanova slide by him and out the door.

He fit in anywhere, Casanova thought to himself as he walked away and down the hospital corridor. He was never going to be caught. He had the perfect mask.

103

There was a fine old upright piano inside the barroom at the Washington Duke Inn. I was there playing Big Joe Turner and Blind Lemon Jefferson tunes between four and five one morning. I played the blues, the blahs, the doldrums, the grumps, the red ass. The hotel maintenance staff sure was impressed.

I was trying to put everything I knew together. I kept circling back to the same big three or four points, my pillars to build the investigation on.

Perfect crimes, both here and in California. The killer's knowledge of crime scenes and police forensics.

Twinning between the monsters. Male bonding as it had never existed.

The disappearing house in the woods. A house had actually disappeared! How could that happen?

Casanova's harem of special women – but even more than that, the 'rejects.'

Dr Wick Sachs was a college professor with questionable morals and actions. But was he a stone-cold murderer without a conscience? Was he the animal who had imprisoned a dozen or more young women somewhere near Durham and Chapel Hill? Was he a modern-day de Sade?

I didn't think so. I believed, I was almost certain, that the Durham police had arrested the wrong man, and that the real Casanova was out there laughing at all of us. Maybe it was even worse than that. Maybe he was stalking another woman.

Later that morning, I made my usual visit to Kate at Duke Medical Center. She was still deep in a coma, still listed as grave. The Durham police no longer had an officer on guard outside her room.

I sat vigil beside her and tried not to think about the way she had been. I held her hand for an hour and quietly talked to her. Her hand was limp, almost lifeless. I missed Kate so much. She couldn't respond, and that created a gaping, painful hole in my chest.

Finally, I had to leave. I needed to lose myself in my work. From the hospital, Sampson and I drove to the home of Louis Freed in Chapel Hill. I had asked Dr Freed to prepare a special map of the Wykagil River area for us.

The seventy-seven-year-old history professor had done his job well. I hoped the map might help Sampson and me find the 'disappearing house.' The idea came to me after reading several newspaper accounts of the golden couple murder case. Over twelve years ago, Roe Tierney's body had been found near 'an abandoned farm where runaway slaves had once been hidden in large underground cellars. These cellars were like small houses under the earth, some with as many as a dozen rooms or compartments.'

Small houses under the earth?

The disappearing house?

There *was* a house out there somewhere. Houses didn't disappear.

104

Sampson and I drove to Brigadoon, North Carolina. We planned to hike through the woods to where Kate had been found in the Wykagil River. Ray Bradbury had once written that 'living at risk is jumping off a cliff, and building your wings on the way down.' Sampson and I were getting ready to jump.

As we trudged into the foreboding woods, the towering oaks and Carolina pines began to shut out all light. A chorus of cicadas was thick as molasses around us. The air wasn't moving.

I could imagine, I could *see*, Kate running through these same dark green woods only a few weeks earlier, fighting for her life. I thought of her now, surviving on life-support systems. I could hear the machine's *whoosh-click, whoosh-click*. Just the thought hurt my heart.

'I don't like it in the deep dark woods,' Sampson confessed as we passed under a thick umbrella of twisted vines and tent-like treetops. He had on a Cypress Hill T-shirt, his Ray-Ban sunglasses, jeans, workboots. 'Reminds me of Hansel and Gretel. Melodramatic bullshit, man. Hated that story when I was a little kid.'

'You were never a little kid,' I reminded him. 'You were six foot when you were eleven, and you already had your cold stare down to a fine art.'

'Maybe so, but I hated those Grimm Brothers. Dark side of the German mind, turning out nasty fantasies to warp the minds of little German children. Must have worked, too.'

Sampson had me smiling again with his warped theories of our warped world. 'You're not afraid going through the D.C. projects at night, but a nice walk in these woods gets you? Nothing can hurt you here. Pine trees. Muscadine grapevines. Brier brambles. Looks sinister, maybe, but it's harmless.'

'Looks sinister. Is sinister. That's my motto.'

Sampson was struggling to get his statuesque body through closely bunched saplings and honeysuckle at the edge of the woods. The honeysuckle was actually like a mesh curtain in places. It seemed to *grow* tangled.

I wondered if Casanova might be watching us. I suspected that he was a very patient watcher. Both he and Will Rudolph were very clever, organized, and careful. They had been doing this for a lot of years and hadn't been caught yet.

'How's your history on the slaves in this area?' I asked Sampson as we walked. I wanted his mind off poisonous snakes and dangling snakelike vines. I needed him concentrating on the killer, or maybe the killers, who might be cohabiting these woods with us.

'I've dabbled with some E. D. Genovese, some Mohamed Auad,' he said. I couldn't tell if he was serious. Sampson is well read for a man of action.

'The Underground Railroad was active in this area.

400

Runaway slaves and whole families heading north were kept safe for days, even weeks, at some of the local farms. They were called stations,' I said. 'That's what Dr Freed's map shows. That's what his book was written about.'

'I don't see any farms, Dr Livingston. Just this muscadine grapevine shit,' Sampson complained and pushed away more branches with his long arms.

'The big tobacco farms used to be west of here. They've been deserted for almost sixty years. Remember I told you that a student from UNC was brutally raped and murdered back in nineteen eighty-one? Her decomposed body was found out here. I think Rudolph, and possibly Casanova, killed her. That's around the time they first met.

'Dr Freed's map shows the locations of the old Underground Railroad, most of the farms in the area where runaway slaves were hidden. Some of the farms had expanded cellars, even underground living quarters. The farms themselves are gone now. There's nothing to see from aerial surveillance. The honeysuckle and brambles have grown thick, too. The cellars are still here, though.'

'Hmmph. Your handy-dandy map tell us where all the old-time tobacco farms used to be?'

'Yup. Got a map. Got a compass. Got my Glock pistol, too,' I said and patted my holster.

'Most important,' Sampson said, 'you got me.'

'That too. God save the miscreants from the two of us.'

Sampson and I walked a long, long way into the hot, damp, buggy afternoon. We managed to find three of the farm sites where tobacco leaf had once flourished; where terrified black men and women, sometimes whole families, had been taken in and hidden in old cellars, as they tried to escape to freedom in the North, to cities like Washington, D.C.

Two of the cellars were located exactly where Dr Freed said they would be. Antique wood planks and twisted, rusted metal were the only signs left of the original farms. It was as if some angry god had come down and destroyed the scenc of the old slave-owning ways.

Around four in the afternoon, Sampson and I arrived at the once-proud-and-successful farm of Jason Snyder and his family.

'How do you know we're *here?*' Sampson looked around at the small, desolate, and deserted area where I had stopped walking.

'Says so on Dr Louis Freed's hand-drawn map. Same compass points. He's a famous historian, so it must be true.'

Sampson was right, though. There was nothing to see. Jason Snyder's farm had completely disappeared. Just as Kate had said it would.

105

'Place gives me the creeps,' Sampson said. 'So-called tobacco farm.'

What was once the Snyder farm was particularly eerie and otherworldly, creepy as hell. There was almost no visual evidence that anyone human had ever lived here. Still, I could feel the blood and bones of the slaves as I stood before the disturbing ruins of the old tobacco farm.

Sassafras trees, arrowwood shrubs, honeysuckle, and poison ivy had grown up to the level of my chin. Red and white oaks, sycamores, and a few sweet gum trees stood tall and mature where a prosperous farm had once been. But the farm itself *had* disappeared.

I felt a cold spot at the center of my chest. Was this the bad place, then? Could we be near the house of horror that Kate had described?

We had worked our way north, and now east. We weren't too far from the state highway, where I wished I had the car parked. According to my rough calculations, we couldn't be more than two or three miles from the state road.

'Search parties for Casanova never came all the way back in here,' Sampson said as he prowled around. 'Undergrowth's real thick, real nasty. Not trampled down anywhere I can see.'

'Dr Freed said he was probably the last person to come out and examine each of the old Underground Railroad sites. The woods were getting too thick and overgrown for casual visitors,' I said.

Blood and bones of my ancestors. That was a powerful, almost overwhelming, notion: to walk where slaves were once held captive *for years*.

No one ever came to rescue them. No one cared. No detectives back then went looking for human monsters who stole entire black families from their homes.

I used natural landmarks from the map to locate where the original Snyder cellar might have been. I was also trying to brace myself – in case we found something I didn't want to find.

'We're probably looking for a very old trapdoor,' I told Sampson. 'There isn't anything specific marked on Freed's map. The cellar is supposed to be forty to fifty feet west of those sycamores. I think those are the right trees, and we should be right over the cellar now. But where the hell is the door?'

'Probably where nobody would walk on it by mistake,' Sampson figured. He was making a path into the thicker, wilder undergrowth.

Beyond the tangle of vines there was an open field or meadow, where tobacco had once been planted and grown. Beyond that was more thick woods. The air was hot and still. Sampson was getting impatient, and he knocked down honey-suckle with a vengeance. He was stamping his feet, trying to locate the hidden door. He listened for a hollow sound, some kind of wood or metal under the tall grass and thickly tangled weeds.

'This was originally a very large cellar on two levels. Casanova might have even expanded it. Built something grander for his house of horror,' I said as I searched through the heavy undergrowth.

I thought of Naomi kept underneath the ground for so long. She had been my obsession all of these days and weeks. She still was. Sampson had been right about these woods. They were eerie, and I felt we were standing at an evil place where forbidden, secretive things had been done. Naomi could be somewhere close by, underneath the ground.

'You're getting hoodoo-spooky on me again. Trying to think like this nutty squirrel. You sure Dr Emeritus Sachs isn't Casanova?' Sampson asked as he worked.

'No, I'm not. But I don't know why the Durham PD arrested him, either. How did they just happen to find out the underwear was there? How did the underwear get in his house in the first place?'

'Because maybe he is Casanova, Sugar. Because maybe he put the victims' underwear there so he could sniff it on rainy afternoons. FBI and Durham crime-fighters going to close down the case now?'

'If there isn't another killing or abduction for a while. Once they shut the case, the real Casanova can relax, plan for the future.'

Sampson stood up tall and stretched his long neck. He sighed, and then he moaned loudly. His T-shirt was soaked through with sweat. He peered up at the overhanging vines. 'We got a long walk back to the car. Long, dark, hot, buggy walk.'

'Not yet. Stick with me on this.'

I didn't want to leave and stop our search for the day. Having Sampson around again was a major plus. There were still three more farms on Dr Freed's map. Two of them sounded promising; the other seemed as if it might be too small. So maybe that was the very one Casanova had chosen for his hideaway. He was a contrarian, wasn't he?

So was I. I wanted to keep searching through the night, dark woods or not, black snakes and copperheads or not, twin killers or not.

I remembered Kate's terrifying stories about the disappearing house and what went on inside. What had really happened to Kate the day she escaped? If the house wasn't in these woods – where in God's name was it? It had to be underground. Nothing else made sense . . .

Nothing made any goddamn sense yet.

Unless someone had purposely cleared away every last remnant of the farm.

Unless someone had used the old wood for other building purposes.

I finally took out my pistol and searched around for something, anything, to shoot at. Sampson watched me out of the corner of his eye. Curious, but not saying anything yet.

I needed to get some anger out. Release some venom, some stress. Right here and now. There was nothing to target-shoot at, though. No underground house of horror.

But also *no rotting planks from the farmhouse or barn.* Not one remnant that I had seen.

I finally fired a round at the knobby trunk of a nearby tree. In my incipient craziness, a knot in the tree resembled the head of a man. A man like Casanova. I fired again and again. All direct hits, dead-solid perfect. I had killed Casanova!

'Feel better now?' Sampson peered over the top of his Ray-Ban sunglasses at me. 'You hit the bogeyman in his evil eye?'

'I feel a little better. Not much.' I showed him my thumb and forefinger, spread about a millimeter apart.

Sampson leaned against a small tree that looked like a human skeleton. The little sapling wasn't getting enough light. 'I *do* think it's time we packed up and left,' he said.

That was when we heard screams!

Women's voices were coming from *under the ground.*

The screams were muffled, but we could hear them clearly all the same. They were to the north of us and even farther into the thick bramble, but closer to the open meadow beyond the old tobacco fields.

A tightly wound ball of tension hit me with tremendous force at the sound of the voices under the ground. My head slumped involuntarily toward my chest.

Sampson took out his Glock and squeezed off two quick shots, more signals for the trapped women, for whoever was screaming under the ground.

The muffled screams were getting louder, rising as if from the tenth circle of hell.

'Sweet Baby Jesus,' I whispered. 'We found them, John. We found the house of horror.'

106

Sampson and I got down on our hands and knees. We searched frantically for the hidden entryway into the underground house, running our fingers and palms over the undergrowth until they were cut and bleeding. I looked down and my hands were shaking.

I fired off several more gunshots, so the women trapped below would know we'd heard them, and that we were still up here. After I fired the shots, I quickly reloaded.

'We're up here!' I yelled, with my head close to the ground. The weeds and grass were scratching my face. 'We're police!'

'Here we go, Alex,' Sampson called to me. 'The door's over here. There's some kind of door, anyway.'

Running through the high thick weeds was like wading in water. The trapdoor was hidden in honeysuckle and waist-high grass, where Sampson had been searching. The door had been covered over with an extra layer of sod and a thick blanket of pine needles. The door wasn't likely to be found by a search party, or anyone else hiking through the woods.

'I'll go down first,' I told Sampson. Blood roared and echoed in my ears. Usually he would have argued. Not this time.

I hurried, rumbling down a steep, narrow wooden stairway that looked as if it had been there for a hundred years. Sampson followed close behind. The *good* twins.

Stop! I told myself. *Slow it down.* At the bottom of the stairs, there was a second doorway. The heavy oak plank door looked new, as if it had been installed recently, possibly in the past year or two. I slowly turned the handle. The door was locked.

'I'm coming in,' I shouted to anyone who might be behind the door. Then I fired two rounds into the lock and it disintegrated. The wooden door heaved open with a hard shove from my shoulder.

I was finally inside the house of horror. What I saw made me retch. A woman's body was laid out on a couch in what appeared to be a well-appointed living room. The corpse had begun to decompose. The features were unrecognizable. Maggots were swarming all over the victim.

Move, I had to tell myself. *Go! Go now.*

'I'm right behind you,' Sampson whispered in his deep, homicide-scene voice. 'Watch yourself now, Alex.'

'This is the police!' I called out. My voice was shaky and getting hoarse. I was afraid of what else we might find in the hideaway. Was Naomi still here? Was she alive?

'We're down here!' a woman called out. 'Can anybody hear me?'

'We hear you! We're coming!' I shouted again.

'Please help us!' A second voice sounded farther away in the underground house. 'Be careful. He's tricky.'

'See. He's tricky,' Sampson whispered. Never at a loss.

'He's in the house! *He's in here now*!' one of the women shouted a warning to us.

Sampson was still standing behind me, keeping close. 'You want to keep the point, partner? Walk on the ridge line?'

'I want to be the one to find her,' I told him. 'I have to find Scootchie.'

He didn't argue. 'You think loverboy is down here someplace? Casanova?' he whispered.

'That's the rumor going around,' I said and moved forward slowly. Both of us had our guns drawn and ready. We had no idea what to expect next. Was loverboy waiting for us? *Move! Move! Move those legs!*

I led the way out of the deserted living room. There were high-tech lamps in the ceiling of the adjoining hallway. How was he able to get electricity in here? A transformer? A generator? What should that tell me? That he was handy? That he had connections with the local electric company?

How long had it taken to get the underground cellar in this condition? I wondered. To fix it up like this? To make his fantasy come true?

The space was extensive. We entered a long hallway that snaked off the living room to the right. There were doors on either side, and they were bolt-locked from the outside, like prison cells.

'Watch our backs,' I said to Sampson. 'I'm going in door number one.'

'I always watch your back,' he whispered.

'Watch *your* back, too.'

I went up to the first door. 'This is the police,' I called out. 'I'm Detective Alex Cross. Everything's going to be all right.'

I yanked open the first door and peered inside. I wanted it to be Naomi. I prayed that it was.

410

107

'Such utter fools,' said the Gentleman, intolerant and impatient as always. 'Two carnival clowns in blackface.'

Casanova smiled thinly, growing impatient with the Gentleman. 'What the hell did you expect? Brain surgeons from Walter Reed in Washington? They're a couple of ordinary street cops.'

'Not so ordinary, perhaps. They found the house, didn't they? They're inside right now.'

The two friends watched everything coming together from a nearby hiding place in the woods. They had tracked the detectives all afternoon, observing them with binoculars. Plotting, planning, but also playing with their prey. They were careful as they moved in for the final confrontation.

'Why didn't they bring the others out here? Why didn't they bring *the FBI*?' Rudolph asked. He was always inquisitive and very logical. A logic machine; a killing machine; but a machine that ran without a human heart.

Casanova looked through the powerful German binoculars again. He could see the open trapdoor that led down into the underground house, the masterpiece that he and Rudolph had built by hand.

'It's their policeman's arrogance,' he finally answered Rudolph's question. 'In some ways, they're like us. Cross is especially. He trusts himself and no one else.'

He glanced over at Will Rudolph, and both men smiled. The irony was beautiful, actually. The two detectives against the two of them.

'Cross probably thinks he understands us, our relationship, that is,' Rudolph said. 'Maybe he does a little bit.' He had been paranoid about Alex Cross since the close call in California. Cross had tracked him down, after all, and that frightened him. But the Gentleman also found Cross interesting as an opponent. He enjoyed the competition, the blood sport.

'He understands some things, he sees *patterns*, so he thinks he knows more than he actually does. Just be patient, and we'll expose Cross's weaknesses.'

As long as they were patient, Casanova believed, as long as they thought everything through carefully, they would win; they would never be caught. It had been that way for years, from the first day they met at Duke University.

Casanova knew that Will Rudolph had been careless out in California. He'd had that disturbing tendency even as a brilliant medical student. He was impatient, and had been sloppy and melodramatic when he killed Roe Tierney and Tom Hutchinson. He had almost been caught back then. He was questioned by the police, and had been a serious suspect in the famous case.

Casanova thought about Alex Cross again, evaluating the detective's strengths and weaknesses. Cross *was* careful, and he was a thorough 'professional.' He almost always

412

thought things through before he acted. He was certainly smarter than the rest of the pack. A cop *and* a psychologist. He'd found the hideaway, hadn't he? He'd gotten this far, closer than all the others.

John Sampson was more impulsive. He was the weak point, though he certainly didn't look it. He was physically powerful, but he would be the one to break first. And breaking Sampson would break Cross. The two detectives were close friends; they were extremely emotional about each other.

'It was stupid for us to split up a year ago, to go our separate ways,' Casanova said to his only real friend in the world. 'If we hadn't begun to compete and play egocentric games, Cross would never have found out anything about us. He wouldn't have found you, and we wouldn't have to kill the girls and destroy the house now.'

'Let me take care of the good Dr Cross,' Rudolph said. He didn't react to the things Casanova had just said. Rudolph never showed much emotion, but actually he'd been lonely, too. He'd come back, hadn't he?

'No one takes care of Dr Cross alone,' Casanova said. 'We'll go after them together. We make it two against one, the way we work best. First, Sampson. Then Alex Cross. I know how he'll react. I know how *he* thinks. I've been watching him. Actually, I've been hunting Alex Cross since he came to the South.'

The two human monsters moved closer to the house.

108

I switched on overhead lights in the first room and I saw one of the captive women. Maria Jane Capaldi cowered like a frightened little girl against the far wall. I knew who she was. I'd met her parents a week or so back; I had seen old, cherished photographs of her.

'Please don't hurt me. I can't take any more of this,' Maria Jane pleaded in a hoarse whisper.

She was hugging herself, rocking gently back and forth. She had on ripped black tights and a wrinkled Nirvana T-shirt. Maria Jane was just nineteen years old, an art major and aspiring painter at North Carolina State in Raleigh.

'I'm a police detective,' I whispered in the softest voice possible. 'Nobody can hurt you now. We won't let them.'

Maria Jane moaned, and she began to cry tears of relief. Her whole body was quivering.

'He can't hurt you now, Maria Jane,' I reassured her in the softest voice I could manage. I could barely speak, actually. 'I have to find the others. I'll be back, I promise you. I'm leaving your door open. You can come out. You're safe now.'

I had to help the others. *His harem of special women was right here. Naomi was one of them.*

I broke into the next room in the passageway. I still couldn't catch my breath. I was exhilarated, frightened, saddened – all at the same time.

A tall blonde woman in the room told me her name was Melissa Stanfield. I remembered the name. She was in nursing school. I had so many questions, but there was time for only one.

I gently touched her shoulder. She shuddered, then collapsed against me. 'Do you know where Naomi Cross is?' I asked her.

'I'm not sure,' Melissa said. 'I don't know the whole layout here.' She shook her head and began to cry. I don't think she even knew who I was talking about.

'You're safe now. The nightmare is finally over, Melissa. Let me help the others,' I whispered.

Out in the hall again, I saw Sampson unbolt a door. I heard him say, 'I'm a police detective. It's safe now.' His voice was soft: *Sampson the Gentle.*

The women we had freed were wandering, dazed and confused, out of the prison rooms. They hugged one another in the hallway. Most of them were sobbing, but I could feel their relief, even their joy. Someone had finally come to help them.

I entered a second hallway at the end of the first. There were more locked doors. Was Naomi here? Was she alive? The pounding in my chest was unbearable.

I opened the first door on the right – and there she was. There was Scootchie. The best sight in the entire world.

Tears finally streamed from my eyes. I was the one who couldn't talk now. I thought that I would have a permanent memory of everything that happened between the two of us. Every word, look, nuance.

'I knew you'd come for me, Alex,' Naomi said. She staggered into my arms and held me tightly.

'Oh, sweet, sweet Naomi,' I whispered. I felt as if thousands of pounds had been lifted off me. 'This makes it worth everything. Well, almost.'

I had to look at her up close. I held her precious face in both my hands. She seemed so fragile and tiny in the room. But she was alive! I had finally found her.

I called out for Sampson. '*I found Naomi! We found her, John! In here! We're in here!*'

Scootchie and I folded into each other's arms, just like old times. If I'd regretted becoming a detective at any other time, this made up for it. I realized now that I'd thought she was dead – I just couldn't give up the fight. Never give up.

'I knew you'd be here, just like this. I dreamed it. I lived for *this instant*. I prayed every day, and here you are.' Naomi managed the most wonderful smile I have ever seen. 'I love you.'

'I love you, too. I missed you like crazy. Everybody did.' After a moment I gently pulled away from Naomi.

I remembered about the monsters, and the way they had to be thinking now. Still plotting everything. Leopold and Loeb all grown up, committing perfect crimes.

'Are you sure you're okay?' I smiled finally, the beginning of a smile, anyway.

I could see some of the old intensity returning to Naomi's eyes. 'Alex, go. Get the others out,' she urged me. 'Please let the others out of these cages he kept us in.'

Just then a strange, terrible sound echoed in the passageway. A scream of pain. I ran from Naomi's room and saw the one thing I could never imagine happening, not in my worst nightmares.

109

The loud, deep-voiced call for help had come from Sampson. My partner was in trouble. Two men, both wearing ghoulish masks, were struggling over him. Casanova and Rudolph? Who else could it be?

Sampson was down in the hallway. His mouth was open in shock and pain. A knife, or ice pick, protruded from the center of his back.

It was a situation I had faced twice before, riding patrol on Washington's streets. A partner in trouble. I had no choice and probably only one chance. I didn't hesitate. I raised my Glock and fired.

I surprised them with the quick shot. They hadn't expected me to shoot while they were holding Sampson. The taller of the monsters grabbed his shoulder and fell back. The other looked down the hallway at me. The cold glare of the fierce death mask was a warning. Still, I'd taken away their edge.

I fired the pistol a second time, aiming at the second death mask. All the lights went out suddenly in the underground house. At the same time, rock 'n' roll music erupted from

417

speakers hidden somewhere in the walls. Axl Rose howled 'Welcome to the Jungle.'

Pitch-blackness fell over the hallway. The rock music shook the foundations of the building. I clung to the walls, and moved steadily toward where Sampson had gone down.

My eyes pressed into the darkness, and a terrible fear swept over me. They had jumped Sampson and that was no easy task. The two of them seemed to have appeared from nowhere. Was there another way in or out?

I heard a familiar low growl. Sampson was up ahead. 'I'm here. Guess I didn't watch my back,' he gasped out the words.

'Don't talk.' I moved closer to where his voice had come from. I knew approximately where he was now. I was afraid that maybe they hadn't left. They had just improved their odds, and I was sure they were waiting to jump me.

They liked to work two on one. They needed to twin. They needed each other. Together they were unbeatable. So far.

I inched my way along the wall, pressing against it with my back. I moved toward shapes and shifting shadows at the end of the passageway.

There was a faint glimmer of amber light ahead. I could see Sampson curled up on the floor. My heart was pounding so fast there was barely a space between the beats. My partner was badly hurt. This had never happened before, not even when we were kids on the streets of D.C.

'I'm here,' I said to Sampson, kneeling beside him. I touched his arm. 'You bleed to death, I'll be pissed off,' I told him. 'Just be real still.'

'Don't sweat it. I'm not going into shock, either. Nothing shocks me anymore,' he groaned.

'Don't be a hero.' I held his head lightly against my side. 'You've got a knife stuck in the middle of your back.'

'I am a hero . . . go on! . . . You can't let them get away now. You already hit one. They headed toward the stairs. The same way we came in.'

'Go, Alex. You have to get them!' I turned at the sound of Naomi's voice. She knelt over Sampson. 'I'll take care of him.'

'I'll be back,' I said. Then I was gone.

I turned a dark corner of the long passageway in a low shooting crouch. I found myself entering the first corridor we'd come to. *They headed toward the stairs*, Sampson had said.

Light at the end of the tunnel? Monsters hiding along the way? I moved faster in the semidarkness. Nothing would stop me now. Well, maybe Casanova and Rudolph could. Two against one weren't the odds I wanted on their home field.

I found the doorway out at last. There was no lock, no doorknob. I'd blown it away.

The stairway was clear, at least it looked that way. The trap-door was open, and I could see dark pine trees and patches of blue sky overhead. Were they waiting up there for me? The two clever monsters!

I climbed the wooden steps as quickly as I could. My finger was light on the Glock's trigger. Everything was surging out of control again.

I exploded up the final stairs like an all-pro fullback through a small hole in the line of scrimmage. I burst from the rectangular opening in the ground. Did a semiacrobatic roll. Came up firing the Glock. At the least, my combat routine might ruin somebody's aim.

No one was there to shoot me, or applaud my performance, either. The deep woods were silent and appeared absolutely empty.

The monsters had disappeared . . . and so had the house.

110

I chose the same general direction that Sampson and I had come in. It was definitely one way out of the woods, and it might be the route Casanova and Will Rudolph would take. I hated leaving Sampson and the women, but there was no other choice, no other way.

I stuck the Glock into my shoulder holster and I started to run. Faster and faster as my legs began to work again, remembered how to *run fast*.

A trail of fresh blood on leaves led a few yards into the thick undergrowth. One of them was bleeding heavily. I hoped he would die soon. I was on the right trail, anyway.

Vines and thorny bushes tore at my arms and legs as I moved through the densely overgrown thicket. The leafy branches whipped across my face. I didn't care about being whipped.

I ran for what must have been a mile, or seemed like it. I was perspiring, and searing pains ripped through my chest. My head felt as hot as the engine of an overheated car. Every footstep seemed heavier than the last.

For all I knew, I was putting distance between myself and the two of them. Or maybe they were right behind me? Maybe they had watched me come out? Trailed me? Circled around behind me? Two on one wasn't how I wanted this to go down.

I looked for more signs of blood or torn clothing. Some sign that they had been through here. My lungs were on fire now, and I was soaked with perspiration. My legs ached and were tightening up.

I had a flashback, a rush of images. I was running with Marcus Daniels in my arms, in Washington, D.C. I saw the poor little boy's face again now. I remembered hearing Sampson scream in shock and pain back at the house. I saw Naomi's face.

Something was up ahead – *two men were running*. One of them was holding his shoulder. Was it Casanova? Or the Gentleman? Didn't really matter – I wanted both of them. Wouldn't settle for less.

The wounded monster showed no signs of slowing. He knew I was bearing down on him, and he unleashed a blood-curdling yell. It reminded me that he was an unpredictable madman of the highest order. The scream – '*Yaaaaahhhhhh*!' – echoed through the fir woods like the howl of a wild animal.

Then another primal scream. '*Yaaaaahhhhhh*!' It was the *other* madman.

Twinning, I thought. They were both natural animals. They couldn't survive anymore without each other.

The sudden sound of gunfire caught me off guard. A chip flew off the bark of a pine tree and whipped past my head. It came within an inch or two of cutting me down, killing me on the spot. *One of the monsters had turned around that fast, fired off a shot.*

421

I crouched behind the tree that had taken a bullet for me. I peered out through leafy branches. I couldn't see either of them up ahead. I waited. Counted off the seconds. Tried to get my heart to start again. Which one of them had fired the shot? Which one was wounded?

They had been near a crest of a steep hill in the woods. Had they gone over the top? If they had, were they waiting for me on the other side? I slowly moved out from the safe cover of the tree and looked around.

It was eerie and quiet again. No screams. No gunshots. No one seemed to be there. What the hell were they up to? *I had just learned something new about them, though.* I had another clue to go on. I'd seen something important a moment ago.

I sprinted to the balding crest of the hill up ahead. Nothing! My heart sank, fell a million miles into the abyss. Had they gotten away? After all this?

I kept running. I couldn't let this abomination happen. I wouldn't let the monsters go free.

111

I thought I knew the direction to the state highway, and I headed that way. I had my second wind, or maybe my third, and ran more easily now. Alex the Pathfinder.

Maybe two hundred yards ahead of me, I spotted them again. Then I saw a familiar flash of gray: a curling ribbon of highway. I could make out a few white-shingled buildings and ancient-looking telephone lines. *A highway. The way for them to escape*.

The two of them were running in the direction of a shambling roadhouse. They still wore their death masks. That told me Casanova was in charge. The natural leader. He loved his masks. They represented who he believed he really was: a dark god. Free to do whatever he chose. Superior to the rest of us.

A red-and-blue neon sign blinked *Trail Dust* on the roadhouse roof. It was one of those country gin mills that got good customer traffic all day. The monsters were heading that way.

Casanova and the Gentleman Caller climbed into a

late-model blue pickup truck parked in the lot. Busy tavern lots were a good place to park a car inconspicuously. I knew that as a detective. I raced across the state road toward the roadhouse.

A man with long, frizzy red hair was just climbing into his Plymouth Duster in the parking area. He wore a wrinkled Coca-Cola workshirt, and had a bulky brown bag shoved under one arm. Liquid groceries.

'Police.' I flashed my badge a foot from his lightly bearded chin. 'I have to take your car!' I had my pistol out, ready for trouble if it came at me. I was definitely taking the car.

'Jesus Christ, man. This here's my girlfriend's car,' he drawled rapidly. His eyes stayed on the Glock. He handed over the car keys.

I pointed back toward where I'd come from. 'Call the police right now. The missing women are back there, maybe a mile and a half. Tell them there's an officer down! Tell them it's Casanova's hideaway.'

I jumped into the Duster, and was doing forty before I got out of the parking lot. In the rearview mirror I could see the man with the six-pack still staring at me. I wanted to call Kyle Craig myself and have him send help, but I couldn't stop now, couldn't lose Casanova and his friend.

The dark blue pickup headed toward Chapel Hill . . . where Casanova had tried to kill Kate, where he had originally kidnapped her. Was that his home base, after all? Was he someone from the University of North Carolina? Another doctor? Someone we had never even heard of? Not only was that possible, it was likely.

I closed to within four car lengths of them inside the city limits. No way to tell if they knew I was there. Probably they did. Chapel Hill's version of rush hour was in progress.

Franklin Street was a narrow winding stream of traffic rolling slowly alongside the tree-lined campus.

Up ahead I could see the funky Varsity Theatre, where Wick Sachs had gone to a foreign movie with a woman named Suzanne Wellsley. It had been adultery, nothing more, nothing less. Dr Wick Sachs had been set up by Casanova and Will Rudolph. Sachs had made a perfect suspect in the case. *The local pornographer.* Casanova had known all about him. How was that?

I was close to getting them now; I could feel it. I had to think like that. They caught a red light at the corner of Franklin and Columbia. Students wearing ratty T-shirts with Champion and Nike and Bass Ale logos jaywalked between the stopped cars. Shaquille O'Neal's 'I Know I Got Skillz' played loudly from somebody's radio.

I waited a few seconds after the stoplight turned red with a noisy *click-click* sound. Then I went for the whole enchilada. *Ready or not, here I come.*

112

I slid out of the Duster and ran in a low crouch down the middle of Franklin Street. The Glock was out, but held flat against my leg to be less conspicuous. *Nobody panic and scream now. Let this go right one time.*

The two of them must have spotted the trailing Duster earlier. I'd figured as much. As soon as I hit the street, they threw themselves out of opposite sides of the pickup.

One turned and fired off three quick shots. *Pop. Pop. Pop.* Only one of them had a gun out. Something clicked inside my head again: I remembered a quick scene from the woods. A connection made. A flash of recognition.

I ducked down behind a black Nissan Z that was waiting for the light, and yelled at the top of my lungs. 'Police! Police! Get down! Get down on the ground! Get out of these cars!'

Most of the drivers and pedestrians did as they were told. What a difference between Chapel Hill and the streets of D.C., in that regard. I took a quick peek up the sheet-metal lane between the cars. I didn't see either of the killers anywhere.

I slid alongside the black sports car, bent over more than double in a low-slung crouch. Students and store owners watched me warily from the sidewalk. 'Police! Get down. Get down. Get that little boy the hell out of here!' I yelled.

I saw crazy things in my mind's eye. Flashing images. Sampson . . . with a knife in his back. Kate . . . after they had beaten her to a bloody, helpless mess. The sunken eyes of the women prisoners back at the house.

I was keeping low to the ground, but one of the monsters saw me and went for a head shot. We both fired at almost the same time.

His bullet barely nicked a sideview mirror that was between us. It probably saved me. I didn't see the final result of my shot.

I went down behind the cars again. The stench of motor oil and gas was almost overpowering. A police siren wailing in the distance told me help was on the way. Not Sampson, though. Not the kind of help I needed.

Just keep moving. Keep them both in sight somehow . . . two of them! Two versus one. Better way to think about it: two for the price of one!

I wondered how well they would deal with this. What they were thinking. Planning. Was Casanova the leader now? Who was he?

I looked up quickly and saw a cop. He was near the corner of the street and his revolver was out. I never had a chance to shout a warning.

A gun fired twice from his left and the patrolman went down hard. People were screaming all over Franklin Street. Jaded college kids didn't look so blasé anymore. Some of the girls were crying. Maybe they finally understood that we're all very mortal.

'Get down!' I shouted again. 'Everybody get the hell down!'

I ducked behind the cars again and inched my way up on the side of a minivan. I saw one of the monsters as my eyes cleared shiny, silver sheet metal.

My next shot wasn't so ambitious, no hero crap. I was willing to settle for a hit anywhere. Chest, shoulders, lower torso. I fired!

Trick shot, fuckhead. Watch this one. The bullet exploded through both passenger windows of a deserted Ford Taurus. It caught one of the bad guys high in the chest, just below the throat.

He dropped as if his legs had been pulled from underneath him. I sprinted as fast as I could toward the place I'd seen him standing last. *Which one went down?* my brain was screaming. *And where is the other one?*

I darted in and out between the parked cars. *He was gone! He wasn't there!* Where the hell was the one I had shot? And where was the other clever boy hiding?

I saw the one I'd hit. He lay spread-eagled under the traffic light at Columbia and Franklin. The death mask still covered his face, but he looked almost ordinary in his white hightops, tan khakis, and Windbreaker.

I didn't see a gun anywhere around him. He wasn't moving, and I knew he was badly hurt. I crouched on my knees over him, my eyes darting around as I checked him out. *Careful! Careful*, I warned myself. I didn't see his partner anywhere. *He's out there someplace. He knows how to shoot.*

I peeled the costume mask off his face, the last façade ripped away. *You're not a god. You bleed like the rest of us.*

It was Dr Will Rudolph. The Gentleman Caller lay close to death in the middle of the street in Chapel Hill. His blue-gray eyes were glazing over. A sopping puddle of arterial blood had already collected under him.

People were pushing in closer from the sidewalk. They were gasping in horror and awe. Their eyes stretched wide. Most of them had probably never seen anyone actually die. I had.

I lifted his head. The Gentleman. The murdering, maiming scourge of Los Angeles. He couldn't believe that he'd been shot, couldn't accept it. His darting, fearful eyes told me that much.

'Who is Casanova?' I asked Dr Will Rudolph. I wanted to shake it out of him. 'Who is Casanova? Tell me.'

I kept looking around behind me. Where was Casanova? He wouldn't let Rudolph die like this, would he? Two patrol cars finally arrived. Three or four local cops ran toward me with their guns drawn.

Rudolph struggled to focus his eyes, to see me clearly, or perhaps to see the world one final time. A bloody bubble formed on his lips and then popped with a soft spray.

His words came slowly. 'You'll never find him.' He smiled up at me. 'You're not good enough, Cross. You're not even close. He's the best ever.'

A raspy howl rose from the Gentleman's throat. I recognized the sound of the death rattle as I placed the death mask back over the monster's face.

113

It was a wild, jubilant scene, one that I would never be able to forget. The immediate families and close friends of the captive women kept arriving at Duke Medical Center all through the night. On the rolling hospital grounds and in the parking lot near Erwin Road, a large, emotional crowd of students and townspeople gathered and stayed on past midnight. There were nothing but indelible images for me.

Photographs of the survivors had been blown up and mounted on placards. Faculty and students held hands and sang spirituals as well as 'Give Peace a Chance.' For at least one night everyone chose to forget that Casanova was still out there somewhere. I tried it for a few hours myself.

Sampson was alive and recovering inside the hospital. So was Kate. People I had never met came up and fiercely shook my hand inside the suddenly festive facility. A father of one of the surviving victims broke down and wept in my arms. It had never felt this good to be a policeman.

I took the elevator to the fourth floor to visit Kate. Before I walked into her room, I took a deep breath. Finally, I went in. She looked like a mysterious mummy with all of her head bandages and wraps. Her condition had stabilized. She wasn't going to die, but she remained in a coma.

I held Kate's hand and I told her the long day's news. 'The captive women are free. I was at the house with Sampson. They're safe, Kate. Now you come back to us. Tonight would be a good night,' I whispered.

I ached to hear Kate's voice again, at least one more time. But no sound came from her lips. I wondered if Kate could hear me, or make any sense of the words. I kissed her softly before I left for the night. 'I love you, Kate,' I whispered against her bandaged cheek. I doubted that she could hear me.

Sampson was located one floor above Kate. Man Mountain had already come out of surgery, and his condition was listed as good.

He was awake and alert when I came in to see him. 'How's Kate and the other women?' he asked me. 'I'm about ready to leave this place myself.'

'Kate's still in a coma. I just came from her room. Your condition is "good," if you're interested.'

'You tell the doctors to upgrade me to "excellent." I hear Casanova got away.' He started to cough, and I could tell he was angry.

'Take it easy. We'll get him.' I knew it was time for me to go.

'Don't forget to bring me my shades,' he said as I left. 'Too much light in this place. Feel like I'm in Kmart.'

At nine-thirty that night I was back in Scootchie's hospital room. Seth Samuel was there. The two of them were impressive to watch together. They were strong, but they were also sweet. I began the happy task of getting to know Naomi-and-Seth.

'Auntie Scootch! Auntie Scootch!'

I heard a familiar voice behind me, and it was the best sound. Nana, Cilla, Damon, and Jannie all trooped into the room. They had flown in from Washington. Cilla broke down and cried as she saw her baby. I saw Nana Mama also wipe away a few tears. Then Cilla and Naomi were giving the word *hug* a new meaning.

My kids watched their Auntie Scootch lying in the scary hospital bed. I could see the fear and confusion shining in their little eyes, especially in Damon's, who tries to rise above all forms of uncertainty and terror in his life.

I went to my kids and scooped them up in my arms. I held them both as tightly as I could. 'Hello, son, little cue ball in the side pocket! How's my Jannie?' I asked. For me, there's nothing like my family, nothing even close. I imagine that's part of why I do what I do. I know it is. Doctor Detective Cross.

'You found Auntie Scootch,' Jannie whispered into my ear. She hugged me tightly with her strong little legs and arms. She was even more excited than I was.

114

It wasn't over for me. The job was only half-done. Two days later, I trudged down a well-worn path through the woods separating Route 22 and the underground house. The local police officers I passed on the way were somber and quiet. They tramped out of the woods with their heads lowered, not talking with one another, their faces drained of color and affect.

They had met the human monsters on an intimate basis now. They had seen the intricate and ghastly handiwork of Dr Will Rudolph and the other monster who called himself Casanova. Some of them had explored the house of horror.

Most of them knew me by now. I was a regular at the hellfires with them. Some nodded or waved hello. I waved back.

I was finally somewhat accepted in North Carolina. Twenty years ago that wouldn't have been possible, not even under these extreme circumstances. I was beginning to like it in the South a little, more than I would have thought possible.

I had a new notion, a plausible theory, about Casanova.

It had to do with something I'd noticed during the gun-battle scene in these woods and on the streets of Chapel Hill. *You'll never find him,* I recalled Rudolph's dying words. Never say never, Will.

Kyle Craig was at the house of horror that warm, hazy afternoon. So were about two hundred men and women from the Chapel Hill and Durham police forces, as well as soldiers from Fort Bragg, North Carolina. They were getting to know the human monsters up close and personal.

'Extraordinary time to be alive, to be a cop,' Kyle said to me. His humor got a shade darker every time I saw him. He worried me. Kyle was such a loner most of the time. Such a careeraholic. Apparently such a straight arrow. He had even looked that way in the Duke yearbook pictures I'd found of him.

'I feel sorry for these local people dragged out here for this,' I said to Kyle. My eyes passed slowly over the ghoulish crime scene. 'They won't be able to forget this until the day they die. They'll dream of it for years.'

'How about you, Alex?' Kyle asked. His intense, grayish-blue eyes leveled mine. Sometimes, he almost seemed to care about me.

'Oh, I have so many nightmare images now, it's hard to pick out just one favorite,' I confessed with a thin smile. 'I'll go home soon. I'll make my kids sleep in with me for a while. They love to, anyway. They won't understand the *real* reason why. I'll be able to sleep okay with the kids there to protect me. They pound on my chest if I have a nightmare.'

Kyle finally smiled. 'You're an unusual man, Alex. You're both incredibly open *and* secretive.'

'Getting more unusual every day,' I said to Kyle. 'You come on a new monster one of these days, don't bother to call.

I'm monstered out.' I stared into his eyes, trying to make contact and not completely succeeding. Kyle was secretive too, not very open with anybody that I knew of.

'I'll try not to call,' Kyle said. 'You rest up, though. There's a monster working in the city of Chicago right now. Another in Lincoln and Concord, Massachusetts. Someone very evil is taking children in Austin, Texas. Little babies, actually. Repeat killers in Orlando and Minneapolis.'

'We've still got work here,' I reminded Kyle.

'Do we?' he asked, his voice dripping with irony. 'What work is that, Alex? You mean spadework?'

Kyle Craig and I watched the terrifying scene that was unfolding near the underground house. Seventy to eighty men were busy digging up the meadow west of the 'disappearing' house. They were working with heavy pickaxes and shovels. Searching for bodies of murder victims. Spadework.

Since 1981, beautiful and intelligent women from all over the South had been abducted by the two monsters and murdered. It was a thirteen-year reign of horror. *First, I fall in love with a woman. Then, I simply take her*. Will Rudolph had written that in his diaries out in California. I wondered if the sentiment was his or his *twin*'s. I wondered how badly Casanova was missing his friend now. How he grieved. How he planned to cope with his loss. Did he already have a plan?

I believed that Casanova had met Rudolph sometime back around 1981. They had shared their forbidden secret: They liked to kidnap, to rape, and, sometimes to torture, women. Somehow, they came up with the idea of keeping a harem of very special women, women who were bright and fascinating enough to hold their interest. They never had anyone to share their secrets with before. Then suddenly they had each other. I tried to imagine never having anyone to confide in – never once in your life – and then finding someone to talk to when you are twenty-one or twenty-two years old.

The two of them had played their wicked games, gathered their harem of beauties in the Research Triangle area and throughout the Southeast. My theory on twinning had been close to the truth. They enjoyed kidnapping and holding beautiful women captive. They also *competed*. So much so, that Will Rudolph finally had to go off on his own for a while. To Los Angeles. He had become the Gentleman Caller out there. He'd tried to make it on his own. Casanova, the more territorial of the two, continued to work in the South, but they communicated. They shared stories. They *needed* to share. Sharing their exploits was part of the thrill for both of them. Rudolph eventually told stories to a reporter at the *Los Angeles Times*. He tasted fame and notoriety, and he liked it. Not so Casanova. He was much more of a loner. He was the genius; the creative one, I believed.

I thought I knew who he might be. I thought that I'd seen Casanova without his mask.

I kept drifting in and out of strange, private thoughts at the dizzying crime scene. I was burnt toast, but that didn't matter anymore; it hadn't mattered for a while.

Casanova, the territorial killer, I was thinking. He was probably still in the area around Durham and Chapel Hill. He had met Will Rudolph around the time of the golden couple murders. So far, he'd thought everything through with almost perfect clarity. He had finally made a mistake during the shootout two days before. A small mistake, but that was all it took sometimes . . . I *thought* I knew who Casanova might be. But I couldn't share it with the FBI. I was their 'loose cannon,' right? The 'outsider' on this case. So be it.

Kyle Craig and I watched the same distant spot in the

high waving grass and honeysuckle, out where the digging was taking place. *Mass graves*, I thought as I watched the horrific scene. *What a concept for the nineties.*

A tall balding man stood up from his deep hole in the soft earth. He waved long arms high over his head, which was shiny with sweat. 'Bob Shaw here!' He called out his name in a loud, clear voice.

The digger's name was the verbal signal that another woman's body had been found. An entire corps of North Carolina medical examiners was at the dreamlike, unbearably grisly scene. One of the MEs ran over to the digger in a strange, lopsided waddle that would have made Kyle and me laugh under different circumstances. He gave Shaw a hand out of the grave.

The TV cameras at the scene moved in on Shaw, who was U.S. Army from Fort Bragg. An attractive woman reporter nearby received a dab of makeup before she spoke into the lens of a camera.

'They've just found victim number twenty-three,' the reporter said with appropriate solemnity. 'All the victims so far appear to have been young women. The grisly murders—'

I turned away from the TV coverage and I had to sigh out loud.

I thought of children like my own Damon and Janelle, watching this spectacle in their homes. This was a world they were inheriting. Human monsters roaming the earth, a majority of them in America and Europe. Why was that? Something in the water? In the high-fat fast food? On Saturday morning TV?

'Go the hell home, Alex,' Kyle said to me. 'It's over now. You won't catch him, I promise you.'

115

Never say never. That's one of my few mottos as a cop. My body was bathed in a cold sweat. My pulse was jumpy and irregular. This was it, wasn't it? I needed to believe that it was.

I waited in the hot, still darkness outside a small wood-shingled house in the Edgemont section of Durham. It was a typical middle-class Southern neighborhood. Nice middle-class houses, American and Japanese cars in about equal numbers, mower-striped lawns, familiar cooking smells. It was where Casanova had chosen to live for the past seven years.

I had spent the early part of that night at the offices of the *Herald Sun*. I had reread everything written in the newspaper about the unsolved murders of Roe Tierney and Tom Hutchinson. A name mentioned in the *Herald Sun* helped put it together for me, confirmed my suspicions and fears, anyway. Hundreds of hours of investigating. Reading and rereading Durham police briefs. Then, pay dirt on a single line of newsprint.

The name was in a story lost in the Durham newspaper's middle pages. It appeared just once. I found it, anyway.

I had stared for a long time at the familiar name in the news article. I thought about something I'd noticed during the shoot-out in Chapel Hill. I thought about the whole subject of 'perfect crimes.' It all fit together for me now. Game, match, set, bingo.

Casanova had blinked just once. I had seen it with my own eyes, though. The name in the news article was verification. It materially linked Will Rudolph and Casanova for the first time. It also explained to me how they had met, and *why* they had talked.

Casanova was sane and completely responsible for his actions. He had planned every step in cold blood. That was the most horrifying and unusual thing about the long trail of crimes. He knew what he was doing. He was a slime who had *chosen* to abduct beautiful young students in their prime. He'd *chosen* to rape and murder again and again. He was obsessed with perfect young women, with *loving* them as he called it.

I conducted an imaginary interview with Casanova as I waited outside his house in the car. I could see his face as clearly as the numbers on the dashboard.

You don't feel anything one way or the other, do you?

Oh, I do. I feel elation. I feel the most tremendous high when I take another lady. I feel varying levels of excitement, anticipation, animal lust. I feel an incredible sense of freedom that most people will never feel.

But not guilt?

I could *see* him smirk as I sat in my car. I'd seen that smirk before, in fact. I knew who he was.

Nothing that would make me want to stop.

Was there any nurturing, any love given and received when you were a boy?

They tried. I wasn't really a boy, though. I don't remember acting or thinking like a boy.

I had begun to think like the monsters again. I was the dragonslayer. I hated the responsibility. I also hated the part of me that was becoming a monster. There was nothing I could do to stop it at this point.

I was outside Casanova's house in Durham. Hammers of fear tapped lightly in my heart. I waited there for four nights.

No partner. No backup.

No problem whatsoever. I could be as patient as he was. I was hunting now.

116

I sucked in a harsh, deep breath and felt a little lightheaded. There he was!

Casanova was leaving the house. *I watched his face, watched his body language. He was confident, very sure of himself.*

Detective Davey Sikes sauntered out to his car at a little past eleven on the fourth night. He was a powerful man, athletic. He wore jeans, a dark Windbreaker, hightopped black sneakers. Sikes climbed into a ten- or twelve-year-old Toyota Cressida he kept in the garage.

The sedan had to be his cruising car; his troller; his anonymous pickup vehicle. 'Perfect crimes.' Davey Sikes definitely had the know-how. He was a detective on the case, and *had been for over a dozen years*. He'd known the FBI would investigate every local policeman when they entered the case. He had been ready with his 'perfect' alibis. Sikes had even altered the date of a kidnapping to 'prove' he was out of town when it happened.

I wondered if Sikes would dare to go after another woman

now. Had he been out carefully stalking and hunting already? What was he feeling now? What was he thinking right at this moment, I wondered, as I watched the dark Toyota back out of the driveway in suburban Durham. Was he missing Rudolph? Would he continue their game, or maybe stop now? Could he stop the game?

I wanted him so badly. Sampson had said at the beginning that this case was too personal for me. He was right on. No case had ever been more personal for me, not even close to this.

I tried to think the way he might. I tried to get into his rhythm. I suspected that he had already picked out a victim, even if he didn't dare take her yet. Would she be another smart, beautiful college student? Maybe he would change his pattern now. I doubted it. He loved his life, his creation, too much.

I followed the human monster down dark, deserted streets in southwest Durham. Blood pumped loudly through my head. I couldn't hear much of anything else. I drove with my headlights off for as long as Davey Sikes stayed on the side streets. Maybe he was just headed to the Circle K for cigarettes and beer.

I thought that I had finally figured out what had happened back in 1981, that I had probably solved the golden couple murder which had shocked the university community here and in Chapel Hill. Will Rudolph had planned and committed the violent sex murders while he was a student. He had 'loved' Roe Tierney, but she was interested in football stars. Detective Davey Sikes had met and questioned Rudolph during the subsequent police investigation.

At some point, he had begun to share his own dark, forbidden secrets with the brilliant medical student. They had known about each other. Felt it, *sensed it*. Both of them desperately wanted to share their secret need with someone. Suddenly, they had each other. *Twinning*.

Now I had killed his only friend. Did Davey Sikes want to kill me for that? Did he know I was coming for him? What was he thinking right at this moment? I didn't just want to catch him, I needed to capture his thoughts.

Casanova turned onto Interstate 40 and headed south. He was traveling toward Garner and McCullers, according to bright white-on-green road signs. There was relatively heavy traffic on the interstate, and I was able to follow him in a safe cluster with four or five other cars. So far, so good. Detective against detective.

He got off at Exit 35, which was boldly marked for McCullers. He'd gone a little over thirty miles. It was approaching eleven-thirty at night. The witching hour.

I was going to take him out tonight, no matter what. I had never done that before, not in all my time as a homicide detective in Washington.

This time it *was* personal.

117

A mile from the exit ramp off 41, a Ford pickup truck swerved out of a hidden driveway. It was unexpected, but good luck for me. The dull red truck fell in between Sikes and me, offering me some cover. Not much, but enough for a few more miles.

The Cressida finally pulled off the main road a couple of miles outside McCullers. Sikes parked in the crowded lot of a bar called the Sports Page Pub. One more car that wasn't likely to be noticed.

That was what had begun to give him away. It was why even Kyle Craig had been on my list of suspects. Casanova seemed to have known every move the police would make *before they made it*. He had probably abducted some of the women by coming up to them as a police officer. *Detective Davey Sikes! He had gone into a professional shooting crouch that afternoon on the street in Chapel Hill*. I knew he was another cop.

When I searched through the newspaper articles on the golden couple murder, I had spotted his name. Sikes had been a young cop on the original investigation team. He had interviewed a student named Will Rudolph back then, but he never mentioned it to any of us, never let on that he had met Will Rudolph in 1981.

I passed by the Sports Page Pub, and pulled off the road as soon as I turned the next bend. I got out of the car and hurried back toward the bar. I was in time to see Davey Sikes cross the highway on foot.

Casanova walked along the side of an intersecting side road with his hands thrust into his trouser pockets. He looked as if he belonged in the small-town neighborhood. *Stun gun in one of those deep pockets, sport? Feeling the familiar, burning itch now? The thrill is back?*

I followed Sikes into a pine-wooded lot, and he began to move quicker. He was fast for a big man. He could lose me now. Somebody's life would be at risk in the peaceful neighborhood. Another Scootchie Cross. Another Kate McTieman. I remembered Kate's words: *Drive a stake through his heart, Alex.*

I slid the Glock nine millimeter out of my shoulder holster. Light. Efficient. Semiautomatic. Twelve deadly shots. My teeth were gritted so tight they hurt. I clicked off the safety. I was ready to take Davey Sikes out.

I eyed the ominous shapes of overhanging pine branches as I moved along. An A-frame house was up ahead, set against the backdrop of a full, pale yellow moon. I moved quickly across the soft floor of pine needles. I made no sound. I had his tempo and rhythm down now.

I saw Casanova rapidly approaching the A-frame house, gaining speed. He knew his way, *He'd been here before, hadn't he? He had been here to scope things out, to study the next victim, to get it just right.*

I sprinted up closer to the house. Then I couldn't see him. I'd lost him for a second. He might have slipped inside.

A single shimmering light had been left on in the house. My heart was going to explode if I didn't blow him up first. My finger was on the semiautomatic's trigger.

Drive a stake through his heart, Alex.

118

Take Sikes out.

I fought to control my emotions, to find the calm pool inside me, as I ran toward a screened-in back porch that lay in shifting shadows and darkness. Suddenly, I could hear the sputtering hum of an air conditioner inside. I noticed a peeling sticker on the whitewashed porch door. It read: *I live for Girl Scout cookies.*

He'd found another nice one out here, hadn't he? He was going to take her tonight. The Beast couldn't stop himself.

'Hello, Cross. Now put down the gun. Very slowly, ace,' said the deep voice behind me in the dark.

Both my eyes closed for a beat. I lowered the pistol, then dropped it on the lawn of grass and pine needles. My body felt like an elevator car in free-fall.

'Turn around now, you son of a bitch. You meddling shithead.'

I turned, and looked into the face of Casanova. He was finally right there, close enough for me to touch. He had a Browning semiautomatic aimed at my chest.

There would be no more overthinking, just gut instincts, I told myself. I let my right leg buckle as if I'd lost my footing. Then I sucker-punched Sikes to the side of his head. It was a hard shot, a crushing, heavyweight-caliber punch.

Sikes went down on one knee, but he came back up in a hurry. I grabbed the front of his jacket and bounced him off the wall of the house. His arm cracked against the shingles and the handgun fell loose. The ground was firm under my feet, and I moved in on him again. The moment had the feeling of a good old-fashioned streetfight. I wanted it. My body ached for physical contact and release.

'C'mon, fucker,' he challenged me. He wanted me, too.

'Oh, don't worry,' I told him. 'I'm coming.'

Another light flashed on inside the house. 'Who's out there?' The sound of the woman's voice caught me off guard. *'Who is out there, please?'*

He threw an arcing roundhouse punch. Pretty good speed and aim. He was a decent fighter, not just a lover. I remembered that Kate said he was scarily strong. I didn't plan to spend a lot of time in his killer grasp, though.

I caught his punch on my upper arm, and it instantly went numb. He was powerful, all right. Stay away from his strength, I warned myself. Hurt him, though. Hurt him a lot.

I fired a hard right uppercut into his lower stomach. I thought of Kate and the beatings she had taken for being disobedient. I vividly remembered the final beating she'd gotten.

I crunched another right hand into his stomach. I felt the stomach soften. I think I hit him below the belt. Sikes groaned and slumped over like a badly beaten club fighter. It was a trick, a slick feint on his part.

He fired a punch and caught the side of my head. He rang

my bell pretty good. I snorted, bobbed a little, showed him he hadn't hurt me. This was streetfighting, D.C. style. *C'mon, white boy. Come to me, monster man.* I needed this time with him so much.

I slammed my fist hard into his lower stomach again. Kill the body, and the head dies. I wanted to mess up the head, too. I hit him for good measure in the nose. My best effort so far. Sampson would have been proud of the shot. I was.

'That's for Sampson,' I told him through gritted teeth. 'He asked me to give you that. Hand-deliver it.'

I hit him in the throat and he started to gag. I continued to bob. I didn't just *look* a little like Ali, I could fight like him when I had to. I could defend what needed to be defended. I could be a street tough when it had to be that way.

'This is for Kate.' I hit Sikes in the nose again, right on the button. Then square in the left eye with another right lead. His face was puffing up nicely. *Drive a stake through his heart, Alex.*

He was strong and well conditioned, and still dangerous, I knew. He came at me again. Charged like a raging bull in the *plaza de toros.* I stepped aside, and he forearmed the wall of the house as if he were trying to level it. The small house rumbled and shook.

I punched Sikes hard on the side of the head. His head snapped back so hard against the house's aluminum siding that he left a dent in it. He was weaving now, his breath coming in gasps. Suddenly, there were wails of sirens in the distance. The woman inside must have called the police. I was the police, wasn't I?

Somebody hit me from behind, hit me real hard. '*Oh, Jesus, no,*' I moaned and tried to shake off the hurt.

This wasn't possible! This couldn't be happening!

Who had hit me? Why? I didn't get it, couldn't understand, couldn't clear my head fast enough.

I was dizzy and hurt but *I turned*, anyway.

I saw a frizzy-haired blonde woman wearing an oversized *Farm Aid* T-shirt. She was still holding the work shovel she'd just clobbered me with.

'Get off my boyfriend!' she screamed at me. Her face and neck were beet red. 'Get away from him or I'll hit you again. You get away from my Davey.'

My Davey? . . . Jesus! My head was spinning, but I got the message. I thought I did, anyway. Davey Sikes had come out here to see his girlfriend. *He wasn't hunting anyone. He wasn't here to murder anyone. He was Farm Aid's boyfriend.*

Maybe I'd lost it, I thought as I backed away from Sikes. Maybe I was finally burned beyond a crisp, beyond recognition or redemption. Or maybe I was like almost every other homicide detective I knew – overworked and fallible as hell. I'd made a mistake. I'd been wrong about Davey Sikes – I just didn't understand how it had happened.

Kyle Craig arrived at the house in McCullers within the hour. He was as calm as ever, completely unruffled. He spoke quietly to me. 'Detective Sikes has been having an affair with the woman in the house for over a year. We knew about it. Detective Sikes isn't a suspect. He isn't Casanova. Go home. Alex. Just go home now. You're through here.'

119

I didn't go home. I went to visit Kate at Duke University Medical Center. She didn't look good; she was pale and haggard; she was rail-thin. She didn't sound good, either. But Kate was much, much improved. She was out of the coma.

'Look who's finally awake,' I said from the doorway into her room.

'You got one of the bad guys, Alex,' Kate whispered as she saw me. She smiled faintly, and she spoke in a slow, uncertain way. It was Kate, but not quite Kate.

'Did you see that in your dreams?' I asked her.

'Yep.' She smiled again, that sweet smile of hers. She was talking so very slowly. 'As a matter of fact, I did.'

'I brought you a little present,' I told her. I held up a teddy bear dressed to look like a doctor. Kate took the bear and she continued to grin. The magical smile almost made her look like her old self.

I put my head down close to Kate's. I kissed her swollen head as if it were the most delicate flower ever put on the earth. Sparks flew, strange ones, but maybe the strongest ones yet.

'I missed you more than I can say,' I whispered against her hair.

'Say it,' she whispered back. Then she smiled again. We both did. Her speech was a little slow maybe, but not her mind.

Ten days later, Kate was up on a clumsy, four-legged metal walker. She was complaining that she hated the 'mechanical contraption' and would be off it within a week. Actually, it took her almost four weeks, but even that was considered miraculous.

She had a half-moon indentation on the left side of her forehead from the terrible beating. So far, she had refused plastic surgery to repair it. She thought her dent added character.

In a way it did. It was pure, unadulterated Kate McTiernan. 'It's also part of my life story, so it stays,' she said. Her speech was closer to normal, getting a little clearer every week.

Whenever I saw Kate's half-moon dent, I was reminded of Reginald Denny, the truck driver who was so savagely beaten during the Los Angeles riots. I remembered how he looked after the first Rodney King verdict. Denny's head was severely dented, actually staved in, on one side. It still looked that way when I saw him on TV a year after the incident. I also thought of a Nathaniel Hawthorne short story called 'The Birthmark.' The dent was Kate's one imperfection. With it, in my eyes, anyway, she was even more beautiful and special than she'd been before.

I spent most of July at home with my family in Washington. I took two short trips back to see Kate in Durham, but that was all. How many fathers get to spend a month with their kids, catching up with their wild-and-wooly run through childhood? Damon and Jannie were both playing organized baseball that summer. They were still music, movie, general noise, and hot chocolate-chip-cookie addicts. They both slept on the quilt with me for the first week or so – while I was recuperating, while I was trying to forget my recent time spent in hell.

I worried that Casanova would come after me for killing his best friend, but so far there was no sign of him. No more beautiful women had been abducted in North Carolina. It was absolutely certain now that he wasn't Davey Sikes. Several area policemen had been investigated; including his partner Nick Ruskin, and even Chief Hatfield. Every cop had alibis, and they all checked out. Who the hell was Casanova then? Was he going to just disappear, like his underground house? Had he gotten away with all those horrifying murders? Could he just stop killing now?

My grandmother still had volumes of psychological and other kinds of useful advice for me to follow. Much of it was directed at the subject of my love life, and my leading a normal life for a change. She wanted me to go into private practice, anything but police work.

'The children need a grandmother, and *a mother*,' Nana Mama told me from the pulpit of her stove where she was fixing her breakfast one morning.

'So I should go out and look for a mother for Damon and Jannie? That what you're telling me?'

'Yes, you should, Alex, and maybe you should do it before you lose your boyish good looks and charm.'

'I'll get right on it,' I said. 'Snare a wife and mother this summer.'

Nana Mama swatted me with her spatula. Swatted me again for good measure. 'Don't get smart with me,' she said. She *always* had the last word.

The phone call came around one o'clock one morning in late July. Nana and the kids had gone up for the night. I was playing some jazz piano, amusing myself, keeping a few junkies out on Fifth Street up with the music of Miles Davis and Dave Brubeck.

Kyle Craig was on the phone line. I groaned when I heard Kyle's calm subaltern voice.

I expected bad news, of course, but not the particular news that I got late that night.

'What the hell is it, Kyle?' I asked him right off, trying to make his unexpected call into a joke. 'I told you not ever to call me again.'

'I had to call on this, Alex. You had to know,' he hissed over the long-distance lines. 'Now listen to me closely.'

Kyle talked to me for almost half an hour, and it wasn't what I had expected. It was much, much worse.

After I got off the phone with Kyle, I went back to the sun porch. I sat there for a long time, thinking about what I should do now. There was nothing I could do, not a thing. 'It doesn't stop,' I whispered to the four walls, 'does it?'

I went and got my pistol. I hated carrying it inside the house. I checked all the doors and windows in our house. Finally, I went to bed.

I heard Kyle's fateful words again as I lay in my darkened bedroom. I heard Kyle tell me his shocker. I saw a face I never wanted to see again. I remembered *everything*.

'Gary Soneji escaped from prison, Alex. He left a note. The note said he'd stop by and see you sometime soon.'

It doesn't stop.

I lay in bed and thought about the fact that Gary Soneji still wanted to kill me. He'd told me so himself. He'd had time in prison to obsess about how, when, and where he was going to do it.

I finally went off to sleep. It was almost morning. Another day was starting. *It really doesn't stop.*

120

There were still two mysteries that had to be solved, or at least dealt with in a better way. There was the mystery of Casanova, and who he was. And there was the one featuring Kate and myself.

Kate and I visited the Outer Banks in North Carolina for six days at the end of August. We stayed near a picturesque resort town called Nags Head.

Kate's clumsy metal walker was gone, though she did carry around a knobby, old-fashioned hickory cane at times. Mostly she practiced karate exercises with the hardwood cane. She used it as a karate stick on the beach, twirling the cane around her body and head with great dexterity and skill.

Watching Kate, I thought that she looked almost luminescent. She was back in good form. Her face was close to the way it had been, except for the dent. 'It's my stubborn streak,' she told me, 'and it's permanent until the day I die.'

It was an idyllic time in many ways. Everything seemed just right for us. Kate and I felt that we both deserved a holiday, and much more.

We ate breakfast together every morning on a porch made from long gray planks, which overlooked the shimmering Atlantic. (I made breakfast on my mornings to cook; Kate went to the Nags Head Market and brought home sticky buns and Bavarian cream doughnuts on her days.) We went for long, long walks along the shoreline. We surf-cast for blues, and cooked the fresh fish right there on the beach. Sometimes, we just watched the shiny boats patrolling the water. We took a day trip to watch the crazy-ass hang gliders off the high dunes in Jockey's Ridge State Park.

We waited on Casanova. We were daring him to come after us. So far he wasn't interested, at least he didn't seem to be.

I thought of the book and movie *The Prince of Tides*. Kate and I were a little bit like Tom Wingo and Susan Lowenstein, only mixed together in a different, though equally complex, way. Lowenstein had brought out Tom Wingo's need to feel and give love, I remembered. Kate and I were learning everything about each other, the important things – and we were both quick learners.

Early one August morning, we waded into the clear, deep blue water in front of the house. Most of the beach community wasn't up yet. A lone brown pelican was skimming the water.

We held hands above the low waves. Everything was picture-postcard perfect. So why was I feeling as if there were a gaping hole where my heart ought to be? Why was I still obsessed with Casanova?

'You're thinking bad thoughts, aren't you?' Kate bumped me hard with her hip. 'You're on vacation. Think vacation thoughts.'

'Actually, I was thinking very good thoughts, but they made me feel bad,' I told her.

'I know that crazy-ass song,' she said. She gave me a hug, to reassure me that we were in this thing together, whatever it was that we were in.

'Let's take a run. I'll race you to Coquina Beach,' she said. 'Ready, set, prepare yourself to lose.'

We started to jog. Kate showed no signs of a limp. The pace picked up. She was so strong – in all ways. We both were. At the end, we were running nearly full-out and we collapsed in a wall of silver-blue surf. I didn't want to lose Kate, I was thinking as I ran. I didn't want this to end. I didn't know what to do about it.

On a warm, breezy Saturday night, Kate and I lay on an old Indian blanket on the beach. We were talking on half a hundred subjects at one sitting. We had already feasted on roast Carolina duckling with blackberry sauce that we'd made together. Kate had on a sweatshirt that read: *Trust me, I'm a doctor.*

'I don't want this to end, either,' Kate said with a heavy sigh. Then, 'Alex, let's talk about some of the reasons we both believe this has to end.'

I shook my head and smiled at her characteristic directness. 'Oh, this will never really end, Kate. We'll always have this time. It's one of those special treasures you get every once in a while in life.'

Kate grabbed and held my arm with both her hands. Her deep brown eyes were intense. 'Then why does it have to end here?'

We both knew some, though not all, of the reasons.

'We're *too much* alike. We're both obsessively analytical. We're both so logical that we *know* the half-dozen reasons this won't work out. We're stubborn and we're strong-willed. Eventually, we would go *boom*,' I said in a half-teasing tone.

'Sounds like the old self-fulfilling prophecy to me,' Kate said.

We both knew I was telling the truth, though. Sad truth? Is there such a thing? I guess that there is.

'We just might go boom,' Kate said, and she smiled sweetly. 'Then we couldn't even be friends. I couldn't stand the idea of losing you as my friend. That's still part of it for me. I can't risk a big loss yet.'

'We're both physically too strong. We'd kill each other eventually. Nidan,' I told her. I was trying to lighten things up.

She squeezed me a little tighter. 'Don't make jokes about it. Don't make me laugh, damn you, Alex. I want this to be our sad time at least. It's so sad I might cry. Now I am. See that?'

'It is sad,' I said to Kate. 'It's the saddest thing.'

We lay on the scratchy wool beach blanket and held each other until the morning. We slept under the stars and listened to the steady beat of the Atlantic. Everything seemed gently touched with the brush of eternity that night on the Outer Banks. Well, almost everything.

Kate turned to me in between catnaps, in between dreams. 'Alex, is he coming after us again? He is, isn't he?'

I didn't know for sure, but that was the plan.

121

Tick-cock.
  Tick-cock.
  Tick-cock.

He was still obsessed with Kate McTiernan, only it was much more disturbing and complex than just the fate of Doctor Kate now. She and Alex Cross had conspired to ruin his unique creation, his precious and very private art, his life as it had been. Nearly everything that he'd ever loved was gone now, or in disarray. It was time for a comeback. Time to show them once and for all. Time to show his true face.

Casanova realized that he missed his 'best friend' above all else. That was proof that he was sane, after all. He could love; he could feel things. He had watched in disbelief as Alex Cross shot down Will Rudolph on the streets of Chapel Hill. Rudolph had been worth ten Alex Crosses, and now Rudolph was dead.

Rudolph had been a rare genius. Will Rudolph *was* Jekyll and Hyde, but only Casanova had been able to appreciate both sides of his personality. He remembered their years together, and couldn't put them out of his thoughts anymore. They had both understood that exquisite pleasure intensified the more it was forbidden. That was a ruling principle behind the hunts, the collection of bright, beautiful, talented women, and eventually the long string of murders. The unbelievable, *matchless* thrill of breaking society's sacred taboos, of living out elaborate fantasies, was absolutely irresistible. These were pleasures not to be believed.

So were the hunts themselves: the choosing, observing, and taking of beautiful women and their most personal possessions.

But now Rudolph was gone. Casanova understood that he wasn't merely alone; he was suddenly afraid to be alone. He felt as if he'd been cut in half. He had to take control again. That's what he was doing now.

He had to give Alex Cross some credit. Cross had come close to catching him. He wondered if Cross knew how close? Alex Cross was obsessed: that was his edge on all the others in the chase. Cross would never give up, not until he was killed.

Cross had set up this delicious little trap in Nags Head for him, hadn't he? Of course he had. Cross had figured that he would come after him and Kate McTiernan, anyway, so why not have it happen under controlled circumstances? Why not, indeed.

It was almost a full moon the night he arrived at the Outer Banks. Casanova could make out two men in the tall, wavering dune grass up ahead. They were the FBI agents assigned to watch over Cross and Dr Kate. The hand-picked guardians.

He flicked on his flashlight so that two of them would see him coming. Yes, he could fit in anywhere. That was just part of his genius, though, just a small part of his act.

461

When he got within voice range, Casanova called out to the agents. 'Yo, it's only me.'

He tilted the flashlight upward to expose his face. He let them see him, see who he was.

Tick-cock.

122

It was my morning to take care of our breakfast, and I democratically decided on Kate's favorite sticky buns to top off my infamous Monterey Jack cheese and sauteed onion omelet.

I figured I would jog to and from the tiny, overpriced bakery in Nags Head. Jogging helps me think in straight lines, sometimes.

I ran on a zigzag path through softly waving, waist-high dune grass that eventually met with the paved road over the marshes and into town. It was a beautiful late-summer day.

I began to relax as I jogged. My guard was down so I almost didn't see him.

A blonde man in a navy blue Windbreaker and stained khaki pants lay spread-eagled in the tall grass, just off the dirt path. He looked as if his neck had been broken. He hadn't been dead very long. His body was still warm when I felt for a pulse.

The dead man was FBI. He was a pro who wouldn't have been easy to take out. He had been stationed out here to watch over Kate and me, to help trap Casanova. The plan was Kyle Craig's, but Kate and I had agreed to it.

'Oh goddammit, no,' I groaned. I took out my gun and began to sprint back to the house and Kate. She was in terrible danger. We both were.

I tried to concentrate on thinking like Casanova, on what he might do next, what he was capable of doing. Clearly, the perimeter defense around the house had been broken.

How did he keep doing that? *Who the hell was he?* Who did I have to fight?

I wasn't expecting the second body and almost tripped over it. It was hidden in the dune grass. The agent also wore a navy blue Windbreaker. He was lying on his back and his red hair was neatly combed. There was no sign of a struggle, his lifeless brown eyes were staring up at circling gulls and a buttery-yellow sun. Another FBI bodyguard dead.

I was in a panic now as I raced through the stiff wind and flowing grass to the beach house. It was quiet and still, just as I had left it.

I was almost certain that Casanova was already there. He had come hunting for us. It was payback time. He had to get this just right, didn't he? He had to make it 'perfect.' Or maybe he just needed revenge for Rudolph.

I raised my Glock pistol and went cautiously inside the front screen door. Nothing moved in the living room. The only sound was the ancient refrigerator humming in the kitchen, singing like a nest of insects.

'Kate!' I yelled at the top of my lungs. 'He's here! Kate! Kate! He's here! Casanova is here!'

I rushed through the living room to the first-floor bedroom and flung open the door.

She wasn't in there.

Kate wasn't where I had left her minutes ago.

I ducked into the hallway again. A closet door opened suddenly. A hand reached out and grabbed me.

I swung around hard to my right.

It was Kate. The look on her face was one of determination and sheer hatred. I saw no fear in her eyes. She put her finger to her lips. 'Shhh. Shhh,' she whispered. 'I'm okay, Alex.'

'Me too. So far.'

We proceeded in lock-step toward the kitchen, where the house phone was located. I had to get the Cape Hatteras police here *now*. They would contact Kyle and the FBI.

It was dark in the narrow hallway, and I didn't see the flash of metal until it was too late. A sharp pain shot through me as a longish dart stuck into the left side of my chest.

It was a heart shot. Perfectly delivered. He'd hit me with a state-of-the-art Tensor stun gun.

A powerful shock of electrical current streaked through my body. My heart fluttered. I could smell my own flesh burning.

I don't know how I did it, but I went at him. That's the problem with stun guns, even an expensive eighty-thousand-volt Tensor. They don't always bring down a big man. Especially a crazed one with a sense of purpose.

I didn't have enough strength left. Not for Casanova. The agile and powerful killer sidestepped me and chopped my neck hard. He hit me a second time and brought me to my knees.

He wore no mask this time.

I looked up at him. He had a light beard now, like Harrison Ford's at the start of *The Fugitive*. His brown hair was slicked straight back, longer now, and unruly. He was letting himself go a little bit. Was he mourning his best friend?

No mask. He wanted me to see who he was. His game had been destroyed, hadn't it.

Here was Casanova, finally.

I had been close with Davey Sikes. I felt sure it had to be someone connected with the Durham police force. I felt it was someone attached to the original golden couple murder case. He had covered every trace, though. He'd had alibis that made it *impossible for him to be the killer.*

He had figured everything out so beautifully. He was a genius – that was why he had succeeded for such a long time.

I stared into the impassive face of Detective Nick Ruskin.

Ruskin was Casanova. Ruskin was the Beast. Ruskin! Ruskin! Ruskin!

'I can do anything I want to do! *Don't you forget that, Cross,*' Ruskin said to me. He had been so perfect at his art. He had fit in, blended so well, created the best possible façade as a detective. The local star; the local hero. The one most above suspicion.

Ruskin stepped toward Kate as I lay helpless from the Tensor dart. 'I missed you, Katie. Did you miss me?'

He laughed easily as he spoke. There was madness in his eyes, though. He had finally gone over the edge. Was it because his 'twin' was dead? What in hell did he want to do now?

'So, did you miss me?' he repeated as he came toward her with the powerful, incapacitating Tensor in hand.

Kate didn't answer the question. She went for him instead. She'd wanted this for so long.

An explosive kick to Casanova's right shoulder spun the gun from Nick Ruskin's outstretched hand. The kick was a beauty, perfectly delivered. *Hit him again, then get out of there,* I wanted to yell at Kate.

I couldn't speak yet. Nothing came out when I tried. I finally managed to get up on one elbow.

Kate was *flowing* the way she did when she practiced on the beach. Casanova was a big man, powerful, but Kate's strength seemed to surge from a rage equal to his. *He comes, we tangle,* she had said once upon a time.

She was a blur, a perfect fighter. Even better than I had expected.

I didn't see the next punch. I was blocked by his body. I saw Nick Ruskin's head snap sharply to the side, and his long hair flew out in every direction. His legs wobbled badly. She'd hurt him.

Kate pivoted and hit him again. A lightning-quick punch caught the left side of his face. I wanted to cheer for her. The punch didn't stop him, though. Ruskin was relentless, but so was she.

He lunged at her and Kate hit him yet again. His left cheek appeared to collapse. It was a mismatch all the way.

She crunched a hard fist into his nose and he went down. He moaned loudly. He was beaten; he wasn't getting up again. Kate had won.

My heart was thundering inside my chest. I saw Ruskin reaching for his ankle holster. Casanova wasn't going to lose to a woman, or anyone else.

The gun appeared like some clever sleight-of-hand trick. It was a semiautomatic. Smith and Wesson. He *was changing the rules of the fight.*

'Nooo!' Kate shouted at him.

'Hey, asshole,' I said in a hoarse whisper. I was changing the rules, too.

Casanova turned. He saw me and pivoted the semiautomatic in my direction. I was holding the Glock with both hands. My arms were shaking some but I was able to sit up. I emptied almost a full clip into him. *Drive a stake through his heart*. That's what I did.

Casanova flew back hard against the wall of the house. His body thrashed. His legs didn't work. Numbness was already spreading through his body. The expression on his face was one of shock. He realized he was human, after all.

His eyeballs seemed to float upward and disappear into the top of his head. Only the whites of his eyes showed. His legs kicked, kicked again, then stopped. Casanova died almost instantly on the beach-house floor.

I stood up on rubbery legs. I noticed that I was glazed with sweat. Icy cold. Unpleasant as hell. I struggled over to Kate, and we held on to each other for a long time. We were both trembling with fear, but also triumph. We had won. We had beaten Casanova.

'I hated him so much,' Kate whispered. 'I never even understood the word before.'

I telephoned the Cape Hatteras police. Then I called the FBI, and my kids and Nana in Washington. It was finally over.

123

I sat on the familiar sun porch of my home sweet home in Washington. I was sipping a cold beer with Sampson.

It was fall, and the crisp, cool bite of winter was already in the air. Our beloved and despised Redskins were already in football training camp; the Orioles were out of the pennant race again. '*And so* it *goes*,' Kurt Vonnegut wrote once upon a time, when I was at Johns Hopkins and susceptible to such easy, breezy sentiments.

I could see my kids in the living room. They were on the couch together watching *Beauty and the Beast* for the leventy-leventh time. I didn't mind. It was a good, strong story and it bore repeating. Tomorrow, it would be *Aladdin* again, my personal favorite.

'I saw today that D.C. deploys three times as many police as the national average,' Sampson was telling me.

'Yeah, but we have twenty times as much crime. We didn't get to be *the capital* city of America for nothing,' I said. 'Like one of our past mayors said, "Outside of the killings, Washington has one of the lowest crime rates in the country."'

Sampson laughed. We both did. Life was finally returning to normal.

'You all right?' Sampson asked me after a while. He hadn't asked that since I'd been back from the South, from the Outer Banks, my 'summer vacation,' as I called it.

'I'm just fine. I'm a big macho, kickass detective like you.'

'You're a lying sack of shit, Alex. Ten pounds in a onepound bag.'

'That, too. Goes without saying.' I admitted to my faults with him.

'I asked you a serious damn question,' he said. He was giving me a flat, cold stare from behind his shades. Kind of reminded me of Hurricane Carter when he was a fighter. 'You miss her, man?'

'Of course I miss her. Hell, yes. I *told* you that I'm all right, though. I never had a woman friend like that. You?'

'No. Not like that. You understand that *both* of you are very *odd*?' He shook his head and didn't know what to make of me. I didn't either.

'She wants to set up practice where she grew up. She made a promise to her family. That's what she's decided to do for the time being. I need to be here right now. Make sure you grow up all right. That's what I decided to do. That's what *we* decided together down in Nags Head. It's the right thing.'

'Uh, huh.'

'It's the right thing, John. It's what the two of us decided.'

Sampson sipped his beer thoughtfully, as us macho men often do. He rocked in his easy chair, and watched me suspiciously over the mouth of the beer bottle. He 'watched over me' is what he did.

Later that night, I sat all alone on the porch.

I played 'Judgment Day,' then 'God Bless the Child' on the

piano. I thought about Kate again and about the thorny subject of loss. Most of us learn to deal with it somehow. We get better at it anyhow.

Kate had told me a powerful story while we were in Nags Head. She was a good storyteller, a reincarnated Carson McCullers.

When she was twenty, she said, she learned that her father was tending bar in a honky-tonk near the Kentucky border, and she went to the bar one night. She told me that she hadn't seen her father in sixteen years. She sat in the seedy, bad-smelling bar and watched him for almost half an hour. She hated what she saw. Finally she left, without ever introducing herself to her own father, without even telling him who she was. Kate just left.

She was so tough, and mostly in good ways. That was how she had survived all of those deaths in her family. It was probably why she was the one who had escaped from Casanova's house.

I remembered what she had told me – *just one night, Alex*. A night neither of us would ever be able to forget. I hadn't been able to forget it. I hoped Kate hadn't either.

As I stared out the porch window into the darkness, I couldn't shake the eerie feeling that I was being watched. I solved the problem in true Doctor-Detective fashion. I stopped staring out the grime-stained window.

I know they are out there, though.

They know where I live.

I finally went up to bed, and had no sooner fallen off to sleep, when I heard a banging sound in the house. Loud banging. Persistent noise. Trouble.

I grabbed my service revolver and hurried downstairs, where the banging noise continued. I glanced at my wristwatch. It was three-thirty. A witching hour. Trouble for me.

I found Sampson lurking at the back door. He was the noisemaker.

'There's been a murder,' he said as I unlocked, unchained, and opened up for him. 'This one is a honey, Alex.'